IN THIS EAGLE'S EYRIE . . . SUZANNE SAT . . . WATCHING EVER

THE WORKS OF

H. RIDER HAGGARD

SWALLOW

A Tale of the Great Trek

McKINLAY, STONE & MACKENZIE

NEW YORK

FIRST EDITION, JANUARY, 1899
REPRINTED MAY, 1899

My dear Clarke,

Over twenty years have passed since we found some unique opportunities of observing Boer and Kaffir character in company; therefore it is not perhaps out of place that I should ask you to allow me to put your name upon a book which deals more or less with the peculiarities of those races—a tale of the great Trek of 1836.

You, as I know, entertain both for Dutchman and Bantu that regard tempered by a sense of respectful superiority which we are apt to feel for those who on sundry occasions have but just failed in bringing our earthly career to an end. The latter of these admirations I share to the full; and in the case of the first of them, as I hope that the dour but not unkindly character of Vrouw Botmar will prove to you, time softens a man's judgment. Nor have I ever questioned, as the worthy Vrouw tells us, that in the beginning of the trouble the Boers met with much of which to complain at the hands of English Governments. Their maltreatment was not intentional indeed, but rather a result of the systematic neglect—to use a mild word—of colonies and their inhabitants, which has culminated within our own experience, only, thanks to a merciful change in public opinion, to pass away for ever. Sympathy with the Voortrekkers of 1836 is easy; whether it remains so in the case of their descendants, the present masters of the Transvaal, is a matter that admits of many opinions. At the least, allowance should always be made for the susceptibilities of a race that *finds its individuality and national life sinking slowly, but without hope of resurrection, beneath an invading flood of Anglo-Saxons.*

But these are issues of to-day with which this story has little to do.

Without further explanations, then, I hope that you will accept these pages in memory of past time and fellowship, and more especially of the providential events connected with a night-long ride which once we took on duty together among the "schanzes" and across the moon-lit paths of Secocoeni's mountain.

Believe me, my dear Clarke,
Your sincere friend,

H. RIDER HAGGARD.

To Lieut.-Colonel Sir Marshal Clarke, R.A., K.C.M.G.

CONTENTS

CONTENTS

SWALLOW

CHAPTER I

WHY VROUW BOTMAR TELLS HER TALE

It is a strange thing that I, an old Boer *vrouw*, should even think of beginning to write a book when there are such numbers already in the world, most of them worthless, and many of the rest a scandal and offence in the face of the Lord. Notably is this so in the case of those called novels, which are stiff as mealie-pap with lies that fill the heads of silly girls with vain imaginings, causing them to neglect their household duties and to look out of the corners of their eyes at young men of whom their elders do not approve. In truth, my mother and those whom I knew in my youth, fifty years ago, when women were good and worthy and never had a thought beyond their husbands and their children, would laugh aloud could any whisper in their dead ears that Suzanne Naudé was about to write a book. Well might they laugh indeed, seeing that to this hour the most that I can do with pen and ink is to sign my own name very large; in this matter alone, not being the equal of my husband Jan, who, before he became paralysed, had so much learning that he could read aloud from the Bible, leaving out the names and long words.

No, no, *I* am not going to write; it is my great-granddaughter, who is named Suzanne after me, who writes. And who that had not seen her at the work could even guess how she does it? I tell you that she has brought up from Durban a machine about the size of a pumpkin which goes tap-tap—like a woodpecker, and prints as it taps. Now, my husband Jan was always very fond of music in his youth, and when first the girl began to tap upon this strange instrument, he, being almost blind and not able to see it, thought that she was playing on a spinet such as stood in my grandfather's house away in the Old Colony. The noise pleases him and sends him to sleep, reminding him of the days when he courted me and I used to strum upon that spinet with one finger. Therefore I am dictating this history that he may have plenty of it, and that Suzanne may be kept out of mischief.

There, that is my joke. Still there is truth in it, for Jan Botmar, my husband, he who was the strongest man among the fathers of the great trek of 1836, when, like the Israelites of old, we escaped from the English, our masters, into the wilderness, crouches in the corner yonder a crippled giant with but one sense left to him, his hearing, and a little power of wandering speech. It is strange to look at him, his white hair hanging upon his shoulders, his eyes glazed, his chin sunk upon his breast, his great hands knotted and helpless, and to remember that at the battle of Vechtkop, when Moselikatse sent his regiments to crush us, I saw those same hands of his seize the only two Zulus who broke a way into our laager and shake and dash them together till they were dead.

Well, well, who am I that I should talk? For has not

the dropsy got hold of my legs, and did not that doctor, who, though an Englishman, is no fool, tell me but yesterday that it was creeping up towards my heart? We are old and soon must die, for such is the will of God. Let us then thank God that it is our lot to pass thus easily and in age, and not to have perished in our youth, as did so many of our companions, the Voortrekkers, they and their children together, by the spear of the savage, or by starvation and fever and wild beasts in the wilderness. Ah! I think of them often, and in my sleep, which has grown light of late, I see them often, and hear those voices that none but I would know to-day. I think of them and I see them, and since Suzanne has the skill to set down my words, a desire comes upon me to tell of them and their deeds before God takes me by the hand and I am borne through the darkness by the wings of God.

Also there is another reason. The girl, Suzanne Kenzie, my great-granddaughter, who writes this, alone is left of my blood, since her father and grandfather, who was our adopted son, and the husband of our only child, fell in the Zulu war fighting with the English against Cetywayo. Now many have heard the strange story of Ralph Kenzie, the English castaway, and of how he was found by our daughter Suzanne. Many have heard also the still stranger story of how this child of ours, Suzanne, in her need, was sheltered by savages, and for more than two years lived with Sihamba, the little witch doctress and ruler of the Tribe of the Mountains, till Ralph, her husband, who loved her, sought her out and rescued her, that by the mercy of the Lord during all this time had suffered neither harm nor violence. Yes, many have heard of these things, for in bygone years there was much talk of them as of events out of nature and marvellous, but few have heard them right. Therefore before I go, I, who remember and know them all, would set them down that they may be a record for ever among my descendants and the descendants of Ralph Kenzie, my foster-son, who, having been brought up amongst us Boers, was the best and bravest Englishman that ever lived in Africa.

And now I will tell of the finding of Ralph Kenzie many years ago.

To begin at the beginning, my husband, Jan Botmar, is one of the well-known Boer family of that name, the most of whom lived in the Graafreinet district in the Old Colony till some of them trekked into the Transkei, when I was still a young girl, to be as far as they could from the heart of the British power. Nor did they trek for a little reason. Listen and judge.

One of the Bezuidenhouts, Frederick, was accused of treating some black slave of his cruelly, and a body of the accursed *Pandours*, the Hottentots whom the English had made into a regiment, were sent to arrest him. He would not suffer that these black creatures should lay hands upon a Boer, so he fled to a cave and fought there till he was shot dead. Over his open grave his brethren and friends swore to take vengeance for his murder, and fifty of them raised an insurrection. They were pursued by the *Pandours* and by burghers more law abiding or more cautious, till Jan Bezuidenhout, the brother of Frederick, was shot also, fighting to the last while his wife and little son loaded the rifles. Then the rest were captured and put upon their trial, and to the rage and horror of all their countrymen the brutal British governor of that day, who was named Somerset, ordered five of them to be hanged, among them my husband's father and uncle. Petitions for mercy availed nothing, and these five were tied to a beam like Kaffir dogs yonder at Slagter's Nek, they who had shed the blood of no man. Yes, yes, it is true, for Jan, my man, saw it; he saw his father and his uncle hanged like dogs. When they pushed them from the beam four of the ropes broke—perhaps they had been tampered with, I know not—but still the devils who murdered them would show no mercy. Jan ran to his father and cast his arms about him, but they tore him away.

"Do not forget, my son," he gasped as he lay there on the ground with the broken rope about his neck, nor did Jan ever forget.

It was after this that the Botmars trekked into the Transkei, and with them some other families, amongst whom were the Naudés, my parents. Here in the Transkei the widow Botmar and my father were near neighbours, their steads being at a distance from each other of about three hours upon horseback, or something over twenty miles. In those days, I may say it without shame now, I was the prettiest girl in the Transkei, a great deal prettier than my granddaughter Suzanne there, although some think well of her looks, but not so well as she thinks of them herself, for that would be impossible. I have been told that I have noble French blood in my veins, though I care little for this, being quite content to be one of the Boers, who are all of noble blood. At least I believe that my great-grandfather was a French Huguenot Count who fled from his country to escape massacre because of his religion. From him and his wife Suzanne, so it is said, we women of the Naudés get our beauty, for we have always been beautiful; but the loveliest of the race by far was my daughter Suzanne who married the Englishman, Ralph

Kenzie, from which time our good looks have begun to fall
off, though it is true that he was no ill-favoured man.

Whatever the cause, in my youth, I was not like the
other Boer girls, who for the most part are stout, heavy,
and slow of speech, even before they are married, nor did
I need to wear a *kapje* to keep a pink and white face from
burning in the sun. I was not tall, but my figure was
rounded and my movements were as quick as my tongue.
Also I had brown hair that curled and brown eyes beneath
it, and full red lips, which all the young men of that district—and there were six of them who can be counted—
would have given their best horse to kiss, with the saddle
and bridle thrown in. But remember this, Suzanne, I
never suffered them to do so, for in my time girls knew
better what was right.

Well, among all these suitors I favoured Jan Botmar, the
old cripple who sits yonder, though in those days he was
no cripple but the properest man a girl could wish to see.
My father was against such a match, for he had the old
French pride of race in him, and thought little of the Botmar family, as though we were not all the children of one
God—except the black Kaffirs, who are the children of the
devil. But in the end he gave way, for Jan was well-to-do;
so after we had "opsitted" together several times according to our customs, and burnt many very long candles,*
we were married and went to live on a farm of our own
at a distance. For my part I have never regretted it, although doubtless I might have done much better for my-

---

* It is customary among the Boers for the suitor to sit up alone at
night with the object of his choice. Should the lady favour him, she
lights long candles, but if he does not please her she produces "ends,"
signifying thereby that she prefers his room to his company.

AUTHOR

self; and if Jan did, he has been wise enough not to say so
to me.   In this country most of us women must choose a
man to look after—it is a burden that Heaven lays upon
us—so one may as well choose him one fancies, and Jan
was my fancy, though why he should have been I am sure
I do not know.   Well, if he had any wits left he would
speak up and tell what a blessing I have been to him, and
how often my good sense has supplied the lack of his, and
how I forgave him, yes, and helped him out of the scrape
when he made a fool of himself with—but I will not write
of that, for it makes me angry, and as likely as not I should
throw something at him before I had finished, which he
would not understand.

No, no; I do not regret it, and, what is more, when my
man dies I shall not be long behind him.   Ah! they may
talk, all these wise young people; but, after all, what is
there better for a woman than to love some man, the good
and the bad of him together, to bear his children and to
share his sorrows, and to try to make him a little better
and a little less selfish and unfortunate than he would have
been alone?   Poor men!   Without us women their lot would
be hard indeed, and how they will get on in heaven, where
they are not allowed to marry, is more than I can guess.

So we married, and within a year our daughter was born
and christened by the family name of Suzanne after me,
though almost from her cradle the Kaffirs called her
" Swallow," I am not sure why.   She was a very beautiful
child from the first, and she was the only one, for I was ill
at her birth and never had any more children.   The other
women with their coveys of eight and ten and twelve used
to condole with me about this, and get a sharp answer for
their pains.   I had one which always shut their mouths,
but I won't ask the girl here to set it down.   An only

daughter was enough for me, I said, and if it wasn't I shouldn't have told them so, for the truth is that it is best to take these things as we find them, and whether it be one or ten, to declare that that is just as we would wish it. I know that when we were on the great trek and I saw the *kinderchies* of others dying of starvation, or massacred in dozens by the Kaffir devils, ah! then I was glad that we had no more children. Heartaches enough my ewe lamb Suzanne gave me during those bitter years when she was lost. And when she died, having lived out her life just before her husband, Ralph Kenzie, went on commando with his son to the Zulu war, whither her death drove him, ah! then it ached for the last time. When next my heart aches it shall be with joy to find them both in Heaven.

CHAPTER II

OUR farm where we lived in the Transkei was not very far from the ocean; indeed, any one seated on the *kopje* or little hill at the back of the house, from the very top of which bubbles a spring of fresh water, can see the great rollers striking the straight cliffs of the shore and spouting into the air in clouds of white foam. Even in warm weather they spout thus, but when the south-easterly gales blow then the sight and the sound of them are terrible as they rush in from the black water one after another for days and nights together. Then the cliffs shiver beneath their blows, and the spray flies up as though it were driven from the nostrils of a thousand whales, and is swept inland in clouds, turning the grass and the leaves of the trees black in its breath. Woe to the ship that is caught in those breakers and ground against those rocks, for soon nothing is left of it save scattered timbers shivered as though by lightning.

One winter—it was when Suzanne was seven years old —such a south-east gale as this blew for four days, and on a certain evening after the wind had fallen, having finished my household work, I went to the top of the *kopje* to rest and look at the sea, which was still raging terribly, taking with me Suzanne. I had been sitting there ten minutes

or more when Jan, my husband, joined me, and I wondered why he had come, for he, as brave a man as ever
lived in all other things, was greatly afraid of the sea, and,
indeed, of any water.　So afraid was he that he did not
like the sight of it in its anger, and would wake at nights at
the sound of a storm—yes, he whom I have seen sleep
through the trumpetings of frightened elephants and the
shouting of a Zulu impi.

"You think that sight fine, wife," he said, pointing to
the spouting foam; "but I call it the ugliest in the world.
Almighty! it turns my blood cold to look at it and to think
that Christian men, ay, and women and children too, may
be pounding to pulp in those breakers."

"Without doubt the death is as good as another," I
answered; "not that I would choose it, for I wish to die
in my bed with the *predicant* saying prayers over me, and
my husband weeping—or pretending to—at the foot of
it."

"Choose it!" he said.　"I had sooner be speared by savages or hanged by the English Government as my father
was."

"What makes you think of death in the sea, Jan?" I
asked.

"Nothing, wife, nothing; but there is that old fool of
a Pondo witch-doctress down by the cattle kraal, and I
heard her telling a story as I went by to look at the ox
that the snake bit yesterday."

"What was the story?"

"Oh! a short one; she said she had it from the coast
Kaffirs—that far away, up towards the mouth of the Umzimbubu, when the moon was young, great guns had been
heard fired one after the other, minute by minute, and that
then a ship was seen, a tall ship with three masts and

many 'eyes' in it—I suppose she meant portholes with the light shining through them—drifting on to the coast before the wind, for a storm was raging, while streaks of fire like red and blue lightnings rushed up from her decks."

" Well, and then? "

" And then, nothing. Almighty! that is all the tale. Those waves which you love to watch can tell the rest."

" Most like it is some Kaffir lie, husband."

" May be, but amongst these people news travels faster than a good horse, and before now there have been wrecks upon this coast. Child, put down that gun. Do you want to shoot your mother? Have I not told you that you must never touch a gun? " and he pointed to Suzanne, who had picked up her father's *roer*—for in those days, when we lived among so many Kaffirs, every man went armed—and was playing at soldiers with it.

" I was shooting buck and Kaffirs, papa," she said, obeying him with a pout.

" Shooting Kaffirs, were you? Well, there will be a good deal of that to do before all is finished in this land, little one. But it is not work for girls; you should have been a boy, Suzanne."

" I can't; I am a girl," she answered; " and I haven't any brothers like other girls. Why haven't I any brothers? "

Jan shrugged his shoulders and looked at me.

" Won't the sea bring me a brother? " went on the child, for she had been told that little children came out of the sea.

" Perhaps, if you look for one very hard," I answered with a sigh, little knowing what fruit would spring from this seed of a child's talk.

On the morrow there was a great to do about the place, for the black girl whose business it was to look after Suzanne came in at breakfast time and said that she had lost the child. It seemed that they had gone down to the shore in the early morning to gather big shells such as are washed up there after a heavy storm, and that Suzanne had taken with her a bag made of spring-buck hide in which to carry them. Well, the black girl sat down under the shadow of a rock, leaving Suzanne to wander to and fro looking for the shells, and not for an hour or more did she get up to find her. Then she searched in vain, for the spoor of the child's feet led from the sand between the rocks to the pebbly shore above, which was covered with tough sea grasses, and there was lost. Now at the girl's story I was frightened, and Jan was both frightened and so angry that he would have tied her up and flogged her if he had found time. But of this there was none to lose, so taking with him such Kaffirs as he could find he set off for the seashore to hunt for Suzanne. It was near sunset when he returned, and I, who was watching from the *stoep*, saw with a shiver of fear that he was alone.

"Wife," he said in a hollow voice, "the child is lost. We have searched far and wide and can find no trace of her. Make food ready to put in my saddle-bags, for should we discover her to-night or to-morrow, she will be starving."

"Be comforted," I said, "at least she will not starve, for the cook girl tells me that before Suzanne set out this morning she begged of her a bottle of milk and with it some biltong and meal cakes and put them in her bag."

"It is strange," he answered. "What could the little maid want with these unless she was minded to make a journey?"

" At times it comes into the thoughts of children to play truant, husband."

" Yes, yes, that is so, but pray God that we may find her before the moon sets."

Then while I filled the saddle-bags Jan swallowed some meat, and a fresh horse having been brought he kissed me and rode away in the twilight.

Oh! what hours were those that followed! All night long I sat there on the *stoep*, though the wind chilled me and the dew wet my clothes, watching and praying as, I think, I never prayed before. This I knew well—that our Suzanne, our only child, the light and joy of our home, was in danger so great that the Lord alone could save her. The country where we lived was lonely, savages still roamed about it who hated the white man, and might steal or kill her; also it was full of leopards, hyenas, and other beasts of prey which would devour her. Worst of all, the tides on the coast were swift and treacherous, and it well might happen that if she was wandering amongst the great rocks the sea would come in and drown her. Indeed, again and again it seemed to me that I could hear her death-cry in the sob of the wind.

At length the dawn broke, and with it came Jan. One glance at his face was enough for me. " She is not dead? " I gasped.

" I know not," he answered, " we have found nothing of her. Give me brandy and another horse, for the sun rises, and I return to the search. The tide is down, perhaps we shall discover her among the rocks," and he groaned and entered the house with me.

" Kneel down and let us pray, husband," I said, and we knelt down weeping and prayed aloud to our God who, seated in the Heavens, yet sees and knows the needs and griefs of His servants upon the earth; prayed that He would pity our agony and give us back our only child. Nor, blessed be His name, did we pray vainly, for presently, while we still knelt, we heard the voice of that girl who had lost Suzanne, and who all night long had lain sobbing in the garden grounds, calling to us in wild accents to come forth and see. Then we rushed out, hope burning up suddenly in our hearts like a fire in dry grass.

In front of the house and not more than thirty paces from it, was the crest of a little wave of land upon which at this moment the rays of the rising sun struck brightly. There, yes, there, full in the glow of them, stood the child Suzanne, wet, disarrayed, her hair hanging about her face, but unharmed and smiling, and leaning on her shoulder another child, a white boy, somewhat taller and older than herself. With a cry of joy we rushed towards her, and reaching her the first, for my feet were the swiftest, I snatched her to my breast and kissed her, whereon the boy fell down, for it seemed that his foot was hurt and he could not stand alone.

"In the name of Heaven, what is the meaning of this?" gasped Jan.

"What should it mean," answered the little maid proudly, "save that I went to look for the brother whom you said I might find by the sea if I searched hard enough, and I found him, though I do not understand his words or he mine. Come, brother, let me help you up, for this is our home, and here are our father and mother."

Then, filled with wonder, we carried the children into the house, and took their wet clothes off them. It was I who undressed the boy, and noted that though his garments were in rags and foul, yet they were of a finer stuff than any that I had seen, and that his linen, which was soft as silk, was marked with the letters R. M. Also I noted other things: namely, that so swollen were his little feet that the boots must be cut off them, and that he was well-nigh dead of starvation, for his bones almost pierced his milk-white skin.

Well, we cleaned him, and having wrapped him in blankets and soft-tanned hides, I fed him with broth a spoonful at a time, for had I let him eat all he would, he was so famished that I feared lest he should kill himself. After he was somewhat satisfied, sad memories seemed to come back to him, for he cried and spoke in English, repeating the word " Mother," which I knew, again and again, till presently he dropped off to sleep, and for many hours slept without waking. Then, little by little, I drew all the tale from Suzanne.

It would seem that the child, who was very venturesome and full of imaginings, had dreamed a dream in her bed on the night of the day when she played with the gun and Jan and I had spoken together of the sea. She dreamed that in a certain kloof, an hour's ride and more away from the stead, she heard the voice of a child praying, and that although he prayed in a tongue unknown to her, she understood the words, which were: " O Father, my mother is dead, send some one to help me, for I am starving." Moreover, looking round her in her dream, though she could not see the child from whom the voice came, yet she knew the kloof, for as it chanced she had been there twice, once with me to gather white lilies for the burial of a neighbour who had died, and once with her father, who was searching for a lost ox. Now Suzanne, having lived so much with her elders, was very quick, and she was sure when she woke in the morning that if she said anything about her dream we should laugh at her and should not allow her to go to the place of which she had dreamt. Therefore it was that she made the plan of seeking for the shells upon the seashore, and of slipping away from the woman who was with her, and therefore also she begged the milk and the biltong.

Now before I go further I would ask, What was this dream of Suzanne's? Did she invent it after the things to which it pointed had come to pass, or was it verily a vision sent by God to the pure heart of a little child, as aforetime He sent a vision to the heart of the infant Samuel? Let each solve the riddle as he will, only, if it were nothing but an imagination, why did she take the milk and food? Because we had been talking on that evening of her finding a brother by the sea, you may answer. Well, perhaps so; let each solve the riddle as he will.

When Suzanne escaped from her nurse she struck inland, and thus it happened that her feet left no spoor upon the hard, dry veldt. Soon she found that the kloof she sought was further off than she thought for, or, perhaps, she lost her way to it, for the hillsides are scarred with such kloofs, and it might well chance that a child would mistake one for the other. Still she went on, though she grew frightened in the lonely wilderness, where great bucks sprang up at her feet and baboons barked at her as they clambered from rock to rock. On she went, stopping only once or twice to drink a little of the milk and eat some food, till, towards sunset, she found the kloof of which she had dreamed. For a while she wandered about in it, following the banks of a stream, till at length, as she passed a dense clump of mimosa bushes, she heard the faint sound of a child's voice—the very voice of her dream. Now she stopped, and turning to the right, pushed her way through the mimosas, and there beyond them was a dell, and in the centre of the dell a large flat rock, and on the rock a boy praying, the rays of the setting sun shining in his golden, tangled hair. She went to the child and spoke to him, but he could not understand our tongue, nor could she understand his. Then she drew out what was left of the bottle of milk and some meal cakes and gave them to him, and he ate and drank greedily.

By this time the sun was down, and as they did not dare to move in the dark, the children sat together on the rock, clasped in each other's arms for warmth, and as they sat they saw yellow eyes staring at them through the gloom, and heard strange snoring sounds, and were afraid. At length the moon rose, and in its first rays they perceived standing and walking within a few paces of them three tigers, as we call leopards, two of them big and one half-grown. But the tigers did them no harm, for God forbade them; they only looked at them a little and then slipped away, purring as they went.

Now Suzanne rose, and taking the boy by the hand she began to lead him homeward, very slowly, since he was footsore and exhausted, and for the last half of the way could only walk resting upon her shoulder. Still through the long night they crawled forward, for the *kopje* at the back of our stead was a guide to Suzanne, stopping from time to time to rest a while, till at the breaking of the dawn with their last strength they came to the house, as has been told.

Well it was that they did so, for it seems that the searchers had already sought them in the very kloof where they were hidden, without seeing anything of them behind the thick screen of the mimosas, and having once sought doubtless they would have returned there no more, for the hills are wide and the kloofs in them many.

CHAPTER III

THE STORY OF THE SHIPWRECK

"WHAT shall we do with this boy whom Suzanne has brought to us, wife?" asked Jan of me that day while both the children lay asleep.

"Do with him, husband!" I answered; "we shall keep him; he is the Lord's gift."

"He is English, and I hate the English," said Jan, looking down.

"English or Dutch, husband, he is of noble blood, and the Lord's gift, and to turn him away would be to turn away our luck."

"But how if his people come to seek him?"

"When they come we will talk of it, but I do not think that they will come; I think that the sea has swallowed them all."

After that Jan said no more of this matter for many years; indeed I believe that from the first he desired to keep the child, he who was sonless.

Now while the boy lay asleep Jan mounted his horse and rode for two hours to the stead of our neighbour, the Heer van Vooren. This Van Vooren was a very rich man, by far the richest of us outlying Boers, and he had come to live in these wilds because of some bad act that he had done; I think that it was the shooting of a coloured person when he was angry. He was a strange man and much feared, sullen in countenance, and silent by nature. It was said that his grandmother was a chieftainess among the red Kaffirs, but if so, the blood showed more in his son and only child than in himself. Of this son, who in after years was named Swart Piet, and his evil doings I shall have to tell later in my story, but even then his dark face and savage temper had earned for him the name of " the little Kaffir."

Now the wife of the Heer van Vooren was dead, and he had a tutor for his boy Piet, a poor Hollander body who could speak English. That man knew figures also, for once when, thinking that I should be too clever for him, I asked him how often the wheel of our big waggon would turn round travelling between our farm and Capetown Castle, he took a rule and measured the wheel, then having set down some figures on a bit of paper, and worked at them for a while, he told me the answer. Whether it was right or wrong I did not know, and said so, whereon the poor creature grew angry, and lied in his anger, for he swore that he could tell me how often the wheel would turn in travelling from the earth to the sun or moon, and also how far we were from those great lamps, a thing that is known to God only, Who made them for our comfort. It is little wonder, therefore, that with such unholy teaching Swart Piet grew up so bad.

Well, Jan went to beg the loan of this tutor, thinking that he would be able to understand what the English boy said, and in due course the creature came in a pair of blue spectacles and riding on a mule, for he dared not trust himself to a horse. Afterwards, when the child woke up from his long sleep, and had been fed and dressed, the tutor spoke with him in that ugly English tongue of which

I could never even bear the sound, and this was the story that he drew from him.

It seems that the boy, who gave his name as Ralph Kenzie, though I believe that really it was Ralph Mackenzie, was travelling with his father and mother and many others from a country called India, which is one of those places that the English have stolen in different parts of the world, as they stole the Cape and Natal and all the rest. They travelled for a long while in a big ship, for India is a great way off, till, when they were near this coast, a storm sprang up, and after the wind had blown for two days they were driven on rocks a hundred miles or more away from our stead. So fierce was the sea and so quickly did the ship break to pieces that only one boat was got out, which, except for a crew of six men, was filled with women and children. In this boat the boy Ralph and his mother were given a place, but his father did not come, although the captain begged him, for he was a man of importance, whose life was of more value than those of common people. But he refused, for he said that he would stop and share the fate of the other men, which shows that this English lord, for I think he was a lord, had a high spirit. So he kissed his wife and child and blessed them, and the boat was lowered to the sea, but before another could be got ready the great ship slipped back from the rock upon which she hung and sank (for this we heard afterwards from some Kaffirs who saw it), and all aboard of her were drowned. May God have mercy upon them!

When it was near to the shore the boat was overturned, and some of those in it were drowned, but Ralph and his mother were cast safely on the beach, and with them others. Then one of the men looked at a compass and they began to walk southwards, hoping doubtless to reach country where white people lived. All that befell afterwards I cannot tell, for the poor child was too frightened and bewildered to remember, but it seems that the men were killed in a fight with natives, who, however, did not touch the women and children. After that the women and the little ones died one by one of hunger and weariness, or were taken by wild beasts, till at last none were left save Ralph and his mother. When they were alone they met a Kaffir woman, who gave them as much food as they could carry, and by the help of this food they struggled on southward for another five or six days, till at length one morning, after their food was done, Ralph woke to find his mother cold and dead beside him.

When he was sure that she was dead he was much frightened, and ran away as fast as he could. All that day he staggered forward, till in the evening he came to the kloof, and being quite exhausted, knelt upon the flat stone to pray, as he had been taught to do, and there Suzanne found him. Such was the story, and so piteous it seemed to us that we wept as we listened, yes, even Jan wept, and the tutor snivelled and wiped his weak eyes.

That it was true in the main we learned afterwards from the Kaffirs, a bit here and a bit there. Indeed, one of our own people, while searching for Suzanne, found the body of Ralph's mother and buried it. He said that she was a tall and noble-looking lady, not much more than thirty years of age. We did not dig her up again to look at her, as perhaps we should have done, for the Kaffir declared that she had nothing on her except some rags and two rings, a plain gold one and another of emeralds, with a device carved upon it, and in the pocket of her gown a little book bound in red, that proved to be a Testament, on the fly leaf of which was written in English, " Flora Gordon, the gift of her mother, Agnes Janey Gordon, on her confirmation," and with it a date.

All these things the Kaffir brought home faithfully, also a lock of the lady's fair hair, which he had cut off with his assegai. That lock of hair labelled in writing—remember it, Suzanne, when I am gone—is in the waggon box which stands beneath my bed. The other articles Suzanne here has, as is her right, for her grandfather settled them on her by will, and with them one thing which I forgot to mention. When we undressed the boy Ralph, we found hanging by a gold chain to his neck, where he said his mother placed it the night before she died, a large locket, also of gold. This locket contained three little pictures painted on ivory, one in each half of it and one with a plain gold back on a hinge between them. That to the right was of a handsome man in uniform, who, Ralph told me, was his father (and indeed he left all this in writing, together with his will); that to the left, of a lovely lady in a low dress, who, he said, was his mother; that in the middle a portrait of the boy himself, as anyone could see, which must have been painted not more than a year before we found him. This locket and the pictures my great-granddaughter Suzanne has also.

Now, as I have said, we let that unhappy lady lie in her rude grave yonder by the sea, but my husband took men and built a cairn of stones over it and a strong wall about it, and there it stands to this day, for not long ago I met one of the folk from the Old Colony who had seen it, and who told me that the people that live in those parts now reverence the spot, knowing its story. Also, when some months afterwards a minister came to visit us, we led him to the place and he read the Burial Service over the lady's bones, so that she did not lack for Christian burial.

Well, this wreck made a great stir, for many were drowned in it, and the English Government sent a ship of war to visit the place where it happened, but none came to ask us what we knew of the matter; indeed, we never learned that the frigate had been till she was gone again. So it came about that the story died away, as such stories do in this sad world, and for many years we heard no more of it,

For a while the boy Ralph was like a haunted child. At night, and now and again even in the daytime, he would be seized with terror, and sob and cry in a way that was piteous to behold, though not to be wondered at by any who knew his history. When these fits took him, strange as it may seem, there was but one who could calm his heart, and that one Suzanne. I can see them now as I have seen them thrice that I remember, the boy sitting up in his bed, a stare of agony in his eyes, and the sweat running down his face, damping his yellow hair, and talking rapidly, half in English, half in Dutch, with a voice that at times would rise to a scream, and at times would sink to a whisper, of the shipwreck, of his lost parents, of the black Indian woman who nursed him, of the wilderness, the tigers, and the Kaffirs who fell on them, and many other things. By him sits Suzanne, a soft kaross of jackal skins wrapped over her nightgown, the dew of sleep still showing upon her childish face and in her large dark eyes. By him she sits, talking in some words which for us have little meaning, and in a voice now shrill, and now sinking to a croon, while with one hand she clasps his wrist, and with the other strokes his brow, till the shadow passes

from his soul and, clinging close to her, he sinks back to
sleep.

But as the years went by these fits grew rarer till at last
they ceased altogether, since, thanks be to God, childhood
can forget its grief. What did not cease, however, was
the lad's love for Suzanne, or her love for him, which, if
possible, was yet deeper. Brother may love sister, but that
affection, however true, yet lacks something, since nature
teaches that it can never be complete. But from the beginning—yes, even while they were children—these twain
were brother and sister, friend and friend, lover and lover;
and so they remained till life left them, and so they will
remain for aye in whatever life they live. Their thought
was one thought, their heart was one heart; in them was
neither variableness nor shadow of turning; they were each
of each, to each and for each, as one soul in their separate
spirits, as one flesh in their separate bodies. I who write
this am a very old woman, and though in many things I
am most ignorant, I have seen much of the world and of
the men who live in it, yet I say that never have I known
any marvel to compare with the marvel and the beauty of
the love between Ralph Kenzie, the castaway, and my
sweet daughter, Suzanne. It was of heaven, not of earth;
or, rather, like everything that is perfect, it partook both
of earth and heaven. Yes, yes, it wandered up the mountain paths of earth to the pure heights of heaven, where
now it dwells for ever.

The boy Ralph grew up fair and brave and strong, with
keen grey eyes and a steady mouth, nor did I know any
lad of his years who could equal him in strength and swift-
ness of foot; for, though in youth he was not over tall, he
was broad in the breast and had muscles that never seemed
to tire. Now, we Boers think little of book learning, hold-

ing, as we do, that if a man can read the Holy Word it is enough. Still Jan and I thought as Ralph was not of our blood, though otherwise in all ways a son to us, that it was our duty to educate him as much in the fashion of his own people as our circumstances would allow. Therefore, after he had been with us some two years, when one day the Hollander tutor man, with the blue spectacles, of whom I have spoken, rode up to our house upon his mule, telling us that he had fled from the Van Voorens because he could no longer bear to witness the things that were practised at their stead, we engaged him to teach Ralph and Suzanne. He remained with us six years, by which time both the children had got much learning from him; though how much it is not for me, who have none, to judge. They learnt history and reading and writing, and something of the English tongue, but I need scarcely say that I would not suffer him to teach them to pry into the mystery of God's stars, as he wished to do, for I hold that such lore is impious and akin to witchcraft of which I have seen enough from Sihamba and others.

I asked this Hollander more particularly why he had fled from the Van Voorens, but he would tell me little more than that it was because of the wizardries practised there. If I might believe him, the Heer Van Vooren made a custom of entertaining Kaffir witch doctors and doctoresses at his house, and of celebrating with them secret and devilish rites, to which his son, Swart Piet, was initiated in his presence. That this last story was true I have no doubt indeed, seeing that the events of after years prove it to have been so.

Well, at last the Hollander left us to marry a rich old vrouw twenty years his senior, and that is all I have to say about him, except that if possible I disliked him more

when he walked out of the house than when he walked
into it; though why I should have done so I do not know,
for he was a harmless body. Perhaps it was because he
played the flute, which I have always thought contemptible
in a man.

CHAPTER IV

Now I will pass on to the time when Ralph was nineteen or thereabouts, and save for the lack of hair upon his face, a man grown, since in our climate young people ripen quickly in body if not in mind. I tell of that year with shame and sorrow, for it was then that Jan and I committed a great sin, for which afterwards we were punished heavily enough.

At the beginning of winter Jan trekked to the nearest drop, some fifty miles away, with a waggon load of mealies and of buckskins which he and Ralph had shot, purposing to sell them and to attend the Nachtmahl, or Feast of the Lord's Supper. I was somewhat ailing just then and did not accompany him, nor did Suzanne, who stayed to nurse me, or Ralph, who was left to look after us both.

Fourteen days later Jan returned, and from his face I saw at once that something had gone wrong.

" What is it, husband? " I asked. " Did not the mealies sell well? "

" Yes, yes, they sold well," he answered, " for that fool of an English storekeeper bought them and the hides together for more than their value."

" Are the Kaffirs going to rise again, then? "

" No, they are quiet for the present, though the accursed

missionaries of the London Society are doing their best to stir them up," and he made a sign to me to cease from asking questions, nor did I say any more till we had gone to bed and everybody else in the house was asleep.

"Now," I said, "tell me your bad news, for bad news you have had."

"Wife," he answered, "it is this. In the dorp yonder I met a man who had come from Port Elizabeth. He told me that there at the port were two Englishmen, who had recently arrived, a Scotch lord, and a lawyer with red hair. When the Englishmen heard that he was from this part of the country they fell into talk with him, saying that they came upon a strange errand. It seems that when the great ship was wrecked upon this coast ten years ago there was lost in her a certain little boy who, if he had lived, would to-day have been a very rich noble in Scotland. Wife, you may know who that little boy was without my telling you his name."

I nodded and turned cold all over my body, for I could guess what was coming.

"Now for a long while those who were interested in him supposed that this lad was certainly dead with all the others on board that ship, but a year or more ago, how I know not, a rumour reached them that one male child who answered to his description had been saved alive and adopted by some Boers living in the Transkei. By this time the property and the title that should be his had descended to a cousin of the child's, but this relation being a just man determined before he took them to come to Africa and find out the truth for himself, and there he is at Port Elizabeth, or rather by this time he is on his road to our place. Therefore it would seem that the day is at hand when we shall see the last of Ralph."

" Never! " I said, " he is a son to us and more than a son, and I will not give him up."

" Then they will take him, wife. Yes, even if he does not wish it, for he is a minor and they are armed with authority."

" Oh! " I cried, " it would break my heart, and, Jan, there is another heart that would break also," and I pointed towards the chamber where Suzanne slept.

He nodded, for none could live with them and not know that this youth and maiden loved each other dearly.

" It would break your heart," he answered, " and her heart; yes, and my own would be none the better for the wrench; yet how can we turn this evil from our door? "

" Jan," I said, " the winter is at hand; it is time that you and Ralph should take the cattle to the bush-veldt yonder, where they will lie warm and grow fat, for so large a herd cannot be trusted to the Kaffirs. Had you not better start to-morrow? If these English meddlers should come here I will talk with them. Did Suzanne save the boy for them? Did we rear him for them, although he was English ? Think how you will feel when he has crossed the ridge yonder for the last time, you who are sonless, and you must go about your tasks alone, must ride alone and hunt alone, and, if need be, fight alone, except for his memory. Think, Jan, think."

" Do not tempt me, woman," he whispered back in a hoarse voice, for Ralph and he were more to each other than any father and son that I have known, since they were also the dearest of friends. " Do not tempt me," he went on; " the lad himself must be told of this, and he must judge; he is young, but among us at nineteen a youth is a burgher grown, with a right to take up land and marry. He must be told, I say, and at once."

"It is good," I said, "let him judge;" but in the
wickedness of my heart I made up my mind that I would
find means to help his judgment, for the thought of losing
him filled me with blind terror, and all that night I lay
awake thinking out the matter.

Early in the morning I rose and went on to the *stoep*,
where I found Suzanne drinking coffee and singing a little
song that Ralph had taught her.   I can see her now as she
stood in her pretty tight-fitting dress, a flower wet with dew
in her girdle, swinging her *kapje* by its strings while the
first rays of the sun glistened on the waves of her brown
and silk-like hair.   She was near eighteen then, and so
beautiful that my heart beat with pride at her loveliness,
for never in my long life have I seen a girl of any nation
who could compare with my daughter Suzanne in looks.
Many women are sweet to behold in this way or in that;
but Suzanne was beautiful every way, yes, and at all ages
of her life; as a child, as a maiden, as a matron and as a
woman drawing near to eld, she was always beautiful if,
like that of the different seasons, her beauty varied.   In
shape she was straight and tall and rounded, light-footed
as a buck, delicate in limb, wide-breasted and slender-
necked.   Her face was rich in hue as a kloof lily, and her
eyes—ah! no antelope ever had eyes darker, tenderer, or
more appealing than were the eyes of Suzanne.   Moreover,
she was sweet of nature, ready of wit and good-hearted—
yes, even for the Kaffirs she had a smile.

"You are up betimes, Suzanne," I said when I had
looked at her a little.

"Yes, mother; I rose to make Ralph his coffee, he does
not like that the Kaffir women should boil it for him."

"You mean that you do not like it," I answered, for I
knew that Ralph thought little of who made the coffee

that he drank, or if he did it was mine that he held to be the best, and not Suzanne's, who in those days was a careless girl, thinking less of household matters than she should have done.

"Did Swart Piet come here yesterday?" I asked. "I thought that I saw his horse as I walked back from the sea."

"Yes, he came."

"What for?"

She shrugged her shoulders. "Oh! mother, why do you ask me? You know well that he is always troubling me, bringing me presents of flowers, and asking me to *opsit* with him and what not."

"Then you don't want to *opsit* with him?"

"The candle would be short that I should burn with Swart Piet," answered Suzanne, stamping her foot; "he is an evil man, full of dark words and ways, and I fear him, for I think that since his father's death he has become worse, and the most of the company he keeps is with those Kaffir witch-doctors."

"Ah! like father, like son. The mantle of Elijah has fallen upon Elisha, but inside out. Well, it is what I expected, for sin and wizardry were born in his blood. Had you any words with him?"

"Yes, some. I would not listen to his sweet talk, so he grew angry and began to threaten; but just then Ralph came back and he went away, for he is afraid of Ralph."

"Where has Ralph gone so early?" I asked, changing the subject.

"To the far cattle-kraal to look after the oxen which the Kaffir bargained to break into the yoke. They are choosing them this morning."

"So. He makes a good Boer for one of English blood,

does he not? And yet I suppose that when he becomes English again he will soon forget that he ever was a Boer."

"When he becomes English again, mother! What do you mean by that saying?" she asked quickly.

"I mean that like will to like, and blood to blood; also that there may be a nest far away which this bird that we have caged should fill."

"A nest far away, mother? Then there is one here which would be left empty; in your heart and father's, I mean;" and dropping her sun-bonnet she turned pale and pressed her hands upon her own, adding, "Oh! speak straight words to me. What do you mean by these hints?"

"I mean, Suzanne, that it is not well for any of us to let our love wrap itself too closely about a stranger. Ralph is an Englishman, not a Boer. He names me mother and your father, father; and you he names sister, but to us he is neither son nor brother. Well, a day may come when he learns to understand this, when he learns to understand also that he has other kindred, true kindred far away across the sea; and if those birds call, who will keep him in the strange nest?"

"Ah!" she echoed, all dismayed, "who will keep him then?"

"I do not know," I answered; "not a foster father or mother. But I forgot. Say, did he take his rifle with him to the kraal?"

"Surely, I saw it in his hand."

"Then, daughter, if you will, get on a horse, and if you can find Ralph, tell him that I shall be very glad if he can shoot a small buck and bring it back with him, as I need fresh meat."

"May I stay with him while he shoots the buck, mother?"

"Yes, if you are not in his way and do not stop too long."

Then, without more words, Suzanne left me, and presently I saw her cantering across the veldt upon her grey mare that Ralph had broken for her, and wondered if she would find him and what luck he would have with the hunt that day.

Now it seems that Suzanne found Ralph and gave him my message, and that they started together to look for buck on the strip of land which lies between the seashore and the foot of the hills, where sometimes the blesbok and springbok used to feed in thousands. But on this day there were none to be seen, for the dry grass had already been burnt off, so that there was nothing for them to eat.

"If mother is to get her meat to-day," said Ralph at length, " I think that we must try the hill side for a duiker or a bush-buck."

So they turned inland and rode towards that very kloof where years before Suzanne had discovered the shipwrecked boy. At the mouth of this kloof was a patch of marshy ground, where the reeds still stood thick, since being full of sap they had resisted the fire.

"That is a good place for a riet-buck," said Ralph, " if only one could beat him out of it, for the reeds are too tall to see to shoot in them."

"It can be managed," answered Suzanne. "Do you go and stand in the neck of the kloof while I ride through the reeds towards you."

"You might get bogged," he said doubtfully.

"No, no, brother; after all this drought the pan is nothing more than spongy, and if I should get into a soft spot I will call out."

To this plan Ralph at length agreed, and having ridden round the pan, which was not more than fifty yards across, he dismounted from his horse and hid himself behind a bush in the neck of the kloof. Then Suzanne rode in among the reeds, shouting and singing, and beating them with her sjambock in order to disturb anything that might be hidden there. Nor was her trouble in vain, for suddenly, with a shrill whistle of alarm by the sound of which this kind of antelope may be known even in the dark, up sprang two riet-buck and dashed away towards the neck of the kloof, looking large as donkeys and red as lions as they vanished into the thick cover. So close were they to Suzanne that her mare took fright and reared; but the girl was the best horsewoman in those parts, and kept her seat, calling the while to Ralph to make ready for the buck. Presently she heard a shot, and having quieted the mare, rode out of the reeds and galloped round the dry pan to find Ralph looking foolish with no riet-buck in sight.

"Have you missed them?" she asked.

"No, not so bad as that, for they passed within ten yards of me, but the old gun hung fire. I suppose that the powder in the pan was a little damp, and instead of hitting the buck in front I caught him somewhere behind. He fell down, but has gone on again, so we must follow him, for I don't think that he will get very far."

Accordingly, when Ralph had reloaded his gun, which took some time—for in those days we had scarcely anything but flintlocks—yes, it was with weapons like these that a handful of us beat the hosts of Dingaan and Moseli-katse—they started to follow the blood spoor up the kloof, which was not difficult, as the animal had bled much. Near to the top of the kloof the trail led them through a thick clump of mimosas, and there in the dell beyond they found the riet-buck lying dead. Riding to it they dismounted and examined it.

" Poor beast," said Suzanne; " look how the tears have run down its face.   Well, I am glad that it is dead and done with," and she sighed and turned away, for Suzanne was a silly and tender-hearted girl who never could understand that the animals—yes, and the heathen Kaffirs, too—were given to us by the Lord for our use and comfort.

Presently she started and said, " Ralph, do you remember this place? "

He glanced round and shook his head, for he was wondering whether he would be able to lift the buck on to the horse without asking Suzanne to help him.

" Look again," she said; " look at that flat stone and the mimosa tree lying on its side near it."

Ralph dropped the leg of the buck and obeyed her, for he would always do as Suzanne bade him, and this time it was his turn to start.

" Almighty! " he said, " I remember now.   It was here that you found me, Suzanne, after I was shipwrecked, and the tigers stared at us through the boughs of that fallen tree," and he shivered a little, for the sight of the spot brought back to his heart some of the old terrors which had haunted his childhood.

" Yes, Ralph, it was here that I found you.   I heard the sound of your voice as you knelt praying on this stone, and I followed it.   God heard that prayer, Ralph."

" And sent an angel to save me in the shape of a little maid," he answered; adding, " Don't blush so red, dear, for it is true that ever since that day, whenever I think of angels, I think of you; and whenever I think of you I think of angels, which shows that you and the angels must be close together."

" Which shows that you are a wicked and silly lad to talk thus to a Boer girl," she answered, turning away with a smile on her lips and tears in her eyes, for his words had pleased her mind and touched her heart.

He looked at her, and she seemed so sweet and beautiful as she stood thus, smiling and weeping together as the sun shines through summer rain, that, so he told me afterwards, something stirred in his breast, something soft and strong and new, which caused him to feel as though of a sudden he had left his boyhood behind him and become a man, aye, and as though this fresh-found manhood sought but one thing more from Heaven to make it perfect, the living love of the fair maiden who until this hour had been his sister in heart though not in blood.

"Suzanne," he said in a changed voice, "the horses are tired; let them rest, and let us sit upon this stone and talk a little, for though we have never visited it for many years the place is lucky for you and me since it was here that our lives first came together."

Now although Suzanne knew that the horses were not tired she did not think it needful to say him nay.

CHAPTER V

A LOVE SCENE AND A QUARREL

PRESENTLY they were seated side by side upon a stone, Suzanne looking straight before her, for nature warned her that this talk of theirs was not to be as other talks, and Ralph looking at Suzanne.

" Suzanne," he said at length.

" Yes," she answered; " what is it? "   But he made no answer, for though many words were bubbling in his brain, they choked in his throat, and would not come out of it.

" Suzanne," he stammered again presently, and again she asked him what it was, and again he made no answer Now she laughed a little and said:

" Ralph, you remind me of the blue-jay in the cage upon the *stoep* which knows but one word and repeats it all day long."

" Yes," he replied, " it is true; I am like that jay, for the word I taught it is 'Suzanne,' and the word my heart teaches me is 'Suzanne,' and—Suzanne, I love you! "

Now she turned her head away and looked down and answered:

" I know, Ralph, that you have always loved me since we were children together, for are we not brother and sister? "

"No," he answered bluntly, "it is not true."

"Then that is bad news for me," she said, "who till to-day have thought otherwise."

"It is not true," he went on, and now his words came fast enough, "that I am your brother or that I love you as a brother. We are no kin, and if I love you as a brother that is only one little grain of my love for you—yes, only as one little grain is to the whole sea-shore of sand. Suzanne, I love you as—as a man loves a maid—and if you will it, dear, all my hope is that one day you will be my wife," and he ceased suddenly and stood before her trembling, for he had risen from the stone.

For a few moments Suzanne covered her face with her hands, and when she let them fall again he saw that her beautiful eyes shone like the large stars at night, and that, although she was troubled, her trouble made her happy.

"Oh! Ralph," she said at length, speaking in a voice that was different from any he had ever heard her use, a voice very rich and low and full, "Oh! Ralph, this is new to me, and yet to speak the truth, it seems as old as—as that night when first I found you, a desolate, starving child, praying upon this stone. Ralph, I do will it with all my heart and soul and body, and I suppose that I have willed it ever since I was a woman, though until this hour I did not quite know what it was I willed. Nay, dear, do not touch me, or at the least, not yet. First hear what I have to say, and then if you desire it, you may kiss me—if only in farewell."

"If you will it and I will it, what more can you have to say?" he asked in a quick whisper, and looking at her with frightened eyes.

"This, Ralph; that our wills, who are young and un-learned, are not all the world; that there are other wills to be thought of; the wills of our parents, or of mine rather, and the will of God."

" For the first," he answered, " I do not think that they stand in our path, for they love you and wish you to be happy, although it is true that I, who am but a wanderer picked up upon the veldt, have no fortune to offer you— still fortune can be won," he added doggedly.

" They love you also, Ralph, nor do they care over much for wealth, either of them, and I am sure that they would not wish you to leave us to go in search of it."

" As for the will of God," he continued, " it was the will of God that I should be wrecked here, and that you should save me here, and that the life you saved should be given to you. Will it not, therefore, be the will of God also that we, who can never be happy apart, should be happy together and thank Him for our happiness every day till we die? "

" I trust so, Ralph; yet although I have read and seen little, I know that very often it has been His will that those who love each other should be separated by death or otherwise."

" Do not speak of it," he said with a groan.

" No, I will not speak of it, but there is one more thing of which I must speak. Strangely enough, only this morning my mother was talking of you; she said that you are English, and that soon or late blood will call to blood and you will leave us. She said that your nest is not here, but there, far away across the sea, among those English; that you are a swallow that has been fledged with sparrows, and that one day you will find the wings of a swallow. What put it in her mind to speak thus, I do not know, but I do know, Ralph, that her words filled me with fear, and now I understand why I was so much afraid."

He laughed aloud very scornfully. "Then, Suzanne," he said, "you may banish your fears, for this I swear to you, before the Almighty, that whoever may be my true kin, were a kingdom to be offered to me among them, unless you could share it, it would be refused. This I swear before the Almighty, and may He reject me if I forget the oath."

"You are very young to make such promises, Ralph," she answered doubtfully, "nor do I hold them binding on you. At nineteen, so I am told, a lad will swear anything to the girl who takes his fancy."

"I am young in years, Suzanne, but I grew old while I was yet a child, for sorrow aged me. You have heard my oath; let it be put to the test, and you shall learn whether or no I speak the truth. Do I look like one who does not know his mind?"

She glanced up at the steady, grey eyes and the stern, set mouth and answered, "Ralph, you look like one who knows his mind, and I believe you. Pray God I may not be deceived, for though we are but lad and girl, if it prove so I tell you that I shall live my life out with a broken heart."

"Do not fear, Suzanne. And now I have heard what you had to say, and I claim your promise. If it be your will I will kiss you, Suzanne, but not in farewell."

"Nay," she answered, "kiss me rather in greeting of the full and beautiful life that stretches before our feet. Whether the path be short or long, it will be good for us and ever better, but, Ralph, I think that the end will be best of all."

So he took her in his arms, and they kissed each other upon the lips, and, as they told me afterwards, in that embrace they found some joy. Why should they not indeed, for if anywhere upon the earth, if it be given and received in youth before the heart has been seared and tainted with bitterness and disillusion, surely in such a pledge as theirs true joy can be found. Yes, and they did more than this, for, kneeling there upon that rock where once the starving child had knelt in bygone years, they prayed to Him who had brought them together, to Him who had given them hearts to love with and bodies to be loved, and the immortality of Heaven wherein to garner this seed of love thus sown upon the earth, that He would guide them, bless them, and protect them through all trials, terrors, sorrows, and separations. As shall be seen, this indeed He did.

Then they rose, and having, not without difficulty, lifted the riet-buck ram upon Ralph's horse and made it fast there, as our hunters know how to do, they started homewards, walking the most part of the way, for the load was heavy and they were in no haste, so that they only reached the farm about noon.

Now I, watching them as we sat at our mid-day meal, grew sure that something out of the common had passed between them. Suzanne was very silent, and from time to time glanced at Ralph shyly, whereon, feeling her eyes, he would grow red as the sunset, and seeing his trouble, she would colour also, as though with the knowledge of some secret that made her both happy and ashamed.

" You were long this morning in finding a buck, Ralph," I said.

" Yes, mother," he answered; " there were none on the flats, for the grass is burnt off; and had not Suzanne beaten out a dry pan for me where the reeds were still green, I think that we should have found nothing. As it was I shot badly, hitting the ram in the flank, so that we were obliged to follow it a long way before I came up with it."

"And where did you find it at last?" I asked.

"In a strange place, mother; yes, in that very spot where many years ago Suzanne came upon me starving after the shipwreck. There in the glade and by the flat stone on which I had lain down to die was the buck, quite dead. We knew the dell again, though neither of us had visited it from that hour to this, and rested there awhile before we turned home."

I made no answer but sat thinking, and a silence fell on all of us. By this time the Kaffir girls had cleared away the meat and brought in coffee, which we drank while the men filled their pipes and lit them. I looked at Jan and saw that he was making up his mind to say something, for his honest face was troubled, and now he took up his pipe, and now he put it down, moving his hands restlessly till at length he upset the coffee over the table.

"Doubtless," I thought to myself, "he means to tell the tale of the Englishmen who have come to seek for Ralph. Well, I think that he may safely tell it now."

Then I looked at Ralph and saw that he also was very ill at ease, struggling with words which he did not know how to utter. I noted, moreover, that Suzanne touched his hand with hers beneath the shelter of the table as though to comfort and encourage him. Now watching these two men, at last I broke out laughing, and said, addressing them:

"You are like two fires of green weeds in a mealie patch, and I am wondering which of you will be the first to break into flame or whether you will both be choked by the reek of your own thoughts."

My gibe, harmless though it was, stung them into speech, and both at once, for I have noticed, however stupid they may be, that men never like to be laughed at.

"I have something to say," said each of them, as though with a single voice, and they paused, looking at one another angrily.

"Then, son, wait till I have finished. Almighty! for the last twenty minutes you have been sitting as silent as an ant-bear in a hole, and I tell you that it is my turn now; why, then, do you interrupt me?"

"I am very sorry, my father," said Ralph, looking much afraid, for he thought that Jan was going to scold him about Suzanne, and his conscience being guilty caused him to forget that it was not possible that he should know anything of the matter of his love-making.

"That is good," said Jan, still glaring at him; "but I am not your father."

"Then why do you call me son?" asked Ralph.

"Almighty! do you suppose that I sit here to answer riddles?" replied Jan, pulling at his great beard. "Why do I call you son, indeed? Ah!" he added in a different voice, a sorrowful voice, "why do I when I have no right? Listen, my boy, we are in sore trouble, I and your mother, or if she is not your mother at least she loves you as much as though she were, and I love you too, and you know it; so why do you seek to make a fool of me by asking me riddles?"

Now, Ralph was about to answer, but Suzanne held up her hand, and he was quiet.

"My son," went on Jan with a kind of sob, "they are coming to take you away from us."

"They! Who?" asked Ralph.

"Who? The English, damn them! Yes, I say, damn the English and the English Government."

"Peace, Jan," I broke in, "this is not a political meeting, where such talk is right and proper."

" The English Government is coming to take me away! "
exclaimed Ralph bewildered. " What has the Government to do with me? "

" No," said Jan, " not the English Government, but two
Scotchmen, which is much the same thing. I tell you that
they are travelling to this place to take you away."

Now, Ralph leaned back in his chair and stared at him,
for he saw that it was little use to ask him questions, and
that he must leave him to tell the tale in his own fashion.
At last it came out.

" Ralph," said my husband, " you know that you are
not of our blood; we found you cast up on the beach like
a storm-fish and took you in, and you grew dear to us; yes,
although you are English or Scotch, which is worse, for if
the English bully us the Scotch bully us and cheat us into
the bargain. Well, your parents were drowned, and have
now been in Heaven for a long time, but I am sorry to say
that all your relations were not drowned with them. At
first, however, they took no trouble to hunt for you when
we should have been glad enough to give you up."

" No," broke in Suzanne and I with one voice, and I
added, " How do you dare to tell such lies in the face of
the Lord, Jan? "

" ——When it would not have been so bad to give you
up," he went on, correcting himself. " But now it seems
that had you lived you would have inherited estates, or
titles, or both."

" Is the boy dead then? " I asked.

" Be silent, wife, I mean—had he lived a Scotchman.
Therefore, having made inquiries, and learned that a lad
of your name and age had been rescued from a shipwreck
and was still alive among the Boers in the Transkei, they
have set to work to hunt you, and are coming here to take

you away, for I tell you that I heard it in the dorp yonder."

"Is it so?" said Ralph, while Suzanne hung upon his
words with white face and trembling lips. "Then I tell
you that I will not go. I may be English, but my home
is here. My own father and mother are dead, and these
strangers are nothing to me, nor are the estates and titles
far away anything to me. All that I hold dear on the
earth is here in the Transkei," and he glanced at Suzanne,
who seemed to bless him with her eyes.

"You talk like a fool," said Jan, but in a voice which
was full of a joy that he could not hide, "as is to be expected of an ignorant boy. Now I am a man who has
seen the world, and I know better, and I tell you that
although they are an accursed race, still it is a fine thing
to be a lord among the English. Yes, yes, I know the
English lords. I saw one once when I went to Capetown;
he was the Governor there, and driving through the streets
in state, dressed as bravely as a blue-jay in his spring
plumage, while everybody took off their hats to him, except I, Jan Botmar, who would not humble myself thus.
Yet to have such clothes as that to wear every day, while
all the people salute you and make a path for you, is not
a thing to be laughed at. See boy, it just comes to this:
here you are poor and little, there you may be rich and
much, and it is our duty not to stand in your road, though it
may break our hearts to lose you. So you had best make up
your mind to go away with the damned Scotchmen when
they come, though I hope that you will think kindly of us
when you get to your own country. Yes, yes, you shall go,
and what is more, you may take my best horse to ride away
on, the thoroughbred *schimmel*, and my new black felt hat
that I bought in the dorp. There, that is done with,

praise be to God, and I am going out, for this place is so thick with smoke that I can't see my own hand," and he rose to go, adding that if the two Scotchmen did not want a bullet through them, it would be as well if they kept out of his way when they came upon the farm.

Now in saying that the room was thick with smoke Jan lied, for both the men's pipes went out when they began to talk. But as I knew why he lied I did not think so much of it. To tell the truth, at that moment I could see little better than he could, since, although I would have poisoned those two Scotchmen before I suffered them to take Ralph away, the very thought of his going was enough to fill my eyes with tears, and to cause Suzanne to weep aloud shamelessly.

"Wait a bit, father,—I beg your pardon, Jan Botmar," said Ralph in a clear and angry voice; "it is my turn now, for you may remember that when we began to talk I had something to say, but you stopped me. Now, with your leave, as you have got off the horse I will get on."

Jan slowly sat down again and said:

"Speak. What is it?"

"This: that if you send me away you are likely to lose more than you bargain for."

Now Jan stared at him perplexedly, but I smiled, for I guessed what was to come.

"What am I likely to lose?" he asked, "beyond my best horse and my felt hat? Allemachter! Do you want my span of black oxen also? Well, you shall have them if you like, for I should wish you to trek to your new home in England behind good cattle."

"No," answered Ralph coolly, "but I want your daughter, and if you send me away I think that she will come with me."

CHAPTER VI

THE COMING OF THE ENGLISHMEN

Now on hearing this Suzanne said, "Oh!" and sank back in her chair as though she were going to faint; but I burst out laughing, half because Ralph's impertinence tickled me and half at the sight of my husband's face. Presently he turned upon me in a fine rage.

"Be silent, you silly woman," he said. "Do you hear what that mad boy says? He says that he wants my daughter."

"Well, what of it?" I answered. "Is there anything wonderful in that? Suzanne is of an age to be married and pretty enough for any young man to want her."

"Yes, yes; that is true now I come to think of it," said Jan, pulling his beard. "But, woman, he says that he wants to take her away with him."

"Ah!" I replied, "that is another matter. That he shall never do with my consent."

"No, indeed, he shall never do that," echoed Jan.

"Suzanne," said I in the pause that followed, "you have heard all this talk. Tell us, then, openly what is your mind in the matter."

"My mind is, mother," she answered very quietly, "that I wish to obey you and my father in all things, as is my duty, but that I have a deeper duty towards Ralph whom

God gave me out of the sea. Therefore, if you send away Ralph without a cause, if he desires it I shall follow him as soon as I am of age and marry him, or if you keep me from him by force then I think that I shall die. That is all I have to say."

"And quite enough, too," I answered, though in my heart I liked the girl's spirit, and guessed that she was playing a part to prevent her father from sending away Ralph against his will.

"All this is pretty hearing," said Jan, staring from one to the other. "Why, now that I think of it, I never heard that you two were more than brother and sister to each other. Say, you shameless girl, when did all this come about, and why do you dare to promise yourself in marriage without my consent?"

"Because there was no time to ask it, father," said Suzanne, looking down, "for Ralph and I only spoke together this morning."

"He spoke to you this morning, and now it seems that you are ready to forsake your father and your mother and to follow him across the world, you wicked and ungrateful child."

"I am not wicked and I am not ungrateful," answered Suzanne; "it is you who are wicked, who want to send Ralph away and break all our hearts."

"It is false, miss," shouted her father in answer, "for you know well that I do not want to send him away."

"Then why did you tell him that he must go and take your roan horse and new hat?"

"For his own good, girl."

"Is it for his good that he should go away from all of us who love him and be lost across the sea?" and choking she burst into tears, while her father muttered:

"Why, the girl has become like a tiger, she who was milder than a sheep!"

"Hush, Suzanne," broke in Ralph, "and you who have been father and mother to me, listen I pray you. It is true that Suzanne and I love each other very dearly, as we have always loved each other, though how much we did not know till this morning. Now, I am a waif and a castaway whom you have nurtured, and have neither lands nor goods of my own, therefore you may well think that I am no match for your daughter, who is so beautiful, and who, if she outlives you, will inherit all that you have. If you decide thus it is just, however hard it may be. But you tell me, though I have heard nothing of it till now, and I think that it may be but idle talk, that I have both lands and goods far away in England, and you bid me be-gone to them. Well, if you turn me out I must go, for I cannot stay alone in the veldt without a house, or a friend, or a hoof of cattle. But then I tell you that when Suzanne is of age I shall return and marry her, and take her away with me, as I have a right to do if she desires it, for I will not lose everything that I love in the world at one stroke. Indeed nothing but death shall part me from Suzanne. Therefore, it comes to this: either you must let me stay here and, poor as I am, be married to Suzanne when it shall please you, or, if you dismiss me, you must be ready to see me come back and take away Suzanne."

"Suzanne, Suzanne," I interrupted angrily, for I grew jealous of the girl; "have you no thought or word, Ralph, for any save Suzanne?"

"I have thoughts for all," he answered, "but Suzanne alone has thought for me, since it seems that your husband would send me away, and you, mother, sit still and say not a word to stop him."

"Learn to judge speech and not silence, lad," I answered. "Look you, all have been talking, and I have shammed dead like a stink-cat when dogs are about; now I am going to begin. First of all, you, Jan, are a fool, for in your thick head you think that rank and wealth are everything to a man, and therefore you would send Ralph away to seek rank and wealth that may or may not belong to him, although he does not wish to go. As for you, Ralph, you are a bigger fool, for you think that Jan Botmar, your foster-father here, desires to be rid of you when in truth he only seeks your good to his own sore loss. As for you, Suzanne, you are the biggest fool of all, for you wish to fly in everybody's face, like a cat with her first litter of kittens; but there, what is the use of arguing with a girl in love? Now listen, and I will ask you some questions, all of you. Jan, do you wish to send Ralph away with these strangers?"

"Almighty! vrouw," he answered, "you know well that I would as soon send away my right hand. I wish him to stop here for ever, and whatever I have is his; yes, even my daughter. But I seek what is best for him, and I would not have it said in after years that Jan Botmar had kept an English lad not old enough to judge for himself from his rank and wealth because he took pleasure in his company and wished to marry him to his girl."

"Good," I said. "And now for you, Suzanne; what have you to say?"

"I have nothing to add to my words," she replied; "you know all my heart."

"Good again. And you, Ralph?"

"I say, mother, that I will not budge from this place unless I am ordered to go, and if I do go, I will come back for Suzanne. I love you all, and with you I wish to live and nowhere else."

"Nay, Ralph," I answered sighing, "if once you go you will never come back, for out yonder you will find a new home, new interests, and, perchance, new loves. Well, though nobody has thought of me in this matter, I have a voice in it, and I will speak for myself. That lad yonder has been a son to me for many years, and I who have none love him as such. He is a man as we reckon in this country, and he does not wish to leave us any more than we wish him to go. Moreover, he loves Suzanne, and Suzanne loves him, and I believe that the God who brought them together at first means them to be husband and wife, and that such love as they bear to each other will give them more together than any wealth or rank can bring to them apart. Therefore I say, husband, let our son, Ralph, stay here with us and marry our daughter, Suzanne, decently and in due season, and let their children be our children, and their love our love."

"And how about the Scotchmen who are coming with power to take him away?"

"Do you and Ralph go to the bush-veldt with the cattle to-morrow," I answered, "and leave me to deal with the Scotchmen."

"Well," said Jan, "I consent, for who can stand up against so many words, and the Lord knows that to lose Ralph would have broken my heart as it would have broken that girl's, perhaps more so, since girls change their fancies, but I am too old to change. Come here, my children."

They came, and he laid one of his big hands upon the head of each of them, saying:—

"May the God in Heaven bless you both, who to me

are one as dear as the other, making you happy with each
other for many long years, and may He turn aside from
you and from us the punishment that is due to all of us
because, on account of our great love, we are holding you
back, Ralph, from the home, the kin and the fortune to
which you were born." Then he kissed each of them on
the forehead and let them go.

"If there be any punishment for that which is no sin,
on my head be it," said Ralph, "since never would I have
gone from here by my own will."

"Aye, aye," answered Jan, "but who can take account
of the talk of a lad in love? Well, we have committed
the sin and we must bear the sorrow. Now I go out to
see to the kraaling of the cattle, which we will drive off
to the bush-veldt to-morrow at dawn, for I will have
naught to do with these Scotchmen; your mother must
settle with them as she wills, only I beg of her that she
will tell me nothing of the bargain. Nay, do not come
with me, Ralph; stop you with your dear, for to-morrow
you will be parted for a while."

So he went, and did not return again till late, and we
three sat together and made pretence to be very happy,
but somehow were a little sad, for Jan's words about sin
and sorrow stuck in our hearts, as the honest words of a
stupid, upright man are apt to do.

Now on the morrow at dawn, as had been arranged, Jan
and Ralph rode away to the warm veldt with the cattle,
leaving me and Suzanne to look after the farm. Three
days later the Scotchmen came, and then it was that for
love of Ralph and for the sake of the happiness of my
daughter I sinned the greatest sin of all my life—the sin
that was destined to shape the fates of others yet unborn.

I was seated on the *stoep* in the afternoon when I saw three white men and some Cape boys, their servants, riding up to the house.

"Here come those who would steal my boy from me," I thought to myself, and, like Pharaoh, I hardened my heart.

Now in those days my sight was very good, and while the men were yet some way off I studied them all and made up my mind about them. First there was a large young man of five-and-twenty or thereabouts, and I noted with a sort of fear that he was not unlike to Ralph. The eyes were the same and the shape of the forehead, only this gentleman had a weak, uncertain mouth, and I judged that he was very good-humoured, but of an indolent mind. By his side rode another man of quite a different stamp, and middle-aged. "The lawyer," I said to myself as I looked at his weasel-like face, bushy eyebrows, and red hair. Indeed, that was an easy guess, for who can mistake a lawyer, whatever his race may be? That trade is stronger than any blood, and leaves the same seal on all who follow it. Doubtless if those lawyers of whom the Lord speaks hard things in the Testament were set side by side with the lawyers who draw mortgage bonds and practise usury here in South Africa, they would prove to be as like to each other as are the grains of corn upon one mealie cob. Yes, when, all dressed the same, they stand together among the goats on the last day few indeed will know them apart.

"A fool and a knave," said I to myself. "Well, perhaps I can deal with the knave and then the fool will not trouble me."

As for the third man, I took no pains to study him, for I saw at once that he was nothing but an interpreter.

Well, up they rode to the *stoep*, the two Englishmen

taking off their hats to me, after their foolish fashion, while the interpreter, who called me " Aunt," although I was younger than he was, asked for leave to off-saddle, according to our custom. I nodded my head, and having given the horses to the Cape boys, they came up onto the *stoep* and shook hands with me as I sat. I was not going to rise to greet two Englishmen whom I already hated in my heart, first because they *were* Englishmen, and secondly because they were about to tempt me into sin, for such sooner or later we always learn to hate.

" Sit," I said, pointing to the yellow-wood bench which was seated with strips of *rimpi*, and the three of them squeezed themselves into the bench and sat there like white-breasted crows on a bough; the young man staring at me with a silly smile, the lawyer peering this way and that, and turning up his sharp nose at the place and all in it, and the interpreter doing nothing at all, for he was a sensible man, who knew the habits of well-bred people and how to behave in their presence. After five minutes or so the lawyer grew impatient, and said something in a sharp voice, to which the interpreter answered, " Wait."

So they waited till, just as the young man was beginning to go to sleep before my very eyes; Suzanne came onto the verandah, whereupon he woke up in a hurry, and, jumping off the bench, began to bow and scrape and to offer her his seat, for there was no other.

" Suzanne," I said, taking no notice of his bad manners. " get coffee," and she went, looking less displeased at his grimaces than I would have had her do.

In time the coffee came, and they drank it, or pretended to, after which the lawyer began to grow impatient once more, and spoke to the interpreter, who said to me that they had come to visit us on a matter of business.

"Then tell him that it can wait till after we have eaten," I answered. "It is not my habit to talk business in the afternoon. Why is the lawyer man so impatient, seeing that doubtless he is paid by the day?"

This was translated, and the lawyer asked how I knew his trade.

"In the same way that I know a weasel by its face and a stink-cat by its smell," I replied, for every minute I hated that advocate more.

At this answer the lawyer grew white with anger, and the young lord burst into a roar of laughter, for, as I have said, these English people have no manners. However, they settled themselves down again on the yellow-wood bench and looked at me; while I, folding my hands, sat opposite, and looked at them for somewhere about another hour, as the interpreter told them that if they moved I should be offended, and, for my part, I was determined that I would not speak to them of their business until Suzanne had gone to bed.

At last, when I saw that they would bear it no longer, for they were becoming very wrathful, and saying words that sounded like oaths, I called for supper and we went in and ate it. Here again I noticed the resemblance between the young man and Ralph, for he had the same tricks of eating and drinking, and I saw that when he had done his meat he turned himself a little sideways from the table, crossing his legs in a peculiar fashion just as it always had been Ralph's habit to do.

"The two had one grandfather, or one grandmother," I said to myself, and grew afraid at the thought.

CHAPTER VII

THE SIN OF VROUW BOTMAR

WHEN the meat was cleared away I bade Suzanne go to bed, which she did most unwillingly, for knowing the errand of these men she wished to hear our talk. As soon as she was gone I took a seat so that the light of the candles left my face in shadow and fell full on those of the three men—a wise thing to do if one is wicked enough to intend to tell lies about any matter—and said:

"Now, here I am at your service; be pleased to set out the business that you have in hand."

Then they began, the lawyer, speaking through the interpreter, asking, "Are you the Vrouw Botmar?"

"That is my name."

"Where is your husband, Jan Botmar?"

"Somewhere on the veldt; I do not know where."

"Will he be back to-morrow?"

"No."

"When will he be back?"

"Perhaps in two months, perhaps in three, I cannot tell."

At this they consulted together, and then went on:

"Have you living with you a young Englishman named Ralph Mackenzie?"

"One named Ralph Kenzie lives with us."

" Where is he? "

" With my husband on the veldt. I do not know where."

" Can you find him? "

" No, the veldt is very wide. If you wish to see him you must wait till he comes back."

" When will that be? "

" I am not his nurse and cannot tell; perhaps in three months, perhaps in six."

Now again they consulted, and once more went on:

" Was the boy, Ralph Mackenzie, or Kenzie, ship-wrecked in the *India* in the year 1824? "

" Dear Lord! " I cried, affecting to lose my patience, " am I an old Kaffir wife up before the Landdrost for stealing hens that I should be cross-questioned in this fashion? Set out all your tale at once, man, and I will answer it."

Thereon, shrugging his shoulders, the lawyer produced a paper which the interpreter translated to me. In it were written down the names of the passengers who were upon the vessel *India* when she sailed from a place called Bombay, and among the names those of Lord and Lady Glenthirsk and of their son, the Honourable Ralph Mackenzie, aged nine. Then followed the evidence of one or two survivors of the shipwreck, which stated that Lady Glenthirsk and her son were seen to reach the shore in safety in the boat that was launched from the sinking ship. After this came a paragraph from an English newspaper published in Capetown, dated not two years before, and headed " Strange Tale of the Sea," which paragraph, with some few errors, told the story of the finding of Ralph—though how the writing man knew it I know not, unless it was through the tutor with the blue spectacles of whom I have spoken—and said that he was still living on the farm of Jan Botmar in the Transkei. This was all that was in the paper. I asked to look at it and kept it, saying in the morning that the Kaffir girl seeing it lying about the kitchen had used it to light the fire; but to this day it is with the other things in the waggon chest under my bed.

When the paper was done with, the lawyer took up the tale and told me that it was believed in England that Lord Glenthirsk had been drowned in the sea, as indeed he was, and that Lady Glenthirsk and her son perished on the shore with the other women and children, for so those sent by the English Government to search out the facts had reported. Thus it came about that after a while Lord Glenthirsk's younger brother was admitted by law to his title and estates, which he enjoyed for some eight years, that is, until his death. About a year before he died, however, someone sent him the paragraph headed " Strange Tale of the Sea," and he was much disturbed by it, though to himself he argued that it was nothing but an idle story, such as it seems are often put into newspapers. The end of the matter was that he took no steps to discover whether the tale were true or false, and none knew of it save himself, and he was not minded to go fishing in that ugly water. So it came about that he kept silent as the grave, till at length, when the grave yawned at his feet, and when the rank and the lands and the wealth were of no more use to him, he opened his mouth to his son and to his lawyer, the two men who sat before me, and to them only, bidding them seek out the beginning of the tale, and if it were true, to make restitution to his nephew.

Now—for all this, listening with my ears wide open, and sometimes filling in what was not told me in words, I gathered from the men before they left the house—as it

chanced the dying lord could not have chosen two worse
people for such an errand, seeing that although the son was
honest, both of them were interested in proving the tale
to be false. Since that time, however, often I have
thought that he knew this himself, and trusted by the
choice both to cheat his own conscience and to preserve
the wealth and dignity for his son. God, to whom he has
gone, alone knows the truth of it, but with such a man it
may very well have been as I think. I say that both were
interested, for it seems, as he told me afterwards, that the
lawyer was to receive a great sum—ten thousand pounds—
under the will of the dead lord for whom he had done
much during his lifetime. But if Ralph were proved to
be the heir this sum would have been his and not the
lawyer's, for the money was part of his father's inheritance; therefore it was worth just ten thousand pounds to
that lawyer to convince himself and the false lord that
Ralph was not the man, and therefore it was that I found
him so easy to deal with.

Now after his father was dead the lawyer tried to persuade the son to take no notice of his dying words, and to
let the matter rest where it was, seeing that he had nothing to gain and much to lose. But this he would not consent to, for, as I have said, he was honest, declaring that
he could not be easy in his mind till he knew the truth,
and that if he did not go to find it out himself he would
send others to do so for him. As the lawyer desired this
least of anything, he gave way, and they set out upon their
journey—which in those days was a very great journey
indeed—arriving at last in safety at our stead in the
Transkei; for, whether he liked it or not, his companion—
who now was called Lord Glenthirsk—would not be turned
aside from the search or suffer him to prosecute it alone.

At length, when all the tale was told, the lawyer looked at me with his sharp eyes and said, through the interpreter:

"Vrouw Botmar, you have heard the story, tell us what you know. Is the young man who lives with you he whom we seek?"

Now I thought for a second, though that second seemed like a year. All doubt had left me, there was no room for it. Ralph and no other was the man, and on my answer might hang his future. But I had argued the thing out before and made up my mind to lie, though, so far as I know, it is the only lie I ever told, and I am not a woman who often changes her mind. Therefore I lied.

"It is not he," I said, "though for his sake I might wish that it were, and this I can prove to you."

Now, when I had told this great falsehood, prompted to it by my love for the lad and my love for Suzanne, his affianced wife, my mind grew as it were empty for a moment, and I remember that in the emptiness I seemed to hear a sound of laughter echoing in the air somewhere above the roof of the house. Very swiftly I recovered myself, and looking at the men I saw that my words rejoiced them, except the interpreter indeed, who being a paid servant coming from far away, from the neighbourhood of Capetown I believe, had no interest in the matter one way or the other beyond that of earning his money with as little trouble as possible. Yes, they smiled at each other, looking as though a great weight had been lifted off their minds, till presently the lawyer checked himself and said:

"Be so good as to set out the proofs of which you speak, Vrouw Botmar."

"I will," I answered, "but tell me first, the ship *India* was wrecked in the year 1824, was she not?"

" Undoubtedly," answered the lawyer.

" Well, have you heard that another ship called the *Flora*, travelling from the Cape I know not whither, was lost on this coast in the same month of the following year, and that a few of her passengers escaped? "

" I have heard of it," he said.

" Good. Now look here," and going to a chest that stood beneath the window, I lifted from it the old Bible that belonged to my grandfather and father, on the white pages at the beginning of which are written the record of many births, marriages, deaths and other notable events that had happened in the family. Opening it I searched and pointed to a certain entry inscribed in the big writing of my husband Jan, and in ink which was somewhat faint, for the ink that the traders sold us in those days had little virtue in it. Beneath this entry were others made by Jan in later years, telling of things that had happened to us, such as the death of his great-aunt who left him money, the outbreak of small-pox on the farm, and the number of people who died from it, the attack of a band of the red Kaffirs upon our house, when by the mercy of God we beat them off, leaving twelve of their dead behind them, but taking as many of our best oxen, and so forth.

" Read," I said, and the interpreter read as follows:

" On the twelfth day of September in the year 1825 (the date being written in letters) our little daughter Suzanne found a starving English boy in a kloof, who had been shipwrecked on the coast. We have taken him in as a gift of the Lord. He says that his name is Rolf Kenzie."

" You see the date," I said.

" Yes," answered the lawyer, " and it has not been altered! "

" No," I added, " it has not been altered; " but I did

not tell them that Jan had not written it down till afterwards, and then by mistake had recorded the year in which
he wrote, refusing to change it, although I pointed out the
error, because, he said, there was no room, and that it
would make a mess in the book.

"There is one more thing," I went on; "you say the
mother of him you seek was a great lady. Well, I saw
the body of the mother of the boy who was found, and it
was that of a common person very roughly clad with coarse
underclothes and hands hard with labour, on which there
was but one ring, and that of silver. Here it is," and going
to a drawer I took from it a common silver ring which
I once bought from a pedlar because he worried me into it.
"Lastly, gentlemen, the father of our lad was no lord,
unless in your country it is the custom of lords to herd
sheep, for the boy told me that in his own land his father
was a shepherd, and that he was travelling to some distant
English colony to follow his trade. That is all I have to
say about it, though I am sorry that the lad is not here to
tell it you himself."

When he had heard this statement of mine, which I
made in a cold and indifferent voice, the young lord,
Ralph's cousin, rose and stretched himself, smiling happily.

"Well," he said, "there is the end of a very bad night-
mare, and I am glad enough that we came here and found
out the truth, for had we not done so I should never have
been happy in my mind."

"Yes," answered the lawyer, the interpreter rendering
their words all the while, "the Vrouw Botmar's evidence
is conclusive, though I shall put her statement in writing
and ask her to sign it. There is only one thing, and that
is the strange resemblance of the names," and he glanced
at him with his quick eyes.

"There are many Mackenzies in Scotland," answered Lord Glenthirsk, "and I have no doubt that this poor fellow was a shepherd emigrating with his wife and child to Australia or somewhere." Then he yawned and added, "I am going outside to get some air before I sleep. Perhaps you will draw up the paper for the good lady to sign."

"Certainly, my lord," answered the lawyer, and the young man went away quite convinced.

After he had gone the lawyer produced pen and ink and wrote out the statement, putting in it all the lies that I had told, and copying the extract from the fly-leaf of the Bible. When he had done the interpreter translated it to me, and then it was that the lawyer told me about the last wishes of the dying lord, the father of the young Scotchman, and how it would have cost him ten thousand pounds and much business also had the tale proved true. Now at last he gave me the paper to sign. Besides the candles on the table, which being of mutton fat had burnt out, there was a lamp fed with whale's oil, but this also was dying, the oil being exhausted, so that its flame, which had sunk low, jumped from time to time with a little noise, giving out a blue light. In that unholy blue light, which turned our faces ghastly pale, the lawyer and I looked at each other as I sat before him, the pen in my hand, and in his eyes I read that he was certain that I was about to sign to a wicked lie, and in mine he read that I knew it to be a lie.

For a while we stared at each other thus, discovering each other's souls. "Sign," he said, shrugging his shoulders, "the light dies."

Then I signed, and as I wrote the lamp went out, leaving us in darkness, and through the darkness once more I heard that sound of laughter echoing in the air above the house.

CHAPTER VIII

THE WISDOM OF SUZANNE

Now, although Suzanne heard not a word of our talk, still she guessed its purport well enough, for she knew that I proposed to throw dust into the eyes of the Englishmen. This troubled her conscience sorely, for the more she thought of it the more did it seem to her to be wicked that just because we loved him and did not wish to part with him, Ralph should be cheated of his birthright. All night long she lay awake brooding, and before ever the dawn broke she had settled in her mind that she herself would speak to the Englishmen, telling them the truth, come what might of her words, for Suzanne, my daughter, was a determined girl with an upright heart. Now feeling happier because of her decision, at length she fell asleep and slept late, and as it happened this accident of fate was the cause of the miscarriage of her scheme.

It came about in this way. Quite early in the morning —at sun-up, indeed—the Englishmen rose, and coming out of the little guest-chamber, drank the coffee that I had made ready for them, and talked together for a while. Then the young lord—Ralph's cousin—said that as they journeyed yesterday at a distance of about an hour on horseback from the farm he had noticed a large *vlei*, or *pan*, where were many ducks and also some antelope. To this *vlei* he proposed to ride forward with one servant only, and to stay there till the others overtook him, shooting the wild things which lived in the place, for to be happy these Englishmen must always be killing something. So he bade me farewell, making me a present of the gold chain which he took off his watch, which chain I still have. Then he rode away, smiling after his fashion; and as I watched him go I was glad to think that he was no knave but only an easy tool in the hands of others. We never met again, but I believe that death finished his story many years ago; indeed, all those of whom I tell are dead; only Jan and I survive, and our course is well-nigh run.

When Suzanne awoke at length, having heard from a Kaffir girl that the strangers had ordered their horses, but not that the young lord had ridden forward, she slipped from the house silently, fearing lest I should stay her, and hid herself in a little patch of bush at the corner of the big mealie field by which she knew the Englishmen must pass on their return journey. Presently she heard them coming, and when she saw that the young lord was not with them, she went to the lawyer, who pulled up his horse and waited for her, the rest of the party riding on, and asked where his master was, saying that she wished to talk with him. And here I must say, if I have not said it before, that Suzanne could speak English, though not well. The Hollander tutor had instructed her in that tongue, in which Ralph also would converse with her at times when he did not wish others to understand what they were saying, for he never forgot his mother language, though he mixed many Dutch words with it.

"He has ridden forward an hour or more ago. Can I take any message to him for you?" said the lawyer. "Or if you wish to talk of business, to speak to me is to speak to him."

"That may be so," answered Suzanne, "still I like to draw my water at the fountain itself. Yet, as he has gone, I beg you to listen to me, for when you have heard what I have to say I think that you will bring him back. You came here about Ralph Kenzie, did you not, and my mother told you that he is not the man whom you seek, did she not?"

The lawyer nodded.

"Well, I tell you that all this tale is false, for he is the very man," and she poured out the true story of Ralph and of the plot that had been made to deceive them about him.

Now, as I have said, Suzanne's English was none of the best and it is possible that the lawyer did not understand. For my part, however, I think that he understood well enough, for she told me afterwards that his face grew grey and anxious as he listened, and that at length he said:

"All this you tell me is very strange and weighty, so much so that I must bring my friend back to look more closely into the matter. Return now to the farm and say nothing of having met me, for by this evening, or to-morrow at the latest, we will come there again and sift out the truth of the question."

To this she agreed, being guileless, and the lawyer rode away after the other. All that day and all the next Suzanne scarcely spoke to me, but I saw that she was expecting something to happen, and that she glanced continually towards the path by which the Englishmen had journeyed, thinking to see them riding back to the farm. But they rode back no more, and I am sure that the cunning lawyer never breathed one word of his meeting with Suzanne and of what took place at it to the young lord. That book was shut and it did not please him to reopen it, since to do so might have cost him ten thousand pounds. On the third morning I found Suzanne still looking down the path, and my patience being exhausted by her silence, I spoke to her sharply.

"What are you doing, girl?" I asked. "Have we not had enough visitors of late that you must stand here all day awaiting more?"

"I seek no new visitors," Suzanne said, "but those who have been here only, and I see now that I seek in vain."

"What do you mean, Suzanne?"

Now of a sudden she seemed to make up her mind to speak, for she turned and faced me boldly, saying:

"I mean, mother, that I told the Englishman with the red hair, the agent, that all the fine tale you spun to him about Ralph was false, and that he *was* the man they came to find."

"You dared do that, girl?" I said, then checked myself and added, "Well, what did the man say?"

"He said that he would ride on and bring the young lord back that I might talk with him, but they have not come."

"No, nor will they, Suzanne, for if they sought they did not wish to find, or at least the lawyer did not wish it, for he had too much at stake. Well, things have gone finely with you, seeing that your hands are clean from sin, and that Ralph still stays at your side."

"The sin of the parents is the sin of the child," she answered, and then of a sudden she took fire as it were, and fell upon me and beat me with her tongue; nor could I hold my own before this girl of eighteen, the truth being that she had right on her side, and I knew it. She told me that we were wicked plotters who, to pleasure ourselves, had stolen from Ralph everything except his life ; and

many other such hard sayings she threw at me till at last
I could bear it no more, but gave her back word for word.
Indeed, it would be difficult to say which had the best of
that quarrel, for if Suzanne's tongue was the nimbler and
her words were winged with truth, I had the weight of
experience on my side and the custom of authority. At
last, as she paused breathless, I cried out:

"And for whose sake was all this done, you ungrateful
chit, if it was not for your own?"

"If that was so, which is not altogether true," she answered, "it would have pleased me better, if, rather than
make me a partner in this crime, and set me as bait to
snare Ralph, you had left me to look after my own wel-
fare."

"What!" I exclaimed, "are you then so shallow hearted
that you were ready to bid farewell to him who for many
years has been as your brother, and is now your affianced
husband? You know well whatever he might promise
now, that if once he had gone across the sea to England,
you would have seen him no more."

"No," she answered, growing calm of a sudden, "I was
not so prepared, for sooner would I die than lose Ralph."

"How, then, do you square this with all your fine talk?"
I asked, thinking that at length I had trapped her. "If
he had gone you must have lost him."

"Not so," she answered, innocently, "for I should have
married him before he went, and then I could have been
certain that he would return here whenever I wished it."

Now when I heard this I gasped, partly because this
girl's cleverness took the breath from me, and partly with
mortification that I should have lived to learn wisdom
from the mouth of a babe and a suckling. For there was
no doubt of it, this plan, of which I had not even thought,

was the answer to the riddle, since by means of it Ralph might have kept his own, and we, I doubt not, should have kept Ralph. Once married to Suzanne he would have returned to her, or if she had gone with him for a little while, which might have been better, she would certainly have brought him back, seeing that she loved us and her home too well to forsake them.

Yes, I gasped, and the only answer that I could make when I reflected how little need there had been for the sin which we had sinned, was to burst into weeping, whereon Suzanne ran to me and kissed me and we made friends again. But all the same, I do not think that she ever thought quite so well of me afterwards, and if I thought the more of her, still I made up my mind that the sooner she was married and had a husband of her own to preach to, the better it would be for all of us.

Thus ended the story of the coming of the Englishmen, and of how Ralph lost his wealth and rank. We never heard or saw more of them, seeing that in those days before the great Trek we did not write letters, and if we had we should not have known where to send them, nor did the post-cart pass the door twice a week as it does in this overcrowded land of Natal.

Now I must go on to tell of the doings of that devil upon earth, Swart Piet, and of how the little Kaffir witch-doctoress, Sihamba Ngenyanga, which means She-who-walks-by-the-moonlight, became the slave and saviour of Suzanne.

At this time the Heer van Vooren, Swart Piet's father, had been dead for two years, and there were strange stories as to the manner of his death which I do not think it necessary to set out here. Whether or no Swart Piet did or did not murder his father I cannot say, nor does it matter, for at the least he worked other crimes as bad. After the death of the Heer van Vooren, however he may have chanced to die, this is certain, that Swart Piet inherited great riches as we used to reckon riches in those days; that is, he had vast herds of cattle and goats and sheep, some of which were kept for him by native chiefs far away, as much land as he wanted, and, it was said, a good sum in English gold.   But he was a strange man, not like to other men, for he married no wife and courted no misses, that is until he took to courting Suzanne, and his only pleasure was to keep the company of Kaffir chiefs and women and to mix himself up with the devilments of the witch-doctors.   Still, as every man has his fate, at last he fell in love with Suzanne, and in love with her he remained during all his wicked life, if that can be love which seeks to persecute and bring misery upon its object. It was just before the coming of the Englishmen that this passion of his manifested itself, for whenever he met the girl—outside the house for the most part, since Jan did not like to have him in it—he made sweet speeches and passed foolish pleasantries which, to be just, I am sure Suzanne never encouraged, since all her heart was elsewhere.

Now Swart Piet had information of everything, for his Kaffir spies brought it to him ; therefore he very soon learned that Jan and Ralph had gone away with the cattle to the warm veldt, and that we two women were alone in the house.   This was his opportunity, and one of which he availed himself, for now two or three times a week he would ride over from his place, take supper and ask leave to sleep, which it was difficult to refuse, all this time wearying the poor girl with his attentions.   At last I spoke my mind to him about it, though not without hesitation, for to tell truth Swart Piet was one of the few men of whom I have ever been afraid. He listened to me politely and answered:

"All this is very true, Aunt, but if you desire a fruit and it will not fall, then you must shake the tree."

"What if it sticks to the bough?" I asked.

"Then, Aunt, you must climb the tree and pluck it."

"And what if by that time it is in another man's pouch?"

"Then, Aunt," he answered with one of those dark smiles that turned my blood cold, "then, Aunt, the best thing which you can do is to kill the other man and take it out, for after that the fruit will taste all the sweeter."

"Get you gone, Swart Piet," I said in anger, "for no man who talks thus shall stay in my house, and it is very well for you that neither my husband nor Ralph Kenzie are here to put you out of it."

"Well," he answered, they are not here, are they?" And as for your house, it is a pretty place; but I only seek one thing in it, and that is not built into the walls. I thank you for your hospitality, Aunt, and now, good-day to you."

"Suzanne!" I called, "Suzanne!" for I thought that she was in her chamber; but the girl, knowing that Piet van Vooren was here, had slipped out, and of this he was aware. He knew, moreover, where she had gone, for I think that one of his Kaffir servants was watching outside and told him, and thither he followed her and made love to her.

In the end—for he would not be put off—he asked her for a kiss, whereat she grew angry. Then, for he was no shy wooer, he tried to take it by force; but she was strong and active and slipped from him. Instead of being ashamed, he only laughed after his uncanny fashion, and said:

"Well, missy, you have the best of me now, but I shall win that kiss yet. Oh! I know all about it; you love the English castaway, don't you? But there, a woman can love many men in her life, and when one is dead another will serve her turn."

"What do you mean, myn Heer van Vooren?" asked Suzanne, afraid.

"Mean? Nothing, but that I shall win that kiss yet, yes, and before very long."

CHAPTER IX

Now in a valley of the hills, something over an hour's ride from the farm, and not far from the road that ran to Swart Piet's place, lived the little Kaffir witch-doc-toress, Sihamba Ngenyanga. This woman did not be-long to any of the Transkei or neighbouring tribes, but had drifted down from the North; indeed, she was of Swazi or some such blood, though why she left her own people we did not know at that time. In appearance Si-hamba was very strange, for, although healthy, perfectly shaped and copper-coloured rather than black, she was no taller than a child of twelve years old—a thing that made many people believe that she was a bush woman, which she most certainly was not. For a Kaffir also she was pretty, having fine small features, beautiful white teeth, and a fringe of wavy black hair that stood out stiffly round her head something after the fashion of the gold plates which the saints wear in the pictures in our old Bible.

This woman Sihamba, who might have been a little over thirty years of age, had been living in our neighbour-hood for some three or four years and practising as a doc-toress. Not that she was a "black" doctoress, for she never took part in the "smelling-out" of human beings for witchcraft or in the more evil sort of rites. Her trade was to sell charms and medicines to the sick, also to cure animals of their ailments, at which, indeed, she was very clever, though there was some who said that when she chose she could "throw the bones" and tell the future better than most, and this without dressing herself up in bladders and snake skins, or falling into fits, or trances, and such mummery. Lastly, amongst the natives about, and some of the Boers too, I am sorry to say, she had the reputation of being the best of rainmakers, and many were the head of cattle that she earned by prophesying the break-up of a drought, or the end of continual rains. Indeed, it is certain that no one whom I ever knew had so great a gift of insight into the omens of the weather at all seasons of the year, as this strange Sihamba Ngenyanga, a name that she got, by the way, because of her habit of wandering about in the moonlight to gather the herbs and the medicine roots which she used in her trade.

On several occasions Jan had sent animals to be doctored by this Sihamba, for she would not come out to attend to them whatever fee was offered to her. At first I did not approve of it, but as she always cured the animals, whatever their ailments might be, I gave in on the matter.

Now it happened that a few months before some traveller who had guested at our house gave Suzanne a little rough-haired dog bred of parents which had been brought from England. Of this dog Suzanne grew very fond, and when it fell sick of the distemper she was much distressed. So it came about that one afternoon Suzanne put the dog in a basket, and taking with her an old Hottentot to carry it, set out upon her grey mare for the valley where Sihamba lived. Now Sihamba had her hut and the huts of the few people in her service in a recess at the end of the valley, so placed that until you were quite on to them you would never have guessed that they were there. Down this valley Suzanne rode, the Hottentot with the basket on his head trotting by her side, till turning the corner she came upon a scene which she had very little expected. In one part of the open space beyond her, herded by some Kaffirs, were a number of cattle, sheep and goats. Opposite to them in the shadow under the hillside stood the huts of Sihamba, and in front of these grew a large tree. Beneath this tree was Sihamba herself with scarcely any clothing on her, for she had been stripped, her tiny wrists bound together behind her back and a rope about her neck, of which one end was thrown over a bough of the tree. In front of her, laughing brutally, stood none other than Swart Piet and with him a small crowd of men, mostly half-breed wanderers of the sort that trek from place to place claiming hospitality on the grounds of cousinship or poverty, until they are turned off as nuisances. Also there were present a few Kaffirs, either headmen in Swart Piet's pay or some of his dark associates in witchcraft.

At first Suzanne was inclined to turn her horse and fly, but she was a brave girl, and the perilous state of the little doctoress moved her to pity, for where Swart Piet was there she suspected cruelty and wicked motive. So she rode on, yes, straight up to Swart Piet himself.

" In the name of Heaven what passes here, myn Heer? " she asked.

" Ah! Miss Suzanne, is it you? " he answered. " Well, you have not chosen a nice time for your visit, for we are about to—hang—this thief and witch, who has been duly convicted after a fair trial."

" A fair trial," said Suzanne, glancing scornfully at the

rabble about her, "and were these friends of yours the jury? What is her offence?"

"Her offence is that she who lives here on my land has stolen my cattle and hid them away in a secret kloof. It has been proved against her by ample evidence. There are the cattle yonder mixed up with her own. I, as Veld-Cornet of the district, have tried the case according to law, and the woman having been found guilty must die according to law."

"Indeed, myn Heer," said Suzanne, "then if I understand you right, you are both accuser and judge, and the law which permits this is one that I never heard of. Oh!" she went on angrily, "no wonder that the English sing a loud song about us Boers and our cruelty to the natives when such a thing as this can happen. It is not justice, myn Heer; it is a crime for which, if you escape the hand of man, God will bring you to account."

Then for the first time Sihamba spoke in a very quiet voice, which showed no sign of fear.

"You are right, lady," she said; "it is not justice, it is a crime born of revenge, and my life must pay forfeit for his wickedness. I am a free woman, and I have harmed none and have bewitched none. I have cured sick people and sick creatures, that is all. The Heer says that I live upon his land, but I am not his slave; I pay him rent to live here. I never stole his cattle ; they were mixed up with mine by his servants in a far-off kloof in order to trump up a charge against me, and he knows it, for he gave orders that the thing should be done, so that afterwards he might have the joy of hanging me to this tree, because he wishes to be avenged upon me for other matters, private matters between me and him. But, lady, do not trouble yourself about the fate of such a poor black creature as I am. Go away and tell the story if you will, but go quickly, for these sights of death are not fit for young eyes like yours to see."

"I will not go," exclaimed Suzanne, "or if I go, it shall be to bring down upon you, Swart Piet, the weight of the law which you have broken. Ah! would that my father were at home; he does not love Kaffirs but he does love justice."

Now when they heard Suzanne speaking such bold words and saw the fire in her eyes, Swart Piet and those with him began to grow afraid. The hanging of a witch-doctoress after a formal trial upon the charge of theft of cattle was no great matter in those days, for such thefts were common and a cause of much trouble to out-lying farmers, nor would anyone in these half-settled regions be likely to look too closely into the rights and wrongs of an execution on account of them. But if a white person who was present went away to proclaim to the authorities, perhaps even to the Governor of the Cape, whose ear could always be won through the missionaries of the London Society, that this pretended execution was nothing but a murder, then the thing became serious. From the moment that Suzanne began to speak on behalf of Sihamba, Swart Piet had seen that it would be impossible to hang her unless he wished to risk his own neck. But he guessed also that the girl could not know this, and therefore he determined to make terms by working on her pity, such terms as should put her to shame before all those gathered there; yes, and leave something of a stain upon her heart for so long as she should live.

"I do not argue law with young ladies," he said, with a little laugh, "but I am always ready to oblige young ladies, especially this young lady. Now, yonder witch and cattle-thief has richly earned her doom, yet, because you ask it, Suzanne Botmar, I am ready to withdraw the prosecution against her, and to destroy the written record of it in my hand, on two conditions, of which the first is that she pays over to me by way of compensation for what she has stolen, all her cattle and other belongings. Do you consent to that, witch?"

"How can I refuse?" said Sihamba, with a bitter laugh, "seeing that if I do you will take both life and goods. But what is the second condition?"

" I am coming to that, witch, but it has nothing to do with you. Suzanne, it is this: that here, before all these people, as the price of this thief's life, you give me the kiss which you refused to me the other day."

Now, before Suzanne could answer, Sihamba broke in eagerly, "Nay, lady, let not your lips be stained and your heart be shamed for the sake of such as I. Better that I should die than that you should suffer defilement at the hands of Swart Piet, who, born of white blood and black, is false to both and a disgrace to both."

"I cannot do it," gasped Suzanne, turning pale and not heeding her outburst, "and, Heer van Vooren, you are a coward to ask it of me."

"Can't you ?" he sneered. "Well, you need not, unless you please, and it is true that young women like best to be kissed alone. Here, you Kaffirs, pull that little devil up; slowly now, that she may learn what a tight string feels like about her throat before it chokes her."

In obedience to his command three of the evil fellows with him caught hold of the end of the rope which hung over the bough, and began to pull, dragging the light form of Sihamba upwards till only the tips of her big toes touched the ground.

"Doesn't she dance prettily?" said Swart Piet with a brutal laugh, at the same time motioning to the men to keep her thus a while.

Now Suzanne looked at the blackening lips and the little form convulsed in its death struggle, and could bear the sight no more.

"Let her down!" she cried, and, springing from the saddle, for all this while she had been seated upon her horse, she walked up to Piet, saying, "Take what you seek, but oh! for your sake I wish to God that my lips were poison."

"No, no," gasped Sihamba, who now was lying half choked upon the ground.

"That is not our bargain, dear," said Piet; "it is that you should kiss me, not I you."

Again Suzanne shrank back, and again at his signal the men began to pull upon the rope. Then seeing it, with her face as pale as death, she leant forward and touched his lips with hers, whereon he seized her round the middle, and, drawing her to him, covered her with kisses till even the brutes with him called to him not to push his jest too far and to let the girl go. This he did, uttering words which I will not repeat, and so weak was Suzanne with shame that when his arms were taken from round her she fell to the ground, and lay there till the old Hottentot, her servant, ran to her, cursing and weeping with rage, and helped her to her feet. For a while she stood saying nothing, only wiping her face, as though filth had bespattered it, with the sun *kapje* which had fallen from her head, and her face was whiter than the white cap. At last she spoke in a hoarse voice:

"Loose that woman," she said, "who has cost me my honour."

They obeyed her, and snatching up her skin rug Si-

hamba turned and fled swiftly down the valley. Then
Suzanne went to her horse, but before she mounted it she
looked Swart Piet straight in the eyes. At the time he
was following her, begging her not to be angry at a joke,
for his madness was satisfied for a while and had left him.
But she only looked in answer, and there was something
so terrible to him in the dark eyes of this young unfriended
girl that he shrank back, seeing in them, perhaps, the
shadow of fate to come. Then Suzanne rode away, and
Swart Piet, having commanded his ruffians to fire the huts
of Sihamba, and to collect her people, goods, and cattle,
went away also.

Just at the mouth of the valley something stirred in a
bush, causing the horse to start, so that Suzanne, who was
thinking of other things, slipped from it to the ground.
Next moment she saw that it was Sihamba, who knelt before her, kissing her feet and the hem of her robe.

"Rise," she said kindly; "what has been cannot be
helped, and at least it was no fault of yours."

"Nay, Swallow," said Sihamba, for I think I have said
that was the name which the natives had given to Suzanne
from childhood, I believe, because of the grace of her
movements and her habit of running swiftly hither and
thither—"Nay, Swallow, in a way it was my fault."

"What do you mean, Sihamba?"

"I mean, Swallow, that although I am so small some
have thought me pretty, and the real reason of Black Piet's
hate for me is—but why should I defile your ears with the
tale?"

"They would only match my face if you did," answered
Suzanne grimly, "but there is no need; I can guess well
enough."

"You can guess, Swallow; then you will see why it was

my fault. Yes, yes, you will see that what I, a black woman, who am less than dirt in the eyes of your people, would not do to save my own life; you, a white chieftainess, and the fairest whom we know, have done of your own will to keep it in me."

"If the act was good," answered Suzanne, "may it go to my credit in the Book of the Great One who made us."

"It will go to your credit, Swallow," answered Sihamba with passion, "both in that Book and in the hearts of all who hear this story, but most of all in this heart of mine. Oh! listen, lady; sometimes a cloud comes over me, and in that cloud I who was born a doctoress see visions of things that are to happen, true visions. Among them I see this: that many moons hence and far away I shall live to save you as you have saved me, but between that day and this the cloud of the future is black to my eyes, black but living."

"It may be so," answered Suzanne, "for I have heard that you have the Sight. And now, farewell; you had best seek out some friends among your people and hide yourself."

"My people," said Sihamba; "then I must seek long, for they are very, very far away, nor do they desire to see me."

"Why not?"

"Because as it chances I am by blood their ruler, for I am the only child of my father's head-wife. But they would not have me set over them as chieftainess unless I married a man, and towards marriage I have no wish, for I am different from other women, both in body and heart. So having quarrelled with them on this and another matter of policy I set out to seek my fortune and left them to theirs."

" Your fortune was not a good one, Sihamba, for it led you to Swart Piet and the rope."

" Nay, lady, it led me to the Swallow and freedom; no, not to freedom but to slavery, for I am your slave, whose life you have bought at a great price.   Now I have nothing left in the world; Swart Piet has taken my cattle which I earned cow by cow and bred up heifer by heifer, and save for the wit within my brain and this kaross upon my shoulders, I have nothing."

" What, then, will you do, Sihamba ?"

" What you do, Swallow, that I shall do, for am I not your slave bought at a great price?   I will go home with you and serve you, yes, to my life's end."

" That would please me well enough, Sihamba, but I do not know how it would please my father."

" What pleases you pleases him, Swallow; moreover, I can save my food twice over by curing his cattle and horses in sickness, for in such needs I have skill."

" Well," she said, " come, and when my father returns we will settle how it shall be."

CHAPTER X

THE OATH OF SIHAMBA

SUZANNE came home and told me her story, and when I heard it I was like a mad woman; indeed, it would have gone ill with Swart Piet's eyes and hair if I could have fallen in with him that night.

"Wait till your father returns, girl," I said.

"Yes, mother," she answered, "I wait for him—and Ralph."

"What is to be done with the little doctoress, Sihamba?" I asked, adding, "I do not like such people about the place."

"Let her bide also till the men come back, mother," she answered, "and then they will see to it. Meanwhile there is an empty hut down by the cattle kraal where she can live."

So Sihamba stopped on and became a body servant to Suzanne, the best I ever saw, though she would do no other work save that of attending to sick animals.

Ten days afterwards Jan and Ralph returned safe and sound, leaving some Kaffirs in charge of the cattle in the bush-veldt. Very glad we were to see them, since, putting everything else aside, it was lonely work for two women upon the place with no neighbour at hand, and in those days to be lonely meant to be in danger.

When we were together Jan's first question to me was:
"Have those Englishmen been here?"

"They have been here," I answered, "and they have
gone away."

Jan asked me nothing more of the matter, for he did not
wish to know what had passed between us. Only he looked
at me queerly, and, as I think, thought the worse of me
afterwards, for he found out that Suzanne and I had quarrelled about the song I sang in the ears of the Englishmen, and what that song was he could guess very well.
Yes, yes, although he had been a party to the fraud, in his
heart Jan put all the blame of it upon me, for that is the
way of men who are mean, and always love to say "The
woman tempted me," a vile habit which has come down
to them with their blood.

Meanwhile another talk was passing between Ralph and
Suzanne. They had rushed to meet each other like two
separated colts bred in the same meadow, but when they
came together it was different. Ralph put out his arms to
embrace her, but she pushed him back and said, "No, not
until we have spoken together."

"This is a cold greeting," said Ralph, amazed and
trembling, for he feared lest Suzanne should have changed
her mind as to their marriage. "What is it that you have
to tell me? Speak on, quickly."

"Two things, Ralph," she answered, and taking the
least of them first, she plunged straightway into a full
account of the coming of the Englishmen, of all that had
passed then, and of her quarrel with me upon the matter.

"And now, Ralph," she ended, "you will understand
that you have been cheated of your birthright, and this I
think it just that you should know, so that, if you will,
you may change your mind about staying here, for there

is yet time, and follow these Englishmen to wherever it is they have gone, to claim from them your heritage."

Ralph laughed and answered, "Why, Sweet, I thought that we had settled all this long ago. That your mother did not tell the men quite the truth is possible, but if she played with it, it was for the sake of all of us and with my leave. Let them go and the fortune with them, for even if I could come to England and find it there, I should be but as a wild buck in a sheep kraal, out of place and unhappy. Moreover, we should be separated, dear, for even if you would all consent, I could never take you from your own people and the land where you were born. So now that there is an end to this, once and for ever, let me kiss you in greeting, Suzanne."

But she shook her head and denied him, saying, "No, for I have another tale to tell you, and an uglier—so ugly indeed that after the hearing of it I doubt much whether you will wish to kiss me any more."

"Be swift with it then," he answered, "for you torment me," and she began her story.

She told how that, after he had gone away, Swart Piet began to persecute her; how he had wished to kiss her and she had refused him, so that he left her with threats. Then she paused suddenly and said:

"And now, before I finish the story, you shall swear an oath to me. You shall swear that you will not attempt to kill Swart Piet because of it."

At first he would swear nothing, for already he was wild with anger against the man, whereupon she answered that she would tell him nothing.

At last, when they had wrangled for a while, he asked her in a hoarse voice, "Say now, Suzanne, have you come to any harm at the hands of this fellow?"

" No," she answered, turning her head away. " God be thanked! I have come to no harm of my body, but of my mind I have come to great harm."

Now he breathed more freely and said:

" Very well, then, go on with your story, for I swear to you that I will not try to kill Swart Piet because of this offence, whatever it may be."

So she went on, setting out everything exactly as it had happened, and before she had finished Ralph was as one who is brain sick, for he ground his teeth and stamped upon the earth like an angry bull. At last, when Suzanne had told him all, she said:

" Now, Ralph, you will understand why I would not let you kiss me before you had heard my story. It was because I feared that after hearing it you would not wish to kiss me any more."

" You talk like a foolish girl," he answered, taking her into his arms and embracing her, " and though the insult can only be paid back in blood, I think no more of it than if some beast had splashed mud into your face, which you had washed away at the next stream."

" Ah!" she cried, " you swore that you would not try to kill him for this offence."

" Yes, Sweet, I swore, and I will keep my oath. This time I will not try to kill Swart Piet."

Then they went into the house, and Ralph spoke to Jan about this matter, of which indeed I had already told him something. Jan also was very angry, and said that if he could meet Piet van Vooren it would go hard with him. Afterwards he added, however, that this Piet was a very dangerous man, and one whom it might be well to leave alone, especially as Suzanne had taken no real hurt from him.

Nowadays, and here in Natal, such a villain could be

made to answer to the law, either for attempting the life of the Kaffir, or for the assault upon the girl, or for both, but in those times it was different. Then the Transkei had but few white people in it, living far apart, nor was there any law to speak of; indeed each man did what was right in his own eyes, according to the good or evil that was in his heart. Therefore, as Jan said, it was not well to make a deadly enemy of one who was restrained by the fear of neither God nor man, and who had great wealth and power, since it might come about that he would work murder in revenge or raise the Kaffirs on us, as he who had authority among them could do very easily. Indeed as will be seen he did both these things, or tried to do them.

When his anger had cooled a little Jan spoke to us in this sense and we women agreed with him; but Ralph, who was young, fearless, and full of rage, set his mouth and said nothing.

As for Sihamba Jan wished to send her away, but Suzanne, who had grown fond of her, begged him that he would not do so, at least until he had spoken with her. So he ordered one of the slaves to fetch her, and presently the little woman came, and having saluted him, sat herself down on the floor of the sitting room after the Kaffir fashion. She was a strange little creature to see in her fur kaross and bead broidered girdle, but for a native she was very clean and pretty, with her wise woman's face set upon a body that had it been less rounded might almost have been that of a child. Also she had adorned herself with great care, not in the cast-off clothes of white people but after her own manner, for her wavy hair which stood out from her head was powdered over with that sparkling blue dust which the Kaffir women use, and round her neck she wore a single string of large blue beads.

At first Jan spoke to her crossly, saying:

"You have brought trouble and disgrace upon my house, Sihamba, and I wish you to begone from it."

"It is true," she answered, "but not of my own will did I bring the trouble, O Father of Swallow," for so she always called Jan. Indeed, for Sihamba, Suzanne was the centre of all things, and thus in her mouth the three of us had no other names than "Father" or "Mother" or "Lover" of Swallow.

"That may be so," answered Jan, "but, doubtless, Black Piet, who hates you, will follow you here, and then we shall be called upon to defend you, and there will be more trouble."

"It is not I whom Black Piet will follow," she replied, "for he has stolen all I have, and as my life is safe there is nothing more to get from me," and she looked at Suzanne.

"What do you mean, Sihamba? Speak plain words," said Jan.

"I mean," she answered, "that it is not I who am now in danger, but my mistress, the Swallow, for he who has kissed her once will wish to kiss her again."

Now at this Ralph cursed the name of Swart Piet aloud, and Jan answered,

"It is a bullet from my *roer* that he shall kiss if he tries it, that I swear."

"I hope it may be so," said Sihamba; "yet, Father of Swallow, I pray you send me not away from her who bought me at a great price, and to whom my life belongs. Look; I cost you but little to keep, and that little I can earn by doctoring your horses and cattle, in which art I have some skill, as you know well. Moreover I have many eyes and ears that can see and hear things to which yours

are deaf and blind, and I tell you that I think a time will
come when I shall be able to do service to all of you who
are of the nest of the Swallow. Now, if she bids me to
go I will go—for am I not her servant to obey?—yet I be-
seech you do not so command her."

Sihamba had risen as she spoke, and now she stood before Jan, her head thrown back, looking up into his eyes
with such strange power that, though he was great and
strong and had no will to it, yet he found himself forced
to look down into hers. More, as he told me afterwards,
he saw many things in the eyes of Sihamba, or it may be
that he thought that he saw them, for Jan was always
somewhat superstitious. At least this is true that more
than once during the terrible after years, when some great
event had happened to us he would cry out, "I have seen
this place, or thing, before, I know not where." Then if
I bade him think he would answer, "Now I remember; it
was in the eyes of Sihamba that I saw it, yonder in the
Transkei before Ralph and Suzanne were married."

Presently she freed his eyes and turned her head,
whereon Jan grew pale and swayed as though he were about
to fall. Recovering himself, however, he said shortly.

"Stay if you will, Sihamba; you are welcome for so long
as it shall please you."

She lifted her little hand and saluted him, and I noticed
that it was after another fashion to that of the Kaffirs who
lived thereabouts, after the Zulu fashion indeed.

"I hear your words, chief," she said, "and I stay.
Though I be but as a lizard in the thatch, yet the nest
of the Swallow shall be my nest, and in the fangs of the
lizard, Sihamba, there is poison and woe to the hawk of
the air or the snake of the grass that would rob this nest
wherein you dwell. Listen now to my oath—you whom

she loves. Cold shall this heart be and stiff this hand, empty shall this head be of thought and these eyes of sight, before shame or death shall touch the swift wings of yonder Swallow who stained her breast for me. Remember this always, you whom she loves, that while I live, I, Sihamba Ngenyanga, Sihamba the walker by moonlight, she shall live, and if she dies I will die also."

Then once more she saluted and went, leaving us wondering, for we saw that this woman was not altogether as other Kaffirs are, and it came into our minds that in the time of need she would be as is a sharp spear in the hand of one who is beset with foes.

That night as we lay abed I talked with Jan, saying:

"Husband, I think there are clouds upon our sky, which for many years has been so blue. Trouble gathers round us because of the beauty of Suzanne, and I fear Swart Piet, for he is not a man to be stopped by a trifle. Now, Ralph loves Suzanne and Suzanne loves Ralph, and, though they are young, they are man and woman full grown, able to keep a house and bear its burdens. Why then should they not marry with as little delay as may be, for when once they are wed Van Vooren will cease from troubling them, knowing his suit to be hopeless?"

"As you will, wife, as you will," Jan answered somewhat sharply, "but I doubt if we shall get rid of our dangers thus, for with you I think that the tide of our lives has turned, and that it sets towards sorrow. Ay," he went on, sitting up in the bed, "and I will tell you when it turned; it turned upon the day that you lied to the Englishmen."

CHAPTER XI

EARLY the next morning I sought for Ralph to speak to him on the matter of his marriage, which, to tell truth, I longed to see safely accomplished. But I could not find him anywhere, or learn where he had gone, though one of the slaves told me that they had seen him mount his horse at the stable.

I went down to the cattle kraal to look if he were there, and as I returned, I saw Sihamba seated by the door of her hut engaged in combing her hair and powdering it with the shining blue dust.

"Greeting, Mother of Swallow," she said. "Whom do you seek?"

"You know well," I answered.

"Yes, I know well. At the break of dawn he rode over yonder rise."

"Why?" I asked.

"How can I tell why? But Swart Piet lives out yonder."

"Had he his gun with him?" I asked again and anxiously.

"No, there was nothing but a sjambock, a very thick sjambock, in his hand."

Then I went back to the house with a heavy heart, for I

was sure that Ralph had gone to seek Piet van Vooren, though I said nothing of it to the others. So it proved indeed. Ralph had sworn to Suzanne that he would not try to kill Piet, but here his oath ended, and therefore he felt himself free to beat him if he could find him, for he was altogether mad with hate of the man. Now he knew that when he was at home it was Swart Piet's habit to ride of a morning, accompanied by one Kaffir only, to visit a certain valley where he kept a large number of sheep. Thither Ralph made his way, and when he reached the place he saw that, although it was time for them to be feeding, the sheep were still in their kraal, baa-ing, stamp-ing, and trying to climb the gate, for they were hungry to get at the green grass.

"So," thought Ralph, "Swart Piet means to count the flock out himself this morning. He will be here presently."

Half an hour afterwards he came sure enough, and with him the one Kaffir as was usual. Then the bars of the gate were let down, and the sheep suffered to escape through them, Swart Piet standing upon one side and the Kaffir upon the other, to take tale of their number. When all the sheep were out, and one of the herds had been brought before him and beaten by the Kaffir, because some lambs were missing, Swart Piet turned to ride homewards, and in a little gorge near by came face to face with Ralph, who was waiting for him. Now he started and looked to see if he could escape, but there was no way of doing it without shame, so he rode forward and bid Ralph good-day boldly, asking him if he had ever seen a finer flock of sheep.

"I did not come here to talk of sheep," answered Ralph, eyeing him.

"Is it of a lamb, then, that you come to talk, Heer Kenzie, a ewe lamb, the only one of your flock?" sneered Piet, for he had a gun in his hand and he saw that Ralph had none.

"Aye," said Ralph, "it is of a white ewe lamb whose fleece has been soiled by a bastard thief who would have stolen her," and he looked at him.

"I understand," said Piet coldly, for he was a bold man; "and now, Heer Kenzie, you had best let me ride by."

"Why should I let you ride by when I have come out to seek you?"

"For a very good reason, Heer Kenzie; because I have a gun in my hand and you have none, and if you do not clear the road presently it may go off."

"A good reason, indeed," said Ralph, "and one of which I admit the weight," and he drew to one side of the path as though to let Piet pass, which he began to do holding the muzzle of the gun in a line with the other's head. Ralph sat upon his horse staring moodily at the ground, as though he was trying to make up his mind to say something or other, but all the time he was watching out of the corner of his quick eye. Just as Swart Piet drew past him, and was shaking the reins to put his horse to a canter, Ralph slid from the saddle, and springing upon him like light, he slipped his strong arm round him and dragged him backwards to the ground over the crupper of the horse. As Piet fell he stretched out his hands to grip the saddle and save himself, so that the gun which he carried resting on his knees dropped upon the grass. Ralph seized it and fired it into the air; then he turned to face his enemy, who by this time had found his feet.

"Now we are more equally matched, myn Heer van Vooren," he said, "and can talk further about that ewe lamb, the only one of the flock. Nay, you need not look for the Kaffir to help you, for he has run after your horse, and at the best he will hardly care to trust himself between two angry white men. Come, let us talk, myn Heer."

Black Piet made no answer, so for a while the two stood facing each other, and they were a strange pair, as different as the light from the darkness. Ralph fair-haired, grey-eyed, stern-faced, with thin nostrils, that quivered like those of a well-bred horse, narrow-flanked, broad-chested, though somewhat slight of limb and body, for he was but young, and had scarcely come to a man's weight, but lithe and wiry as a tiger. Piet taller and more massive, for he had the age of him by five years, with round Kaffir eyes, black and cruel, coarse black hair that grew low upon his brow, full red lips, the lower drooping so that the large white teeth and a line of gums could be seen within. Great-limbed he was also, firm-footed and bull-strengthed, showing in his face the cruelty and the cunning of a black race, mingled with the mind and mastery of the white; an evil and a terrible man, knowing no lord save his own passions, and no religion but black witchcraft and vile superstition; a foe to be feared indeed, but one who loved better to stab in the dark than to strike in the open day.

"Well, myn Heer van Vooren," mocked Ralph, "you could fling your arms about a helpless girl and put her to shame before the eyes of men, now do the same by me if you can," and he took one step towards him.

"What is this monkey's chatter?" asked Piet, in his slow voice. "Is it because I gave the girl a kiss that you would fix a quarrel upon me? Have you not done as much yourself many times, and for a less stake than the life of one who has been doomed to die?"

"If I have kissed her," answered Ralph, "it is with her

consent, and because she will be my wife; but you worked
upon her pity to put her to shame and now you shall pay
the price of it. Do you see that whip?" and he nodded
toward the sjambock that was lying on the grass. "Let
him who proves the best man use it upon the other."

"Will be your wife——" sneered Piet, "the wife of the
English castaway! She might have been, but now she
never shall, unless she cares to wed a carcase cut into rimpis. You want a flogging, and you shall have it, yes,
to the death, but Suzanne shall be——not your wife
but——"

He got no further, for at that moment Ralph sprang at
him like a wild cat, stopping his foul mouth with a fearful
blow upon the lips. Then there followed a dreadful
struggle between these two. Swart Piet rushed again and
again, striving to clasp his antagonist in his great arms
and crush him, whereas Ralph, who, like all Englishmen,
loved to use his fists, and knew that he was no match for
Piet in strength, sought to avoid him and plant blow after
blow upon his face and body. This, indeed, he did with
such success that soon the Boer was covered with blood
and bruises. Again and again he charged at him, roaring
with pain and rage, and again and again Ralph first struck
and then slipped to one side.

At length Piet's turn came, for Ralph in leaping back ·
caught his foot against a stone and stumbled, and before
he could recover himself the iron arms were round his
middle, and they were wrestling for the mastery.

Still, at the first it was Ralph who had the best of it,
for he was skilful at the game, and before Swart Piet
could put out his full strength he tripped him so that he
fell heavily upon his back, Ralph still locked in his arms.
But he could not keep him there, for the Boer was the

stronger; moreover, as they fought they had worked their way up the steep side of the kloof so that the ground was against him. Thus it came about that soon they began to roll down hill fixed to each other as though by ropes, and gathering speed at every turn. Doubtless, the end of this would have been Ralph's defeat, and perhaps his death, for I think that, furious as he was, Black Piet would certainly have killed him had he found himself the master. But it chanced that his hand was stayed, and thus. Near the bottom of the slope lay a sharp stone, and as they rolled in their fierce struggle, Piet's head struck against this stone so that for a few moments he was rendered helpless. Feeling the grip of his arms lessen, Ralph freed himself, and running to the sjambock snatched it from the ground. Now Piet sat up and stared at him stupidly, but he made no effort to renew the fight, whereon Ralph gasped:

"I promised you a flogging, but since it is chance that has conquered you more than I, I will take no advantage of it, save this——" and he struck him once or twice across the face with the whip, but not so as to draw blood, and added: "Now, at least, I am free from a certain promise that I made—that I would not kill you—and should you attempt further harm or insult towards Suzanne Botmar, kill you I will, Piet van Vooren."

At first Swart Piet did not seem to feel the blows, but presently he awoke, as it were, and touched his cheeks where the sjambock had struck him as though to assure himself that he was not dreaming some evil dream. Then he spoke in a hollow, unnatural voice. "You have won for this time, Ralph Kenzie," he said, "or, rather, Fate fighting for you has won. But it would have been better for you and your dear also, if you had never struck those blows, for I tell you, Ralph Kenzie, that as your whip

touched me something broke in my brain, and now I think
that I am mad."

"Mad or bad, it is all one to me," replied Ralph. "You
have had your warning, and you had best keep sane enough
to remember it." Then turning he went to his horse,
which was standing close by, mounted and rode away,
the other answering him nothing.

Still Ralph did not get home without another adven-
ture, for when he had gone a little way he came to a stream
that ran from a hillside which was thick with trees, and
here he stopped to doctor his hurts and bruises, since he
did not wish to appear at the house covered with blood.
Now this was a foolish enough thing to do, seeing the sort
of man with whom he had to deal, and that there was bush
where anyone could hide to within a hundred and twenty
yards of his washing place. So it proved indeed, for just
as Ralph had mounted his horse and was about to ride on,
he felt a sharp stinging pain across his shoulders, as
though someone had hit him on the back with a stick, and
heard the sound of a gunshot fired from the cover of the
bush, for there above the green leaves hung a cloud of
smoke.

"That is Swart Piet who has crept round to cut me off,"
Ralph thought to himself, and for a moment was minded
to ride to the smoke to seek him. Then he remembered
that he had no gun, and that that of his enemy might be
loaded again before he found him, and judged it wisest to
canter into the open plain and so homewards. Of the
hurt which he had taken from the bullet he thought little,
yet when he reached the house it was seen that his escape
had been narrow indeed, for the great ball had cut through
his clothes beneath his shoulders, so that they hung down
leaving his back naked. Also it had furrowed the skin,

causing the blood to flow copiously, and making so horrible a sight of him that Suzanne nearly fainted when she saw it. For my part I made certain that the lad was shot through the body, although, as it turned out, in a week, except for some soreness he was as well as ever.

Now this matter caused no little stir among us, and Jan was so angry that, without saying a word to anyone, he mounted his horse and, taking some armed servants with him, set out to seek Black Piet, but not to find him, for the man had gone, nobody knew whither. Indeed this was as well, or so we thought at the time, for though Jan is slow to move, when once he is moved he is a very angry man, and I am sure that if he had met Piet van Vooren that day the grasses would have been richer by the blood of one or both of them. But he did not meet him and so the thing passed over, for afterwards we remembered that Ralph had been the aggressor, since no one would take count of this story of the kissing of a girl, and also that there was no proof at all that it was Piet who had attempted his life, as that shot might have been fired by anyone.

Now from this day forward Suzanne went in terror of Swart Piet, and whenever Ralph rode, he rode armed, for though it was said that he had gone on one of his long journeys trading among the Kaffirs, both of them guessed that they had not seen the last of Van Vooren. Jan and I were afraid also, for we knew the terrible nature of the man and of his father before him, and that they came of a family which never forgot a quarrel or left a desire ungratified.

About fourteen days after Ralph had been shot at and wounded, a Kaffir brought a letter for Jan, which, on being opened, proved to have been written by Swart Piet, or on his behalf, since his name was set at the bottom of it. It read thus:—

" To the Heer Jan Botmar.

" Well-beloved Heer, this is to tell you that your daughter, Suzanne, holds my heart, and that I desire to make her my wife. As it is not convenient for me to come to see you at present, I write to ask you that you will consent to our betrothal. I will make a rich woman of her as I can easily satisfy you, and you will find it better to have me as a dear son-in-law and friend than as a stranger and an enemy, for I am a good friend and a bad enemy. I know there has been some talk of love between Suzanne and the English foundling at your place; but I can overlook that, although you may tell the lad that if he is impertinent to me again as he was the other day, he will not for the second time get off with a whipping only. Be so good as to give your answer to the bearer, who will pass it on to those that can find me, for I am travelling about on business, and do not know where I shall be from day to day. Give also my love to Suzanne, your daughter, and tell her that I think often of the time when she shall be my wife.

"I am, well-beloved Heer, your friend,

"Piet van Vooren."

Now, when Ralph had finished reading this letter aloud, for it had been given to him as the best scholar among us, you might have thought there were four crazy people in the room, so great was our rage. Jan and Ralph said little indeed, though they looked white and strange with anger, and Suzanne not over much, for it was I who talked for all of them.

"What is your answer, girl?" asked her father presently with an angry laugh.

"Tell the Heer Piet van Vooren," she replied, smiling faintly, "that if ever his lips should touch my face again it will be only when that face is cold in death. Oh! Ralph," she cried, turning to him suddenly and laying her hand upon his breast, "it may be that this man will bring trouble and separation on us; indeed, my heart warns me of it, but, whatever chances, remember my words, dead I may be, but faithful I shall be—yes, to death and through death."

"Son, take pen and write," said Jan before Ralph could answer. So Ralph wrote down these words as Jan told them to him:

"Piet van Vooren,

"Sooner would I lay my only child out for burial in the grave than lead her to the house of a coloured man, a consorter with witch-doctors and black women and a would-be murderer. That is my answer, and I add this to it. Set no foot within a mile of my house, for here we shoot straighter than you do, and if we find you on this place, by the help of God we will put a bullet through your carcase."

At the foot of this writing, which he would not suffer to be altered, Jan printed his name in big letters; then he went out to seek the messenger, whom he found talking to Sihamba, and having given him the paper bade him begone swiftly to wherever it was he came from. The man, who was a strong red-coloured savage, marked with a white scar across the left cheek, and naked except for his moocha and the kaross rolled up upon his shoulders, took the letter, hid it in his bundle, and went.

Jan also turned to go, but I who had followed him and was watching him, although he did not know it, saw him hesitate and stop.

"Sihamba," he said, "why were you talking to that man?"

"Because it is my business to know of things, Father of Swallow, and I wished to learn whence he came."

"Did he tell you then?"

"Not altogether, for someone whom he fears had laid a weight upon his tongue, but I learned that he lives at a kraal far away in the mountains, and that this kraal is owned by a white man who keeps wives and cattle at it, although he is not there himself just now. The rest I hope to hear when Swart Piet sends him back again, for I have given the man a medicine to cure his child, who is sick, and he will be grateful to me."

"How do you know that Swart Piet sent the man?" asked Jan.

She laughed and said: "Surely that was easy to guess; it is my business to twine little threads into a rope."

Again Jan turned to go and again came back to speak to her.

"Sihamba," he said, "I have seen you talking to that man before. I remember the scar upon his face."

"The scar upon his face you may remember," she answered, "but you have not seen us talking together, for until this hour we never met."

"I can swear it," he said angrily. "I remember the straw hut, the shape of the man's bundle, the line where the shadow fell upon his foot, and the tic-bird that came and sat near you. I remember it all."

"Surely, Father of Swallow," Sihamba replied, eyeing him oddly, "you talk of what you have just seen."

" No, no," he said, " I saw it years ago."

" Where? " she asked, staring at him.

He started and uttered some quick words. " I know now," he said. " I saw it in your eyes the other day."

" Yes," she answered quietly, " I think that, if any-where, you saw it in my eyes, since the coming of this messenger is the first of all the great things that are to happen to the Swallow and to those who live in her nest. I do not know the things; still, it may happen that another who has Vision may see them in the glass of my eyes."

CHAPTER XII

WHAT THE COW SHOWED ZINTI

TWELVE days passed, and one morning when I went out to feed the chickens, I saw the red Kaffir with the scar on his face seated beyond the *stoep* taking snuff.

" What is it? " I asked.

" A letter," he answered, giving me a paper.

I took it into the house, where the others were gathered for breakfast, and as before Ralph read it. It was to this effect:

" WELL-BELOVED HEER BOTMAR,—I have received your honoured letter, and I think that the unchristian spirit which it shows cannot be pleasing to our Lord. Still, as I seek peace and not war, I take no offence, nor shall I come near your place to provoke the shedding of the blood of men. I love your daughter, but if she rejects me for another, I have nothing more to say, except that I hope she may be happy in the life she has chosen. For me, I am leaving this part of the country, and if you, Heer Botmar, like to buy my farm, I shall be happy to sell it to you at a fair price; or perhaps the Heer Kenzie will buy it to live on after he is married; if so, he can write to me by this messenger. Farewell."

Now, when they heard this letter, the others looked more happy; but for my part I shook my head, seeing guile in it, since the tone of it was too humble for Swart

Piet. There was no answer to it, and the messenger went away, but not, as I learned, before he had seen Sihamba. It seems that the medicine which she gave him had cured his child, for which he was so grateful that he drove her down a cow in payment, a fine beast, but very wild, for handling was strange to it; moreover, it had been but just separated from its calf. Still, although she questioned him closely, the man would tell Sihamba but little of the place where he lived, and nothing of the road to it.

Here I will stop to show how great was the cunning of this woman, and yet how simple the means whereby she obtained the most of her knowledge. She desired to learn about this hiding-place, since she was sure that it was one of the secret haunts of Swart Piet, but when she asked him the messenger grew deaf and blind, and she could find no one else who knew anything of the matter. Still she was certain that the cow which had been brought to her would show the way to its home, if there were anybody to follow it thither and make report of the path.

Now when Sihamba had been robbed and sentenced to death by Swart Piet, the most of her servants and people who lived with her had been taken by him as slaves. Still two or three had escaped, either then or afterwards, and settled about in the neighbourhood of the farm where they knew that their mistress dwelt. From among these people, who still did her service, she chose a young man named Zinti, who, although he was supposed to be stupid, was still very clever about many things, especially the remembering of any path that he had once trodden, and of every *kopje*, stream, or pan by which it could be traced. This youth she bade to herd the cow which had been given her, telling him to follow it whithersoever it should wander, even if it led him a ten days' journey, and when he saw that it had reached home, to return himself without being seen, and to give to her an exact report of the road which it had travelled.

Now all happened as Sihamba expected, for on the first day that the cow was turned out, watched by the lad, who was provided with food and a blanket, so soon as it had filled itself it started straight over the hills, running at times, and at times stopping to graze, till night came on. Then it lay down for a while and its herd beside it, for he had tied his wrist to its tail with a rimpi lest it should escape in the darkness.

At the first breaking of the light the cow rose, filled itself with grass and started forward on its homeward path, followed by Zinti. For three days they travelled thus, the herd milking the cow from time to time when its udder was full. On the evening of the third day, however, the beast would not lie down, but walked forward all night, lowing now and again, by which Zinti, who found it difficult to keep it in sight because of the darkness, guessed that it must be near its home. So it proved indeed, for when the sun rose Zinti saw a kraal before him hidden away in a secret valley of the mountains over which they had been travelling. Still following the cow, though at a distance, he moved down towards the kraal and hid himself in a patch of bush. Presently the cattle were let out to graze, and the cow rushed to them lowing loudly, till a certain calf came to it, which it made much of and suckled, for it was its own calf.

Now Zinti's errand was done, but still he lay hid in the bush a while, thinking that he might learn some more, and lying thus he fell asleep, for he was weary with travel. When he woke the sun was high, and he heard women talking to each other close by him, as they laboured at their task of cutting wands, such as are used for the making of huts. He rose to run away, then thought better of it and sat down again, remembering that should he be found, it would be easy to tell them that he was a wanderer who had lost his path. Presently one of the women asked:

"For whom does Bull-Head build this fine new hut in the secret krantz yonder?"

Now Zinti opened his ears wide, for he knew that this was the name which the natives had given to Swart Piet, taking it from his round head and fierce eye, according to their custom when they note any peculiarity in a man.

"I do not know," answered a second woman, who was young and very pretty, "unless he means to bring another wife here; if so, she must be a chief's daughter, since men do not build such huts for girls of common blood."

"Perhaps," said the other; "but then I think that he has stolen her from her father without payment: else he would not wish to hide her away in the secret krantz. Well, let her come, for we women must work hard here where there are so few men, and many hoes clean a field quickly."

"For my part I think there are enough of us already," said the young girl, looking troubled, for she was Swart Piet's last Kaffir wife, and did not desire to be supplanted by a new favourite. "But be silent, I hear Bull-Head coming on his horse," and she began to work very hard at cutting the wands.

A few minutes later Zinti saw Swart Piet himself ride up to the women, who saluted him, calling him "Chief" and "Husband."

"You are idle," he said, eyeing them angrily.

"These wands are tough to cut, husband," murmured the young woman in excuse.

"Still you must cut them quicker, girl," he answered,

" if you would not learn how one of them feels upon your back. It will go hard with all of you if the big hut is not finished in seven days from now."

" We will do our best," said the girl, " but who is to dwell in the hut when it is done? "

" Not you, be sure of that," he answered, roughly, " nor any black woman, for I am weary of you, one and all. Listen: I go to-morrow with my servants to fetch a chieftainess, a white lady, to rule over you, but if any of you speak a word of her presence here you will pay for it, for I shall turn you away to starve. Do you understand? "

" We hear you, husband," they replied, somewhat sullenly, for now they understood that this new wife would be a mistress, and not a sister to them.

" Then be careful that you do not forget my words, and —hearken—so soon as you have cut a full load of hut-poles, let two of you carry them up to the krantz yonder, where they are wanted, but be careful that no one sees you going in or coming out."

" We hear you, husband," they said again, whereon Swart Piet turned and rode away.

Now, although Zinti was said to be foolish, chiefly, as I think, because he could not, or would not, work, yet in many ways he was cleverer than most Kaffirs, and especially always did he desire to see new places, the more so if they chanced to be secret places. Therefore, when he heard Swart Piet command the women to carry the rods to the hidden krantz, he determined that he would follow them, and this he did so skilfully that they neither heard nor saw him. At first he wondered whither they could be going, for they walked straight to the foot of what seemed to be an unclimbable wall of rock more than a hundred feet high. On the face of this rock, however, shrubs grew here and there like the bristles on the back of a hog, and having first glanced round to see that no one was watching them, the women climbed to one of these shrubs, which was rooted in the cliff about the height of a man above the level of the ground, and vanished so quickly that Zinti, who was watching, rubbed his eyes in wonder. After waiting a while, however, he followed in their steps to find that behind the shrub was a narrow cleft or crack such as are often to be seen in cliffs, and that down this cleft ran a pathway which twisted and turned in the rock, growing broader as it went, till at last it ended in the hidden krantz. This krantz was a very beautiful spot about three morgen, or six English acres, in extent, and walled all round with impassable cliffs. Down the face of one of these cliffs fell a waterfall forming a deep pool, out of which a stream ran, and on the banks of this stream the new hut was being built in such a position that the heat of the sun could strike it but little.

While he was taking note of these and other things Zinti saw some of those who were working at the hut leave it and start to walk towards the cleft. So having learnt everything that he could he thought that it was time to go, and slipped away back to the bush, and thence homewards by the road which the cow had shown him.

Now, it chanced that as he went Zinti pierced his foot with a large thorn so that he was only able to travel slowly. On the fifth night of his journey he limped into a wood to sleep, which wood grew not much more than two hours on horseback from our farm. When he had been asleep for some hours he woke up, for all his food was done, and he could not rest well because of his hunger, and was astonished to see the light of a fire among the trees at some distance from him. Towards this fire he crept, thinking that there were herds or travellers who would give him food, but when he came to it he did not ask for any, since the first thing he saw was Swart Piet himself walking up and down in front of the fire, while at some distance from it lay a number of his men asleep in their karosses. Presently another man appeared slipping through the tree trunks, and coming to Swart Piet saluted him.

"Tell me what you have found out," he said.

"This, Baas," answered the man; "I went down to Heer Botmar's place and begged a bowlful of meal there, pretending that I was a stranger on a journey to court a girl at a distant kraal. The slaves gave me meal and some flesh with it, and I learned in talk with them that the Heer Botmar, his vrouw, his daughter Suzanne and the young Englishman, Heer Kenzie, all rode away yesterday to the christening party of the first-born of the Heer Roozen, who lives about five hours on horseback to the north yonder. I learned also that it is arranged for them to leave the Heer Roozen to-morrow at dawn, and to travel homewards by the Tiger's Nek, in which they will off-saddle about two hours before mid-day, for I forgot to say that they have two servants with them to see to their horses."

"That makes six in all," said Swart Piet, "of whom two are women, whereas we are twenty. Yes, it is very good, nothing could be better, for I know the off-saddling place by the stream in Tiger's Nek, and it is a nice place for men to hide behind the rocks and trees. Listen now to the plan, and be sure you understand it. When these people are off-saddled and eating their food, you Kaffirs will fall on them—with the spear and the kerry alone, mind—and they will come to their end."

"Does the master mean that we are to kill them?" asked the man doubtfully.

"Yes," answered Swart Piet, with some hesitation. "I do not want to kill them indeed, but I see no other way, except as regards the girl, of course, who must be saved. These people are to be attacked and robbed by Kaffirs, for it must never be known that I had a hand in it, and you brutes of Kaffirs always kill. Therefore, they must die, alas! especially the Englishman, though so far as I am concerned I should be glad to spare the others if I could, but it cannot be done without throwing suspicion upon me. As for the girl, if she is harmed the lives of all of you pay for it. You will throw a kaross over her head, and bring her to the place which I will tell you of to-morrow, where I shall come upon you with some men and seem to rescue her. Do you understand, and do you think the plan good!"

"I understand, and I think the plan good—for you—and yet, Baas, there is one thing that I have not told you which may mar it."

"What is it?"

"This: When I was down there at the Heer Botmar's place, I saw the witch-doctoress Sihamba, who has a hut upon the farm. I was some way off, but I think that she recognised me, as she might well do seeing that it was I who set the rope about her neck when you wished to hang her. Now if she did know me all your plans may be in vain, for that woman has the Sight and she will guess them. Even when the cord was round her she laughed at me and told me that I should die soon, but that she would live for years, and therefore I fear her more than anyone living."

"She laughed at you, did she?" said Swart Piet; "well, I laugh at her, for neither she nor anyone who breathes shall stand between me and this girl, who has preferred the suit of another man to mine."

"Ah, master!" said the Kaffir, with admiration, "you are a great one, for when a fruit pleases you, you do not wait for it to drop into your lap, you pluck it."

"Yes," said Swart Piet, striking his breast with pride, "if I desire a fruit I pluck it as my father did before me. But now go you and sleep, for to-morrow you will need all your wit and strength."

When the herd Zinti had heard this talk he crept away, heading straight for the farm, but his foot was so bad, and he was so weak from want of food, that he could only travel at the pace of a lame ox, now hopping upon one leg and now crawling upon his knees. In this fashion it was that at length, about half-past eight in the morning, he reached the house, or rather the hut of Sihamba, for she had sent him out, and therefore to her, after the Kaffir fashion, he went to make report. Now, when he came to Sihamba, he greeted her and asked for a little food, which she gave him. Then he began to tell his story, beginning as natives do at the first of it, which in his case were all the wanderings of the cow which he had followed, so that although she hurried him much, many minutes went by before he came to that part of the tale which told of what he had heard in the wood some eight hours before.

So soon as he began to speak of this, Sihamba stopped him, and calling to a man who lingered near, she bade him bring to her Jan's famous young horse, the roan *schimmel*, bridled but not saddled. Now this horse was the finest in the whole district, for his sire was the famous blood stal-lion which the Government imported from England, where it won all the races, and his dam the swiftest and most enduring mare in the breeding herds at the Paarl. What Jan gave for him as a yearling I never learned, because he was afraid to tell me; but I know that we were short of money for two years after he bought him. Yet in the end that *schimmel* proved the cheapest thing for which ever a man paid gold.

Well, the Kaffir hesitated, for, as might be guessed, Jan was very proud of this horse, and none rode it save himself, but Sihamba sprang up and spoke to him so fiercely that at last he obeyed her, since, although she was small in stature, all feared the magic of Sihamba, and would do her bidding. Nor had he far to go, for the *schimmel* did not run wild upon the veldt, but was fed and kept in a stable, where a slave groomed him every morning. Thus it came about that before Zinti had finished his tale, the horse was standing before Sihamba bridled but not saddled, arching his neck and striking the ground with his hoof, for he was proud and full of corn and eager to be away

"Oh! fool," said Sihamba to Zinti, "why did not you begin with this part of your story? Now, to save five from death and one from dishonour, there is but a short hour left and twenty long miles to cover in it. Ho! man, help me to mount this horse."

The slave put down his hand, and setting her foot in it, the little woman sprang on to the back of the great stallion, which knew and loved her as a dog might do, for she had tended it day and night when it was ill from the sickness we call "thick head," and without doubt had saved its life by her skill Then, gripping its shoulders with her knees, Sihamba shook the reins and called aloud to the *schimmel*, waving the black rod she always carried in her hand, so that the fiery beast, having plunged once, leapt away like an antelope, and in another minute was nothing but a speck racing towards the mountains.

CHAPTER XIII

THE SCHIMMEL'S FIRST RACE

So hard did Sihamba ride, and so swift and untiring proved the horse, to whose strength her light weight was as nothing, that, the veldt over which they travelled being flat and free from stones or holes, she reached the mouth of Tiger's Nek, twenty miles away, in very few minutes over the hour of time. But the Nek itself was a mile or more in length, and for aught she knew we might already be taken in Black Piet's trap, and she but riding to share our fate. Still she did not stay, but though it panted like a blacksmith's bellows, and its feet stumbled with weariness among the stones in the Nek, she urged on the *schimmel* at a gallop. Now she turned the corner, and the off-saddling place was before her. Swiftly and fearfully Sihamba glanced around, but seeing no signs of us, she uttered a cry of joy and shook the reins, for she knew that she had not ridden in vain. Then a voice from the rocks called out:

"It is the witch-doctoress, Sihamba, who rides to warn them. Kill her swiftly." With the voice came a sound of guns and of bullets screaming past her, one of which shattered the wand she carried in her hand, numbing her arm. Nor was that all, for men sprang up across the further end of the off-saddling place, where the path was narrow, to bar her way, and they held spears in their hands. But Sihamba never heeded the men or the spears, for she rode straight at them and through them, and so soon was she gone that, although six or seven assegais were hurled at her, only one of them struck the horse, wounding it slightly in the shoulder.

A few minutes later, three perhaps, or five, just as the four of us with our Kaffir servants were riding quietly up to the mouth of the Nek, we saw a great horse thundering towards us, black with sweat and flecked with foam, its shoulder bloody, its eyes staring, its red nostrils agape, and perched upon its bare back a little woman who swayed from side to side as though with weariness, holding in her hand a shattered wand.

"Allemachter!" cried Jan. "It is Sihamba, and the witch rides my roan *schimmel!*"

By this time Sihamba herself was upon us. "Back," she screamed as she came, "death waits you in the pass;" whereon, compelled to it as it were by the weight of the words and the face of her who spoke them, we turned our horses' heads and galloped after the *schimmel* for the half of a mile or more till we were safe in the open veldt.

Then of a sudden the horse stopped, whether of its own accord or because its rider pulled upon the reins I know not. At the least it stood there trembling like a reed and Sihamba lay upon its back clinging to the mane, and as she lay I saw blood running down her legs, for her skin was chafed to the flesh beneath. Ralph sprang to her and lifted her to the ground and Suzanne made her take a draught of peach brandy from Jan's flask, which brought the life into her face again.

"Now," she said, "if you have it to spare, give the

schimmel yonder a drink of that stuff, for he has saved all
your lives and I think he needs it."

" That is a wise word," said Jan, and he bade Ralph and
the Kaffirs pour the rest of the spirit down the horse's
throat, which they did, thereby, as I believe, saving its
life, for until it had swallowed it the beast looked as
though its heart were about to burst.

" Now," said Jan, " why do you ride my best horse to
death in this fashion? "

" Have I not told you, father of Swallow," she answered,
" that it was to save you from death? But a few minutes
over an hour ago, fifteen perhaps, a word was spoken to me
at your stead yonder and now I am here, seven leagues
away, having ridden faster than I wish to ride again, or
than any other horse in this country can travel with a man
upon its back."

" To save us from death! What death? " asked Jan
astounded.

" Death at the hands of Swart Piet and his Kaffir tribes-
men for the three of you and the two slaves, and for the
fourth, the lady Swallow here, a love which she does not
seek, the love of the murderer of her father, her mother,
and her chosen."

Now we stared at each other; only Suzanne ran to
Sihamba, and putting her arms about her, she kissed
her.

" Nay," said the little woman smiling, " nay, Swallow, I
do but repay to you one-hundredth part of my debt, and all
the rest is owing still."

Then she told her story in few words, and when it was
done, having first looked to see that Swart Piet and his
men were not coming, at the bidding of Jan we all knelt
down upon the veldt and thanked the Almighty for our

deliverance. Only Sihamba did not kneel, for she was a heathen, and worshipped no one unless it were Suzanne.

"You should pray to the horse, too," she said, "for had it not been for his legs, I could never have reached you in time."

"Peace, Sihamba," I answered, "it is God who made the horse's legs, as God put it into your mind to use them;" but I said no more, though at any other time I should have rated her well for her heathen folly.

Then we consulted together as to what was to be done and decided to make our way to the house by a longer path which ran through the open veldt, since we were sure that there, where is no cover, Swart Piet would not attack us. Ralph, it is true, was for going into the Nek and attacking him, but, as Jan showed him, such an act would be madness, for they were many and we were few; moreover, they could have picked us off from behind the shelter of the rocks. So we settled to leave him alone, and that night came home safely, though not without trouble, for we carried Sihamba the most of the way, and after he grew stiff the *schimmel* could only travel at a walking pace. Very soon that horse recovered, however, for he was a good feeder, and lived to do still greater service, although for a while his legs were somewhat puffed and had to be poulticed with cabbage leaves.

Now Jan and Ralph were mad against Swart Piet, and would have brought him to justice. But this road of justice was full of stones and mud-holes, since the nearest land-drost, as we call a magistrate, lived a hundred miles off, and it would not have been easy to persuade Piet to appear and argue the case before him. Moreover, here again we had no evidence against the man except that of a simple black fellow, who would never have been believed, for, in fact, no attack was made upon us, while that upon Sihamba might very well have been the work of some of the low Kaffirs that haunt the kloofs, runaway slaves, and other rascals who desired to steal the fine horse upon which she rode. Also we learned that our enemy, acting through some agent, had sold his farm to a stranger for a small sum of ready money, giving it out that he had no need of the land, as he was leaving this part of the country.

But if we saw Piet's face no more, we could still feel the weight of his hand, since from that time forward we began to suffer from thefts of cattle and other troubles with the natives, which—so Sihamba learned in her underground fashion—were instigated by him, working through his savage tools, while he himself lay hidden far away and in safety. Also he did us another ill turn—for it was proved that his money was at the bottom of it—by causing Ralph to be commandeered to serve on some distant Kaffir expedition, out of which trouble we were obliged to buy him, and at no small cost.

All these matters weighed upon us much, so much, indeed, that I wished Jan to trek from the Transkei and found a new home; but he would not, for he loved the place which he had built up brick by brick, and planted tree by tree; nor would he consent to be driven out of it through fear of the wicked practices of Swart Piet. To one thing he did consent, however, and it was that Ralph and Suzanne should be married as soon as possible, for he saw that until they were man and wife there would be little peace for any of us. When they were spoken to on the matter, neither of them had anything to say against this plan; indeed, I believe that in their hearts, for the first and last time in their lives, they blessed the name of Black Piet, whose evildoing, as they thought, was hurrying on their happiness.

Now it was settled that the matter of this marriage should be kept secret for fear it should come to the ears of Van Vooren through his spies, and stir him up to make a last attempt to steal away Suzanne.　And, indeed, it did come to his ears, though how to this hour I do not know, unless, in spite of our warning, the *predicant* who was to perform the ceremony, a good and easy man but one who loved gossip, blabbed of it on his journey to the farm, for he had a two days' ride to reach it

It was the wish of all of us that we should continue to live together after the marriage of Ralph and Suzanne, though not beneath the same roof.　Indeed, there would have been no room for another married pair in that house, especially if children came to them, nor did I wish to share the rule of a dwelling with my own daughter after she had taken a husband, for such arrangements often end in bitterness and quarrels.　Therefore Jan determined to build them a new house in a convenient spot not far away, and it was agreed that during the two or three months while this house was building Ralph and his wife should pay a visit to a cousin of mine, who owned a very fine farm on the outskirts of the dorp which we used to visit from time to time to partake of *Nachtmahl.** This seemed wise to us for several reasons beyond that of the building of the new house.　It is always best that young people should begin their married life alone, as by nature they wish to do, and not under the eyes of those who have bred and nurtured them, for thus face to face, with none to turn to, they grow more quickly accustomed to each other's faults and weaknesses, which, perhaps, they have not learned or taken count of before.

Moreover, in the case of Ralph and Suzanne we thought

* That is, Holy Communion.

it safer that they should be absent for a while from their own district and the neighbourhood of Swart Piet, living in a peopled place where they could not be molested, although, not knowing the wickedness of his heart, we did not believe it possible that he *would* molest them when once they were married. Indeed, there was some talk of their going to the dorp for the wedding, and I wish that they had done so, for then much trouble. might have been spared to us. But their minds were set against this plan, for they desired to be married where they had met and lived so long, so we did not gainsay them.

At length came the eve of the wedding day and with it the *predicant*, who arrived hungry and thirsty but running over with smiles and blessings. That night we all supped together and were full of joy, nor were Ralph and Suzanne the least joyous of us, though they said little, but sat gazing at each other across the table as though the moon had struck them.

Before I went to bed I had occasion to go out of the house for I remembered that some linen which Suzanne was to take with her had been left drying upon bushes after the wash, and I feared that if it remained there the Kaffir women might steal it. This linen was spread at a little distance from the house, near the huts where Sihamba lived, but I took no lantern with me, for the moon was bright.

As I drew near the spot I thought that I heard a sound of chanting which seemed to come from a little circle of mimosa trees that grew a spear's throw to my left, of chanting very low and sweet. Wondering who it was that sung thus, and why she sang—for the voice was that of a woman —I crept to the nearest of the trees, keeping in its shadow, and peeped through the branches into the grassy space beyond, to perceive Sihamba crouched in the centre of the

circle. She was seated upon a low stone in such fashion
that her head and face shone strangely in the moonlight,
while her body was hidden in the shadow Before her,
placed upon another stone, stood a large wooden bowl,
such as the Kaffirs cut out of the trunk of a tree, spending
a month of labour, or more, upon the task, and into this
bowl, which I could see was filled with water, for it reflected the moonrays, she was gazing earnestly, and, as she
gazed, chanting that low, melancholy song whereof I could
not understand the meaning

Presently Sihamba ceased her singing, and turning from
the bowl as though she had seen in it something that
frightened her, she covered her eyes with her hands and
groaned aloud, muttering words in which the name of
Suzanne was mixed up, or of Swallow, as she called her.
Now I guessed that Sihamba was practising that magic of
which she was said to be so great a mistress, although she
denied always that she knew anything of the art. At
first I made up my mind to call to her to cease from such
wickedness, which, as the Holy Book tells us, is a sin in the
eyes of the Lord, and a cause of damnation to those who
practise it. But I was curious and longed greatly in my
heart to know what it was that Sihamba saw in the bowl,
and what it had to do with my daughter Suzanne. So I
changed my mind, thereby making myself a partaker of
the sin, and coming forward said instead:

"What is it that you do here by night, in this solitary
place, Sihamba?"

Now although, as I suppose, she had neither seen nor
heard me, for I came up from behind her, Sihamba did not
start or cry out as any other woman would have done; she
did not even turn to look at me as she answered in a clear
and steady voice:

" Now while she is still a girl I read the fate of Swallow and of those who love her according to my lore, O mother of Swallow. Look, I read it there."

I looked and saw that the large bowl was filled to the brim with pure water. At the bottom of it lay some white sand, and on the sand were placed five pieces of broken looking-glass, all of which had been filed carefully to a round shape. The largest of these pieces was of the size of a crown of English money. This lay in the exact centre of the bowl. Above it and almost touching its edge, was another piece of the size of a half-crown, then to the right and left at a little distance, two more pieces of the size of a shilling, and below, but some way off, where the bowl began to curve, a very small piece not larger than a six-penny bit.

" Swallow," said Sihamba, pointing to the two largest of the fragments, " and husband of Swallow. There to the right and left father and mother of Swallow, and here at her feet, a long way off and very small, Sihamba, servant of Swallow, made all of them from the broken glass that shows back the face, which she gave me, and set, as they must be set, like the stars in the Cross of the Skies."

Now I shivered a little, for in myself I was afraid of this woman's magic, but to her I laughed and said roughly:

" What fool's plaything made of bits of broken glass is this that you have here, Sihamba? "

" It is a plaything that will tell a story to those who can read it," she answered without anger, but like one who knows she speaks the truth.

" Make it tell its story to me, and I will believe you," I said laughing again.

She shook her head and answered, " Lady, I cannot, for you have not the Sight; but bring your husband here, and perhaps he will be able to read the story, or some of it."

Now at this I grew angry, for it is not pleasant to a woman to hear that a man whom all know to be but as a child compared to her can see things in water which she is not able to see, even though the things are born only of the false magic of a witch-doctoress. Still, as at that moment I chanced to hear Jan seeking me, for he wondered where I had gone, I called to him and set out the matter, expecting that he would be very angry and dismiss Sihamba, breaking up her magic bowl. But all the while that I talked to him the little woman sat, her chin resting upon her hand, looking into his face, and I think that she had some power over him. At the least, he was not at all angry, although he said that I must not mention the business to the *predicant*, who was well known to be a prejudiced man. Then he asked Sihamba to show him the wonders of the bowl. Replying that she would if she might, and always keeping her eyes fixed upon his face, she bade him kneel down and look into the water in such fashion that he did not shut the moonlight off from it, and to tell us what he saw.

So he knelt and looked, whispering presently that on the midmost piece of glass there appeared the image of Suzanne, and on the others respectively those of Ralph, Jan himself, me his wife, and of Sihamba. I asked him what they were doing, but he could give me no clear answer, so I suppose that they were printed there like the heads on postage stamps, if indeed they existed anywhere except in Jan's brain, into which Sihamba had conjured them.

"What do you see more?" asked Sihamba.

"I see a shadow in the water," he answered, "a dark shadow, and—it is like the head of Swart Piet cut out of black paper—it spreads till it almost hides all the faces on the bits of glass. Almost, I say, but not quite, for things are passing beneath the shadow which I cannot distinguish. Now it shrinks quite small, and lies only over your likeness, Sihamba, which shows through it red—yes, and all the water round it is red, and now there is nothing left;" and Jan rose pale with fright, and wiped his brow with a coloured pocket-handkerchief, muttering "Allemachter! this is magic indeed."

"Let me look," I said, and I looked for a long while and saw nothing except the five bits of glass. So I told Jan outright that he was a fool whom any conjurer could play with, but he waited until I had done and then asked Sihamba what the vision meant.

"Father of Swallow," she answered, "what I saw in the water mirror you have seen, only I saw more than you did because my sight is keener. You ask me what it means, but I cannot tell you altogether, for such visions are uncertain; they sum up the future but they do not show it all. This, however, is sure, that trouble waits us every one because of Swart Piet, for his shadow lay thick upon the image of each of us; only note this, that while it cleared away from the rest, it remained upon mine, staining it blood-red, which means that while in the end you will escape him, I shall die at his hands, or through him. Well, so be it, but meanwhile this is my counsel—because of other things that I saw in the water which I cannot describe, for in truth I know not rightly what they were— that the marriage of the Swallow and her husband should be put off, and that when they are married it should be at the dorp yonder, not here."

Now when I heard this my anger overflowed like water in a boiling pot. "What!" I cried, "when all is settled and the *predicant* has ridden for two days to do the thing, is the marriage to be put off because forsooth this little black idiot declares that she sees things on bits of glass in a bowl, and because you, Jan, who ought to know better, take the lie from her lips and make it your own? I say that I am mistress here and that I will not allow it. If we are to be made fools of in this fashion by the peepings and mutterings of Kaffir witch-doctors we had better give up and die at once to go and live among the dead, whose business it is to peep and mutter. Our business is to dwell in the world and to face its troubles and dangers until such time as it pleases God to call us out of the world, paying no heed to omens and magic and such like sin and folly. Let that come which will come, and let us meet it like men and women, giving glory to the Almighty for the ill as well as for the good, since both ill and good come from His hands and are part of His plan. For my part I trust to Him who made us and who watches us, and I fear not Swart Piet, and therefore chance what may the marriage shall go on."

"Good words," said Jan, "such as my heart approves of;" but he still mopped his head with the coloured pocket-handkerchief and looked troubled as he added, "I pray you, wife, say nothing of this to anybody, and above all to the predicant, or he will put me out of the church as a wizard."

"Yes, yes," said Sihamba, "good words, but the Sight is still the Sight for those who have the power to see. Not that I wished you to see, indeed I did not wish it, nor did I think that you would be turned from your purpose by that which you have seen. Father and mother of Swallow, you are right, and now I will tell you the truth. What you beheld in the water was nothing but a trick, a clever trick of the little doctoress, Sihamba, by the help of which and others like it, she earns her living, and imposes on the foolish, though she cannot impose upon you, who are wise, and have the Lord of the skies for a friend. So think no more of it, and do not be angry with the little black monkey whose nature it is to play tricks;" and with a motion of her foot she upset the bowl of water, and collecting the pieces of mirror hid them away in her skin pouch.

Then we went, but as I passed through the thorn trees I turned and looked at Sihamba, and lo! she was standing in the moonlight, her face lifted towards the sky, weeping softly and wringing her hands. Then for the first time I felt a little afraid.

CHAPTER XIV

THE WEDDING

THE marriage morning of Ralph and Suzanne broke brightly; never have I seen a fairer. It was spring time, and the veldt was clothed with the fresh green grass and starred everywhere with the lily blooms that sprang among it. The wind blew softly, shaking down the dewdrops from the growing corn, while from every bush and tree came the cooing of unnumbered doves. Beneath the eave of the *stoep* the pair of red-breasted swallows which had built there for so many years were finishing their nest, and I watched them idly, for to me they were old friends, and would wheel about my head, touching my cheek with their wings. Just then they paused from their task, or perhaps it was at length completed, and flying to a bough of the peach tree a few yards away, perched there together amidst the bright bloom, and nestling against each other, twittered forth their song of joy and love.

It was at this moment that Sihamba walked up to the *stoep* as though to speak to me.

"The Swallow and the Swallow's mate," she said, following my eyes to where the little creatures swung together on the beautiful bough.

"Yes," I answered, for her fancy seemed to me of good omen, "they have built their nest, and now they are thanking God before they begin to live there together and rear their young in love."

As the words left my lips a quick shadow swept across the path of sunlit ground before the house, two strong wings beat, and a brown hawk, small but very fierce, being of a sort that preys upon little birds, swooped downwards upon the swallows. One of them saw it, and slid from the bough, but the other the hawk caught in its talons, and mounted with it high into the air. In vain did its mate circle round it swiftly, uttering shrill notes of distress; up it went steadily as pitiless as death.

" Oh! my swallow," I cried aloud in grief, " the accursed hawk has carried away my swallow."

" Nay, look," said Sihamba, pointing upwards.

I looked, and behold! a black crow that appeared from behind the house, was wheeling about the hawk, striking at it with its beak until, that it might have its talons free to defend itself, it let go the swallow, which, followed by its mate, came fluttering to the earth, while the crow and the falcon passed away fighting, till they were lost in the blue depths of air.

Springing from the *stoep* I ran to where the swallow lay, but Sihamba was there before me and had it in her hands.

" The hawk's beak has wounded it," she said pointing to a blood stain among the red feathers of the breast, " but none of its bones are broken, and I think that it will live. Let us put it in the nest and leave it to its mate and nature."

This we did, and there in the nest it stayed for some days, its mate feeding it with flies as though it were still unfledged. After that they vanished, both of them together, seeking some new home, nor did they ever build again beneath our eaves.

"Would you speak with me, Sihamba?" I asked when this matter of the swallows was done with.

"I would speak with the Baas, or with you, it is the same thing," she answered, "and for this reason. I go upon a journey; for myself I have the good black horse which the Baas gave me after I had ridden to warn you in Tiger Kloof yonder, the one that I cured of sickness. But I need another beast to carry pots and food and my servant Zinti, who accompanies me. There is the brown mule which you use little because he is vicious, but he is very strong and Zinti does not fear him. Will you sell him to me for the two cows I earned from the Kaffir whose wife I saved when the snake bit her? He is worth three, but I have no more to offer."

"Whither do you wish to journey, Sihamba?" I asked.

"I follow my mistress to the dorp," she answered.

"Did she bid you follow her, Sihamba?"

"No! is it likely that she would think of me at such a time, or care whether I come or go? Fear not, I shall not trouble her, or put her to cost; I shall follow, but I shall not be seen until I am wanted."

Now I had made up my mind to gainsay Sihamba, not that I could find any fault with her plan, but because if such arrangements are made, I like to make them myself, as is the business of the head of the house. I think Sihamba guessed this; at any rate she answered me before I spoke, and that in an odd way, namely, by looking first at the swallow's nest, then at the blooming bough of the peach tree, and lastly into the far distances of air.

"It was the black crow that drove the hawk away," she said, reflectively, as though she were thinking of something else, "though I think, for my eyes are better than yours, that the hawk killed the crow, or perhaps they killed each other; at the least I saw them falling to the earth beyond the crest of the mountain."

At this I was about to break in angrily, for if there was one thing in the world I hated it was Sihamba's nonsense about birds and omens and such things, whereof, indeed, I had had enough on the previous night, when she made that lump Jan believe that he saw visions in a bowl of water. And yet I did not—for the black crow's sake. The cruel hawk had seized the swallow which I loved, and borne it away to devour it in its eyrie, and it was the crow that saved it. Well, the things that happened among birds might happen among men, who also prey upon each other, and—but I could not bear the thought.

"Take the mule, Sihamba," I said; "I will answer for it to the Baas. As for the two cows, they can run with the other cattle till your return."

"I thank you, Mother of Swallow," she answered, and turned to go, when I stopped her and asked:

"Have you heard anything that makes you afraid, Sihamba?"

"I have heard nothing," she replied, "still I am afraid."

"Then you are a fool for your pains, to be afraid of nothing," I answered roughly; "but watch well, Sihamba."

"Fear not, I will watch till my knees are loosened and my eyes grow hollow." Then she went away, and that was the last I saw of her for many a weary month. Ah! Suzanne, child, had it not been for the watching of little Sihamba, the walker-by-moonlight, you had not been sitting there to-day, looking much as she used to look, the Suzanne of fifty years ago."

The marriage was to take place at noon, and though I had much to see to, never have I known a longer morning.

Why it was I cannot say, but it seemed to me as though twelve o'clock would never come. Then, wherever I went there was Ralph in my way, wandering about in a senseless fashion with his best clothes on, while after him wandered Jan holding his new hat in his hand.

" In the name of Heaven," I cried at length as I blundered into both of them in the kitchen, " be off out of this. Why are you here? "

" Allemachter! " said Jan, " because we have nowhere else to go. They are making the sitting-room ready for the service and the dinner after it; the *predicant* is in Ralph's room writing; Suzanne is in yours trying on her clothes, and the *stoep* and even the stables are full of Kaffirs. Where, then, shall we go? "

" Cannot you see to the waggon? " I asked.

" We have seen to it, mother," said Ralph; " it is packed, and the oxen are already tied to the yokes for fear lest they should stray."

" Then be off and sit in it and smoke till I come to call you," I replied, and away they walked shamefacedly enough, Ralph first, and Jan following him.

At twelve o'clock I went for them, and found them both seated on the waggon-chest smoking like chimneys, and saying nothing.

" Come, Ralph," I said, " it is quite time for you to be married," and he came, looking very pale, and walking unsteadily as though he had been drinking, while after him, as usual, marched Jan, still pulling at the pipe which he had forgotten to take out of his mouth.

Somehow I do not recollect much of the details of that wedding; they seem to have slipped my mind, or perhaps they are buried beneath the memories of all that followed hard upon it. I remember Suzanne standing before the little table, behind which was the *predicant* with his book. She wore a white dress that fitted her very well, but had no veil upon her head after the English fashion, which even Boer girls follow nowadays, only in her hand she carried a bunch of rare white flowers that Sihamba had gathered for her in a hidden kloof where they grew. Her face was somewhat pale, or looked so in the dim room, but her lips showed red like coral, and her dark eyes glowed and shone as she turned them upon the lover at her side, the fair-haired, grey-eyed, handsome English lad, whose noble blood told its tale in every feature and movement, yes, and even in his voice, the man whom she had saved from death to be her life-mate.

A few whispered words, the changing of a ring, and one long kiss, and these two, Ralph Kenzie and Suzanne Botmar, were husband and wife in the eyes of God and man. Ah! me, I am glad to think of it, for in the end, of all the many marriages that I have known, this proved the very best and happiest.

Now I thought that it was done with, for they had knelt down and the *predicant* had blessed them; but not so, for the good man must have his word, and a long word it was. On and on he preached about the duties of husbands and wives, and many other matters, till at last, as I expected, he came to the children. Now I could bear it no longer.

"That is enough, reverend Sir," I said, "for surely it is scarcely needful to talk of children to people who have not been married five minutes."

That pricked the bladder of his discourse, which soon came to an end, whereon I called to the Kaffirs to bring in dinner.

The food was good and plentiful, and so was the Hol--

lands, or Squareface as they call it now, to say nothing of the Constantia and peach-brandy which had been sent to me many years before by a cousin who lived at Stellenbosch; and yet that meal was not as cheerful as it might have been. To begin with, the *predicant* was sulky because I had cut him short in his address, and a holy man in the sulks is a bad kind of animal to deal with. Then Jan tried to propose the health of the new married pair and could not do it. The words seemed to stick in his throat, for at the best Jan never was a speaker. In short, he made a fool of himself as usual, and I had to fill up the gaps in his head.

Well, I talked nicely enough till in an evil moment I overdid it a little by speaking of Ralph as one whom Heaven had sent to us, and of whose birth and parents we knew nothing. Then Jan found his tongue and said: "Wife, that's a lie, and you know it," for, doubtless, the Hollands and the peach-brandy had got the better of his reason and his manners. I did not answer him at the time, for I hate wrangling in public, but afterwards I spoke to him on the subject once and for all. Luckily, the *predicant* took no notice of this incident, for he was thinking about himself as he was too prone to do.

Then, to make matters worse, Suzanne must needs throw her arms round her father's neck and begin to cry—thanks be to my bringing up of her, she knew better than to throw them round mine. "Good Lord!" I said, losing my temper, "what is the girl at now? She has got the husband for whom she has been craving, and the first thing she does is to snivel. Well, if I had done that to my husband I should have expected him to box my ears, though Heaven knows that I should have had excuse for it."

Here the *predicant* woke up, seeing his chance.

"Vrouw Botmar," he said, blinking at me like an owl, "it is my duty to reprove your irreverent language even at this festive board, for a word must be spoken both in and out of season, and without respect of persons. Vrouw Botmar, I fear that you do not remember the Third Commandment, therefore I will repeat it to you," and he did so, speaking very slowly.

What I answered I cannot recollect, but even now I seem to see that *predicant* flying out of the door of the room holding his hands above his head. Well, for once he met his match, and I know that afterwards he always spoke of me with great respect.

After this again I remember little more till the pair started upon their journey. Suzanne asked for Sihamba to say good-bye to her, and when she was told that she was not to be found she seemed vexed, which shows that the little doctoress did her injustice in supposing that just because she was married she thought no more of her. Then she kissed us all in farewell—ah! we little knew for how long that farewell was to be—and went down to the waggon to which the sixteen black oxen, a beautiful team, were inspanned, and standing there ready to start. But Ralph and Suzanne were not going to ride in the waggon, for they had horses to carry them. At the last moment, indeed, Jan, whose head was still buzzing with the peach-brandy, insisted upon giving Ralph the great *schimmel*, that same stallion which Sihamba had ridden when she warned us of the ambush in the pass, galloping twenty miles in the hour. This shows me that Providence can turn even a man's vices to account, for afterwards the *schimmel* was very useful.

So there was much kissing and many good-byes; Ralph

and Suzanne saying that they would soon be back, which indeed was the case with one of them, till at last they were off, Jan riding with them a little way towards their first outspan by the sea, fourteen miles distant, where they were to sleep that night.

When they had gone I went into my bedroom, and sitting down, I cried, for I was sorry to lose Suzanne, even for a little and for her own good, and my heart was heavy. Also my quarrel with the *predicant* had put me out of temper. When I had got over this fit I set to work to tidy Suzanne's little sleeping place, and that I found a sad task. Then Jan returned from the waggon, having bid farewell to the young couple, an hour's trek away, and his head being clear by now, we talked over the plans of the new house which was to be built for them to live in, and, going down to the site of it, set it out with sticks and a rule, which gave us occupation till towards sunset, when it was time for him to go to see to the cattle.

That night we went to bed early, for we were tired, and slept a heavy sleep, till at length, about one in the morning, we were awakened by the shoutings of the messengers who came bearing the terrible news.

CHAPTER XV.

RALPH RETURNS INTO THE SEA.

RALPH and Suzanne reached their outspan place in safety a little before sunset. I used to know the spot well; it is where one of the numerous wooded kloofs that scar the mountain slopes ends on a grassy plain of turf, short but very sweet. This plain is not much more than five hundred paces wide, for it is bordered by the cliff, that just here is not very high, against which the sea beats at full tide.

When the oxen had been turned loose to graze, and the voorlooper set to watch them, the driver of the waggon undid the cooking vessels and built a fire with dry wood collected from the kloof. Then Suzanne cooked their simple evening meal, of which they partook thankfully. After it was done the pair left the waggon and followed the banks of the little kloof stream, which wandered across the plain till it reached the cliff, whence it fell in a trickling waterfall into the sea. Here they sat down upon the edge of the cliff, and locked in each other's arms, watched the moon rise over the silver ocean, their young hearts filled with a joy that cannot be told.

" The sea is beautiful, is it not, husband? " whispered Suzanne into his ear.

" To-night it is beautiful," he answered, " as our lives

seem to be; yet I have seen it otherwise," and he shuddered a little.

She nodded, for she knew of what he was thinking, and did not wish to speak of it. " Neither life nor ocean can be always calm," she said, " but oh! I love that great water, for it brought you to me."

" I pray that it may never separate us," answered Ralph.

" Why do you say that, husband? " she asked. " Nothing can separate us now, for even if you journey far away to seek your own people, as sometimes I think you should, I shall accompany you. Nothing can separate us except death, and death shall but bind us more closely each to each for ever and for ever."

" I do not know why I said it, Sweet," he answered uneasily, and just then a little cloud floated over the face of the moon, darkening the world, and a cold wind blew down the kloof, causing its trees to rustle and chilling the pair, so that they clung closer to each other for comfort.

The cloud and the wind passed away, leaving the night as beautiful as before, and they sat on for a while to watch it, listening to the music of the waterfall that splashed into the deep sea pool below, and to the soft surge of the waves as they lapped gently against the narrow beach.

At length Ralph spoke in a low voice. " Sweet, it is time to sleep," he said, and kissed her.

" It is time," she whispered back, " but, husband, first let us kneel together here and pray to the Almighty to bless our married life and make us happy."

" That is a good thought," he answered, for in those days young men who had been brought up as Christians were not ashamed to say their prayers even in the presence of others.

So they knelt down side by side upon the edge of the cliff, with their faces set towards the open sea.

"Pray for us both aloud, Ralph," said Suzanne, "for though my heart is full enough I have no words."

So Ralph prayed very simply, saying: "Oh, God, Who madest us, hear us, Thy son and daughter, and bless us. This night our married life begins; be Thou with us ever in it, and if it should please Thee that we should have children, let Thy blessing go with them all their days. Oh! God, I thank Thee that Thou didst save me alive from the sea and lead the feet of the child who is now my wife to the place where I was starving, and Suzanne thanks Thee that through the whisperings of a dream her feet were led thus. Oh! God, as I believe that Thou didst hear my prayer when as a lost child I knelt dying on the rock, so I believe that Thou dost hear this the first prayer of our wedded life. We know that all life is not made up of such joy as Thou hast given us this day, but that it has many dangers and troubles and losses, therefore we pray Thee to comfort us in the troubles, to protect us in the dangers, and to give us consolation in the losses; and most of all we pray Thee that we who love each other, and whom Thou hast joined together, may be allowed to live out our lives together, fearing nothing, however great our peril, since day and night we walk in the shadow of Thy strength, until we pass into its presence."

This was Ralph's prayer, for he told it to me word by word afterwards when he lay sick. At the time the answer to it seemed to be a strange one, an answer to shake the faith out of a man's heart, and yet it was not lost or mocked at, for the true response came in its season. Nay, it came week by week and hour by hour, seeing that every day through those awful years the sword of the Strength

they had implored protected those who prayed, holding
them harmless in many a desperate peril to reunite them
at the last. The devil is very strong in this world of ours, or
so it seems to me, who have known much of his ways, so
strong that perhaps God must give place to him at times,
for if He rules in heaven, I think that Satan shares His
rule on earth. But in the end it is God who wins, and
never, never, need they fear, who acknowledge Him and
put their faith in Him, trying the while to live uprightly
and conquer the evil of their hearts. Well, this is only
an old woman's wisdom, though it should not be laughed
at, since it has been taught to her by the experience of a
long and eventful life. Such as it is I hope that it may
be of service to those who trust in themselves and not
in their Maker.

As the last words of his prayer left Ralph's lips he heard
a man laugh behind him. The two of them sprang to
their feet at the sound, and faced about to see Swart Piet
standing within five paces of them, and with him eight or
ten of his black ruffians, who looked upon him as their
chief, and did his needs without question, however wicked
they might be.

Now Suzanne uttered a low cry of fear and the blood
froze about Ralph's heart, for he was unarmed and their
case was hopeless. Black Piet saw their fear and laughed
again, since like a cat that has caught a mouse for which
it has watched long, he could not resist the joy of torture
before he dealt the death blow.

"This is very lucky," he said, "and I am glad that I
have to do with such pious people, since it enabled us to
creep on you unawares; also I much prefer to have found
you engaged in prayer, friend Englishman, rather than in

taking the bloom off my peach with kisses, as I feared might be the case. That was a pretty prayer, too; I almost felt as though I were in church while I stood listening to it. How did it end? You prayed that you might be allowed to live together, fearing nothing, however great your peril, since you walked always in the shadow of God's strength. Well, I have come to answer your petition, and to tell you that your life together is ended before it is begun. For the rest, your peril is certainly great, and now let God's strength help you if it can. Come, God, show Your strength. He does not answer, you see, or perhaps He knows that Swart Piet is god here and is afraid."

"Cease your blasphemy," said Ralph in a hoarse voice, "and tell me what you want with us."

"What do I want? I want her whose scorn and beauty have driven me mad, her for whom I have been seeking this long time—Suzanne Botmar."

"She is my wife," said Ralph; "would you steal away my wife?"

"No, friend, for that would not be lawful. I will not take your wife, but I shall take your widow, as will be easy, seeing that you are armed with God's strength only."

Now understanding all this man's devilish purpose, Suzanne fell upon her knees before him, imploring him with many piteous words. But knowing that death was at hand Ralph's heart rose to it, as that of a high-couraged man will do, and he bade her to cease her supplications and rise. Then in a loud, clear voice he spoke in the Kaffir tongue, so that those who were with Piet Van Vooren should understand him.

"It seems, Piet Van Vooren," he said, "that you have stolen upon us here to carry off my wife by violence after you have murdered me. These crimes you may do, though

I know well that if you do them they will be revenged
upon you amply, and upon you men also who take part in
them. And now I will not plead to you for mercy, but I
ask one thing which you cannot refuse, because those with
you, Kaffirs though they be, will not suffer it—five short
minutes of time in which to bid farewell to my new-wed
wife."

"Not an instant," said Swart Piet, but at the words the
black men who were with him, and whose wicked hearts
were touched with pity, began to murmur so loudly, that
he hesitated.

"At your bidding, Bull-Head," said one of them, "we
have come to kill this man and to carry away the white
woman, and we will do it, for you are our chief and we
must obey you. But, if you will not give him the little
space for which he asks, wherein to bid farewell to his wife
before she becomes your wife, then we will have nothing
more to do with the matter. I say that our hearts are
sick at it already, and, Bull-Head, you kill a man, not a
dog, and that by murder, not in fair fight."

"As you will, fool," said Swart Piet. "Englishman, I
give you five minutes," and he drew a large silver watch
from his pocket and held it in his hand.

"Get out of hearing then, murderer," said Ralph, "for I
have no breath left to waste on you," and Piet obeying
him, fell back a little and stood gnawing his nails and
staring at the pair.

"Suzanne, wife Suzanne," whispered Ralph, "we are
about to part, since, as you see, I must die, and your fate
lies in the Hand of God. Yes, you are made a widow before you are a wife ; and, Suzanne, ah! that is the worst of
it, another takes you, even my murderer."

Now Suzanne, who till this moment had been as one

stupefied, seemed to gather up her strength and answered him calmly, saying:

" Truly, husband, things appear to be as you say, though what we have done that they should be so, I cannot tell. Still comfort yourself, for death comes to all of us soon or late, and whether it comes soon or late makes little difference in the end, seeing that come it must."

" No, not death, it is your fate that makes the difference. How can I bear to die and leave you the prey of that devil? Oh my God! my God! how can I bear to die! "

" Have no fear, husband," went on Suzanne in the same clear, indifferent voice, " for you do not leave me to be his prey. Say, now; if we walk backwards swiftly before they could catch us we might fall together into the pit of the sea beneath."

" Nay, wife, let our deaths lie upon their heads and not upon ours, for self-murder is a crime."

" As you will, Ralph; but I tell you, and through you I tell Him who made me, that it is a crime which I shall dare if need be. Have no fear, Ralph, as I leave your arms, so shall I return to them, whether it be in Heaven or upon earth. That man thinks he has power over me, but I say that he has none, seeing that at the last God will protect me with His hand, or with my own."

" I cannot blame you, Suzanne, for there are some things which are not to be borne. Do therefore as your conscience teaches you, if you have the means."

" I have the means, Ralph. Hidden about me is a little knife which I have carried since I was a child; and if that fails me there are other ways."

" Time is done," said Swart Piet, replacing the watch in his pocket.

" Farewell, sweet," whispered Ralph.

10

" Farewell, husband," she answered bravely, " until we meet again, whether it be here on earth or above in Heaven; farewell until we meet again," and she flung her arms about his neck and kissed him.

For a moment Ralph clung to her muttering some blessing above her bowed head; then he unloosed her clasping arms, letting her fall gently upon the ground and saying: " Lie thus, shutting your ears and hiding your eyes till all is done. Afterwards you must act as seems best to you. Escape to your father if you can, if not—tell me, do you understand? "

" I understand," she murmered, and hid her face in a tuft of thick grass, placing her hands upon her ears.

Ralph bowed his head for an instant in prayer. Then he lifted it and there was no fear upon his face.

" Come on, murderer," he said, addressing Swart Piet, " and do your butcher's work. Why do you delay? You cannot often find the joy of slaughtering a defenceless man in the presence of his new-made wife. Come on then and win the everlasting curse of God."

Now Swart Piet glanced at him out of the corners of his round eyes; then he ordered one of the Kaffirs to go up to him and shoot him.

The man went up and lifted his gun, but presently he put it down again and walked away, saying that he could not do this deed. Thrice did Van Vooren issue his command, and to three separate men, the vilest of his flock, but with each of them it was the same; they came up lifting their guns, looked into Ralph's grey eyes and slunk away muttering. Then, cursing and swearing in his mad fury, Swart Piet drew the pistol from his belt and rushing towards Ralph fired it into him so that he fell. He stood over him and looked at him, the smoking pistol in his hand, but the wide grey eyes remained open and the strong mouth still smiled.

" The dog lives yet," raved Swart Piet; " cast him into the sea, and let the sea finish him."

But no man stirred; all stood silent as though they had been cut in stone, and there, a little nearer the cliff edge, lay the silent form of Suzanne.

Then Van Vooren seized Ralph and dragged him by the shoulders to the brink of the precipice. His hair brushed the hair of Suzanne as his body was trailed along the ground, and as he passed he whispered one word, " Remember," into her ear, and she raised her head to look at him and answered, " Now, and always." Then she let her head fall again.

Stooping down, Swart Piet lifted Ralph in his great arms, and crying aloud: " Return into the sea out of which you came," he hurled him over the edge of the cliff. Two seconds later the sound of a heavy splash echoed up its sides; then, save for the murmer of the waterfall and the surge of the surf upon the beach, all was still again.

CHAPTER XVI

For a few moments Swart Piet and his black ruffians stood staring now at each other and now over the edge of the cliff into the deep sea-hole. There, however, they could see nothing, for the moonbeams did not reach its surface, and the only sound they heard was that of the dripping of the little waterfall, which came to their ears like the tinkle of distant sheep-bells. Then Swart Piet shivered and laughed aloud, a laugh that had more of fear than of merriment in it.

"The Englishman called down the everlasting curse of God on me," he cried. "Well, I have waited for it, and it does not come, so now for man's reward," and going to where Suzanne lay, he set his arms beneath her and turned her over upon her back. "She has swooned," he said; "perhaps it is as well," and he stood looking at her, for thus in her faint she seemed wonderfully fair with the moonbeams playing upon her deathlike face.

"He had good taste, that Englishman," went on Swart Piet. "Well, now our account is squared; he has sown and I shall harvest. Follow me, you black fellows, for we had best be off," and, stooping down he lifted Suzanne in his arms and walked away with her as though she were a child. For a while they followed the windings of the stream, keeping under cover of the reeds and bushes that grew upon its banks. Then they struck out to the right, taking advantage of a cloud which dimmed the face of the moon for a time, for they wished to reach the kloof without being seen from the waggon. Nor, indeed, were they seen, for the driver and voorlooper were seated by the cooking-fire on its further side, smoking, and dozing as they smoked. Only the great thoroughbred horse winded them and snorted, pulling at the reim with which he was tied to the hind wheel of the waggon.

"Something has frightened the *schimmel*," said the driver waking up.

"It is nothing," answered the other boy drowsily; "he is not used to the veldt, he who always sleeps in a house like a man; or, perhaps, he smells a hyena in the kloof."

"I thought I heard a sound like that of a gun a while ago down yonder by the sea," said the driver again. "Say, brother, shall we go and find what made it?"

"By no means," answered the voorlooper, who did not like walking about at night, fearing lest he should meet spooks. "I have been wide awake and listening all this time, and I heard no gun; nor, indeed, do people go out shooting at night. Also it is our business to watch here by the waggon till our master and mistress return."

"Where can they have gone?" said the driver, who felt frightened, he knew not why. "It is strange that they should be so long away when it is time for them to sleep."

"Who can account for the ways of white people?" answered the other, shrugging his shoulders. "Very often they sit up all night. Doubtless these two will return when they are tired, or perhaps they desire to sleep in the veldt. At any rate it is not our duty to interfere with

them, seeing that they can come to no harm here where
there are neither men nor tigers."

" So be it," said the driver, and they both dozed off again
till the messenger of ill came to rouse them.

Now Black Piet and his men crept up the kloof carrying
Suzanne with them, till they came to a little patch of rocky
ground at the head of it where they had left their horses.

" That was very well managed," said Piet as they loosed
them and tightened their girths, " and none can ever know
that we have made this journey. To-morrow the bride
and bridegroom will be missed, but the sea has the one
and I have the other, and hunt as they may they will never
find her, nor guess where she has gone. No, it will be
remembered that they walked down to the sea, and folk
will think that by chance they fell from the cliff into the
deep water and vanished there. Yes, it was well managed
and none can guess the truth."

Now the man to whom he spoke, that same man with
whom the boy Zinti had heard him plot our murder in the
Tiger Kloof, shrugged his shoulders and answered.

" I think there is one who will guess."

" Who is that, fool? "

" She about whose neck once I set a rope at your bidding, Bull-Head, and whose life was bought by those lips,"
and he pointed to Suzanne, " Sihamba Ngenyanga."

" Why should she guess? " asked Piet angrily.

" Has she not done so before? Think of the great
schimmel and its rider in Tiger Kloof. Moreover, what
does her name mean? Does it not mean ' Wanderer-by-
moonlight,' and was not this great deed of yours a deed
at the telling of which all who hear of it shall grow sick
and silent, done in the moonlight, Bull-Head?"

Now as we learned afterwards from a man whom Jan took prisoner, and who told us everything which passed that night, hoping to buy his life, Piet made no an wer to this saying, but turned to busy himself with his sad-dle, for, after his ill dealings with her, he was always afraid of Sihamba, and would never mention her name unless he was obliged. Soon the horses, most of which were small and of the Basuto breed, were ready to start. On one of the best of them there was a soft pad of sheep-skins, such as girls used to ride on when I was young, before we knew anything about these new-fangled English saddles with leather hooks to hold the rider in her place. On this pad, which had been prepared for her, they set Su-zanne, having first tied her feet together loosely with a riem so that she might not slip to the ground and attempt to escape by running. Moreover, as she was still in a swoon, they supported her, Black Piet walking upon one side and a Kaffir upon the other. In this fashion they travelled for the half of an hour or more, until they were deep in among the mountains, indeed, when suddenly with a little sigh Suzanne awoke, and glanced about her with wide, frightened eyes. Then memory came back to her, and she understood, and, opening her lips, she uttered one shriek so piercing and dreadful that the rocks of the hills multiplied and echoed it, and the blood went cold even in the hearts of those savage men.

"Suzanne," said Swart Piet in a low, hoarse voice, "I have dared much to win you, and I wish to treat you kindly, but if you cry out again, for my own safety's sake and that of those with me, we must gag you."

She made no answer to him, nor did she speak at all except one word, and that word "*Murderer.*" Then she closed her eyes as though to shut out the sight of his face,

and sat silent, saying nothing and doing nothing, even
when Piet and the other man who supported her had
mounted and pushed their horses to a gallop, leading that
on which she rode by a riem.

It might be thought after receiving a pistol bullet
fired into him at a distance of four paces, and being cast
down through fifty feet of space into a pool of the sea,
that there was an end of Ralph Kenzie for ever on this
earth. But thanks to the mercy of God this was not so,
for the ball had but shattered his left shoulder, touching
no vital part, and the water into which he fell was deep,
so that, striking against no rock, he rose presently to the
surface, and the pool being but narrow, was able to swim
to one side of it where the beach shelved. Up that beach
Ralph could not climb, however, for he was faint with loss
of blood and shock. Indeed, his senses left him while he
was in the water, but it chanced that he fell forward and
not backward, so that his head rested upon the shelving
edge of the pool, all the rest of his body being beneath its
surface. Lying thus, had the tide been rising, he would
speedily have drowned, but it had turned, and so, the water
being warm, he took no further harm.

Now Sihamba did not leave the stead till some hours
after Ralph and his bride had trekked away. She knew
where they would outspan, and as she did not wish that
they should see her yet, or until they were too far upon
their journey to send her back, it was her plan to reach the
spot, or rather a hiding-place in the kloof within a stone's
throw of it, after they had gone to rest. So it came
about that at the time when Ralph and Suzanne were sur-
prised by Swart Piet, Sihamba was riding along quietly
upon the horse which Jan had given her, accompanied by

the lad Zinti, perched on the strong brown mule in the midst of cooking pots, bags of meal, biltong, and rolls of blankets Already, half a mile off or more, she could see the cap of the waggon gleaming white in the moonlight, when suddenly away to the left they heard the sound of a pistol shot

" Now who shoots in this lonely place at night? " said Sihamba to Zinti " Had the sound come from the waggon yonder I should think that someone had fired to scare a hungry jackal, but all is quiet at the waggon, and the servants of Swallow are there, for, look, the fire burns."

" I know not, lady," answered Zinti, for Sihamba was given the title of Chieftainess among the natives who knew something of her birth, " but I am sure that the sound was made by powder "

" Let us go and see," said Sihamba turning her horse.

For a while they rode on towards the place whence they had heard the shot, till, suddenly, when they were near the cliff and in a little fold of ground beyond the ridge of which ran the stream, Sihamba stopped and whispered, " Be silent, I hear voices." Then she slipped from her horse and crept like a snake up the slope of the rise until she reached its crest, where at this spot stood two tufts of last season's grass, for no fires had swept the veldt. From between these tufts, so well hidden herself that unless they had stepped upon her body, none could have discovered her, she saw a strange sight.

There beneath her, within a few paces indeed, for the ground sloped steeply to the stream, men were passing. The first of these was white, and he carried a white woman in his arms; the rest were Kaffirs, some of whom wore karosses or cotton blankets, and some tattered soldiers' coats and trousers, while all were well armed with " *roers* " or other guns, and had powder flasks hung about their necks. Sihamba knew at once that the white man was Swart Piet, and the woman in his arms her mistress, Suzanne. She could have told it from her shape alone, but as it happened, her head hung down, and the moonlight shone upon her face so brightly that she could see its every feature. Her blood boiled in her as she looked, for now she understood that her fears were just, and that the Swallow whom she loved above everything in the world, had fallen into the power of the man she hated. At first she was minded to follow, and if might be, to rescue her. Then she remembered the pistol-shot, and remembered also that this new-made wife would have been with her husband and no other. Where, then, was he now? Without doubt, murdered by Bull-Head. If so, it was little use to look for him, and yet something in her heart told her to look.

At that moment she might not help Suzanne, for what could one woman and a Kaffir youth do against so many men? Moreover, she knew whither Van Vooren would take her, and could follow there, but first she must learn for certain what had been the fate of the Baas Ralph her husband. So Sihamba lay still beneath the two tufts of grass until the last of the men had passed in silence, glancing about them sullenly as though they feared vengeance for a crime. Then, having noted that they were heading for the kloof, she went back to where Zinti stood in the hollow holding the horse with one hand and the mule with the other, and beckoned him to follow her.

Very soon, tracing the spoor backwards, they reached the edge of the cliff just where the waterfall fell over it into the sea pool. Here she searched about, noting this thing and that, till at last all grew clear to her. Yonder Suzanne had lain, for the impress of her shape could still be seen upon the grass   And there a man had been stretched out, for his blood stained the ground.   More, he had been dragged to the edge of the cliff, for this was the track of his body and the spoor of his murderer's feet. Look how his heels had sunk into the turf as he took the weight of the corpse in his arms to hurl it over the edge.

"Tie the horse and the mule together, Zinti," she said, "and let us find a path down this precipice."

The lad obeyed, wondering, though he too guessed much of what had happened, and after a little search they found a place by which they could descend.   Now Sihamba ran to the pool and stood upon its brink scanning the surface with her eyes, till at length she glanced downwards, and there, almost at her feet, three parts of his body yet hidden in the water, lay the man she sought.

Swiftly she sprang to him, and, aided by Zinti, dragged him to dry ground.

"Alas! lady," moaned the Kaffir, "it is of no use, the Baas is dead.   Look, he has been shot."

Taking no heed of the words, Sihamba opened Ralph's garments, placing first her hand, then her ear, upon his heart.   Presently she lifted her head, a light of hope shining in her eyes, and said:

"Nay, he lives, and we have found him in time.   Moreover, his wound is not to death.   Now help me, for between us we must bear him up the cliff."

So Zinti took him on his back as a man takes a sack of flour, while Sihamba supported his legs, and thus between them, with great toil, for the way was very steep, they carried him by a sloping buck's path to the top of the precipice, and laid him upon the mule.

"Which way now?" gasped Zinti, for being strong he had borne the weight.

"To the waggon if they have not yet stolen it," said Sihamba, and thither they went.

When they were near she crept forward, searching for Swart Piet and his gang, but there were no signs of them, only she saw the driver and his companion nodding by the fire. She walked up to them.

"Do you then sleep, servants of Kenzie," she said, "while the Swallow is borne away to the Hawk's Nest and the husband of Swallow, your master, is cast by Bull-Head back into the sea whence he came?"

Now the men woke up and knew her. "Look, it is Sihamba," stammered one of them to the other, for he was frightened. "What evil thing has happened, Lady Sihamba?"

"I have told you, but your ears are shut. Come then and see with your eyes," and she led them to where Ralph lay in his blood, the water yet dripping from his hair and clothes.

"Alas! he is dead," they groaned and wrung their hands.

"He is not dead, he will live; for while you slept I found him," she answered. "Swift now, bring me the waggon box that is full of clothes, and the blankets off the cartel."

They obeyed her, and very quickly and gently—for of all doctors Sihamba was the best—with their help she drew off his wet garments, and, having dried him and dressed his wounds with strips of linen, she put a flannel shirt upon him and wrapped him in blankets. Then she poured brandy into his mouth, but, although the spirit brought a little colour into his pale face, it did not awaken him, for his swoon was deep.

"Lay him on the cartel in the waggon," she said, and, lifting him, they placed him upon the rimpi bed. Then she ordered them to inspan the waggon, and this was done quickly, for the oxen lay tied to the trek-tow. When all was ready she spoke to the two men, telling them what had happened so far as she knew it, and adding these words:

" Trek back to the stead as swiftly as you may, one of you sitting in the waggon to watch the Baas Kenzie and to comfort him should he wake out of his swoon. Say to the father and mother of Swallow that I have taken the horses to follow Swart Piet and to rescue her by cunning if so I can, for as will be plain to them, this is a business that must not wait; also that I have taken with me Zinti, since he alone knows the path to Bull-Head's secret hiding-place in the mountains. Of that road Zinti will tell you all he can and you will tell it to the Baas Botmar, who must gather together such men as he is able, and start to-morrow to follow it and rescue us, remembering what sort of peril it is in which his daughter stands. If by any means I can free the Swallow, we will come to meet him, if not, who knows? Then he must act according to his judgment and to what he learns. But let him be sure of this, and let her husband be sure also, that while I have life in me I will not cease from my efforts to save her, and that if she dies—for I know her spirit and no worse harm than death will overtake her—then if may be, I will die with her or to avenge her, and I have many ways of vengeance. Lastly, let them not believe that we are dead until they have certain knowledge of it, for it may chance that we cannot return to the stead, but must lie hid in the mountains or among the Kaffirs. Now hear what Zinti has to say as to the path of Bull-Head's den and begone, forgetting no one of my words, for if you linger or forget, when I come again I, Sihamba, will blind your eyes and shrivel your livers with a spell."

" We hear you," they answered, " and remember every

word of your message.   In three hours the Baas shall
know it."

Five minutes later they trekked away and so swiftly
did they drive and so good were the oxen, that in less
than the three hours we were awakened by the barking of
the dogs and one knocking on our door, and ran out to
learn all the dreadful tidings and to find Ralph bleeding
and still senseless, stretched upon that cartel where we
thought him sleeping happily with his bride.

Oh! the terror and the agony of that hour, never may I
forget them!   Never may I forget the look that sprang
into Ralph's eyes when at last he awoke and, turning them
to seek Suzanne, remembered all.

"Why am I here and not dead?" he asked hoarsely.

"Sihamba saved you and you have been brought back
in the waggon," I answered.

"Where then is Suzanne?" he asked again.

"Sihamba has ridden to save her also, and Jan starts
presently to follow her, and with him others."

"Sihamba!" he groaned.   "What can one woman do
against Piet Van Vooren and his murderers, and for the
rest they will be too late.   Oh! my God, my God, what
have we done that such a thing should fall upon us?   Think
of it, think of her in the hands of Piet Van Vooren.   Oh!
my God, my God, I shall go mad!"

Indeed I, who watched him, believe that this would have
been so, or else his brain must burst beneath its shock of
sorrow, had not nature been kind to him and plunged him
back into stupor.   In this he lay long, until well on into
the morrow indeed, or rather the day, for by now it was
three o'clock, when the doctor came to take out the pistol
ball and set his shattered bone.   For, as it chanced, a
doctor, and a clever one, had been sent for from the dorp

to visit the wife of a neighbour who lay sick not more than twenty miles away, and we were able to summon him. Indeed but for this man's skill, the sleeping medicines he gave him to quiet his mind, and, above all, a certain special mercy which shall be told of in its place, I think that Ralph would have died. As it was, seven long weeks went by before he could sit upon a horse.

CHAPTER XVII

THE HIDDEN KRANTZ

BEFORE the waggon left her, Sihamba took from it
Ralph's gun, a very good *roer*, together with powder and
bullets. Also she took tinder, a bottle of peach-brandy,
a blanket, mealies in a small bag, wherewith to bait the
horses in case of need, and some other things which she
thought might be necessary. These she laded among her
own goods upon the mule that with her horse had been
fetched by Zinti and hastily fed with corn. Now, at her
bidding, Zinti set Suzanne's saddle upon the back of the
schimmel, and Ralph's on that of Suzanne's grey mare,
which he mounted that the mule might travel lighter
Then Sihamba got upon her own horse, a good and quiet
beast which she rode with a sheepskin for a saddle, and
they started, Sihamba leading the *schimmel* and Zinti the
mule that, as it chanced, although bad tempered, would
follow well on a riem.

Riding up the kloof they soon reached the spot where
Van Vooren's band had tethered their horses and tracked
the spoor of them with ease for so long as the ground was
soft. Afterwards when they reached the open country,
where the grass had been burnt off and had only just
begun to spring again, this became more difficult, and at
length, in that light, impossible. Here they wasted a long

time, searching for the hoof-marks by the rays of the waning moon, only to lose them again so soon as they were found.

" At this pace we shall take as long to reach Bull-Head's kraal as did the cow you followed," said Sihamba presently. Say, now, can you find the way to it? "

" Without a doubt, lady; Zinti never forgets a road or a landmark."

" Then lead me there as fast as may be."

" Yes, lady, but Bull-Head may have taken the Swallow somewhere else, and if we do not follow his spoor how shall we know where he has hidden her? "

" Fool, I have thought of that," she answered angrily, " else should I have spent all this time looking for hoof-marks in the dark? We must risk it, I say. To his house he has not taken her, for other white folk are living in it, and it is not likely he would have a second, or a better hiding-place than that you saw. I say that we must be bold and risk it since we have no time to lose."

" As you will, mistress," answered Zinti. " Who am I that I should question your wisdom? " and, turning his horse's head, he rode forward across the gloomy veldt as certainly as a homing rock-dove wings its flight.

So they travelled till the sun rose behind a range of distant hills. Then Zinti halted and pointed to them.

" Look, lady," he said. " Do you see that peak among the mountains which has a point like a spear, the one that seems as though it were on fire? Well, behind it lies Bull-Head's kraal."

" It is far, Zinti, but we must be there by night."

" That may be done, lady, but if so we must spare our horses."

" Good," she answered. " Here is a spring; let us off-saddle a while."

So they off-saddled and ate of the food which they had brought, while the horses filled themselves with the sweet green grass, the *schimmel* being tied to the grey mare, for he would not bear a knee-halter.

All that day they rode, not so very fast but steadily, till towards sunset they off-saddled again beneath the shadow of the spear-pointed peak. There was no water at this spot, but seeing a green place upon the slope of a hill close by, Zinti walked to it, leading the thirsty beasts. Presently he threw up his hand and whistled, whereon Sihamba set out to join him, knowing that he had found a spring. So it proved to be, and now they learned that Sihamba had been wise in heading straight for Swart Piet's hiding-place, since round about this spring was the spoor of many horses and of men. Among these was the print of a foot that she knew well, the little foot of Suzanne.

" How long is it since they left here? " asked Sihamba, not as one who does not know, but rather as though she desired to be certified in her judgment.

" When the sun stood there," answered Zinti, pointing to a certain height in the heavens.

" Yes," she answered, " three hours. Bull-Head has travelled quicker than I thought."

" No," said Zinti, " but I think that he knew a path through the big *vlei*, whereas we rode round it, two hours' ride, fearing lest we should be bogged. Here by this spring they stayed till sunset, for it was needful that the horses should feed and rest, since they would save their strength in them.

" Lady," went on Zinti presently, " beyond the neck of

the hill yonder lies the secret kraal of Bull-Head. Say, now, what is your plan when you reach it? "

" I do not know," she answered, " but tell me again of the hidden krantz where the women built the new hut, and of the way to it."

He told her and she listened, saying nothing.

" Good," she said, when he had done. " Now lead me to this place, and then perhaps I will tell my plan if I have one."

So they started on again, but just as they reached the crest of the Nek a heavy thunderstorm came up, together with clouds and rain, hiding everything from them.

" Now I suppose that we must stay here till the light comes," said Sihamba.

" Not so, lady," answered Zinti, " I have been the path once and I can go it again in storm or shine," and he pressed forward, with the lightning flashes for a candle.

Well was that storm for them indeed, since otherwise they would have been seen, for already Swart Piet had set his scouts about the kraal.

At length Sihamba felt that they were riding among trees, for water dripped from them upon her and their branches brushed her face.

" Here is the wood where the women cut poles for the new hut," whispered Zinti in her ear.

" Then let us halt," she answered, and dismounting they tied the three horses and the mule to as many small trees close together, but not near enough for them to kick each other.

Now Sihamba took a piece of biltong from a saddle-bag and began to eat it, for she knew that she would need all her cleverness and strength " Take the bag of mealies," she said, " and divide it among the horses and the mule, giving a double share to the *schimmel*."

Zinti obeyed her, and presently all four of the beasts were eating well, for though they had travelled far their loads were light, nor had the pace been pressed.

Sihamba turned, and, holding out her hands towards the horses, muttered something rapidly.

" What are you doing, mistress? " asked Zinti.

" Perhaps I am throwing a charm upon these animals, that they may neither neigh nor whinny till we come again, for if they do so we are lost. Now let us go, and—stay, bring the gun with you, for you know how to shoot."

So they started, slipping through the wet wood like shadows. For ten minutes or more they crept on thus towards the dark line of cliff, Zinti going first and feeling the way with his fingers, till presently he halted.

" Hist! " he whispered. " I smell people."

As he spoke, they heard a sound like to that of someone sliding down rocks. Then a man challenged, saying, " Who passes from the krantz? " and a woman's voice answered, " It is I, Asika, the wife of Bull-Head." " I hear you," answered the man. " Now tell me, Asika, what happens yonder."

" What happens? How do I know what happens? " she answered crossly. " About sunset Bull-Head brought home his new wife, a white chieftainess, for whom we built the hut yonder; but the fashions of marriage among these white people must be strange indeed, for this one came to her husband, her feet bound, and with a face like to the face of a dead woman, the eyes set wide, and the lips parted. Yes, and they blindfolded her in the wood there and carried her through this hole in the rock down to the hut where she is shut in."

" I know something of this matter," answered the man; " the white lady is no willing wife to Bull-Head, for he killed her husband and took her by force. Yes, yes, I know, for my uncle was one of those with him when the deed was done, and he told me something of it just now."

" An evil deed," said Asika, " and one that will bring bad luck upon all of us; but then, Bull-Head, our chief, is an evil man. Oh! I know it who am of the number of his Kaffir wives. Say, friend," she went on, " will you walk a little way with me, as far as the first huts of the kraal, for there are ghosts in the wood, and I fear to pass it alone at night."

" I dare not, Asika," he answered, " for I am set here on guard."

" Have no fear, friend, the chief is within, seeing to the comfort of his new wife."

" Well, I will come with you a little way if you wish it, but I must be back immediately," he said, and the listeners heard them walk off together."

" Now, Zinti," whispered Sihamba, " lead me through the hole in the rock."

So he took her by the hand and felt along the face of the cliff till he found the bush which covered the entrance. To this he climbed, dragging her after him, and presently they were in the secret krantz.

" We have found our way into the spider's nest," muttered Zinti, who grew afraid; " but say, lady, how shall we find our way out of it?"

" Lead on and leave that to me," she answered. " Where I, a woman, can go, surely you who are a man can go also."

" I trust to your magic to protect us—therefore I come," said Zinti, " though if we are seen our death is sure."

On they crept across the glen, till presently they heard the sound of the small waterfall and saw it glimmering faintly through the gloom and drizzling rain. To their left ran the stream, and on the banks of it stood something large and round.

"There stands the new hut where Swallow is," whispered Zinti.

Now Sihamba thought for a moment and said:

"Zinti, I must find out what passes in that hut. Listen: do you lie hid among the reeds under the bank of the stream, and if you hear me hoot like an owl, then come to me, but not before."

"I obey," answered Zinti, and crept down among the reeds, where he crouched for a long time up to his knees in water, shivering with cold and fear.

CHAPTER XVIII

WHAT PASSED IN THE HUT

GOING on to her hands and knees Sihamba crawled to-wards the hut. Now she was within ten paces of it and could see that a man stood on guard at its doorway. "I must creep round to the back," she thought, and began to do so, heading for some shrubs which grew to the right. Already she had almost reached them, when of a sudden, and for an instant only, the moon shone out between two thick clouds, revealing her, though indistinctly, to the eyes of the guard. Now Sihamba was wearing a fur cape made of wild dog's hide, and, crouched as she was upon her hands and knees, half-hidden, moreover, by a tuft of dry grass, the man took her to be a wild dog or a jackal, and the hair which stood out round her head for the ruff upon the animal's neck.

"Take that, you four-legged night thief," he said aloud, and hurled the assegai in his hand straight at her. The aim was good; indeed, had she been a dog it would have transfixed her. As it was, the spear passed just beneath her body, pinning the hanging edges of the cape and re-maining fixed in the tough leather. Now if Sihamba's wit had left her, as would have happened with most, she was lost, but not for nothing had she been a witch-doctoress from her childhood, skilled in every artifice and accustomed to face death. From his words she guessed that the sentry had mistaken her for a wild beast, so instead of springing to her feet she played the part of one, and uttering a howl of pain scrambled away among the bushes. She heard the man start to follow her, then the moonlight went out and he returned to his post grumbling over his lost assegai and saying that he would find it in the jackal's body on the morrow. Sihamba, listening not far away, knew his voice; it was that of the fellow who had set the noose about her neck at Swart Piet's bidding and who was to have done the murder in the pass.

" Now, friend, you are unarmed," she thought to herself, " for you have no gun with you, and perhaps we shall settle our accounts before you go to seek that dead jackal by to-morrow's light." Then drawing the assegai from the cloak and keeping it in her hand, she crept on till she came to the back of the hut in safety. Still she was not much nearer to her end, for the hut was new and very well built, and she could find no crack to look through, though when she placed her ear against its side she thought that she could hear the sound of a man's voice. In her perplexity Sihamba cast her eyes upwards and saw that a fine line of light shone from the smoke-hole at the very top of the hut, which was hive-shaped, and a thought came into her head.

" If I climb up there," she said to herself, " I can look down through the smoke-hole and see and hear what passes in the hut. Only then if the moon comes out again I may be seen lying on the thatch; well, that I must chance with the rest."

So very slowly and silently, by the help of the rimpis which bound the straw, she climbed the dome of the hut, laughing to herself to think that this was the worst of omens for its owner, till at length she reached the smoke-hole at the top and looked down.

This was what she saw: Half seated, half lying upon a rough bedstead spread with blankets, was Suzanne. Her hair had come undone and hung about her, her feet were still loosely bound together, and as the Kaffir, Asika, had said, her face was like the face of a dead woman, and her eyes were set in a fixed unnatural stare. Before her was a table cut by natives out of a single block of wood, on which were two candles of sheep's fat set in bottles, and beyond the table stood Swart Piet, who was addressing her.

"Suzanne," he said, "listen to me. I have always loved you, Suzanne, yes, from the time when I was but a boy: we used to meet now and again, you know, when you were out riding with the Englishman who is dead"—here Suzanne's face changed, then resumed its deathlike mask—"and always I worshipped you, and always I hated the Englishman whom you favoured. Well, as you grew older you began to understand and dislike me, and Kenzie began to understand and insult me, and from that seed of slight and insult grew most that is bad in me. Yes, Suzanne, you will say that I am wicked; and I am wicked. I have done things of which I should not like to tell you. I have done such things as you saw last night; I have mixed myself up with Kaffir wizardries and cruelties; I have forgotten God and taken another master, and so far from honouring my own father, why, I struck him down when he was drunk and dared me to do it, and of that blow they say he died. Well, I owed him nothing less for begetting me into such a world as this, and teaching me how to find the devil before my time.

"And now," he went on after a pause, for Suzanne answered nothing, "standing before you as I do here with your husband's blood upon my hands, and seeking your love over his grave, you will look at me and say—

‘ This man is a monster, a madman, one who should be cast from the earth and stamped deep, deep into hell.’ Yes, all these things I am, and let the weight of them rest upon your head, for you made me them, Suzanne. I am mad, I know that I am mad, as my father and grandfather were before me, but my madness is mixed with knowledge, for in me runs the blood of the old Pondo witch-doctoress, my grandmother, she who knew many things that are not given to white men. When I saw you and loved you I became half mad—before that I was sane—and when the Englishman, Kenzie, struck me with the whip after our fight at the sheep-kraal, ah! then I went wholly mad, and see how wisely, for you are the first-fruits of my madness, you and the body that to-night rolls to and fro in the ocean.

“ You do not answer: Well, look you, Suzanne, I have won you by craft and blood, and by craft and blood I will keep you. Here you are in my power, here Heaven itself could not save you from me, in Bull-Head's secret krantz which none know of but some few natives. Choose, therefore; forget the sins that I have committed to win you and become my wife willingly, and no woman shall ever find a better husband, for then the fire and the tempest will leave my brain and it will grow calm as it was before I saw you.

“ Have you still no answer? Well, I will not hurry you. See, I must go—do you know what for? To set scouts lest by any chance your father or other fools should have found my hiding-place, though I think that they can never find it except it be through the wisdom of Sihamba, which they will not seek. Still I go, and in an hour I will return for your answer, which you must make then, Suzanne, since whether you desire it, or desire it not, fortune has given you to me. Have you no word for me before I go? ”

Now during all this long, half-insane harangue, Suzanne had sat quite silent, making no reply at all, not even
seeming to hear the demon, for such he was, whose wicked
talk defiled her ears. But when he asked her whether she
had nothing to say to him before he went, still looking
not at him, but beyond him, she gave him his answer in
one word, the same that she had used when she awoke
from her swoon:

"*Murderer.*"

Something in the tone in which she spoke, or perhaps
in the substance of that short speech, seemed to cow him;
at the least he turned and left the hut, and presently
Sihamba heard him talking to the sentry without, bidding
him to keep close watch till he came back within an hour.

When Piet went out he left the door-board of the hut
open, so that Sihamba dared neither act nor speak, fearing
lest the guard should hear or see her through it. Therefore
she still lay upon the top of the hut, and watched through
the smoke-hole. For a while Suzanne sat quiet upon the
bed, then of a sudden she rose from it, and shuffling across
the hut as well as her bound feet would allow her, she
closed the opening with the door-board, and secured it by
its wooden bar. Next she returned to the bed and, seating
upon it, clasped her hands and began to pray, muttering
aloud and mixing with her prayer the name of her husband
Ralph. Ceasing presently, she thrust her hand into her
bosom and drew from it a knife, not large, but strong and
very sharp. Opening this knife she cut the thong that
bound her ankles, and made it into a noose. Then she
looked earnestly first at the noose, next at the knife, and
thirdly at the candles, and Sihamba understood that she
meant to do herself to death, and was choosing between
steel and rope and fire.

Now all this while, although she dared not so much as whisper, Sihamba had not been idle, for with the blade of the assegai she was working gently at the thatch of the smoke-hole, and cutting the rimpis that bound it, till at last, and not too soon, she thought that it was wide enough to allow of the passage of her small body.   Then watching until the guard leaned against the hut, so that the bulge of it would cut her off from his sight, during the instant that her figure was outlined against the sky, she stood up, and thrusting her feet through the hole, forced her body to follow them, and then dropped lightly as a cat to the floor beneath.   But now there was another danger to be faced, and a great one, namely, that Suzanne might cry out in fear, which doubtless she would have done, had not the sudden sight of some living creature in the hut where she thought herself alone, so startled her that for a moment she lost her breath.   Before she could find it again Sihamba was whispering in her ear, saying:

"Keep silence for your life's sake, Swallow.   It is I, Sihamba, who am come to save you."

Suzanne stared at her, and light came back into the empty eyes, then they grew dark again, as she answered below her breath:

"Of what use is my life?   Ralph is dead, and I was about to take it that I may save myself from shame and go to seek him, for surely God will forgive the sin."

Sihamba looked at her and said:

"Swallow, prepare yourself for a great joy, and, above all, do not cry out.   Your husband is not dead, he was but wounded, and I drew him living from the sea.   He lies safe at the stead in your mother's care."

Suzanne heard her, and, notwithstanding the caution, still she would have cried aloud in the madness of her joy, had not Sihamba, seeing her lips opened, thrust her hands upon her mouth and held them there till the danger was past.

"You do not lie to me?" she gasped at length.

"Nay, I speak truth; I swear it. But this is no time to talk. Yonder stand food and milk; eat while I think."

As Sihamba guessed, nothing but a little water had passed Suzanne's lips since that meal which she and her husband took together beside the waggon, nor one minute before could she have swallowed anything had her life been the price of it. But now it was different, for despair had left her, and hope shone in her heart again, and behold! of a sudden she was hungry, and ate and drank with gladness, while Sihamba thought.

Presently the little woman looked up and whispered:

"A plan comes into my head; it is a strange one, but I can find no other, and it may serve our turn, for I think that good luck goes with us. Swallow, give me the noose of hide which you made from the riem that bound your feet."

Suzanne obeyed her wondering, whereon Sihamba placed the noose about her own neck, then bade Suzanne stand upon the bed and thrust the end of the riem loosely into the thatch of the hut as high up as she could reach, so that it looked as though it were made fast there. Next, Sihamba slipped off her fur cloak, leaving herself naked except for the moocha round her middle, and, clasping her hands behind her back with the assegai between them, she drew the riem taut, and leaned against the wall of the hut after the fashion of one who is about to be pulled from the ground and strangled.

"Now, mistress, listen to me," she said earnestly. "You have seen me like this before, have you not, when I was about to be hanged, and you bought my life at a price? Well, as it chances, that man who guards the hut is he who took me at Bull-Head's bidding and set the rope round my neck, whereon I said some words to him which made him afraid. Now if he sees me again thus in a hut where he knows you to be alone, he will think that I am a ghost and his heart will turn to ice and the strength of his hands to water, and then before he can find his strength again I shall make an end of him with the spear, as I know well how to do although I am so small, and we will fly."

" Is there no other way?" murmured Suzanne aghast.

" None, Swallow. For you the choice lies between witnessing this deed and—Swart Piet or—Death. Nay, you need not witness it even, if you will do as I tell you. Presently, when I give the word, loosen the bar of the doorboard, then crouch by the hole and utter a low cry of fear, calling to the man on guard for help. He will enter and see me, whereon you can creep through the door-hole and wait without, leaving me to deal with him. If I succeed I will be with you at once; if I fail, run to the stream and hoot like an owl, when Zinti, who is hidden there, will join you. Then you must get out of the krantz as best you can. Only one man watches the entrance, and if needful Zinti can shoot him. The *schimmel* and other horses are hidden in the wood, and he will lead you to them. Mount and ride for home, or anywhere away from this accursed place, and at times when you talk of the matter of your escape with your husband, think kindly of Sihamba Ngenyanga. Nay, do not answer, for there is little time to lose. Quick, now, to the door-hole, and do as I bade you."

So, like one in a dream, Suzanne loosened the bar, and, crouching by the entrance to the hut, uttered a low wail of terror, saying, " Help me, soldier, help me swiftly," in the Kaffir tongue. The man without heard, and, pushing down the board, crept in at once, saying, " Who harms you, lady? " as he rose to his feet. Then suddenly, in this hut, where there was but one woman, a white woman, whom he himself had carried into it, he beheld another woman—Sihamba; and his hair stood up upon his head and his eyes grew round with terror. Yes, it was Sihamba herself, for the light of the candles shone full upon her, or, rather, her ghost, and she was hanging to the roof, the tips of her toes just touching the ground, as once he had seen her hang before.

For some seconds the man stared in his terror, and while he stared Suzanne slipped from the hut. Then muttering, " It is the spirit of the witch, Sihamba, who prophesied my death—her spirit that haunts me," he dropped to his knees, and, trembling like a leaf, turned to creep from the hut. Next second he was *dead*, dead without a sound, for Sihamba was a doctoress, and knew well where to thrust with the spear.

Of all this Suzanne heard nothing and saw nothing, till presently Sihamba stood by her side holding the skin cape in one hand and the spear in the other.

" Now one danger is done with," she said quietly, as she put on the cape, " but many still remain. Follow me, Swallow," and, going to the edge of the stream, she hooted like an owl, whereupon Zinti came out of the reeds, looking very-cold and frightened.

" Be swift," whispered Sihamba, and they started along the krantz at a run. Before they were half way across it, the storm-clouds, which had been thinning gradually, broke up altogether, and the moon shone out with a bright light, showing them as plainly as though it were day; but as it chanced they met nobody and were seen of none.

12

At length they reached the cleft in the rock that led to the plain below. "Stay here," said Sihamba, "while I look," and she crept to the entrance. Presently she returned and said:

"A man watches there, and it is not possible to slip past him because of the moonlight. Now, I know of only one thing that we can do; and you, Zinti, must do it. Slip down the rock and cover the man with your gun, saying to him that if he stirs a hand or speaks a word you will shoot him dead. Hold him thus till we are past you on our way to the wood, then follow us as best you can, but do not fire except to save your life or ours."

Now the gifts of Zinti lay rather in tracking and remembering paths and directions than in fighting men, so that when he heard this order he was afraid and hesitated. But when she saw it, Sihamba turned upon him so fiercely that he feared her more than the watchman, and went at once, so that this man who was half asleep suddenly saw the muzzle of a *roer* within three paces of his head and heard a voice command him to stand still and silent or die. Thus he stood indeed until he perceived that the new wife of his chief was escaping. Then remembering what would be his fate at the hands of Bull-Head he determined to take his chance of being shot, and, turning suddenly, sped towards the kraal shouting as he ran, whereon Zinti fired at him, but the ball went wide. A cannon could scarcely have made more noise than did the great *roer* in the silence of the night as the report of it echoed to and fro among the hills.

"Oh! fool to fire, and yet greater fool to miss," said Sihamba. "To the horses! Swift! swift!"

They ran as the wind runs, and now they were in the wood, and now they had found the beasts.

"Praise to the Snake of my house!" said Sihamba, "they are safe, all four of them," and very quickly they untied the riems by which they had fastened the horses to the trees.

"Mount, Swallow," said Sihamba, seizing the head of the great *schimmel*.

Suzanne set her foot upon the shoulder of Zinti, who knelt to receive it, and sprang into the saddle. Then having lifted Sihamba on to the grey mare Zinti mounted the other horse himself, holding the mule by a leading riem.

"Which way, mistress?" he asked.

"Homewards," she answered, and they cantered forward through the wood.

On the further side of this wood was a little sloping plain not more than three hundred paces wide, and beyond it lay the seaward Nek through which they must pass on their journey to the stead. Already they were out of the wood and upon the plain, when from their right a body of horsemen swooped towards them, seven in all, of whom one, the leader, was Swart Piet himself, cutting them off from the Nek. They halted their horses as though to a word of command, and speaking rapidly, Sihamba asked of Zinti: "Is there any other pass through yonder range, for this one is barred to us?"

"None that I know of," he answered; "but I have seen that the ground behind us is flat and open as far as the great peak which you saw rising on the plain away beyond the sky-line."

"Good," said Sihamba. "Let us head for the peak, since we have nowhere else to go, and if we are separated, let us agree to meet upon its southern slope. Now, Zinti, loose the mule, for we have our lives to save, and ride on, remembering that Death is behind you."

CHAPTER XIX

WHEN they turned their horses' heads, Swart Piet and his men were not much more than a hundred paces from them, but in the wood they gained much ground, for he did not think that they would dare to leave it, and hunted for them there while they were racing over the open plain more than a mile away At last he caught sight of them crossing a distant ridge, and the long chase began. For hour after hour they galloped on through the moonlight across the wide and rolling veldt until the moon sank, and they must pick their way as best they could in the darkness. Then came the dawn, and still they rode forward, though now the horses were beginning to grow weary, except the *schimmel*, who pulled upon his bit as though he were fresh from the stable. In front of them, some twenty miles away, rose the lofty peak for which they were heading, and behind lay the great expanse of plain which they had passed. Suzanne looked back over her shoulder, but there was no one in sight.

"Let us halt," she said, "and rest ourselves and the horses." So they pulled up by a stream and suffered the beasts to drink some water, though not much, while they themselves devoured biltong, of which they had a little in the saddle-bags.

" Why do we ride for the peak? " asked Suzanne.

" Because there are places where we may lie hid," Sihamba answered, " and thence we can make our way down to the seashore and so back homewards, whereas here upon the plain we can be seen from miles away."

" Do any people live on the peak? "

" Yes, Swallow; it is the home of the great chief Sigwe, the chief-paramount of the Red Kaffirs, who counts his spears by thousands, but I have heard that he is away to the north upon a war which he makes against some of the Swazi tribes with whom he has a quarrel."

" Will the people of Sigwe protect us, Sihamba? "

" Perhaps. We shall see. At least, you are safer with them than in the hands of Swart Piet."

At this moment, Zinti, who was watching the plain over which they had travelled, uttered a cry of warning. Looking back, they saw the reason of it, for there, crossing the crest of a wave of ground, not more than a mile away, were five horsemen riding hard upon their spoor.

" Swart Piet and four of his men," said Sihamba, " and by my Spirit, they have fresh horses; they must have taken them from the kraal of the half-breed which we passed at daybreak, and that is why we lost sight of them for a while."

Now even as Zinti helped her to mount the *schimmel* Suzanne turned so faint with terror that she almost fell to the ground again.

" Have no fear, Swallow," said Sihamba, " he has not caught us yet, and a voice in me says that we shall escape him."

But though she spoke thus bravely, in her heart Sihamba was much afraid, for except the *schimmel* their horses were almost spent, whereas Van Vooren was fresh mounted, and not a mile behind. Still they galloped forward till they reached a more broken stretch of veldt, where trees grew singly, and here and there were kloofs with bush in them.

"Mistress," cried Zinti, "my horse can go no more, and Bull-Head is hard upon us. Of your wisdom tell me what I should do or presently I must be killed."

"Ride into that kloof and hide yourself," answered Sihamba, "for Bull-Head will never seek you there; he hunts the white Swallow, not the black finch. Afterwards you can follow on our spoor, and if you cannot find us, make your way back to the Baas Botmar and tell him all you know Quick, into the kloof, for here they cannot see you."

"I hear you, lady," said Zinti, and the next minute they saw him leading his weary horse into the shelter of the thick bush, for the poor beast could carry him no more.

For the next three miles the ground trended downwards to the banks of a great river, beyond which were the gentle rising slopes that surrounded the foot of the high peak. On they galloped, the *schimmel* never faltering in his swinging stride, although his flanks grew thin and his eyes large. But with the grey mare it was otherwise, for though she was a gallant nag her strength was gone. Indeed, with any heavier rider upon her back, ere this she would have fallen. But still she answered to Sihamba's voice and plunged on, rolling and stumbling in her gait.

"She will last till the river," she said, seeing Suzanne look at the mare.

"And then——?" gasped Suzanne, glancing behind her to where, not five hundred yards away, Swart Piet and his Kaffirs hunted them sullenly and in silence, as strong dogs hunt down a wounded buck.

"And then—who knows?" answered Sihamba, and they

went on without more words, for they had no breath to spare.

Now, not half a mile away, they came in sight of the river, which had been hidden from them before by the lie of the ground, and a groan of despair broke from their lips, for it was in flood. Yes, the storms in the mountains had swollen it, and it rolled towards the sea a red flood of foam-flecked water, well-nigh two hundred yards from bank to bank. Still they rode on, for they dared not stop, and presently behind them they heard a shout of triumph, and knew that their pursuers had also seen the Red Water, and rejoiced because now they had them in a trap.

Within ten yards of the lip of the river, the grey mare stopped suddenly, shivered like a leaf in the wind and sank to the ground.

"Now, Swallow," said Sihamba as she slipped from the saddle, "you must choose between that raging torrent and Swart Piet. If you choose the torrent the great horse is still strong and he may swim through; I can say no more."

"And you?" asked Suzanne.

"I? I bide here, and oh! I would that Zinti had left the gun with me."

"Never," cried Suzanne. "Together we will live or die. Mount, I say—mount. Nay, if you refuse I will throw myself into the water before your eyes."

Then seeing that she would indeed do no less, Sihamba took her outstretched hand, and placing her foot upon the foot of Suzanne, scrambled up upon the pad in front of her, whereat the pursuers, who now were little over two hundred yards away, laughed out loud, and Swart Piet shouted to Suzanne to yield. But they did not laugh long, for Sihamba, having first bent her head and kissed

Suzanne on the hand, leaned forward and began to stroke
the *schimmel's* neck and to whisper into his ear, till indeed
it seemed as though the great brute that loved her understood.   At the least he pricked his ears and tossed his
head, then looked, first round at the horses that drew near,
and next at the foaming flood in front.

"Sit fast, Swallow," said Sihamba, and then she cried
a word aloud to the horse, and struck it lightly with her
hand.   At the sound of that word the stallion drew himself
together, sprang forward with two bounds over the ten
paces of level bank and leapt far out. into the flood that
foamed beneath.   Down sank the horse and his riders till
the Red Water closed over their heads, then they rose again
and heard the shout of wonder of their enemies, who by
now had almost reached the bank.   With a yell of rage
Black Piet rode his horse at the river, for to do him justice
he was a brave man, but do what he might it would not
face it, so with the others he sat still and watched.

Now the *schimmel* struck out bravely, heading for the
other bank, but in the fierce current it was not possible
that any horse should reach it swimming in a straight line,
for the weight of the stream was too great.   Sihamba had
noted, however, that from the further shore, but two or
three hundred paces lower down the river, a little point of
land projected into it, and this the horse had seen also, or
perhaps she told him of it, at least for that point he swam
steadily.   In five minutes they were in the centre of the
torrent, and here it ran with a roar and mighty force so
that its waves began to break over the *schimmel's* head,
and they feared that he would drown.   So much did Sihamba fear it, indeed, that she slipped from his back, and
leaving Suzanne to cling to the saddle, caught hold of his
mane, floating alongside of him and protected by his neck

from the whirl of the water. Lying thus she continued to call to the horse and to urge him forward, and ever he answered to her words, so that although twice he nearly sank, in the end he set his feet upon a sandbank and, having rested there a while, plunged forward, half wading and half swimming, to the projecting point of land, up which he scrambled, still carrying Suzanne and dragging Sihamba with him, until once more they found themselves safe upon the solid earth, where he stood shaking himself and snorting.

Suzanne slipped from the saddle and lay flat upon the ground, looking at the awful water they had passed, and by her lay Sihamba. Presently the little doctoress spoke.

"It is well to have lived," she said, "if only to have dared that deed, for no others have ever made the passage across the Red Water in flood, two of them on one tired horse," and she caught in her arms the muzzle of the *schimmel* that hung above her, pressing it to her breast as though it had been a child, whereon the brute whinnied faintly, knowing well that she was thanking him for his toil and courage.

"I pray God that I may never be called upon to make it again," answered Suzanne, staggering to her feet, the water running from her dripping dress as she turned to look across the river.

Now, when Van Vooren's horse refused to face the stream, he had ridden up and down shouting like a madman; once even he lifted his gun and pointed it, then let it fall again, remembering that he could not make sure of hitting the horse, and that if he did so Suzanne must certainly be drowned. When they were quite beyond his reach in the middle of the stream, he stood still and watched until he saw them come to the further shore in safety. Then he called his men about him and consulted with them, and the end of it was that they rode off in a body up the bank of the river.

"They go to seek a ford," said Suzanne.

"Yes, Swallow, but now we shall have the start of them. Come, let us mount."

So they climbed upon the back of the *schimmel*, and once more he went on with them, not fast, for now he could not even canter, but ambling or walking, according to the nature of the ground, at a rate perhaps of seven miles the hour. Soon they had left the river and were toiling up the slopes of the peak, until presently they struck a well-worn footpath.

"I think that this must lead to the town of Sigwe," said Sihamba.

"I pray that it does," answered Suzanne, "and that it is not far, for I feel as though Death were near to me."

"Keep a great heart," said Sihamba, "for we have met Death face to face and conquered him."

So still they toiled on till at length the path took a turn, and there, in a fold of the hill, they beheld the great kraal of Sigwe, a very large Kaffir town. Before the kraal was a wide open space, and on that space armed men were assembled, several full regiments of them. In front of this impi was gathered a company of chiefs.

"Now we have no choice," said Sihamba, and turned the *schimmel* towards them, while all that army stared at this strange sight of two women, one tall and fair, one black and little, riding towards them mounted together upon a great blood horse which was so weary that he could scarcely set one foot before the other.

When they reached the captains Sihamba slipped to the ground, but Suzanne remained seated upon the *schimmel*.

" Who are you? " asked a broad man in a leopard-skin cloak, of Sihamba; but although she was small and dishevelled, her hair and garments being wet with water, he did not laugh at her, for he saw that this stranger had the air of one who is of the blood of chiefs.

" I am Sihamba Ngenyanga, the doctoress, of whom you may have heard," she answered; and some of the people said, " We have heard of her; she is a great doctoress."

" To what people do you belong, Sihamba? " asked the captain again.

" I belong to the people of Zwide, whom Chaka drove from Zululand, and by birth I am the chieftainess of the Umpondwana, who live in the mountain Umpondwana, and who were the Children of Zwide, but are now the Children of Chaka."

" Why then do you wander so far from home, Sihamba? "

" For this reason. When Zwide and his people, the Endwandwe, were driven back, my people, the Umpondwana, who were subject to Zwide, made peace with Chaka against my will. Therefore, because I would not live as a Zulu dog, I left them."

" Although your body is small you have a large heart," said the captain, and one of his people cried out: " The story of Sihamba is true, for when you sent me as messenger to the Endwandwe, I heard it—it is a tale there."

Then the captain asked, " And who is the beautiful white woman who sits upon the great horse? "

" She is my mother and my sister and my mistress, whom I serve till death, for she saved me from death, and her name is Swallow."

Now at this word *Swallow*, most of those present started, and some uttered exclamations of wonder, especially a little band of people, men and women, who stood to the left, and who from their dress and other tokens it was easy to see were witch-doctors and diviners. Sihamba noted the movements and words of wonder, but pretending to see nothing she went on:

"The lady Swallow and I have fled hither from far, hoping to find the chief Sigwe, for we need his counsel and protection, but he is away, making war to the north, is it not so?"

"Nay," answered the captain. "I am the chief Sigwe, and I have not yet begun my war."

"I am glad," said Sihamba. "Chief, listen to my tale and suffer us to creep into the shadow of your strength——" and in a few words she told them the story of the capture of Suzanne by Swart Piet and of their flight from him. Now when she spoke of Van Vooren, or of Bull-Head rather, for she called him by his native name, she saw that Sigwe and the captains looked at each other, and when she told how they had swum the Red Water in flood, the two of them upon one horse, she was sure that they did not believe her, for such a deed they thought to be impossible. But still Sihamba went on and ended— "Chief, we seek this from you; protection from Bull-Head, who doubtless will be here ere long, and an escort of spears to lead us down the coast to the home of the Swallow, a hundred miles away, where they and you will be well rewarded for the service. Answer us quick, chief, I pray you, for our need is great and we are weary."

CHAPTER XX

Now Sigwe and two of his captains walked to where the diviners stood and took counsel with them, speaking low and earnestly. Then he returned and said:

" Sihamba, Walker-by-Moonlight, and you, Lady Swallow, listen to me. A wonderful thing has come to pass in the kraal of Sigwe this day, such a thing as our fathers have not known. You see that my host is gathered yonder: well, to-morrow they start to make war upon these very Endwandwe of whom you have spoken because of a deadly insult which they have put upon me and my house. Therefore, according to custom, this morning the soldiers were assembled at dawn to be doctored and that the diviners might search out the omens of the war. So the diviners searched, and she who was chosen among them ate the medicine and sank into the witch sleep here before us all. Yes, this one," and he pointed to a tall woman with dreamy eyes who was bedizened with bones and snake-skins.

" Now in her sleep she spoke, and we hung upon her words, for we knew that they would be the words of omen. Sihamba, these were the words, as all can testify:

" Thus say the spirits of your fathers, and thus speaks the Snake of your tribe. Unless a *White Swallow* guide your footsteps in the war with the Men of the Mountains you

shall perish and your impis shall be scattered, but if a
White Swallow flies before your spears then but little of
your blood shall be shed, and you shall return with honour
and with you one whom you seek.   Only the Swallow shall
not return with you, for if she set her face southward, then,
Sigwe, woe to you and your armies.'

"Sihamba, these were the words of the dreamer.
Scarcely was she awake again, while he wondered at their
strangeness, and asked her questions of their meaning,
which she could not answer, for here the wisdom of the
wisest was at fault, lo! you rode over the hill, and with you
a beautiful white woman whose name you say is Swallow.
Yes, this is the White Swallow who shall fly in front of
my regiments, bringing me honour and good fortune in
the war, and therefore, Sihamba, your prayer is granted,
though not all of it, for you shall go northward and not
southward, and among your own people I will leave you and
the Swallow with you, and for her sake I will spare your
people, the people of Umpondwana, although they are subject to my foes, the Endwandwe, and of the same blood.
Moreover, while you are among us all honour shall be done
to you and the Swallow, and of the cattle we capture a
tenth part shall be the Swallow's.   Still, I tell you this,
that had it not been for the omen of the diviner I would
have refused your prayer and delivered you and the Swallow over to Bull Head, for with him I have sworn friendship long ago.   But now the face of things is changed, and
should he come with a hundred men armed with guns yet
I will protect you from him, and the Swallow also; yes,
though oaths must be broken to do it."

When they heard this saying, Suzanne and Sihamba
looked at each other in dismay.

"Alas!" said Suzanne, "it seems that we do but change

one prison for another, for now we must be borne away to
the far north to do battle with this Kaffir chief, and there
be left among your people, so that none will know what has
become of us, and the heart of Ralph will break with doubt
and sorrow; yes, and those of my parents also."

"It is bad," answered Sihamba, "but had not yonder
diviner dreamed that dream of a swallow, it would have
been worse. Better is it to travel in all honour with the
impis of Sigwe than to be dragged back by Bull-Head to
his secret kraal—I to be done to death there and you to the
choice of which you know. For the rest we must take our
chance and escape when the time comes, and meanwhile
we will send a message to the stead."

Now Suzanne heard her, and sat upon the horse thinking, for her trouble was sore; still, she could see no way
out of the net which had meshed her. As she thought, a
man who was herding cattle on the mountain ran up to the
chief and saluted him, saying that five men, one of them
white, rode towards his kraal. When Suzanne heard this
she hesitated no more, but cried out to the chief
Sigwe, speaking in the Kaffir tongue, which she knew
well:

"Chief Sigwe, swear to me that you will not suffer Bull-
Head so much as to touch me or my sister Sihamba, and
that while we dwell with you you will treat us with all
honour, and I, who am named Swallow, yes, I, the White
Swallow of the diviner's dream, will lead your armies to
the northern land, bringing you the good fortune which
is mine to give to others, though myself I know it not."

"I swear it by the spirits of my fathers, lady," answered
Sigwe, "and these my counsellors and headmen swear it
also."

"Yes," echoed the counsellors, "we swear it, all of it.

and while one of us is left alive the oath shall be fulfilled, O White Bird of good omen."

Then Sigwe gave an order, and at his bidding five hundred soldiers, the half of a regiment, ran up and formed a circle about Sihamba and Suzanne, who still sat upon the *schimmel,* white faced and wearied, her hair hanging down her back. Scarcely was the circle made when from round the shoulder of the hill appeared Swart Piet and with him his four after-riders.

Seeing all the great array, he halted for a moment astonished, then catching sight of Suzanne set up above the heads of the ring of soldiers, he rode straight to Sigwe, who, with his counsellors and guards, was standing outside the circle.

"Chief Sigwe," he said, "a wife of mine with her servant has escaped from me, and as I suspected taken refuge in your kraal, for I see her sitting yonder surrounded by your soldiers. Now, in the name of our friendship, I pray you hand them over to me that I may lead them back to their duty."

"I give you greeting, Bull-Head," answered Sigwe courteously, "and I thank you for your visit to my town; presently an ox shall be sent for you to eat. As for this matter of the white lady and her companion it is one that we can inquire into at leisure. I hear that she is the daughter of the big Boer whom the natives of the coast name Thick-Arm; also that you murdered the lady's husband and carried her off by force to be your wife instead of his. Now here, as you know, I am chief paramount, for having of our blood in your veins you understand our customs, and, therefore, I must see justice done, especially as I do not wish to bring a quarrel with the white people upon our heads. So off-saddle a while, and to-morrow before I start upon a certain journey, I will summon my counsellors and we will try the case."

Now by this time Swart Piet, who, as Sigwe had said, understood the customs of the Kaffirs, knew very well that the chief was making excuses, and would not surrender Suzanne to him. For a while he had kept himself calm, but when this knowledge came home to his mind his reason left him, and he grew more than commonly mad with rage and disappointment, for after all his crimes and toil Suzanne was now as far from him as ever. Springing from his horse, but still keeping the gun in his hand, he ran up to the triple ring of soldiers, pausing only at the hedge of assegais which shone about it.

"Open," he said, "open, you red dogs!" but not a spear moved. Twice he ran round the circle, then he stopped and cried, "Sihamba. Is Sihamba here?"

"Surely, Bull-Head," answered the little woman, walking forward from where she stood behind the *schimmel*. "Where else should I be? I pray you, soldiers, draw a little way but not far apart, that yonder half-breed may satisfy his eyes with the sight of me. So, a little way, but not far, for I who know him like him best at a distance. Now, Bull Head," she went on, "what is it that you wish to talk about—the Englishman, Ralph Kenzie, the husband of Swallow yonder? You thought you killed him. Well, it was not so; I lifted him living from the water, and I, who am a doctoress, tell you that his wound is of no account, and that soon he will be strong again and seeking a word with you, Half-breed. No, not of him? Then perhaps it is of your hidden krantz and the new hut you built in it. Bah! I knew its secret long ago and—that hut has too wide a smoke-hole. Go back and ask him who guarded it if this is not true. What! Not of that either?

Then would you speak of the ride which we have taken? Ah! man, I thought at least that you were no coward, and yet even when you had us in your hand, you did not dare to face the Red Water which two women swam on one tired horse. Look at him, soldiers, look at the brave cross-bred chief who dared not swim his horse across one little stream."

Now while the soldiers laughed Swart Piet stamped upon the ground, foaming with rage, for Sihamba's bitter words stuck in him like barbed assegais.

"Snake's wife, witch!" he screamed, "I will catch you yet, and then you shall learn how slowly a woman may die, yes, and her also, and she shall learn other things, for if that husband of hers is not dead I will kill him before her eyes. I tell you I will follow you both through all Africa and across the sea if needful; yes, whenever you lie down to sleep, you may be sure that Piet van Vooren is not far from you."

"Do you say so?" mocked Sihamba. "Well, now I think of it you have no luck face to face with me, Half-breed, and were I you, I should look the other way when you saw me coming, for I who have the Sight tell you that when you behold the Walker-by-Moonlight for the last time, you will very soon become a walker in the darkness for ever. Bah!" she went on, her clear voice rising to a cry. "Bastard, dog, thief, murderer that you are! I, Si-hamba, who have met and beaten you in every pool of the stream, will beat you for the last time where the stream falls into the sea. Be not deceived, yonder Swallow never shall be yours; for many and many a year after you are dead, your rival shall fold her close, and when men name your name they shall spit upon the ground. Nothing, nothing shall be yours, but shame and empty longing and black death, and after it the woe of the wicked. Get you back to your secret krantz and your Kaffir wives, Half-breed, and tell them the tale of your ride, and of how you did not dare to face the foam of the Red Water."

Now Van Vooren went mad indeed; so mad that, forgetting he was not on the lonely veldt, he lifted his gun and fired straight at Sihamba. But her eye was quick, and seeing the muzzle rise, she threw herself upon the ground, so that the ball passed over her.

"Why, Half-breed, have you even forgotten how to shoot?" she called, springing to her feet again and mocking him. Then the voice of Sigwe broke in, for his anger was deep.

"One thing you have certainly forgotten, Bull-Head," he said, "that these two are my guests and wrapped in my kaross, and therefore from this hour we are enemies. Ho! men," he cried to his guard, " I spare Bull-Head's life because once we were friends, therefore do not take his life, but beat him and those with him out of my town with the shafts of your assegais, and if ever he sets foot within it again then use their blades upon him."

At their chief's bidding the soldiers of the guard sprang forward, and, falling upon Van Vooren and those with him, they flogged them with sticks and the shafts of their spears until from head to foot they were nothing but blood and bruises, and thus they drove them out of the town of Sigwe back to the ford of the Red River.

When they were gone, Suzanne, who through it all had sat upon the horse watching in silence, now urged him forward to where Sigwe stood, and said:

"Chief, I thank you for that deed, and now, I pray you, give us food and a hut to rest in, for we are wet and hungry and worn out with long travel."

So the guest masters led them into the fence of the town and gave them the guest hut, the largest in the kraal, and the best food that they had—milk and meal and beef and eggs, as much as they would of it. The *schimmel* also was fastened to a post in the little courtyard of the hut, and a Kaffir who once had served as groom to a white man, washed him all over with warm water. Afterwards he was given a mash of meal to eat, and, later, when he was a little rested, his fill of good forage, which he ate gladly, for, though he was very tired and his legs were somewhat swollen, otherwise he was none the worse for that great ride.

In the shelter of the hut Suzanne took off her clothes, remembering with a sort of wonder how she had put them on on the morning of her marriage, which now seemed years ago, and bathed herself with water. Then Sihamba having given the garments to a waiting woman to wash, wrapped her in a soft kaross of fur, and after drinking some milk and eating a little, Suzanne laid herself down upon a mattress made of the husks of mealie cobs, and even as she thanked God Who had brought her safely through so many dangers past, and prayed Him to protect her in those that were to come, and to comfort the heart of her husband in his sickness and affliction, she fell asleep. When she saw her sleeping, but not before, Sihamba crept to her feet, for now that all was over she could scarcely walk, and laying herself down there slept also.

All the rest of the day they slept, and all the night that followed, nor did they wake till sunrise of the next morning, when women of the household of the chief knocked upon the door-board to ask if they needed aught. Then they rose feeling well and strong again except for the stiffness of their limbs, and Suzanne clothed herself in the garments that the woman had washed, combing her dark hair with a Kaffir comb. Afterwards they ate heartily of the good food that was brought to them, and left the hut to visit the *schimmel*, that they found almost recovered and devouring Kaffir sugar-cane, though like themselves he was somewhat stiff.

Presently, while they stroked and fondled him, a messenger came, saying that if it pleased the lady Swallow, the chief Sigwe would take counsel with her in the place of audience. So after a little while they went, and as they passed out of the kraal fence, Suzanne was received with a chief's salute by the escort that was waiting for her. Then surrounding her and Sihamba, they led them to the place of audience, a circle of ground enclosed by a high double fence, and as Suzanne entered it once more all present there, including Sigwe himself, gave her the salute of chiefs.

But though it was strange enough that such a thing should happen to a white woman, at the time Suzanne took little notice of the salute or aught else, for there standing before her, looking much bewildered and very weary, was none other than Zinti and with him Sihamba's horse, and also that mule laden with goods, which they had abandoned in the wood nearly a hundred miles away, when they came face to face with Van Vooren and his riders and turned to begin their long flight for life and liberty.

CHAPTER XXI

THE VISION OF RALPH AND SUZANNE

"SIHAMBA," said the chief Sigwe, "this man who was found wandering upon the outskirts of the town, declares that he is your servant, and that he comes to seek you. Is it so?"

"It is so, indeed, chief," she answered, "though I scarcely expected to see him again," and she told how they two and Zinti had parted.

Then Zinti was commanded to tell his tale, and from it it seemed that after he had rested some hours in the kloof he crept to the mouth of it, and, hidden behind a stone, saw Swart Piet and his servants pass quite close to him on their homeward way. A sorry sight they were, for three of their horses were lame, so that the riders were obliged to walk and lead them, and the men themselves had been so bruised with the spear-shafts that they seemed more dead than alive. Swart Piet rode last of all, and just then he turned, and looking towards the peak shook his fist as though threatening it, and cursed aloud in Dutch and Kaffir. Indeed, Zinti said that his head and face were so swollen with blows that had it not been for his large round eyes he could not have known him, and Sihamba thought that very good tidings.

Well, when they had gone Zinti took heart, for it was

plain that they had been roughly handled, and had failed to catch his mistress or the Swallow. So he went back to where he had left his horse eating a little grass, and since it was too weak to carry him he led it, following Van Vooren's spoor backwards till in the evening he came to the ford of the Red River. Here he halted for the night, knee-haltering the horse, and leaving it loose to graze, though he himself had nothing to eat. At the first grey of dawn he awoke, and was astonished to see a second animal feeding with the horse, which proved to be none other than the mule that, as these creatures sometimes will, had followed the spoor of his companion, Sihamba's horse, till it found it again. After this he crossed the drift, riding slowly and leading the mule, till shortly after sunrise he came to the outskirts of the town, where Sigwe's watchmen found him and brought him to the chief.

" This man is a servant worth having," said Sigwe when he had heard the story. " Let food be given to him and to the beasts."

When Zinti had gone Sigwe spoke to Suzanne.

" Lady Swallow," he said, " as you have heard, by the command of the spirits of my ancestors speaking through the mouth of the diviner, while you are with us, you and not I are the captain of my army, and must lead it in this great war which I make against the Endwandwe. Now the regiments are ready to march, and I ask if it be your pleasure that we should set out to-morrow at the dawn, for time presses, and the Endwandwe live very far away? "

" Your will is my will, chief," she answered, for she could see no way of escape from this strange journey, " but I desire to learn the cause of this war which I must lead by the decree of the spirits of your ancestors."

Now Sigwe gave an order to some attendants waiting

upon him, who went away to return presently leading with them a woman. This woman was about fifty years of age, very fat in person, sour-faced, yellow-toothed, and with one eye only.

"There is the cause," exclaimed the chief, at the same time turning his back upon the woman and spitting upon the ground as though in disgust.

"I do not understand," said Suzanne.

"Then listen, Lady Swallow. Sikonyana, the chief of the Endwandwe, has a sister named Batwa, whose beauty is famous throughout all the world, and for her by my envoys I made an offer of marriage, intending that she should be my head wife, for I desired to be the husband of the most beautiful woman in the world."

"I saw Batwa when she was still a child," broke in Sihamba; "indeed, she is my cousin, and it is true that she is most beautiful."

"The chief Sikonyana," went on Sigwe, "answered me that he was much honoured by my offer since he knew me to be the greatest man of all this country, but that at the same time his sister was not to be won with a small price; yet if I would send a thousand head of cattle, half of them black and half white, she should be mine. Then with much pain I collected these cattle, two years did it take me to gather them together, for here oxen and cows pure white and pure black are not common, and I sent them with an impi to guard them, for nothing less would suffice, to the kraal of the chief of the Endwandwe.

"Four moons was that impi gone, while I awaited its return, eating out my heart with impatience. At length it did return, bringing with it my bride. At nightfall it marched into the town hungry and tired, for it had suffered much upon the journey, and twice had been forced

to give battle to the armies of other chiefs, but although
I was eager to see her I did not look upon my new wife
that night. No, I sent out messengers and gathered together all my army and all the people young and old,
yonder in the plain of assembly. Then when they were
mustered from far and near, I commanded that Batwa, the
sister of Sikonyana, should be produced in the face of the
people that her loveliness might shine upon me and upon
them as the sun shines equally upon us all.

"Lady Swallow, the moment came, and this old woman
was brought out; yes, she strutted before us proudly, this
one-eyed hag, this cat of the mountains. For her I had
sent an impi, for her I had paid a thousand head of cattle,
half of them pure black and half pure white——" and
Sigwe ceased, gasping with rage.

Now at this story Suzanne, who had not smiled for days,
laughed aloud, while even Sihamba the wise looked down
studying the earth. But there was one who did not laugh,
and it was the one-eyed woman. No, she sprang up and
screamed aloud:

"Dog of a red Kaffir, who are you that dare to talk
thus of a princess of the blood of the Endwandwe, a princess whom Chaka, the great king, wished to take to wife?
You asked for Batwa in marriage, Batwa, the sister to
Sikonyana, and I am Batwa the sister of Sikonyana."

"Then, hag, there must be two Batwas," shouted Sigwe
in answer.

"Two Batwas!" she screamed. "Fool and beast, there
are *four!* In our race all the women of royal blood are
named Batwa, and I am the eldest and the wisest and the
best of them, for I am older than my brother Sikonyana
by twenty years, I, who have had three husbands and out-
lived them all; whereas the chit of whom you talk, a thing

with a waist like a reed and an eye like a sick buck, is his junior by ten years, being a child of our father's last wife."

"It may be so," answered Sigwe, "for aught I know, every woman of your accursed tribe is named Batwa, but this I say, that very soon there will be few Batwas left to look upon the sun, for to-morrow I march against them and I will stamp the house of Batwa flat, and you I will hang to the roof-tree of the hut of the chief your brother; yes, I keep you alive that I may hang you there, so until then you have nothing to fear from me."

"Is it so, is it so, indeed?" shrieked the virago; "then I am safe, for, little red Kaffir, I shall live to see you and your cowards beaten out of the country of the Endwandwe with whips of hide."

"Take her away," groaned Sigwe, "before I break my word and hang her at once, which I do not wish to do," and Batwa the eldest was led off still screaming curses.

When she had gone, after consulting apart for a while with Sihamba, Suzanne spoke.

"Now, chief," she said, " I understand the cause of this war and in truth it is a strange one. Still, as I must lead your armies, and as I do not love to see men killed for such a quarrel, here and before we start I will lay down the terms of peace if it should please Sikonyana and the people of the Endwandwe to accept them. Subject to your wisdom they shall be these: If Sikonyana will give to you that Batwa whom you desire in the place of the Batwa whom you do not desire, paying back to you the thousand head of cattle, and by way of fine for his deceit, if indeed he meant to deceive you, for you do not seem to have told him which of the many Batwas you sought, two thousand other head of cattle, then no blood shall be shed

and you and your impi shall return in peace and honour.
If he will not do this, then the war must go as it is fated.
Say, do you consent as I counsel you to do? for otherwise,
although I go with you my goodwill will not go, since I
am the Swallow of peace and not the Hawk of war."

Now there followed a great *indaba* or debate between
Sigwe and his counsellors and captains, some of them taking one view of the matter, and some of them the other,
but the end of it was that the party of peace prevailed, it
being agreed between them that if the Endwandwe would
grant these terms and in addition an ox for every man
who might die or be killed upon the journey, the impi
should return without putting the matter to the chance of
war, and this the chief and his counsellors swore solemnly
to Suzanne. Indeed Sigwe was glad to swear it, for he
sought that Batwa for whom he longed rather than the
dangers of battle and the risk of defeat in a far land, while
those who were for fighting at all costs thought that the
oath meant little, since they did not believe that the great
Sikonyana would make peace upon such terms.

When this matter was settled Suzanne prayed the chief
that he would allow her to send Zinti as a messenger to
her husband and father to tell them that she lived and was
well. But on this matter, and this only, Sigwe would not
listen to her, and though he gave many reasons for his
refusal, the true one was that he feared lest the white men,
on learning her whereabouts, should gather a commando
and send it to take her from him, as doubtless we should
have done had it been in any way possible.

Indeed, the foolish dream of the diviner as to the leading of his army by a white swallow, followed as it chanced
to be by the arrival at his town of a woman who was
named Swallow, had taken such a hold of Sigwe—who,

like all savages, was very superstitious—that for nothing which could have been offered to him would he have consented to let Suzanne go until the war with the End-wandwe was finished. Rather than do so he would have fought till the last, and he issued an order that if any man, woman, or child spoke of Suzanne's presence in his town to strangers they should be put to death without mercy. Moreover, in his terror lest she should escape, he set a guard over her and Sihamba day and night and other guards over the horses and the lad Zinti, so that they soon learned that all hopes of flight must be abandoned and that it was not possible even to send a messenger or a letter.

As may be guessed this was a sore grief to Suzanne, so great a grief that when they were back in the guest-hut she wept long and bitterly, for her heart ached with her own sorrow, and she knew well how deep would be the torment of mind of Ralph if he still lived, and of us, her father and mother, when we learned that she had vanished quite away, and that none could tell what her fate had been. At first she thought of bidding Zinti slip away under cover of the night, but Sihamba showed her that even if he could do so, which was not likely, the end of it must be that he would be followed and put to death, and that then his blood would be upon their hands and no good done. Afterwards she tried to bribe and to command several men of her guard to take the message, but in this matter alone the people of Sigwe would not obey her, for they knew the doom which awaited them if they listened to her pleading. So, when she spoke, they looked into the air over her head, and did not seem to hear, although after-wards they reported her words to Sigwe, whereupon that chief doubled the guard, setting a second to watch the first.

And now I have to tell you one of the strangest things in the strange story of the love of Ralph Kenzie and my daughter Suzanne. It will be remembered that it was by means of a dream—or so the child declared—that Suzanne was led to where the boy Ralph lay alone and starving in the kloof. So now in this second great crisis of their lives, it was by means of a dream that comfort was brought to the hearts of both of them, enabling them, as I believe, to bear the terrors of those long years of tidingless terror and separation, that otherwise would have broken down their minds and perhaps have killed them.

It seems, as Suzanne told me in after days, that before she slept that night, there in the guest-hut of Sigwe, she prayed long and earnestly as those who have faith do pray when they lie under the shadow of an overwhelming grief. She prayed that God would bring about what she was unable to bring about, namely, that her husband should learn that she was unharmed and well, and that she might learn how it went with him, seeing that for aught she knew, by now he might be dead of his wounds. Well, that prayer was heard, for I myself can testify to it, as the prayer of faith is so often heard; yes, that which seemed to be impossible was done, for in the watches of the night these two who lay a hundred miles apart, one of them a prisoner in the town of a savage, and the other helpless upon a bed of pain, had sight and speech of each other.

Still praying, Suzanne fell asleep. Then of a sudden it seemed as though space had no bars for her, for she awoke, or thought that she awoke, in the guest-hut of Sigwe, since she could hear the breathing of Sihamba at her side, and stretching out her hand she touched her face. But in the twinkling of an eye there came a change, for, still wide awake, now she was standing in the stead at home just within the door of her own sleeping-room. There upon the bed lay her husband, fevered and unconscious, but muttering to himself, while bending over him were I, her mother, and a strange man whom she did not know, but who, as she guessed, must have been roused from his sleep, for his hair was dishevelled and he was half-clothed.

To this man she heard me—her mother—talking. " The fever runs so high, doctor," I said, " that I made bold to wake you from your rest, for I fear lest it should burn his life away." Thereupon she saw the man look at Ralph, feeling his pulse, and heard him answer as he examined the bandages of the wound, " His hurt does well, and I do not think that the fever comes from it. It comes from his mind, and it is there that the danger lies, for who can doctor a broken heart? "

" Heaven only," I replied.

" Yes," he said, " Heaven only. And now, Vrouw Botmar, go and rest awhile, hoping for the best, for you will hear him if he wakes up, but he will not wake, since the sleep-draught that I gave him holds him fast."

Then she saw us both go—the doctor back to his bed and me to a settle with a mattress on it, which was placed just outside his door.

Here I would stop my tale to say that *this thing happened*, and that those words which Suzanne heard while her body lay in Sigwe's guest-hut, passed between the doctor, who was sleeping at the stead, and myself at one o'clock of the morning on the third night after the night of the taking of Suzanne, and moreover, that I never spoke of them to any living creature until Suzanne repeated them to me in later years. Nor could the doctor have told them to her, for he went away to the province of Graff Reinet, where shortly afterwards he was killed by a fall from his horse.

Then it seemed to Suzanne that she moved to the bed-side of her husband, and bending down, kissed him upon the forehead, which was hot to her lips, saying, "Awake, dear love." Instantly, in her vision, he awoke with a cry of joy, and said, "Suzanne, how came you here?" to which she answered, "I am not here. I have escaped un-harmed from Swart Piet, but I am a prisoner in the hands of red Kaffirs, and to-morrow I lead their army to the north. Yet it has been permitted me to visit you, husband, and to tell you to be of good comfort and to fear no evil tidings, for you will recover and we shall meet again, un-harmed in any way, though not till many days are passed."

"Where shall we meet?" he asked. "I do not know," she answered. "Yes, I see now. Look before you."

Then they looked, both of them, and there painted in the air they saw the picture cf a great mountain, standing by itself upon a plain, but with other mountains visible to the north and south of it. This mountain was flat-topped, with precipices of red rock, and down its eastern slope ran five ridges shaped like the thumb and fingers of a mighty hand, while between the thumb and the first finger, as it were, a stream gushed out, upon the banks of which grew flat-topped trees with thick green leaves and white bloom.

"You have seen and you will remember, fearing noth-ing," she said in her vision.

"I have seen and I shall remember, fearing nothing," Ralph answered, and with the sound of his voice still echo-ing in her ears, Suzanne awoke in the guest-hut of Sigwe, and once more heard Sihamba breathing at her side, and felt the hand which she had outstretched to find her, pressed against her cheek. But now there was a new sense of comfort in her heart, for she believed that without any doubt she had seen her husband, and that although they were separated, still the day would come when they should meet again, not in the spirit but in the flesh.

Now I, Suzanne Botmar, who tell this tale, had scarcely left Ralph's room upon that very night and laid myself down upon the settle when he called to me. I ran back to the bed to find him sitting up in it wide awake and calm-eyed.

"Mother," he said, for so he still named me, "did you see Suzanne?"

"Hush, Ralph," I answered, "you are talking foolishly; wherever Suzanne may be, alas! she is not here."

"She was here just now," he said, smiling, "for we have been talking together. She has escaped from Swart Piet and is unharmed, but a prisoner among the Kaffirs. And, mother, she and I will meet again upon a great mountain like a fortress, which has ridges on its eastern side resembling the thumb and fingers of a man, and a stream of water gushing out between the thumb and first finger."

"Doubtless, doubtless," I said, for I saw that he was wandering in his mind.

"Ah!" Ralph answered, "you do not believe me, but it is true. I tell you that I saw Suzanne just now wearing a fine kaross of tiger skins upon her shoulders, and that she kissed me on the forehead," and even as he spoke he sank into a deep and quiet sleep, and when he awoke in the morning we found that the fever had left him and that he was out of danger of his life.

CHAPTER XXII

WHEN Sihamba arose next day, Suzanne asked her if the home of her people, the Umpondwana, was a great mountain faced round with slab-sided precipices and having ridges on its eastern face like to the thumb and fingers of a hand, with a stream of water gushing from between the thumb and first finger, upon the banks of which grew flat-topped trees with thick green leaves and white flowers.

Sihamba stared at her, saying:

"Such is the place indeed, and there are no trees like to those you speak of to be found anywhere else. The maidens use the flowers of them to adorn their hair, and from the leaves is made a salve that is very good for wounds. But, say, Swallow, who told you about the mountain Umpondwana that is so far away, since I never described it to you?"

"Nobody told me," she answered, and she repeated the vision to her, or as much of it as she wished.

Sihamba listened, and when the tale was done she nodded her little head, saying:

"So even you white people have something of the power which has been given to us Kaffir witch-doctors from the beginning. Without a doubt your spirit spoke to the spirit of your husband last night and I am glad of it, for now, although you are apart from each other, the hearts of both of you will be rested. Now also I am sure that we must go to my people and live among them for so long as may be appointed, seeing that there and nowhere else you and the Baas Kenzie will come together again."

" I had sooner go back to the stead," sighed Suzanne.

" That cannot be, Swallow, for it is not fated, and for the rest, if you meet, what does it matter where you meet? "

That morning Suzanne, mounted upon the great *schimmel*, which by now had almost recovered from his weariness, although he was still somewhat stiff, and followed by Sihamba and Zinti riding the horse and the mule, passed up and down before Sigwe's regiments that saluted her as chieftainess. Then amongst much wailing of women and children, the impi started northward, Suzanne, preceded only by scouts and a guard to feel the way, riding in front of it that she might escape the dust raised by so many feet and the hoofs of the great herd of oxen that were driven along to serve as food for the soldiers.

For fourteen days' journey they travelled thus, and during that time nothing of note happened to them, except that twelve men and Sihamba's brown mule were lost in crossing a flooded river, whereof there were many in their path. The country through which they passed was populated by Kaffirs, but these tribes were too small and scattered to attempt to oppose so large an army, nor did the men of Sigwe do them any mischief beyond taking such grain and meal as they required for food.

On the fourteenth day, however, they reached the boundary of the territories of a very powerful tribe of Pondo blood, and here they halted while messengers were sent forward to the Pondo chief, saying that with him Sigwe had no quarrel, and asking for a safe-conduct for the army while passing through his lands. On the third day these messengers returned, accompanied by an embassy from the Pondo chief, that after much talk, though to all appearance unwillingly, gave Sigwe the promise of safe-conduct upon condition that he made a present of cere-mony of one ox to their ruler. Now Sihamba noticed that while the envoys were talking, their eyes wandered all about, taking note of every thing, and especially of the number of the soldiers and of Suzanne, who sat beside Sigwe during the *indaba,* or council.

"These are no true men," she thought to herself, and made a plan. In the evening she visited the camp of the envoys who had heard already that she was a famous doc-toress, and offered her services to them for payment should any of them chance to need the boon of her magic arts. They laughed, answering that they wanted neither charms nor divinations, but that she should see a certain young man, a servant in their train, who was very sick with love and had bought philtres from every doctor in their coun-try without avail, wherewith to soften the heart of a girl who would have nothing to do with him. When Sihamba, without seeming to speak much of it, had drawn from them all that she wished to know of the story of this man and girl, and with it other information, though they won little enough from her, she took her leave, and so set her trap that at night when all were asleep the young man came to consult her in a place apart.

Now she looked at him, and said at once, without suf-fering him to speak:

"Let me see. Your name is so-and-so, and you are in love with such a girl, who turns away from you;" and she went on to tell him things which he thought were known only to himself.

"Wonderful!" he said, "wonderful! But say, lady doctoress, can you help me, for my heart is water because of this girl?"

"It is difficult," she answered. "Do you know that when you come to consult a wise woman you should keep your mind fixed upon the matter about which you would take counsel with her from the first moment that you set out to visit her until you stand in her presence? Now this you have not done, for as you came you were thinking of other things; yes, you were thinking about the ambush which is to be set for these people in the pass yonder, and therefore I cannot see the girl's heart clear, and do not quite know what medicine I should give you to soften it."

"It is true, lady," answered the stupid fellow, "that I was thinking about the ambush of which I have heard some talk, though I do not know who told you of it."

"Who told me? Why to my sight your thoughts are written on your face, yes, they ran before you and reached me as I heard your footsteps. But now, think no more of that matter, which has nothing to do with you or me, think only of the girl, and go on thinking of her, and of her only, until you get back home, and give her the medicine— that is if you wish it to work."

"I am thinking, lady," he muttered, turning his stupid face up to the skies.

"Fool, be quiet. Do I not know that? Ah! now I see her heart, and I tell you that you are lucky, for when you have done as I bid you, she will love you more than if you were the greatest chief in all the land." Then Sihamba gave him a certain harmless powder to sprinkle in the hut where the girl slept, and bade him wait for her on six different days when she came up from bathing, giving her on each day a garland of fresh flowers, a new flower for every day.

The man thanked her and asked what he must pay her for a fee, to which she replied that she took no fee in matters of love, since her reward was to know that she had made two people happy; but she added:

" Remember what I tell you, or instead of earning love you will earn hate. Say nothing of your visit to me, and if you can avoid it, do not speak at all until you have sprinkled the powder in the hut; especially put all things which do not concern you and her out of your mind and think only of her face and how happy you will be when you have married her, which, if you follow my instructions, you will shortly do."

Now the young man went away as though he were walking upon air, and indeed so closely did he obey her that he was dismissed by his masters as a dumb fool before· he reached home again. But whether or no Sihamba's medicine softened the heart of the maid I have not heard.

So soon as he was gone Sihamba sent Zinti to bring Sigwe and two of his generals to the place where she and Suzanne were encamped in a booth made of branches and long grass. When they were come, she told them what she had learned from the love-stricken lad, adding that this plan of making sure of what already she suspected, had been born in the brain of the Swallow, although she had carried it out. For when she deemed that she could serve her mistress or win her honour, Sihamba thought less of the truth than she should have done.

On learning this tidings Sigwe and his captains were

full of wrath, and spoke of making war upon the Pondo chief at once, but Sihamba said:

" Listen; the Swallow has whispered a better way into my ear. It is this: the embassy of the Pondos leaves at dawn, and you must bid them farewell, telling them that you will follow and camp to-morrow night at the mouth of the pass, which you will enter at the next daybreak. Meanwhile now at once we will send out my servant, Zinti, dressed like a Pondo lad, to search the country, and find if there is not another path by which the pass can be turned, for if such a way exists he will discover it and report to us to-morrow at nightfall, since he, who is stupid in many things, was born with the gift of seeking out roads and remembering them; also he knows how to be silent if questioned."

The chief and his captains thought this plan good, and thanked the Swallow for it, praising her wisdom, and within an hour, having been instructed what he must do and where he should meet them, Zinti was despatched upon his errand.

Next morning the envoys departed suspecting nothing, and taking with them gifts and the ox of ceremony; and that night the army of Sigwe encamped within a mile of the pass, to the right and left of which stretched tall and difficult cliffs.

About an hour after sunset Zinti crept into the camp and asked for food to eat, for he had travelled far and was hungry; moreover, he had been chased by some Pondo soldiers to whom, feigning the fool he was commonly supposed to be, he would make no answer when they questioned him. When he had eaten he made his report to Sigwe, Suzanne, and Sihamba, and the gist of it was that he had found a good road by which men might safely

ascend the cliffs, though not so easily as they could travel
through the gorge. Following this road, he added, they
could pass round the Pondo town, avoiding its fortifications, and coming out at the cattle kraals at the back of the
town, for he had climbed a high tree and mapped out the
route with his eye. Then followed a council of war, and
the upshot of it was that, under the leadership of Zinti,
the army marched off in silence an hour before midnight,
leaving its cooking fires burning to deceive the Pondos.

They climbed the cliffs by the path he showed them,
and, travelling all night, at dawn found themselves before
the cattle kraals, which, as no enemy was expected, were
unguarded except by the herds. These they cleared of the
cattle, some thousands of them, and marched on at speed,
sending a message back to the town by the herds that this
was the luck which those must expect who attempted to
trap the Swallow in a snare set for a rock-rabbit.

The Pondos were very angry at their loss, and, gathering their strength, followed them for some days, but before
they could come up with them Sigwe and his army had
reached country so difficult and so far away that the Pondo
chief thought it wisest to leave them alone. So they
marched on, taking the captured cattle with them, and
after this bloodless victory Suzanne and Sihamba were
greatly honoured by the soldiers, and even the lad Zinti
was treated like a chief.

Now once more they reached wild lands, inhabited only
by scattered tribes, and passed through them at their
leisure, for they had plenty of food to eat, although from
time to time they were obliged to encamp upon the banks
of flooded rivers, or to hunt for a road over a mountain.
It was on the thirty-first day of their journey that at length
they entered the territories of the Endwandwe, against

whom they had come to make war, where at once they were
met by messengers sent by Sikonyana, the chief of the
Endwandwe, desiring to know why they came upon him
with so great a force. To these men the case was set out
by Sigwe, speaking in his own name and in that of the
Swallow. As he had promised Suzanne, for this was a
savage who kept his word, he offered to refrain from attack if the young Batwa was exchanged for her one-eyed
sister and sent to him, together with the thousand head of
cattle which he had paid, and two thousand more by way
of fine. At first these terms were refused, but afterwards
an embassy came of whom the captain was the brother of
the king, who said that he was charged to discuss this
matter with the white chieftainess named Swallow, herself,
and with none other.

So Suzanne, accompanied only by Sihamba, and mounted
upon the great *schimmel* that had come safe and well
through all the journey, though the black horse had died
of sickness, rode out a hundred paces in front of the army
and met the man. There she spoke to him well and wisely,
pointing out to him that without doubt a trick had been
played upon Sigwe which he was mad to avenge. The
captain answered that they were well able to fight. She
replied that this might be so, that they might even conquer Sigwe and drive him back, but it could not be done
without great loss to themselves, and that if his tribe were
at all weakened the Zulus, who hated them, would hear of
it, and take the opportunity to stamp them out.

Well, the end of it was that the Endwandwe yielded, and
upon the promise of Suzanne—for they would take no
other—that no spear should be lifted against them, they
sent the true Batwa, a beautiful but sullen girl, to Sigwe,
taking back the old Batwa, who departed cursing him and

all his race. With her they returned also the thousand head of cattle which he had paid and twelve hundred more by way of fine, for the balance was remitted by agreement.

And so came to an end the war of Sigwe with the Endwandwe, which among the Kaffirs is still spoken of as the " War of the White Swallow," or sometimes as " The War of the Clean Spear," because no blood at all was shed in it, and not a man was killed by violence, although when Sigwe passed through that country on his journey home, by means of a clever trick the Pondo chief re-captured most of the cattle that had been taken from him.

CHAPTER XXIII

HOW SUZANNE BECAME A CHIEFTAINESS

So the cattle were handed over, and the girl Batwa was given to Sigwe, whom by the way she made unhappy for the rest of his days. Indeed, she brought about his ruin, for being ambitious she persuaded him to make war upon the white people in the Transkei, of which the end was that from a great chief he became a very small one. When all was accomplished Sigwe waited upon Suzanne.

"Lady Swallow," he said, "in three days I begin my homeward march, and now I have come to ask whither you wish to go, since you cannot stop here in the veldt alone."

"I would return with you to the Transkei," she answered, "and seek out my own home."

"Lady," he said shamefacedly, "alas! that may not be. You remember the dream of the diviner, and you know how that all which she foretold, and more, has come to pass, for you, the White Swallow, appeared and flew in front of my impi, and from that hour we have had the best of luck. By your wisdom we outwitted the Pondos and seized their cattle; by your wisdom we have conquered the Endwandwe without lifting a single spear, and that Batwa, whom I desired, is mine; while of the great force which came out with me to war but twenty-and-one are dead, twelve by drowning, eight by sickness, and one by snakebite. All things have gone well, and she who dreamed the dream of the White Swallow is the greatest of diviners.

"But, lady, this was not all the dream, for it said that if you, the Swallow, should set your face southward with us then the best of luck would turn to the worst, for then utter misfortune should overwhelm me and my regiments. Now, lady, I cannot doubt that as the first part of the prophecy has come true, so the last part would come true also did I tempt the spirits of my ancestors by disregarding it, and, therefore, White Swallow, though all I have is yours, yet you cannot fly home with us."

Now Suzanne pleaded with him long and earnestly, as did Sihamba, but without avail, for he could not be moved. Indeed, had he consented the captains and the army would have disobeyed his order in this matter, for they believed, every man of them, that to take the Swallow with them homewards would be to run to their own deaths. Nor was it safe that she should attempt to follow in the path of the impi, since then in their superstitious fear they might send back and kill her to avert the evil fate.

"Now, Swallow," said Sihamba, "there is but one thing for us to do, and it is to seek refuge among my people, the Umpondwana, whose mountain stronghold lies at a distance of four days' journey from this place. But to speak truth, I am not sure how they will receive me, seeing that I parted from them in anger twelve years ago, having quarrelled with them, first about a matter of policy, and secondly about a matter of marriage, and that my half-brother, the son of my father by a slave, was promoted to rule in my place. Still to them we must go, and with them we must stay, if they will suffer it, until we find an opportunity of travelling south in safety "

"If it must be so," answered Suzanne, sighing, " perhaps Sigwe will escort us to the house of the Umpondwana before he turns homewards, for they will think the more of us if they see us at the head of a great army."

To this plan Sigwe and his captains assented with gladness, for they loved and honoured the Swallow, and were sore at heart because their fears forced them to leave her alone in the wilderness. But first they made sure that the mountain Umpondwana lay to the west, and not to the south, for not one step to the southward would they allow Suzanne to travel with them.

On the morrow, then, they marched, and the evening of the third day they set their camp in a mountain pass which led to a wide plain. Before sunrise next morning Sihamba woke Suzanne.

"Dress yourself, Swallow," she said, "and come to see the light break on the house of my people."

So they went out in the grey dawn, and climbing a koppie in the mouth of the pass, looked before them. At first they could distinguish nothing, for all the plain beneath was a sea of mist through which in the distance loomed something like a mountain, till presently the rays of the rising sun struck upon it and the veils of vapour parted like curtains that are drawn back, and there before them was the mountain-fortress of Umpondwana separated from the pass by a great space of mist-clad plain. Suzanne looked and knew it.

"Sihamba," she said, "it is the place of my vision and none other. See, the straight sides of red rock, the five ridges upon the eastern slope fashioned like the thumb and fingers of the hand of a man. Yes, and there between the thumb and first finger a river runs."

"I told you that it was so from the beginning, Swallow, for in all the country there is no other such hill as this, and because of the aspect of those ridges when seen from a distance it is named the Mountain of the Great Hand."

Before the words had left her lips another voice spoke, at the sound of which Suzanne nearly fell to the earth.

" Good day to you, Suzanne," it said in Dutch and was silent.

" Sihamba, did you hear, Sihamba? " she gasped. " Do I dream, or did Piet Van Vooren speak to me? "

"You did not dream," answered Sihamba, "for that voice was the voice of Swart Piet and no other, and he is hidden somewhere among the rocks of yonder cliff wall. Quick, Swallow, kneel behind this stone lest he should shoot."

She obeyed, and at that moment the voice spoke again out of the shadows of the cliff that bordered the pass twenty or thirty paces from them.

" What, Suzanne," it said, " is that little witch-doctoress telling you that I shall fire on you? Had I wished I could have shot you three times over while you were standing upon that rock. But why should I desire to kill one who will be my lover? Sihamba I wished to shoot indeed, but her familiar set her so that the bullet must pass through you to reach her heart. Suzanne, you are going to hide yourself among the people of the Umpondwana. Oh! yes, I know your plan. Well, when once you are behind the walls of that mountain it may be difficult to speak to you for a while, so listen to me. You thought that you had left me far away, did you not? but I have followed you step by step and twice I have been very near to you, although I could never find a chance to carry you off safely. Well, I wish to tell you that sooner or later I shall find that chance; sooner or later you will come out of the mountain or I shall get into it, and then it will be my turn; so, love,

till that hour fare you well. Stay, I forgot, I have news
for you; your husband, the English castaway, is dead."

At this tidings a low moan of pain broke from Suzanne's
lips.

"Be silent and take no heed," whispered Sihamba, who
was kneeling at her side behind the shelter of the stone,
"he does but lie to torment you."

"The bullet and the water together were too much for
him," went on Swart Piet, "and he died on the second
night after he reached the stead. Your father came to
seek me in the place you know, and was carried home badly
wounded for his pains, but whether he lived or died I
cannot tell you, but I heard that your mother, the good
Vrouw Botmar, is very sick, for things have so fallen out
lately that her mind is troubled, and she flies to drink to
comfort it."

Now when she heard this, Sihamba could keep silence
no longer, but cried in a mocking voice:

"Get you gone, Bull-Head, and take lessons in lying
from your friends of my trade, the Kaffir witch-doctors,
for never before did I hear a man bear false witness so
clumsily. On the third night of his illness the husband of
Swallow was alive and doing well; the Heer Jan Botmar
was not wounded at all, and as for the Vrouw Botmar,
never in her life did she drink anything stronger than
coffee, for the white man's firewater is poison to her. Get
you gone, you silly half-breed, who seek to deceive the
ears of Sihamba, and I counsel you, hold fast to your
business of theft and murder and give up that of lying,
in which you will never succeed. Now be off, you stink-
cat of the rocks, lest I send some to hunt you from your
hole who this time will use the points and not the shafts
of their assegais. Come, Swallow, let us be going."

So they went, keeping under cover all the way to the camp, which, indeed, was quite close to them, and if Swart Piet made any answer they did not hear it. So soon as they reached it Sihamba told Sigwe what had passed and he sent men to scour the cliff and the bush behind it, but of Van Vooren they could find no trace, no, not even the spot where he had been hidden, so that Sigwe came to believe that they had been fooled by echoes and had never heard him at all.

But both Suzanne and Sihamba knew that this was not so; indeed, this hearing of the voice of Swart Piet filled Suzanne with fear, since where the voice was, there was the man, her hateful enemy, who had given his life to her ruin and to that of those she loved. Whatever lies he might have spoken—and her heart told her that all his ill tidings were but a cruel falsehood—this at least was true, that he had dogged her step by step through the vast wilderness, and so craftily that none guessed his presence. What might not be feared from such a foe as this, half mad and all wicked, armed with terrible cunning and untiring patience? If the Umpondwana would not receive her she must fall into his hands at once, and if they did receive her she would never dare to leave their kraal, for always, always he would be watching and waiting for her. Little wonder then that she felt afraid, though, just as the sun shines ever behind the blackest cloud, still in her heart shone the sure comfort of her hope, and more than hope that in the end God would give her back her husband and her to him unharmed. Yet, which ever way she looked the cloud was very black, and through it she could see no ray of light.

When the mists had vanished and the air was warm with

the sun, the army of Sigwe marched from the pass heading for the great mountain. As they drew near they saw that the Umpondwana were much terrified at the sight of them, for from all the kraals, of which there were many on the slopes of the mountain, they ran hither and thither like ants about a broken nest, carrying their goods and children upon their shoulders, and driving herds of cattle in towards the central stronghold. Noting this, Sigwe halted and sent heralds forward to say that he came in peace and not in war, and he desired to speak with their chief. In less than two hours the heralds returned, bringing with them some of the headmen of the Umpondwana, who stared round with frightened eyes, for they did not believe that any general would come upon a message of peace with so many regiments. When the *indaba* was set Sigwe told them his name and tribe, of both of which they had heard, and then, before speaking of his business, asked which of them was the chief of the Umpondwana.

"Alas!" answered an old man, "we are in sore trouble here, and wander in the darkness, for our chief, who was named Koraanu, died two days ago of the small-pox which has raged among us for many months, leaving no children behind him, for the sickness killed them also. Moreover, we are suffering from a great drought, for as you may see, the veldt is still brown, and there is no green upon the cornfields, and if rain does not fall soon famine will follow the sickness, and then it will only need that the Zulus should follow the famine to make an end of us once and for all."

"It seems that your tribe must have sinned deeply and brought down upon itself the curse of the spirits of its ancestors," said Sigwe, when they had done their melancholy tale, "that so many misfortunes should overtake you. Tell me now, who by right is ruler of the Umpond-wana?"

"We do not know, chief," they answered, "or rather, we cannot tell if our ruler is alive or dead, and if she is dead then none are left of the true blood. She was a small woman, but very pretty and full of wisdom as a mealie-cob with grains of corn, for in all this country there was no doctoress or diviner like to her. Her name was Sihamba Ngenyanga, the Wanderer-by-Moonlight, which name was given her when she was little, because of her habit of walking in the dark alone, and she was the only child of our late chief's *inkosikaas*, a princess of the Swazis, the father of that lord, Koraanu, who lies dead of the small-pox. But when this chief died and Sihamba was called upon to rule our tribe, quarrels arose between her and the *indunas* of the tribe, for she was a very headstrong woman.

"We, the *indunas*, wished her to marry, but for her own reasons she would not marry; also we wished to swear allegiance to Chaka, but she was against it, saying that as well might a lamb swear allegiance to a wolf as the Um-pondwana to the Zulus. The end of it was that in a temper she took a bowl of water, and before us all washed her hands of us, and that same night she vanished away we know not where, though rumours have reached us that she went south. From the day of her departure, however, things have gone ill with us; the Zulus with whom we made peace threaten us continually; her half-brother, Koraanu, the slave-born, was not a good chief, and now he is dead of the sickness. So our heart is heavy and our head is in the dust, and when we saw your impi we thought that Dingaan, who now rules over the Zulus, had sent it to eat us up and to take the cattle that still remain to us.

"But you say that you come in peace, so tell us, chief,

what it is you desire, and I trust that it may be little, for
here we have nothing to give, unless," he added with meaning, " it be the small-pox, although we are ready to fight
to the death for what is left to us, our liberty and our
cattle; and, chief, even a larger army than yours might fail
to take that stronghold which has but one gate."

When the councillor had finished speaking, Sigwe called
aloud:

" Lady Sihamba, I pray you come hither, and with you
the lady Swallow, your companion."

Then Sihamba, who was prepared for this event, for
her hair was freshly dressed and powdered with blue mica,
wearing her little cape of fur and the necklace of large
blue beads, stepped from the screen of bush behind which
she had hidden. With her, and holding her hand, came
Suzanne, who covered the raggedness of her clothes beneath a splendid kaross of leopards' skins that Sigwe had
given her, down which her dark hair flowed almost to her
knee. A strange pair they made, the tall Suzanne in the
first bloom of her white beauty which had suffered nothing
in their journeying, and the small, quick-eyed, delicate-
featured Kaffir woman.

" Who are these? " asked Sigwe of the council.

The old man looked at them and answered:

" Of the white lady we can say nothing except that she
is very beautiful; but, unless our eyes deceive us, she whom
she holds by the hand is Sihamba Ngenyanga, who was
our chieftainess, and who left us because she was angry."

" She is Sihamba and no one else," said Sigwe. " Sihamba come back to rule you in the hour of need, and now
with her own tongue she shall tell you her story and the
story of the White Swallow who holds her by the hand."

So Sihamba began, and for an hour or more she spoke

to them, for when she chose this little woman had the gift
of words, telling them all about herself, and telling them
also the story of the Swallow, and of how she had brought
good luck to the army of Sigwe, and how she was destined
to bring good luck wherever she made her home. At the
end of her speech she said:

" Now, my people, although I have wandered from you,
yet my eyes, which are far-seeing, have not been blind to
your griefs, and in the hour of your need I return to you,
bringing with me the White Swallow to sojourn among you
for a while. Receive us if you will and be prosperous, or
reject us and be destroyed; to us it matters nothing, it is
for you to choose. But if we come, we come not as servants but as princes whose word cannot be questioned,
and should you accept us and deal ill with us in any way,
then your fate is sure. Ask the chief Sigwe here whether
or no the flight of the Swallow is fortunate, and whether
or no there is wisdom in the mouth of Sihamba, who is not
ashamed to serve her."

Then Sigwe told them of all the good fortune that had
come to him through Suzanne, and of how wise had been
the words of Sihamba, and told them, moreover, that if
they dealt ill by either of them he would return from his
own country and stamp them flat.

Thus it came about that the *indunas* of the Umpondwana took back Sihamba to be their chieftainess with all
powers, and with her Suzanne as her equal in rule, and this
their act was confirmed that same day by a great council
of the tribe. So that evening Suzanne, mounted on the
schimmel, rode down the ranks of the Red Kaffirs, while
they shouted their farewells to her. Then having parted
with Sigwe, who almost wept at her going, she passed

with Sihamba, the lad Zinti, and a great herd of cattle—
her tithe of the spoil—to the mountain Umpondwana,
where all the tribe were waiting to receive them. They
rode up to the flanks of the mountain, and through the
narrow pass and the red wall of rock to the tableland upon
its top, where stood the chief's huts and the cattle-kraal,
and here they found the people gathered.

"Give us a blessing," these cried. "Grant to us that
rain may fall."

Sihamba spoke with Suzanne and answered:

"My people, I have entreated of the White Swallow, and
for your sake she will pray that rain may fall ere long."

Now Sihamba knew the signs of the weather, and as it
happened rain began to fall that night in torrents, and fell
for three days almost without ceasing, washing the sickness away with it. So the Umpondwana blessed the name
of Sihamba and the White Swallow, and these two ruled
over them without question, life and death hanging upon
their words.

And there, a chieftainess among savages, Suzanne was
fated to dwell for more than two long years.

CHAPTER XXIV

Now my story goes back to that night at the stead when I, Suzanne Botmar and my husband, Jan Botmar, were awakened from our sleep to learn that our daughter had been carried off by that mad villain, Piet Van Vooren, and that her husband Ralph lay senseless and wounded in the waggon at the door. We carried him in, groaning in our bitter grief, and despatched messengers to arouse all the Kaffirs on and about the place whom we could trust and to a party of Boers, six men in all, who chanced to have outspanned that night upon the borders of our farm to shoot vildebeest and blesbok. Also we sent another messenger mounted on a good horse to the house of that neighbour who was being attended by the doctor from the dorp, praying that he would come with all speed to visit Ralph, which indeed he did, for he was with us by half-past eight in the morning.

Within an hour of the despatch of the messengers the Boers rode up from their waggons, and to them, as well as to ourselves and to the Kaffirs who had gathered, the driver and voorlooper told all they knew of the terrible crime that had been done upon the persons of Ralph Kenzie and his wife by Piet Van Vooren and his band. Also they repeated all that Zinti had taught them of the road to the secret krantz whither it was believed that he had carried off Suzanne. Then Jan asked those present if they would help him in this trouble, and being true men, one and all, they answered yes, so by seven in the morning the little commando, numbering twenty-one guns —eight white men and thirteen Kaffirs—started to seek for Swart Piet's hiding-place, and to rescue Suzanne if they might.

"Alas!" I said to Jan as he bade me farewell, "at the best I fear that you will be too late."

"We must trust in God," he answered heavily.

"Never had we more need of trust, husband, but I think that God turns His face from us because of the lies we told to the Englishmen, for now the punishment which you foresaw has fallen."

"Then, wife, it were more just that it should have fallen on us who were guilty, and not on these two who are innocent. But still I say I trust in God—and in Sihamba" —he added by an afterthought, "for she is brave and clever, and can run upon a path which others cannot even see."

Then they went, and were away five days, or it may have been six. They started early on Tuesday, and upon the Thursday morning, after much trouble, by the help of a native whom they captured, they found Swart Piet's kraal, but of Swart Piet or Suzanne or the hidden krantz they could see nothing. Indeed, it was not until they had gathered together every man they could find in the kraal and tied them to trees, saying that they would shoot them, that a woman, the wife of one of the men, led them to a rock wall and showed the secret of the kloof. They entered and found the big hut with the body of the man whom Sihamba had killed still lying in it, and also the knife with which Suzanne had intended to destroy herself, and which her father knew again.

Then by degrees they discovered the whole story, for the woman pointed out to them the man who had guarded the entrance to the kloof, at whom Zinti had fired, and under fear of death this man confessed all he knew, which was that Suzanne, Sihamba, and Zinti had escaped northward upon their horses, followed by Swart Piet and his band.

Accordingly northwards they rode, but they never found any traces of them, for rain had fallen, washing out their spoor, and as might be expected in that vast veldt they headed in the wrong direction. So at last worn out, they returned to the stead, hoping that Suzanne and Sihamba would have found their way back there, but hoping in vain.

After that for days and weeks they searched and hunted, but quite without result, for as it chanced the Kaffirs who lived between the territory of Sigwe and the stead rose in arms just then, and began to raid the Boer farms, stealing the cattle, including some of our own, so that it was impossible to travel in their country, and therefore nobody ever reached the town of Sigwe to make inquiries there.

The end of it was that, exhausted by search and sorrow, Jan sat down at home and abandoned hope; nor could the prayers and urgings of Ralph, who all this while was unable even to mount a horse, persuade him to go out again upon so fruitless an errand.

"No, son," he answered, "long before this the girl is either dead or she is safe far away, and in either event it is useless to look for her about here, since Van Vooren's kraal is watched, and we know that she is not in it." To which Ralph would answer:

"She is not dead, I know that she is not dead," and we understood that he spoke of the vision which had come to him, for I had told the tale of it to Jan. But in his heart Jan put no faith in the vision, and believed that Suzanne, our beloved child, had been dead for many days, for he was certain that she would die rather than fall again into the hands of Van Vooren, as I was also, and indeed of this we were glad to be sure.

To Ralph, however, that we might comfort him in his sorrow, which was even more terrible than our own, we made pretence that we believed Suzanne to be hiding far away, but unable to communicate with us, as in fact she was.

Oh! our lives were sad during those bitter months. Yes, the light had gone out of our lives, and often we wished, the three of us, that already we were resting in the grave. As he recovered from his wounds and the strength of his body came back to him, a kind of gentle madness took hold of Ralph which it wrung our hearts to see. For hours, sometimes for days indeed, he would sit about the place brooding and saying no word. At other times he would mount his horse and ride away none knew whither, perhaps not to return that night or the next, or the next, till we were terrified by the thought that he too might never come back again. It was useless to be angry with him, for he would only answer with a little smile.

" You forget; I must be seeking my wife, who is waiting for me upon the Mountain of the Hand," and then we learned that he had ridden to a far off hill to examine it, or to see some travellers or natives and ask of them if they knew or had heard of such a mountain, with ridges upon its eastern slopes fashioned like the thumb and fingers of a man's hand. Indeed, in all that countryside, among both Boers and natives, Ralph won the by-name of the " Man of the Mountain " because he rarely spoke of aught else. But still folk, black and white, knew the reason of his madness and bore with him, pitying his grief.

It was, I remember, in the season after Suzanne had vanished that the Kaffirs became so angry and dangerous. For my part I believe that those in our neighbourhood were stirred up by the emissaries of Swart Piet, for though he had gone none knew where, his tools and agents remained behind him. However this may have been, all over the country the black men began to raid the stock, and in our case they ended by attacking the stead also, a great number of them armed with guns. Fortunately we had a little warning, and they were very sad Kaffirs that went away next day; moreover, forty of them never went away at all. Just at dawn, when they had been besieging the house for some hours, shouting, banging off their guns, and trying to fire the roof by means of assegais with tufts of blazing grass tied on to them, Jan, Ralph, and about twenty of our people crept down under cover of the orchard wall and sallied out upon them.

Almighty ! how those men fought, especially Jan and Ralph. It was a pleasure to see them, for I watched the whole thing from the *stoep*, though I admit that I was anxious, since it was evident that neither of them seemed to care whether he lived or died. However, as it turned out, it was not they who died, but the Kaffirs, who went off with some few cattle and afterwards left us in peace.

And now comes the strange part of the affair, though I scarcely like to tell it, lest after all these years it should not be believed. Someone connected with the London Missionary Society reported us to the Government at the Cape for shooting poor, innocent black men, and it was threatened that Jan and Ralph would be put upon their trial for murder by the British Government. Indeed, I

believe that this would have been done had not we and
others of our neighbours let it be clearly known that before
they were dragged to the common gaol there would be
killing not of black but of white men.

Our case was only one of many, since in those times
there was no security for us Boers—we were robbed, we
were slandered, we were deserted. Our goods were taken
and we were not compensated; the Kaffirs stole our herds,
and if we resisted them we were tried as murderers; our
slaves were freed, and we were cheated of their value, and
the word of a black man was accepted before our solemn
oath upon the Bible.

No wonder that we grew tired of it and trekked, seeking
to shake the dust of British rule from off our feet, and to
find a new home for ourselves out of the reach of the hand
of the accursed British Government. Oh! I know that
there are two sides to the story, and I daresay that the
British Government meant well, but at the least it was a
fool, and it always will be a fool with its Secretaries of
State, who know nothing sitting far away there in London,
and its Governors, whose only business is to please the
Secretaries of State, that when the country they are sent
to rule grows sick of them, they may win another post with
larger pay.

Well, this tale is of people and not of politics, so I will
say no more of the causes that brought about the great
trek of the Boers from the old Colony and sent them forth
into the wilderness, there to make war with the savage
man and found new countries for themselves. I know
those causes, for Jan and Ralph and I were of the number
of the voortrekkers; still, had it not been for the loss of
Suzanne, I do not think that we should have trekked, for we
loved the home we had made upon the face of the wild veldt.

But now that she was gone it was no home for us; every room of the house, every tree in the garden, every ox and horse and sheep reminded us of her. Yes, even the distant roar of the ocean and the sighing of the winds among the grasses seemed to speak of her. These were the flowers she loved, that was the stone she sat on, yonder was the path which day by day she trod. The very air was thick with memories of her, and the tones of her lost voice seemed to linger in the echoes of the hills at night.

It was upon the anniversary of the marriage of Ralph and Suzanne, yes, on the very day year of her taking by Piet Van Vooren, that we made up our minds to go. We had dined and Ralph sat quite silent, his head bowed a little upon his breast, as was his custom, while Jan spoke loudly of the wrongs of the Boers at the hand of the British Government. I do not think that he was much troubled with those wrongs just then, but he talked because he wished to interest Ralph and turn his mind from sad thoughts.

"What think you of it, son?" said Jan at length, for it is hard work talking all by oneself, even when one has the British Government to abuse, which was the only subject that made Jan a wordy man.

"I, father?" answered Ralph with a start, which showed me that his mind was far away. "I do not quite know what I think. I should like to hear what the English Government say about the matter, for I think that they mean to be fair, only they do not understand the wants and troubles of us Boers who live so far away. Also, without doubt the missionaries mean well, but they believe that a black man has a bigger soul than a white man, whereas we who know the black man see that there is a difference."

"Allemachter, son," said Jan, looking at him out of

the corner of his eye, " cannot you show some spirit? I
hoped that being an Englishman you would have stood up
for your own people, and then we might have quarrelled
about it, which would have done us both good, but you
only sit and talk like a magistrate in his chair, looking at
both sides of the case at once, which is an evil habit for
men who have to make their way in the world. Well, I
tell you that if you had seen the cursed British Government hang your father and uncle at Slagter's Nek, and not
satisfied with that, hang them a second time, when the
ropes broke, just because they tried to shoot a few Hottentot policemen, you would not think much of its fairness.
And as for the missionaries of the London Society, well,
I should like to hang *them*, as would be right and proper,
seeing that they blacken the names of honest Boers."

Ralph only smiled at this onslaught, for he was not to be
stirred from his lethargy by talk about Slagter's Nek and
the missionaries. For a while there was silence, which
presently was broken by Jan roaring at me in a loud voice
as though I were deaf.

" *Vrouw, let ons trek*," and, to give weight to his words,
he brought his great fist down with a bang upon the table,
knocking off a plate and breaking it.

I stooped to pick up the pieces, rating him for his care-
lessness as I gathered them, for I wished to have time to
think, although for a long while I had expected this.
When I had found them all I placed them upon the table,
saying:

" They cannot be mended, and—hearts or plates—what
cannot be mended had best be hidden away. Hearts and
plates are brittle things, but the last can be bought in
iron, as I wish the first could be also. Yes, husband, we
will trek if you desire it."

"What say you, son?" asked Jan.

Ralph answered his question by another. "In which direction will the emigrants trek?"

" North, I believe, to the Vaal River."

"Then, father, I say let us go," he replied with more spirit than he had shown for a long while, "for I have searched and inquired to the south and the east and the west, and in them I can hear of no mountain that has ridges upon its eastern slopes shaped like the thumb and fingers of a man's hand with a stream of water issuing from between the thumb and first finger."

Now once more we were silent, for we saw that his madness had again taken hold of Ralph's mind, and that was a sad silence.

CHAPTER XXV

On the morrow we began to make ready, and a month later we trekked from our much loved home. Jan tried to sell the farm, which was a very good one of over six thousand morgen, or twelve thousand English acres, well watered, and having on it a dwelling house built of stone, with large kraals and out-buildings, an orchard of fruit-trees, and twenty morgen of crop lands that could be irrigated in the dry season, well fenced in with walls built of loose stones. But no one would make a bid for it, for there were few English about, and most of the farmers were trekking, so at last he parted with it to a cowardly fellow, a Boer by birth, but, as I believe, a spy of the British Government, who gave him fifty pounds and an old waggon in exchange for the place and everything upon it except the stock which we took with us.

Some years ago I heard that this man's grandson sold that same farm for twenty thousand pounds in cash, and that now it is a place where they breed horses, angora goats, and ostriches in great numbers. It makes me mad to think that the descendant of that low spy should have profited so largely out of the land which was ours, but so it often chances that those whose hearts are small and mean reap the reward of the courage and misfortunes of braver men. Nor should we grumble indeed, seeing that the Lord has blessed us greatly in land and goods.

Ah! It was a sad home leaving. The day before we trekked Ralph rode to visit his mother's grave for the last time, and then, following the track which he had taken as a child, he went to the kloof where Suzanne had found him, and sat down upon that stone on which as a child he had knelt in prayer, and where in after years he and his lost wife had told their love. Jan accompanied him upon this dismal journey, for to speak truth we did not like to leave him more alone than we could help, since his manner remained strange, and when he set out on his solitary rides we could not be certain that we should ever see him come back again.

Next morning we trekked away, and my eyes were so full of tears as I sat beneath the tent of the first waggon that the familiar landscape and the home where I lived for twenty years and more were blotted from my sight. But I could still hear the long-nosed spy who had bought the farm, and who was waiting to enter into possession, talking to Jan.

"Good-bye, Heer Botmar," he said, "and good fortune to you upon your journey. For my part I cannot understand you emigrants. The English Government is an accursed Government, no doubt; still I would not sell a farm and a house like this for fifty pounds and an old waggon in order to wander in the wilderness to escape from it, there to be eaten by lions or murdered by Kaffirs. Still, good-bye, and good luck to you, and I hope that you are as content with your bargain as I am with mine."

"The Lord will be our guide, as He was to the Israelites of old," answered Jan in a somewhat troubled voice.

"Yes, yes; they all say that, Heer Botmar, and I trust

that they are right, for you will need nothing less than a cloud by day and a pillar of fire in the darkness to protect you from all the dangers in your path. Also I hope that the hosts of Pharaoh, in the shape of English soldiers, will not fetch you back before you cross the border, for then, when you have sold your birthright in Egypt, and are cut off from the Promised Land, your lot will be hard, Heer Botmar."

"The Lord will guide and protect us," repeated Jan, and gave the word to trek.

In my heart at the time I was inclined to agree with that cheat's sneering words; and yet Jan was right, and not I, for of the truth the Lord did guide and protect us. Has anything more wonderful happened in the world than this journey of a few farmers, cumbered with women and children, and armed only with old-fashioned muzzle-loading guns, into a vast, unknown land, peopled by savages and wild beasts? Yet, look what they did. They conquered Moselikatse; they broke the strength of Dingaan and all his Zulu impis; they peopled the Free State, the Transvaal, and Natal. That was the work of those few farmers, and I say that of their own strength they could never have done it; the strength was given to them from above; the Sword of God was in their hand, and He guided that hand and blessed it.

Our first outspan was at the spot where Van Vooren had tried to murder Ralph and carried off Suzanne upon her wedding-day. We did not stop there long, for the place was bad for Ralph, who sat upon the box of a waggon staring moodily at some blackened stones, which, as one of the drivers told me—the same man who accompanied them upon their wedding journey—had been brought by Ralph from the kloof and used by Suzanne to set the kettle on when they took their meal together. Led by this same driver I walked to the edge of the cliff—for I had never visited the place before—and looked at the deep sea-pool, forty feet below me, into which Swart Piet had thrown Ralph after he had shot him. Also I went down to the edge of the pool and climbed up again by the path along which Zinti and Sihamba had staggered with his senseless body. Afterwards I returned to the waggons with a heart full of thankfulness and wonder that he should still be alive among us to-day, although alas, there was much for which I could not feel thankful, at least not then.

Now it is of little use that I should set down the history of this trek of ours day by day, for if I did my story would have no end. It is enough to tell that in company with other emigrants we crossed the Orange River, heading for Thaba Nchu, which had been the chief town of Maroko before Moselikatse drove him out of the Marico country. Here several bands of emigrants were to meet, and here they did meet, but not until a year or more had passed since we left the colony and wandered out into the veldt.

Ah! I tell you, my child, the veldt in those days was different indeed from what it is now. The land itself remains the same except where white men have built towns upon it, but all else is changed. Then it was black with game when the grass was green; yes, at times I have seen it so black for miles that we could scarcely see the grass. There were all sorts of them, springbucks in myriads, blesbok and quagga and wildebeeste in thousands, sable antelope, sassaby and hartebeeste in herds, eland, giraffe and koodoo in troops; while the forests were full of elephant and the streams of sea-cow. They are all gone now, the beautiful wild creatures; the guns of the white men have killed them out or driven them away, and I suppose that it is as well that they are gone, for while the game is in such plenty the men will not work. Still I for one am sorry to lose the sight of them, and had it not been for their numbers we Boers should never have lasted through that long trek, for often and often we lived upon buck's flesh and little else for weeks together.

At Thaba Nchu we camped, waiting for other bands of emigrants, but after four or five months some of our number grew so impatient that they started off by themselves. Among these were the companies under the Heer Triegaart and the Heer Rensenburg, who wished us to accompany him, but Jan would not, I do not know why. It was as well, for the knob-nosed Kaffirs killed him and everybody with him. Triegaart, who had separated from him, trekked to Delagoa Bay, and reached it, where nearly all his people died of fever.

After that we moved northwards in detachments, instead of keeping together as we should have done, with the result that several of our parties were fallen upon and murdered by the warriors of Moselikatse. Our line of march was between where Bloemfontein and Winburg now stand in the Orange Free State, and it was south of the Vaal, not far from the Rhenoster River that Moselikatse attacked us.

I cannot tell the tale of all this war, I can only tell of what I saw myself. We were of the party under the leadership of Carl Celliers, afterwards an elder of the church at Kronnstadt. Celliers went on a commission to Zoutpansberg to spy out the land, and it was while he was away that so many families were cut off by Moselikatse, the remainder of them, with such of their women and children as were left alive, retreating to our laager. Then Celliers returned from his commission, and we retired to a place called Vechtkop, near the Rhenoster River; altogether we numbered not more than fifty or sixty souls, including women and children.

Here we heard that Moselikatse was advancing to make an end of us, so we made our laager as strong as we could, lashing the disselboom of each waggon beneath the framework of that before it and filling the spaces beneath and between with the crowns and boughs of sharp-thorned mimosa trees, which we tied to the trek tows and brake chains so that they could not be torn away. Also in the middle of the laager we made an inner defence of seven waggons, in which were placed the women and children, with the spare food and gunpowder, but the cattle we were obliged to leave outside. Early on the morning when we had finished the laager we heard that the impi of Moselikatse was close to us, and the men to the number of over thirty rode out to look for it, leaving but a few to defend the camp.

About an hour's ride away they found the Kaffirs, thousands of them, and a Hottentot who could speak their tongue was instructed to call to them and ask them why they attacked us. By way of answer they shouted out the name of their chief and began to charge, whereupon our men dismounted from their horses and opened fire upon them, mounting again before they could come near. So the fight went on until the laager was reached, and many Kaffirs were killed without any loss to the Boers, for luckily in those days the natives had no firearms.

I remember that we women were moulding bullets when the men rode in, and very thankful we were to find that not one of them was even wounded. While they ate something we washed out their guns, and at intervals near the places where each man must stand behind the waggons we piled little heaps of powder and bullets upon buckskins and pieces of canvas laid on the ground; also we did all we could to strengthen our defences still further by binding ox-hides over the waggon wheels and thrusting in more thorns between them.

Then, as the enemy was still preparing to attack us, the Heer Celliers called us together, and there in the laager, while all knelt around him, even to the smallest child, he put up a prayer to God asking that we might be forgiven our sins, and that He would look upon us and protect us in our great need.

It was a strange sight. There we all knelt in the quiet sunshine while he prayed in an earnest voice, and we followed his words with our hearts, every one of us, men and women, holding guns or axes in our hands. Never had human beings more need for prayer, for through the cracks between the waggons we could see Moselikatse's Zulus, six or seven thousand of them, forming themselves into three bodies to rush upon us and murder us, and that was a dreadful sight for fifty or sixty people, of whom some were little children.

When we had finished praying, husbands and wives and parents and children kissed each other, and then the little ones and some of the women who were sick or aged were put behind the seven waggons in the centre of the laager, round which were tied the horses, while the rest of us went to our stations, men and women together. I stood behind Jan and Ralph, who fought side by side, and, assisted by a girl of fourteen years of age, loaded their spare guns. Now there was a great silence in the camp, and suddenly in the silence, Jan, who was looking through his loophole, whispered:

" Allemachter! here they come."

And come they did, with a rush and a roar from three sides at once, while men drew in their breath and set their faces for the struggle. Still no one fired, for the order was that we were to save our powder until Celliers let off his gun. Already the savages were within thirty paces of us, a countless mass of men packed like sheep in a kraal, their fierce eyes shewing white as ivory in the sunlight, their cruel spears quivering in their hands, when the signal was given and every gun, some loaded with slugs and some with bullets, was discharged point-blank into the thick of them.

Over they rolled by dozens, but that did not stop the rest, who, in spite of our pitiless fire, rushed up to the waggons and gripped them with their hands, striving to drag them apart, till the whole line of them rocked and surged and creaked like boats upon the sea, while the air grew thick with smoke rising straight up towards the sky, and through the smoke assegais flashed as thick as rain.

But although some of the heavy laden waggons were dragged a foot or more outward they held together, and the storm of spears flying over our heads did little harm. Heavens! what a fight was that, the fight of fifty against six thousand.

Not more than seven feet of space divided us from that shrieking sea of foes into which we poured bullets at hazard, for there was no need to aim, as fast as the guns could be loaded. Suddenly I heard the girl call out:

" *Kek, tante, da is een swartzel!* " (Look, aunt, there is a black man.)

I looked, and just at my side I saw a great savage who had forced his way through the thorns and crawled beneath the waggon into the laager. The gun in my hand was empty, but by me lay an axe which I snatched up, and as he rose to his knees I struck him with all my strength upon the neck and killed him at a blow. Yes, my child, that was the kind of work to which we wives of the voortrekkers had to put a needle.

Jan had just fired his gun, and seeing the man he sprang to help me, whereon three more Kaffirs following on the dead soldier's path crawled out from under the waggon. Two of them gained their feet and ran at him lifting their assegais. I thought that all was lost, for one hole in our defence was like a pin prick to a bladder, but with a shout Jan dropped the empty gun and rushed to meet them. He caught them by the throat, the two of them, one in each of his great hands, and before they could spear him dashed their heads together with such desperate strength that they fell down and never stirred again. This was always thought something of a feat, for as everybody knows the skulls of Kaffirs are thick.

By this time the girl had handed Ralph his second gun loaded, and with it he shot the third Kaffir; then he also did a brave thing, for seeing that more Zulus were beginning to creep through the hole, he snatched the assegai from a dead man's hand, and stopped the gap with his own body, lying flat upon his stomach and thrusting at their heads with the spear. Soon we dragged him out with only one slight wound, pushing the bodies of the Kaffirs into his place, and over them spare branches of thorn, so that the breach was made good.

This was the turning point of the fight, for though after it one other Kaffir managed to get into the laager, where he was cut down, and two Boers, Nicholas Potgieter and Pieter Botha were killed by assegais thrown from without, from that moment the attack began to slacken. In thirty minutes from the time that Celliers had fired the first shot, Moselikatse's general, whose name was Kalipi, had given the order to retire, and his hosts drew off sullenly, for we had beaten them.

Thirty minutes! Only thirty minutes—the shadows had shifted but a few inches on the grass, and yet now that it was done with it seemed like half a lifetime. Panting and begrimed with smoke and powder, we stood looking at each other and around us. The tents of the waggons were ripped to pieces, in our own I counted more than sixty spear cuts, and the trampled turf inside the laager was like the back of an angry porcupine, for from it we gathered nearly fourteen hundred heavy assegais. For the rest, the two men lay dead where they had fallen, their faces turned towards the sky, each of them pierced through by a spear, and out of our little number twelve others were wounded, though none of them died of their wounds. Not a woman or a child was touched.

Outside the laager there was a sight to see, for there on the red grass, some lying singly and some in heaps, were over four hundred Zulu soldiers, most of them dead, and how many wounded they carried away with them I cannot tell.

Now we saw that the Kaffirs were collecting our cattle, and about twenty men under Potgieter saddled up and rode out to try and recapture them, since without oxen to draw the waggons we were helpless. Till sunset they followed them, killing many, but being so few they could not recapture the cattle, and in the end were obliged to return empty handed. Ralph went with his party, and, because of an act of mercy which he did then it came about in the end that Suzanne was found and many lives were saved.

So plenteously do our good deeds bear fruit, even in this world.

Yes, you may have thought that this tale of the battle of Vetchkop was only put in here because it is one of the great experiences of an old woman's life. But it is not so; it has all to do with the story of Ralph and of my daughter Suzanne,

CHAPTER XXVI

HOW GAASHA BROUGHT GOOD LUCK

WHEN Ralph returned from pursuing the Zulus, as he drew near to the laager he lingered a little behind the others, for he was very weary of all this work of killing, also the flesh-wound that he had got from the Kaffir's spear having stiffened pained him when his horse cantered. There was no more danger now, for the savages were gone, leaving their path marked by the corpses of those who had been shot down by the Boers, or of men who had limped away wounded either to die upon the road or to be killed by their comrades because their case was hopeless. Following this black trail of death backwards Ralph rode on, and when he was within a hundred yards of the waggons halted his horse to study the scene. He thought that he would never see such another, although, in fact, that at the Blood River when we conquered the Zulu king, Dingaan, was even more strange and terrible.

The last crimson rays of the setting sun were flooding the plain with light. Blood-red they shone upon the spear-torn canvas of the waggons and upon the stained and trampled veldt. Even the bodies of the Kaffirs looked red as they lay in every shape and attitude; some as though they slept; some with outstretched arms and spears gripped tight; some with open mouths as they had died shouting

their war-cry. Ralph looked at them and was thankful
that it was not we white people who lay thus, as it might
well have been. Then, just as he was turning towards the
laager, he thought that he saw something move in a tussock
of thick grass, and rode towards it. Behind the tussock
lay the body of a young Kaffir, not an uncommon sight
just there, but Ralph was so sure that he had seen it move
that, stirred by an idle curiosity, he dismounted from his
horse to examine it. This he did carefully, but the only
hurt that he could see was a flesh wound caused by a slug
upon the foot, not serious in any way, but such as might
very well prevent a man from running.

"This fellow is shamming dead," he thought to himself,
and lifted his gun, for in those times we could not afford
to nurse sick Kaffirs.

Then of a sudden the young man who had seemed to be a
corpse rose to his knees, and, clasping his hands, began to
beg for mercy. Instead of shooting him at once, as most
Boers would have done, Ralph, who was tender-hearted,
hesitated and listened while the Kaffir, a pleasant-faced
lad and young, besought him for his life.

"Why should I spare you," asked Ralph, who understood his talk well, "seeing that, like all the rest of these,
you set upon my people to murder them?"

"Nay, chief," answered the young man, "it is not so.
I am no Zulu. I belong to another tribe, and was but a
slave and a carrier in the army of Kalipi, for I was taken
prisoner and forced to carry mats and food and water,"
and he pointed to a bundle and some gourds that lay beside
him.

"It may be so," answered Ralph, "but the dog shares
his master's fate."

"Chief," pleaded the man, "spare me. Although it

prevented me from running away with the others, my wound is very slight and will be healed in a day or two, and then I will serve you as your slave and be faithful to you all my life. Spare me and I shall bring you good luck."

" I need that enough," said Ralph, " and I am sure that you are no Zulu, for a Zulu would not stoop to beg for his life thus," and he stood thinking.

While he thought, Jan, who had seen him from the laager, came up behind.

" What are you doing, son," he asked in an angry voice, " talking to this black devil here alone among the dead? Stand aside and let me settle him if you have not the heart," and he lifted his gun.

" No, father," said Ralph, pushing it aside, " this man is not a Zulu; he is but a slave-carrier and he has prayed me to spare his life, swearing that he will serve me faithfully. Also he says that he brings good luck."

" Certainly he brought good luck to these," answered Jan, pointing to the scattered dead with his hand, and laughing grimly. " Allemachter! scn, you must be mad to play the fool thus, for doubtless the sneaking villain will murder you the first time your back is turned. Come, stand aside and I will finish it."

Now the young man, whose name was Gaasha, seeing that he was about to be shot, threw himself upon the ground, and clasping Ralph round the knees, implored for mercy.

" Save me, Baas," he prayed, " save me, and you will always be glad of it, for I tell you I bring you good luck, I tell you I bring you good luck."

" Father," said Ralph, setting his mouth, " if you kill this Kaffir it will be a cause of quarrel between us, and we never quarrelled yet."

"Quarrel or no quarrel, he shall die," said Jan in a rage, for he thought it the strangest folly that Ralph should wish to spare a black man.

At that moment, however, something seemed to strike his mind, for his face grew puzzled, and he looked about him almost anxiously.

"Where have I seen it before?" he said, as though he were speaking to himself. "The veldt all red with blood and sunset, the laager behind and the Kaffir with the wounded foot holding Ralph by the knees. Allemachter! I know. It was that day in the *sit-kammer* * at the stead yonder, when the little doctoress, Sihamba, made me look into her eyes; yes, yes, I have seen it all in the eyes of Sihamba. Well, let the lad live, for without a doubt Sihamba did not show me this picture that should be for nothing. Moreover, although I am stupid, as your mother says, I have learned that there are many things in the world which we cannot understand but which play a part in our lives nevertheless."

So the lad Gaasha was brought to the laager, and upon the prayer of Jan and Ralph, the commandant gave him his life, ordering, however, that he should sleep outside the waggons.

"Well," I said when I heard the tale, "one thing is, that you will never see him again, for he will be off during the night back to his friends the Zulus." But I was wrong, for next morning there was Gaasha, and there he remained even after his foot was quite well, making the best Kaffir servant that ever I had to do with.

After that day we saw no more of the Zulus at Vetchkop, although later with the help of other Boers we attacked them twice, killing more than four thousand of them, and

* Sitting room.

capturing six thousand head of cattle, so that they fled
north for good and all, and founded the nation of the
Matabele far away.

But oh! our fate was hard there at Vetchkop; never have
I known worse days. The Zulus had taken away all our
cattle, so that we could not even shift the waggons from
the scene of the fight, but must camp there amidst the
vultures and the mouldering skeletons, for the dead were
so many that it was impossible to bury them all. We sent
messengers to other parties of Boers for help, and while
they were gone we starved, for there was no food to eat,
and game was very scarce. Yes, it was a piteous sight to
see the children cry for food and gnaw old bits of leather
or strips of hide cut from Kaffir shields to stay the craving
of their stomachs. Some of them died of that hunger,
and I grew so thin that when I chanced to see myself in a
pool of water where I went to wash I started back
frightened.

At length, when we were all nearly dead, some oxen
came and with them we dragged a few of the waggons to
Moroko, where an English clergyman and his wife, taking
pity on us, gave us corn, for which reason I have always
held that among the British the clergymen must be a great
deal better than the rest of that proud and worthless race,
for it is true that we judge of people as they deal by us.
Yes, and I will go so far as to say that I do not believe
that the Reverend Mr. Owen, the English missionary at the
kraal of the Zulu King Dingaan, did in truth advise him
to massacre Retief and his seventy Boers, as was generally
reported among my countrymen.

Well, after Moselikatse's Zulus were finally defeated the
question arose whether we should proceed to Zoutpansberg
and settle there, or follow our brethren who in large num-

bers had already crossed the Quathlamba Mountains into Natal under the leadership of Retief. In the end we decided for Natal because it was nearer the sea, for in those days we never dreamed that the treacherous British Government would steal that land also; so trekking slowly, we headed for Van Reenen's Pass, our party then numbering thirty waggons and about sixty white people.

It was when we were about four days trek, or sixty miles, from the pass that one evening, as we sat eating our food, Jan, Ralph, and I—I remember it was the fried steaks of an eland that Ralph had shot—the lad Gaasha, who had now served us for some six months, came up to the fire, and having saluted Ralph, squatted down before him Kaffir fashion, saying that he had a favour to ask.

" Speak on," said Ralph. " What is it? "

" Baas," replied Gaasha, " it is this; I want a week or ten days leave of absence to visit my people."

" You mean that you want to desert," I put in.

"No, lady," answered Gaasha; "you know that I love the Baas who saved my life far too well ever to wish to leave him. I desire only to see my parents and to tell them that I am happy, for doubtless they think me dead. The Baas proposes to cross into Natal by Van Reenen's Pass, does he not? Well, not so very far from my home, although none would guess it unless he knew the way, is another pass called Oliver's Hook, and by that pass, after I have spoken with my father and my mother if they still live, I would cross the Quathlamba, finding the Baas again on the further side of the mountains, as I can easily do."

" I think that I will let you go as I can trust you, Gaasha," said Ralph, " but tell me the name of your home, that I may know where to send to seek you if you should not come back as you promise."

"Have I not said that I will come back, Baas, unless the lions or the Zulus should eat me on the way? But the name of the house of my tribe is Umpondwana. It is only a little tribe, for the Zulus killed many of us in the time of Chaka, but their house is a very fine house."

"What does Umpondwana mean?" asked Ralph idly as he lit his pipe.

"It means the Mountain of the Man's Hand, Baas."

Ralph let his pipe fall on the ground, and I saw his face turn white beneath the sunburn, while of a sudden his grey eyes looked as though they were about to leap from their sockets.

"Why is it called the Mountain of the Man's Hand?" he asked in a hollow voice. "Speak quick now, and do not lie to me."

Gaasha looked up at him astonished. "How should I know, Baas, when the place was named so before I was born, and none have told me? But I think that it may be because upon one of the slopes of the mountain, which has great cliffs of red rock, are five ridges, which, seen from the plain below, look like the four fingers and the thumb of a man. Also the place has another name, which means 'where the water springs out of the rock,' because from between two of the ridges, those that are like the thumb and first finger, flows a stream which comes from the heart of the mountain."

"On which side of the mountain are the ridges and the stream?" asked Ralph in the same unnatural voice.

"Baas, when the sun rises it strikes on them."

Now Ralph swung to and fro like a drunken man, and had I not put my arm about him I believe that he would have fallen.

"It is the mountain of my vision," he gasped.

"Be not foolish," I answered, for I feared lest when he found that all this strange resemblance was a chance, the bitterness of his disappointment might overwhelm him. "Be not foolish, son; are there not many hills in this great land with ridges on their flanks, and streams of water running down them?"

Then, as Ralph seemed unable to answer me, I asked of Gaasha:

"Who is the chief of this tribe of yours?"

"He is named Koraanu," he answered, "if he still lives, but a man I met some months ago told me that he has been dead these two years, and that she who used to rule us when I was a little child had come back from the lands whither she had wandered, and is now *Inkoosikaas* of the Umpondwana."

"What is the name of this chieftainess?" I asked in the midst of a great silence.

Gaasha answered at once; that is, after he had taken a pinch of snuff, but to us it seemed a year before the words crossed his lips.

"Her name, lady," and he sneezed, "is"—and he sneezed again, rocking himself to and fro. Then slowly wiping away the tears which the snuff had brought to his eyes with the back of his hand he said, "Ow! this is the best of snuff, and I thank the Baas for giving it to me."

"Answer," roared Jan, speaking for the first time, and in such a fierce voice that Gaasha sprang to his feet and began to run away.

"Come back, Gaasha, come back," I called, and he came doubtfully, for Gaasha was not very brave, and ever since he had wished to shoot him he trembled even at the sight of Jan. "Be silent, you fool," I whispered to the latter as the lad drew near, then said aloud, "Now, Gaasha."

"Lady," he answered, "it is indeed as I have told you; the Baas gave me the snuff a long time ago; he took it out of the ear-boxes of the dead men at Vetchkop. He gave it to me. I did not steal it. He will say so himself."

"Never mind the snuff, Gaasha," I said in a voice half-choked with doubt and anxiety, for the sight of Ralph's piteous face and the strangeness of it all were fast overwhelming me, "but tell us what is the name of this chieftainess whom you have heard is now the ruler of your tribe?"

"Her name, lady," he answered, much relieved, "why it is well known, for though she is small, it is said that she is the best of doctoresses and rain-makers."

Now Jan could no longer be restrained, for stretching out his great hand he gripped Gaasha by the throat, saying:

"Accursed *swartzel*, if you do not tell us the name at once I will kill you."

"Madman," I exclaimed, "how can the lad speak while you are choking him?"

Then Jan shifted his grip and Gaasha began to cry for pity.

"The name, the name," said Jan.

"Why should I hide it? Have I not told it? Baas, it is *Sihamba Ngenyanga*."

As the words passed his lips Jan let go of him so suddenly that Gaasha fell to the ground and sat there staring at us, for without doubt he thought that we had all gone mad.

Jan looked up to the skies and said, "Almighty, I thank Thee, Who canst make dreams to fly to the heart of a man as a night-bird to its nest through the darkness, and Who, because of what I saw in the eyes of Sihamba, didst turn aside my gun when it was pointed at the breast of this Kaffir."

Then he looked at Ralph, and was quiet, for Ralph had swooned away.

CHAPTER XXVII

IT was a strange life that Suzanne led among the Umpondwana during the two years or more that, together with Sihamba, she ruled over them as chieftainess. Upon the top of the mountain was a space of grass land measuring about five hundred morgen, or a thousand acres in extent, where were placed the chief's huts and those of the head men and soldiers, surrounding a large cattle kraal, which, however, was only used in times of danger. The rest of the people dwelt upon the slopes of the mountain, and even on the rich plains at the foot of it, but if need were they could all retreat to the table-land upon its crest. Here they might have defied attack for ever, for beneath the cattle kraal grain was stored in pits, only there was but one spring, which in dry seasons was apt to fail. Therefore it was that the Umpondwana had built stone schanzes or fortifications about the mouth of the river which gushed from the mountain between the thumb and finger like ridges on the eastern slope, although it lay below their impregnable walls of rock, seeing that to this river they must look for their main supply of water.

The table-top of the hill, which could only be approached by one path that wound upwards through a ravine cut by water, being swept by every wind of heaven, and so high in the air, was very cold and naked. Indeed, in the winter season, rain fell there twice or thrice a week, and there were many days when it was wrapt in a dense white mist. Still, during the two years and more that she dwelt with the Umpondwana, Suzanne scarcely left this plain, not because she did not desire to do so, but because she did not dare, for word was brought that the foot, and even the slopes, of the mountain were patrolled by men in the employ of Swart Piet. Moreover, soon it became clear that he had knowledge of all her movements, doubtless from spies in his pay who dwelt among the Umpondwana themselves. During the first few months of her sojourn on the mountain, it is true that now and again Suzanne rode out on to the veldt mounted on the *schimmel*, but this pastime she was forced to abandon because one day Swart Piet and his men saw her and gave chase, so that she was only saved from him by the fleetness of the great horse.

After this, both she and the *schimmel* stayed upon the table-land, where daily they took exercise together, galloping round a prepared path which was laid about the fence of the cattle kraal, and thus kept themselves in good health.

Swart Piet had Kaffir blood in his veins, as I have said, and from boyhood it had been his custom to live two lives, one as a white man with white men, and one as a Kaffir with Kaffirs. About three miles distant from the Umpondwana Mountain was a strong koppie with fertile valleys to the back of it, and here, being rich and having a great name as a white man, he found it no trouble to establish himself as a native chief, for refugees of all sorts gathered themselves about him, so that within a year he ruled over a little tribe of about a hundred men together with women.

With these men Van Vooren began to harass the Umpondwana, cutting off their cattle if they strayed, and from
time to time killing or enslaving small parties of them
whom he caught wandering on the plains out of reach
of help from the mountain. Whenever he captured such
a party he would spare one of them, sending him back
with a message to the Umpondwana. They were all to one
effect, namely, that if the tribe would deliver over to him
the lady Swallow who dwelt among them he would cease
from troubling it, but if this were not done, then he would
wage war on it day and night until in this way or in that
he compassed its destruction.

To these messages Sihamba would reply as occasion
offered, that if he wanted anything from the Umpondwana
he had better come and take it.

So things went on for a long while. Swart Piet's men did
them no great harm indeed, but they harassed them continually, until the people of the Umpondwana began to murmur, for they could scarcely stir beyond the slopes of the
mountain without being set upon. Happily for them these
slopes were wide, for otherwise they could not have found
pasturage for their cattle or land upon which to grow their
corn. So close a watch was kept upon them, indeed, that
they could neither travel to visit other tribes, nor could
these come to them, and thus it came about that Suzanne
was as utterly cut off from the rest of the world as though
she had been dead. She had but one hope to keep her
heart alive, and it was that Ralph and Jan would learn of
her fate through native rumours and be able to find her
out. Still, as she knew that this could not be counted
on, she tried to let us have tidings of her, for when she had
been only a week on the mountain Umpondwana she despatched Zinti and two men to bear him company, with

orders to travel back over all the hundreds of miles of veldt to the far-off stead in the Transkei.

As she had neither pen nor ink, nor anything with which she could write, Suzanne was obliged to trust a long message to Zinti's memory, making him repeat it to her until she was sure that he had it by heart. In this message she told all that had befallen her, and prayed us to take Zinti for a guide and to come to her rescue, since she did not dare to set foot outside the walls of rock, for fear that she should be captured by Van Vooren, who watched for her continually.

Zinti, being brave and faithful, started upon his errand, though it was one from which many would have shrunk. But as ill-luck would have it, one night when they were camped near the kraal of a small Basuto tribe, his companions becoming hungry, stole a goat and killed it. Zinti ate of the goat, for they told him that they had bought it for some beads, and while they were still eating the Basutos came upon them and caught them red-handed. Next day they were tried by the councillors of the tribe and condemned to die as thieves, but the chief, who wanted servants, spared their lives and set them to labour in his gardens, where they were watched day and night.

Zinti was a prisoner among these Basutos for nearly a year, but at length he made his escape, leaving his two companions behind, for they were afraid lest if they ran away with him they should be recaptured and killed. As soon as he was free Zinti continued his journey, for he was a man not easily turned from his purpose, nor because it was now over a year old did he cease from his attempt to deliver the message that had been set in his mouth.

Well, after many dangers, footsore and worn-out with travelling, at length he reached the stead, to find that we had all gone, none knew whither, and that the long-nosed cheat to whom we had sold the farm ruled in our place. Zinti sought out some Kaffirs who lived upon the land, and abode with them awhile till he was rested and strong again. Then once more he turned his face northward towards the mountain Umpondwana, for though he greatly feared the journey, he knew that the heart of Suzanne would be sick for news. War raged in the country that he must pass, and food was scarce; still at length he won through, although at the last he was nearly captured by Black Piet's thieves, and one year and nine months after he had left it, a worn and weary figure, he limped up the red rock path of Umpondwana.

Suzanne had been watching for him. It seems strange to say it, but after six months had gone by, which time at the best must be given to his journey, she watched for him every day. On the top of the highest and most precipitous cliff of the mountain fortress of Umpondwana was a little knoll of rock curiously hollowed out to the shape of a chair, difficult to gain and dizzy to sit in, for beneath it was a sheer fall of five hundred feet, which chair-rock commanded the plain southward, and the pass where Van Vooren had spoken to Suzanne from his hiding-place among the stones. By this pass and across this plain help must reach her if it came at all, or so she thought; therefore in that eagle's eyrie of a seat Suzanne sat day by day watching ever for those who did not come. A strange sight she must have been, for now long ago such garments as she had were worn to rags, so that she was forced to clothe herself in beautiful skins fashioned to her fancy, and to go sandal-footed, her lovely rippling hair hanging about her.

At length one day from her lonely point of outlook she

saw a solitary man limping across the plain, a mere black speck dragging itself forward like a wounded fly upon a wall. Descending from her seat she sought out Sihamba.

"Swallow," said the little woman, "there is tidings in your eyes. What is it?"

"Zinti returns," she answered, "I have seen him from far away."

Now Sihamba smiled, for she thought Zinti lost; also she did not believe it possible that Suzanne could have recognised him from such a distance. Still before two hours were over Zinti came, gaunt and footsore, but healthy and unharmed, and sitting down before Suzanne in her private enclosure, began at the very beginning of his long story, after the native fashion, telling of those things which had befallen him upon the day when he left the mountain nearly two years before.

"Your news? Your news?" said Suzanne.

"Lady, I am telling it," he answered.

"Fool!" exclaimed Sihamba. "Say now, did you find the Baas Kenzie and the Baas Botmar?"

"No, indeed," he replied, "for they were gone."

"Gone where? Were they alive and well?"

"Yes, yes, they were alive and well, but all the Boers in those parts have trekked, and they trekked also, believing the lady Swallow to be dead."

"This is a bitter cup to drink," murmured Suzanne, "yet there is some sweetness in it, for at least my husband lives."

Then Zinti set out all his story, and Suzanne listened to it in silence, praising him much and thanking him when he had done. But after that day her heart failed her, and she seemed to give up hope. Ralph had vanished, and we, her parents, had vanished, and she was left alone a prisoner among a little Kaffir tribe, at the foot of whose stronghold her bitter enemy waited to destroy her. Never was white woman in a more dreadful or more solitary state, and had it not been for Sihamba's tender friendship she felt that she must have died.

Now also Swart Piet grew bolder, appearing even on the slopes of the mountain where his men harried and stole. He did more than this even, for one morning just before dawn he attacked the pass leading to the stronghold so secretly and with such skill that his force was halfway up it before the sentries discovered them. Then they were seen, and the war-horns blew, and there followed a great fight. Indeed, had it not been for a lucky chance, it is doubtful how that fight would have ended, for his on-slaught was fierce, and the Umpondwana, who at the best were not the bravest of warriors, were taken by surprise.

It will be remembered that Zinti had brought Ralph's gun with him when first they fled north, and this gun he still had, together with a little powder and ball, for, fearing lest it should be stolen from him, he had not taken it on his great journey to the Transkei and back. Now, hearing the tumult, he ran out with it, and fired point blank at the stormers, who were pushing their way up the narrow path, driving the Umpondwana before them. The *roer* was loaded with slugs, which, scattering, killed three men; moreover, by good fortune, one of the slugs struck Van Vooren himself through the fleshy part of the thigh, caus-ing him to fall, whereon, thinking him mortally wounded, in spite of his curses and commands, his followers lost heart and fled, bearing him with them. Sihamba called upon her people to follow, but they would not, for they feared to meet Swart Piet in the open.

In truth they began to weary of this constant war, which

was brought upon them through no fault or quarrel of
their own, and to ask where was that good luck which the
White Swallow had promised them. Had it not been
that they loved Suzanne for her beauty and her gentle
ways, and that Sihamba, by her cleverness and good rule,
had mastered their minds, there is little doubt indeed but
that they would have asked Suzanne to depart from among
them.

On the day following the attack Sihamba learned that
Swart Piet lay very sick, having lost much blood, and
sought to persuade her people to attack him in turn, and
make an end of him and his robbers. But they would
not, and so the council broke up, but not before Sihamba
had spoken bitter words, telling them that they were
cowards, and would meet the end of cowards, whereat they
went away sullenly. Afterwards they learned through
their spies that Van Vooren had gone to Zululand to visit
the King Dingaan, which Sihamba thought evil tidings,
for she scented fresh danger in this journey, and not without reason. But to Suzanne she said nothing.

Two more months went by peacefully, when one morning a herd who was tending the cattle that belonged to
Suzanne and Sihamba, sought audience of the chieftainess.

" What is it? " asked Sihamba, for she saw by the man's
face that something strange had happened.

" This, lady," he answered. " When I went down to
the kloof at dawn, where your cattle and those of the Lady
Swallow are kraaled, I found among them strange oxen
to the number of more than a hundred. They are beautiful oxen, such as I have never seen, for every one of them
is pure white—white from the muzzle to the tail, and I
cannot understand how they came among your cattle, for

the mouth of the kraal was closed as usual last night; moreover, I found it closed this morning."

When Sihamba heard this she turned cold to the heart, for she knew well that these spotless white cattle must come from the royal herd of Dingaan, king of the Zulus, since none other were known like them in all the land. Also she was sure that Swart Piet had stolen them and placed them among her cattle so as to bring down upon her and her tribe the terrible wrath of Dingaan, for she remembered that this mingling of cattle was a trick which he had played before. But to the herd she said only that doubtless they were cattle which had strayed, and that she would make enquiry as to their owner. Then she dismissed him, bidding him to keep a better watch in future.

Scarcely had he gone when another man appeared saying that he had met a Kaffir from beyond the mountains, who told him that a party of white men with women and children had crossed the Quathlamba range by what is now known as Bezuidenhout's Pass, and were camped near the Tugela River. This was strange news to Sihamba, who had heard nothing of the whereabouts of the Trek Boers, so strange that she would not speak of it to Suzanne, fearing lest it should fill her with false hopes. But she sent for Zinti, and bade him cross the Quathlamba by a little-used pass that was known to her near to the place where the Tugela takes its rise, and which to-day is called Mont aux Sources, and following the river down, to find out whether or no it was true that white men were encamped upon its banks. When he had done this he was to return as swiftly as possible with whatever information he could gather.

This task Zinti undertook gladly, for he loved following a spoor, which was a gift that Nature had given him; also he was weary of being cooped up like a fatting fowl upon the mountain Umpondwana.

When Zinti had gone Sihamba summoned other messengers, and commanded them to travel swiftly to the kraal Umgungundlhovo, bearing her homage to Dingaan, king of the Amazulus, and asking whether he had lost any of the cattle from his royal herds, since certain white oxen had been found among her beasts, though how they came there she could not tell. These men went also, though in fear and trembling, since in those days none loved to approach the Lion of the Zulu with tales of cattle of his that had strayed among their herd. Still they went, and with doubt in her heart Sihamba sat awaiting their return.

CHAPTER XXVIII

SIHAMBA had not very long to wait, for on the evening of the fifth day from the starting of the messengers they came back at great speed, having run so fast that they could scarcely speak for want of breath, and telling her that a Zulu impi, numbering more than three thousand spears, was advancing upon the Umpondwana to destroy them. It seemed that long before the king's oxen had been found mixed with her herd it had been reported to Dingaan that Sihamba had stolen them, which was not altogether strange, seeing that Swart Piet travelled with the impi. As she suspected, he had caused the oxen to be stolen, and now he had fixed the deed upon her, knowing well that Dingaan only sought a pretext to destroy her tribe, with which the Zulus had an ancient quarrel.

Now there was but one thing to be done—to make ready their defence, so, without more ado, Sihamba summoned her council and told them that a Zulu impi was at hand to eat them up because of the white cattle that had been placed among their herds. Then the councillors wrung their hands, and some of them shed tears even, although they were aged men, for the name of the Zulus struck terror to their hearts, and they expected nothing less than death for themselves, their wives, and their children.

"It is best that we should fly while there is yet time," said the captain of the council.

"There is no time," answered Sihamba; "the impi will be here by dawn and will cut you up upon the plain."

"What then shall we do?" they asked; "we who are already dead."

"Do?" she cried. "You shall fight as your fathers fought before you, and beat back these dogs of Dingaan. If you will but be brave, what have you to fear from them? You have water, you have food, you have spears, and even the Zulus have not wings like eagles with which to fly over your walls of cliff. Let them come, and if you will but obey me, I promise you that they shall return again to make report to the 'Elephant' many fewer than they left his kraal."

So the Umpondwana made ready to fight, not because they loved it, but because they must, for they knew that no humbleness would help them in face of the spears of Dingaan. The cattle were driven into the centre kraal, and great supplies of grass and green corn were cut to feed them. Except for one manhole the pass leading to the top of the mountain was closed, and the schanzes, or walls, which protected the mouth of the river that welled from the hillside between the eastern ridges were strengthened and garrisoned. Here, as Sihamba knew, was their weak place, for this river flowed out beneath the impregnable precipices of rock, and to it they must look for their main supply of water, since, although the spring upon the table-land, if husbanded, would suffice for a supply to the tribe, it was not sufficient for the cattle. It was for this reason that Sihamba wished to turn the kine loose and let the Zulus capture them if they would, for she knew that then they could never take the mountain or harm a hair of the head of one of its inhabitants. But the Umpondwana were greedy, and would not consent to the loss of their cattle, forgetting that cattle are of no value to dead men. They said that they could very well defend the schanzes which surrounded the source of the river, and that from it sufficient water could be carried to keep the beasts alive, even if the siege were long

"As you will," answered Sihamba shortly, "but see that you do defend them when the Zulu warriors leap upon the walls, for if you fail then you will lose cattle and life together."

All this time, according to her daily custom, Suzanne had been seated in her chair of rock upon the highest point of the precipice looking for that help which never came. Presently, as she watched with sad eyes, far away upon the plain she saw a cloud of dust in which moved and shone the sheen of spears. Now she climbed down from her seat, and ran to seek Sihamba, whom she found surrounded by her councillors.

"What is it, Swallow?" asked the little chieftainess looking up, though already she had guessed the answer.

Suzanne told her, adding, "Who can it be that travels towards the mountain with so great a force?"

"Lady Swallow," said Sihamba gravely, "it is an army of the Zulus sent by Dingaan to destroy us, and with them marches Bull-Head." And she told her of the trick of the cattle and of what the messengers had seen.

Suzanne heard, and her face grew white as the goatskin cloak she wore.

"Then at last the long story is at an end," she faltered, for she knew the terrible prowess of the Zulus, and how none could stand before their onslaught.

"Yes, of that impi there is an end," answered Sihamba

proudly, " if these children of mine will but take heart and fight as their fathers fought. Fear not, Lady Swallow, nothing that has not wings can storm the mountain of Umpondwana."

But for all that she could say Suzanne still felt much afraid, which was not strange, for she knew that the heart was out of these soldiers of Sihamba, and knew, moreover, that a Zulu army did not dare to be defeated, for which reason it must either take the mountain or fight till it was destroyed.

Now all was confusion; the horns blew and women wailed, while the captains of the Umpondwana issued their commands, and the men piled up stones upon the brink of the precipice to roll down upon the foe, and drove the herds of cattle into the great kraal upon the table-land.

Marching quickly, the impi drew near and the defenders could see that it numbered about four thousand spears and was composed of two separate regiments. At a distance of a mile it halted and throwing out horns or wings surrounded the mountain, up the slopes of which it advanced in a thin circle, much as beaters do who are driving game to a certain point. As the circle drew near to the cliffs it thickened, having less ground to cover, though still there was a gap here and there.

Presently those who were watching saw a man dart through one of these gaps and run up hill at great speed, followed by Zulu soldiers, who tried to kill him. But he was the swifter of foot, moreover he knew the path, so that before they could come up with him he reached the great stone walls which were built about the source of the river, and was dragged over them by the defenders.

A while later this man appeared upon the top of the

mountain and proved to be none other than Zinti, who had returned from his errand, and, having news to tell, risked his life to pass through the impi before the stronghold was altogether surrounded. Sihamba received him at once, Suzanne standing at her side, and bade him be brief for she had little time to listen to long stories.

"I will be brief," Zinti answered. "Lady, as you bade me I crossed the mountains by the road of which you told me. It is a good road for men on foot or horseback, but waggons could not travel it. Having reached the plain on the further side I followed the bank of the river, till suddenly I came in sight of thirty waggons drawn up in a laager upon a knoll of ground, and among the waggons I saw Boers with their wives and children. I tried to go up to speak to them, but a young Boer, seeing me, shot at me with his gun, so I thought it safer to lie hid. At nightfall, however, I met the driver of one of the waggons, a Kaffir man, at some distance from the laager, where he was watching by a pit made to catch bucks, and fell into talk with him. He told me that this was a party of the Boers who had trekked from Cape Colony, and were taking possession of Natal, and that there were other such parties scattered about the country. He said that in this party there were five-and-twenty men with women and children, but he did not know the names of any of them. Also he told me that he meant to run away, as he heard that Dingaan was going to attack the white people, and was sure that if he did so they would be eaten up, for these Boers, thinking themselves quite safe, had grown very careless, and neither made their laager as strong as it should be nor set any watch at night. Having learned this I returned at once to make report to you, nor did I come too quickly, for the Zulus nearly caught me as I passed their ranks. I saw Bull-Head as I ran, he is riding a brown horse, and seems quite recovered from his wound."

"How far is the Boer laager from this place?" asked Sihamba before Suzanne could speak.

"Lady, a man on a good horse could reach it in seven hours, nor is it possible to mistake the way. After crossing the plain you enter the gorge by the saw-edged rock yonder, and follow its windings across the mountains till you come out the other side, where the river runs down to the flat country. Then you can keep along the bank of the river as I did when I went, or if you wish to go more quickly you must head for a large white-topped hill, or koppie, which can be seen from the mountains, and when you come to it you will find the Boer laager upon the knoll at its foot, but near to the banks of the river, which winds round it."

"Oh! let us go; let us go quickly," said Suzanne springing to her feet, for the thought even of seeing a white man again made her drunk with hope.

"Alas! sister," answered Sihamba sadly, "an hour ago we might have gone, or rather you might have gone, mounted on the great *schimmel*, but now—look," and she pointed to where the Zulus clustered like bees along the banks of the river by which the path ran. "See," she added, "there is but one road out of this stronghold, for nowhere else can the surest-footed climber in the world descend its cliffs, no, not with a rope to help him, and that road is thick with Zulu spears; moreover, a certain man whom you do not wish to see waits for you upon it."

Suzanne looked. "Too late," she moaned "Oh! surely my God has forsaken me! Within six hours of safety and doomed to perish here, oh! surely my God has

forsaken me!" and she burst out weeping in the bitterness
of her disappointed hope.

"Say not so," answered Sihamba gently, "for I think
that the Great One whom you worship will save you yet."

As she spoke a messenger arrived saying that the Zulus
had sent forward heralds who desired to speak with her,
and that these heralds waited within earshot of the first
wall.

"I will come," said Sihamba, and she passed down the
cleft and through the man hole into the fortifications
which were built about the source of the river. But she
would not allow Suzanne to accompany her.

When she reached the outer wall she climbed it and
stood upon it, for Sihamba was a woman who knew no fear,
and there, about forty paces away, she saw three great
Zulus standing, and with them him whom she dreaded
more than all the Zulus on the earth—Piet Van Vooren himself. When the Zulu captains caught sight of her upon
the wall, they jeered aloud and asked whether this was indeed Sihamba Ngenyanga, or if a she-monkey had been
sent to talk with them.

"I am Sihamba," she answered quietly, "or I am a
monkey, as it may please you, though the white man with
you can tell you what I am."

"I can," said Piet with a laugh. "You are a witch and
a thief, and the fate that I promised you long ago is with
you at last."

"Murderer," mocked Sihamba in answer, "I see Death
standing behind you, and with him shadows of the Fear to
come. But I would speak with these chiefs and not with
an outcast half-breed. Tell me, chiefs, why do you come
up against my stronghold with so great a force?"

"Because that 'Elephant whose tread shakes the earth,'

our master, Dingaan the king, has sent us," answered the
spokesman of the captains.

" Say, now, on what errand, chief? "

" On this errand; to take your stronghold and cattle, to
burn your kraal, and to kill your people, all of them save
the marriageable girls and such children as are old enough
to travel, who must be brought with the cattle to Dingaan.
But you yourself and the white woman who is called Swallow who rules with you are to be handed over to Bull-Head
here to do with as he will, for that is the bargain between
him and the king."

" And why are these things to come upon us who have
done no wrong? " asked Sihamba.

" Why, little woman! " answered the chief, " because you
have dared to steal cattle from the king's herd, even the
royal white cattle; yes, and they have been traced to your
mountain and seen among your oxen."

" It is true that the cattle are here," said Sihamba, " but
it is not true that we have stolen them, seeing that they
were lifted by the white man, Bull-Head, and mixed up
with our herds to bring us into trouble with the king."

" A fit tale for the king's ears," replied the captain,
laughing. " Why it was Bull-Head who told the king
of the theft; but let that pass. Dingaan the king is merciful, and he makes you this offer through my mouth: If
you will return the cattle together with all your own by
way of fine, and hand over your councillors and head men
to be killed, then he will grant the rest their lives. But
all the young men and the girls must come with me to pass
into the service of the king, the married women and the
children going where they will. Perhaps Bull-Head here
will take them with yourself and White Swallow. What is
your word, little chieftainess? "

" My word is that we will have none of such mercy.   It is better that we should die together, but I tell you, men of Dingaan, that these rocks will be white with your bones before ever you drive our cattle and maidens back to Dingaan."

" As you will, little chieftainess.   We captains of the Zulus have heard many such proud words in our time, but ah! where are those who spoke them?   Ask the jackals and the vultures, little chieftainess."

CHAPTER XXIX

WHEN Sihamba finished her talk with the captains of Dingaan the sun was already sinking. Still the Umpond-wana thought that the Zulus would attack at once, but these shouted to the defenders that they might rest easily till the dawn, since they wished to have daylight by which to divide the spoil. And at daylight the attack came. Driving the men of Bull-Head in front of them much against their will, for they knew these to be cowards, and wished to make mock of them, company by company the Zulus rushed at the stone wall, though many of them were killed and often they were driven back. But always they came on laughing and shouting their war-cry till the arms of the Umpondwana grew weary with stabbing at them as their plumed heads appeared above the level of the wall. Still, fighting under the eye of Sihamba, whose bitter tongue they feared, her people held their own, for indeed the place was almost impregnable to the attacks of men armed only with spears however brave they might be, and had it been defended by warriors of true Zulu blood it could never have been taken.

When the fight had raged for an hour or more the Zulu captains withdrew their men, and went apart to consult with Van Vooren, for their loss was heavy, and they saw

that if they were to capture the head waters of the river
they must seek some other plan. Very soon they found it.
The river issued from the side of the mountain not as a
little stream but as a broad fierce water. So deep and
rapid was it that the triple line of defence works of the
Umpondwana were built only to its edge, for the water
ran through a rocky gorge, although thorn trees fastened
by their trunks were thrust out for ten or twelve feet over
the banks of the gorge from either side of the stream.
Now, in the centre of this river, which may have been
thirty paces wide, ran a long ridge or saddle of rock over
which the water boiled furiously, although here it was not
more than three feet deep. This ridge began at a point
within the last line of walls and ran down to some five-and-
twenty paces below the first wall. Swart Piet had noted
the ridge.

"There is a saddle on which you may ride to victory,"
he said.

"How so, Bull-Head?" asked the captain.

"Thus. Yonder stand trees with tall stems and green
tops; cut them down and make a bridge from the bank to
the saddle; then wade up the saddle where the water is not
more than waist deep, till you are past the third wall and
reach the bank inside it as best you can."

Now although he was a brave man, as were all the Zulus
in those days, the captain looked long and doubtfully at
the white water which foamed upon the ridge.

"There is death in that water," he said.

"Death for some and victory for others," answered Van
Vooren, "but if you fear it, go back to Dingaan and tell
him so, for in no other way can this mountain be taken,
seeing that it is impregnable, and that thirst alone can conquer it."

" I fear nothing, white man," answered the Zulu, " but if you are so brave, why, show us black people the way along yonder ridge! "

Piet shrugged his shoulders. " I wish to keep alive for reasons of my own; besides, I am not a soldier of Dingaan," he answered.

Then the captain turned and commanded such men as had battle axes to cut down three of the longest trees, which they did, although the task was difficult, for the wood was hard and their axes were light. When at length the trees were down they rolled them uphill to a spot where the ridge of rock ended, which was not more than thirty paces from the face of the outer wall. Now it was that Sihamba guessed their purpose for the first time, for until then she had believed that they were cutting the trees to use them as battering rams against the walls.

" They are coming on us by the path of the river," she said, and called for men to sally out and prevent them making the bridge from the bank to the saddle. But none answered her, for they dared not face the Zulus in the open.

" The water will sweep them away," they said; " moreover, when they try to land we can spear them."

" Cowards," she moaned, " on your own heads be your doom."

So the Umpondwana contented themselves with standing behind the first wall and casting volleys of spears at those who thrust out the trees within thirty paces of them, while Zinti shot at them with his gun, killing several. But coming between, the Zulus made a shield hedge to protect their comrades, so that the light throwing assegais did little hurt, and of the few that the gun killed they thought nothing.

Presently the ends of the trees lay beneath the water on the ridge of rock, and the captain commanded a certain *induna* to lead his men across. Now all natives fear a wet death, and though he was a brave man who would gladly have rushed at the fortifications alone had he been so commanded, this soldier to whom the captain spoke looked askance at the furious torrent and hesitated. But that captain had served under Chaka, and knew how to deal with those who showed doubt or fear. Lifting his heavy assegai, he drove it through the man, so that he fell dead, and as he smote cried, " Coward, take this gift from the king! "

Then, calling to the soldiers, he himself ran out upon the bridge of tree-trunks and leaped into the water that rose to his middle. In an instant he would have been swept away, for the current was very fierce, had not those who followed sprung down at his side and behind him. For a moment they managed to keep their feet till others came, giving them support and being themselves protected by a breakwater built of the men who had gone first. Then, forming in a double line, each man linked his arms round the middle of his comrade in front, as Kaffir girls link themselves in a dance, and very slowly this human chain began to struggle forward along the back of the ridge. At times, indeed, the weight of the stream was almost too much for them, and swept some of them off into the deep water which ran on either side, but the strong rope of human muscles held, and they were dragged back again. Now they were between the lip of the first walls, and the Umpondwana soldiers hurled spears at them from the banks, killing many. But if a man was slain, or even badly wounded, his companion who held him let go, and, if needful, thrust him into the water, who could no longer serve the king. Then he gripped the soldier who stood in front of the lost one, and the chain dragged on.

"Oh! men of the Umpondwana," cried Sihamba, "had you but half the heart of these, who are brave, we need fear nothing from Dingaan," and the Zulus in the stream who heard her called in answer:—

"You are right, little chieftainess, we are brave."

Slowly the black snake-like line pressed forward through the white foam, never heeding the storm of spears that slew continually, till the point of it was well within the third line of walls. Then the captain, who by some chance had escaped, called an order to those behind him, and the head of the double line leapt off the ridge of rock into deep water, and swimming with their feet, but still gripping with their hands, suffered themselves to be swung round by the current towards the bank, twenty yards away. Here some rocks jutted out, and these, after a great struggle, they were able to grasp and hold.

Then followed what Suzanne, who was watching from above, afterwards declared to be the strangest sight she had ever seen, for these men, who swung to and fro in the current, anchored, as it were, to the ridge and the bank, made of their living bodies a bridge for their fellows. Yes, their companions ran and crawled over them, springing from shoulder to shoulder, and driving their heads beneath the water with the push of their clinging feet. Half-drowned and almost torn in two as they were, still they held on till enough men were safe on shore to finish the fray. For when the Umpondwana saw that the Zulus had won the bank they did not stay to kill them while they landed, as might easily have been done; no, dragging Sihamba with them, they ran into the gorge leading to the flat top of the mountain, and blocked it with great stones

that were ready. And so it came about that the Zulus won
this fight, though with great loss to themselves, and cut
off the Umpondwana from their main supply of water.

But though they had won the fight they had not won
the mountain. After resting a while they began the work
of storming the narrow gorge that led upwards to the table-
land, for this gorge was its only gate, and at first were
suffered to pull down or climb over the walls which were
built across it with but little resistance. Soon, however,
they found out the reason of this, for when a number of
them were in the gorge stones began to roll upon them
from the edges of the cliffs above, crushing the life out of
many, so that presently they were driven back to the head
of the river. Afterwards they searched long and earnestly
but could find no other path by which to attack, for there
was none.

" Well," said the Zulu captain, " it seems that we must
fight the fight of ' sit-down,' and since these rock-rabbits
will not let us come to them we must wait till they come to
us to ask for water."

So they waited for seven whole days, setting guards
about the mountain in case there should be secret ways of
egress of which they knew nothing.

When they reached the tableland Sihamba spoke words
so bitter to her councillors and captains that some of them
stopped their ears that they might hear no more, while
others answered that they could do nothing against men
who walked upon the boiling waters.

" Now, indeed, you can do nothing against them," Sihamba cried, " for Thirst will fight for them, and he is the
best of friends. Because of your cowardice we must perish,
everyone of us, and for my part I should be glad of it were

it not that you have given the Lady Swallow to death also."

Then she buried her face in the ground and would say no more, even when they told her that the Zulus had been beaten back by the rocks that were rolled down upon them.

For some days the little spring gave enough water for the thousands of people who were crowded upon the mountain top, though there was none to spare for the cattle. But on the third night the poor beasts being maddened by thirst, broke out of the kraal and rushing to the spring, so trampled it with their hoofs that its waters were sealed up, and only very little could be obtained even by digging, for here the rock came near to the surface of the soil, and it would seem as though the course of the spring was turned or choked beneath it.

Then all those upon that mountain began to suffer the horrors of thirst. Soon the cattle were altogether mad and rushed to and fro in herds, bellowing furiously and goring everyone they met, or trampling them to the earth. Now the Umpondwana strove to be rid of them by driving them down the gorge, but the Zulus, guessing the trouble that the presence of these beasts was bringing upon the besieged would not suffer them to pass. Next they attempted to force them over the edge of the precipice, but when they were driven to it the oxen turned and charged through them, killing several men. After this they contented themselves with stabbing the most dangerous of the animals, and leaving the rest to rush to and fro as they would, for they did not care to kill them all lest their carcasses should breed a pestilence.

The sixth day came, and, oh! the great kraal of the Umpondwana was but as a hell wherein lost souls wandered in torment, for the sun beat down upon it fiercely and everywhere roamed or lay men, women and children overcome with the torture of thirst; indeed, of the last, some were already dead, especially those who were at the breast, for their mothers' milk was dry. Here three men had dragged an old wife from her hut, and were beating her to make her reveal the store of water which she was believed to have hidden; there others were cutting the throat of an ox that they might drink its blood, and yonder a little girl was turning stones to lick the damp side of them with her poor parched tongue.

In the midst of these scenes which passed outside her hut, sat Sihamba brooding. As chieftainess she still had about a pint of water stored in a jar, but though she had made Suzanne drink, herself she drank but little, for she would not consent to suffer less than those about her.

Now Sihamba's eyes fell upon the child who was licking stones, and her heart was wrung with pity. Going into the hut she fetched most of the water in a gourd, and calling to the child, who staggered towards her, for she could scarcely walk, she gave it to her, bidding her drink slowly.

In a moment it was gone, every drop of it, and, behold! the dim eyes brightened, and the shrunken limbs seemed to grow round again, while the young voice, no longer high and cracked, praised and blessed her name. Sihamba motioned the child away, then she went into the hut to weep, only weep she could not, since her eyes were too dry for tears.

"Three more days," she thought to herself, "and they will all be dead unless rain should fall. Yes, the cowards, and those whom their cowardice has betrayed will all be dead together."

As she thought thus, Suzanne entered the hut, and there was tidings in her eyes.

"What is it, sister," asked Sihamba, "and whence do you come?"

"I come from the high seat upon the edge of the cliff," she answered, "where I have sat all day, for I can no longer bear these sights, and I have this to tell, that the Zulus are marching across the plain, but not towards Zulu-land, since they head for the Quathlamba Mountains."

CHAPTER XXX

SIHAMBA PREVAILS

Now a fire of hope shot up in Sihamba's eyes, but soon it died out again.

"It is a trick, it must be a trick," she said, "for who ever heard of a Zulu loosing the prey that was in his hand? Never dare he do it save by the command of the king," and she left the hut to be met by others running with the same tidings. Of these she sent some down the gorge to bring her report of what had happened, and with them Zinti, for she could not altogether trust the word of her own people.

Within an hour the messengers returned, and on their faces was a strange look which, clever as she was, Sihamba did not understand.

"Is the path clear?" she asked.

"No, chieftainess," they replied, "it is still blocked, for though the Zulus have gone we know not where by order received from Dingaan, Bull-Head holds it with such of his own men as are left alive."

"Had you speech with the white man?" she asked.

"Yes, lady."

"Say on."

Now they looked about them like people that are ashamed, but at last the oldest of them spoke.

"Chieftainess," he said, "Bull-Head made us this offer

and in these words: ' You people of the Umpondwana, you are dying of thirst and I know it; yes, though the Zulus have gone and but few of us are left here, yet you cannot force the narrow way against us, so that I have only to sit here for a few days longer and you will be dead of thirst, everyone of you, you and your cattle together. But I do not wish that you should die, for with you I have no quarrel; also if you die one will perish among you whom I desire to keep alive. Therefore I make you this offer. Hand over to me your ruler, Sihamba Ngenyanga, and with her the white woman named Swallow, and you yourselves shall go free, everyone of you; more, although I will take this stronghold of yours to live in myself, I will give back to you the half of the cattle. Now, answer.'

" Lady, when he had finished speaking we consulted together and answered Bull-Head thus: ' We cannot give over to you our chieftainess and her white sister, for it is better to die than that such dishonour should lie upon our names. But if you will let us go, you can take them from among our number as we pass before you, for that will be no fault of ours, or if they do not choose to accompany us, after we have gone by you can ascend the mountain and take them.'

" To this Bull-Head assented, saying, ' Set the Lady Swallow in her chair upon the cliff edge and Sihamba at her side so that my eyes seeing them may know that they are safe, and you shall go.' So it was agreed between us that to-morrow at the dawn he will open the wall and let us down to the river to drink, after which we may pass whither we will."

Now when Sihamba heard these shameful words her rage was so great that for a while she could not even speak. At length she found her tongue and gasped out:

" Oh! father of cowards, do you dare to sing such a song in my ears? Why do not you, who are many, storm the pass and take the water? "

" Lady," answered the old man coldly, " we dare because we must, for honour cannot live before the assegai of thirst. You talk to us of storming the pass; we cannot storm it, for ten men can hold that place against a hundred; also our arms are weak and we are weary of war. Listen; on the one hand are the lives of thousands, with them your own and that of the White Swallow, and on the other this dishonour. We choose the dishonour, since if you and the Swallow do not desire to fall into the hands of Bull-Head, you can still do what you must have done had we chosen honour. Lady, you can die, knowing that by your death you have saved the lives of the multitude over whom you rule.

" Listen again, lady, we did not seek you, it was you who came back to us after the death of the chief, your brother. We accepted you and you have ruled us justly for these two years, but you wish to make of us a fighting people who are and who desire to remain a people of peace. Moreover, you promised that the white chieftainess, your companion, would bring us prosperity and good, whereas to us she has been a bird of ill-omen, for since she came here on her account there has been war and nothing but war. Yes, because of her we have been cooped up on this mountain and killed whenever we ventured on to the plains beyond; therefore we will have no more of her, she must find her own fortune, for we have our lives and those of our wives and children to save.

" Further, I say this: the news of the offer of Bull-Head has gone abroad among the people, and had we refused they would have torn us limb from limb, yes, and you and the

White Swallow also. Our hearts are sad, but lady, who can fight against fate? "

" I can," answered Sihamba, " but have no fear; to-morrow at the dawn you shall see us sit out upon the cliff point; and now, father of cowards, begone, and let me see your face no more. Betray us if you will, you who were not men enough to hold the water, you who are not men enough to cut a path to it as you might, and therefore must complete your cowardice with treachery. Betray us if you will, but I tell you that you shall not go free from this disgrace. The curse of Chaka shall fall upon you and the blade of the spear shall be the inheritance of you who are afraid to grasp its shaft. Begone!" and withered by her words and the fire of her eyes, the spokesmen of the Umpondwana crept like beaten hounds from the presence of their deserted chieftainess.

Here I will stop the tale to say that this prophecy of Sihamba's came true, as did all the prophecies of that strange woman, who, with other gifts, without doubt had that of foresight. A few years later, when Panda was king, and their wars with us Boers were ended, the Zulus, who never forget a quarrel, swooped down upon the Umpondwana unawares, and storming the mountain by night, put all the men on it to the spear, and carried away the women and children to Zululand, so that of this tribe there remains nothing but some crumbling walls and a name of shame.

Now the sun set upon that home of thirst, and all was silent in it save for the sound of the hoofs of the galloping cattle as they rushed hither and thither, and the groaning of the women and children, who wandered about seeking grass to chew, for the sake of the night damps that gathered on it. Sihamba went into the great hut where she always slept with Suzanne, whom she found seated upon a stool, wan-faced, and her eyes set wide with misery of mind and body.

"What passes now?" asked Suzanne.

The little woman came to her, and throwing her arms about her neck she kissed her, answering:

"Alas! sister, all things pass, and with them our lives," and she told her of the surrender of the Umpondwana and its terms.

Suzanne listened in silence, for grief and despair had done their worst with her, and her heart could hold no more pain.

"So it is finished at last," she said, when Sihamba had spoken, "and this is the end of all our toil and strivings and of our long fight against fate. Yes, this is the end: that we must die, or at the least I must die, for I will choose death rather than that Van Vooren should lay a finger upon me. Well, I should care little were it not that now I believe my husband to be still alive, and it is hard to go before him into yonder darkness, though I believe also that the darkness which we fear will prove such a happy light as does not shine upon this earth," and she laid her head upon Sihamba's breast and they wept together.

Presently Sihamba said, "My mind, that was wont to be clear, is darkened. Pray to your God, you who are of His people that He may send light upon it, so that I can think once more while there is yet time. Now we wander in the forest of despair, but never yet was there a forest so thick that it cannot be passed. Pray then that I may be given light, for your life hangs upon it."

So Suzanne prayed, and presently, as she prayed, her

weariness overcame her and she slept, and Sihamba slept also. When Sihamba awoke it was within an hour of midnight A little lamp of oil burnt in the hut, and by the light of it she could see the white face of Suzanne lying at her side, and groaned in her bitterness to think that before the sun set again that face must be whiter still, for she knew that the Swallow was not of the mind of the Umpondwana, who preferred dishonour to death. " Oh! that my wisdom might' come back to me," she murmured. " Oh! Great-Great, God of my sister, give me back my wisdom and I will pay my life for it. Oh! Lighter of the stars, for myself I ask nothing, who am not of Thy children. Let eternal death be my portion, but give me back my wisdom that I may save my sister who serves Thee."

Thus prayed Sihamba out of the depth of her untutored heart, not for herself but for another, and it would seem that her prayer was heard; though many among our people think that God does not listen to the black creatures. At the least, as her eyes wandered around the hut, they fell upon certain jars of earthenware. Now during the years that she dwelt among the Umpondwana Suzanne had but two pastimes. One of them was to carve wood with a knife, and the other to paint pictures upon jars, for which art she always had a taste, these jars being afterwards burnt in the fire. For pigments she used certain clays or ochres, red and black and white and yellow, which were found in abundance on the slopes of the mountain, and also a kind of ink that she made by boiling down the kernels of the fruit of the green-leaved tree which grew by the banks of the river

Now it was as she gazed at these jars of pigments and the brushes of goat's hair that the wisdom which she sought came to Sihamba; yes, in a moment it came to her, in a moment her plan was made, and she knew that it would not fail. To-morrow at the dawn the Umpondwana, to the number of several thousands, would pour through the pass on to the plain beyond. Well, Suzanne should go with them, she should go *as a black woman!* Already her hair and eyes were dark, and with those pigments her snow-white flesh could be darkened also, and then in the crowd who would know her from a Kaffir girl, she who could talk the language as though she had been born a Kaffir. Stay! Bull-Head was artful and clever, and perhaps he might be ready for such a trick. How could she deceive him?

Again she looked at the jars, and again wisdom came to her. It was the habit of Suzanne to sit in her dizzy chair of rock and watch the sunrise, hoping ever that in the light of it she might see white men riding to rescue her, and this Van Vooren knew, for she could be seen from the mouth of the pass below, where from hour to hour he would stand gazing at her five hundred feet above his head.

Well, to-morrow at the dawn another white woman should be seated yonder to satisfy his eyes, or at least a woman who seemed to be white. On the cliff edge, not far from this very rock lay the body of a poor girl who that day had died of thirst. If its face and arms and feet were painted white, and Suzanne's cloak of white goat's hair were set upon its shoulders, and the corpse itself placed upright in the chair, who, looking at it from hundreds of feet beneath, could guess that it was not Suzanne, and who, seeing it set aloft, would seek for Suzanne among the crowd of escaping Kaffirs? The plan was good; it could scarcely fail, only time pressed.

"Sister, awake," whispered Sihamba. Suzanne sat up at once, for the sleep of the doomed is light. "Listen, sister," went on Sihamba, "that wisdom for which you prayed has come to me," and she told her all the plan.

"It is very clever, and it may serve," answered Suzanne, "for I understand these paints and can stain myself so that if my hair is cut none would know me from a Kaffir. But, Sihamba, there is one thing which I do not understand. What will you do? For if you attempt to escape your stature will betray you."

"I?" hesitated the little woman, "nay, I do not know, I have never thought of it. Doubtless I shall win through in this way or in that."

"You are deceiving me, Sihamba. Well, there is an end, I will not go without you."

"Can you think of death and say that you will not go without me?"

"I can Sihamba."

"Can you think of your father and your mother and say that you will not go without me?"

"I can, Sihamba."

"Can you think of your husband and say that you will not go without me?"

"I can," faltered Suzanne.

"Truly you are brave," laughed the little woman. "There is more courage in that white heart of yours than in those of all the Umpondwana. Well, sister, I also am brave, or at the least for these many moons I have set myself a task, nor will I shrink from it at the end, and that is to save you from Piet Van Vooren as once at a dearer price you saved me. Now, hearken, for myself I have no fear; as I have said, doubtless in this way or in that I shall win through, but it cannot be at your side. I must rejoin you afterwards. What, you refuse to go? Then, Lady Swallow, you send me down to death and your hands are red with my blood. I am weary, I will not live to see more trouble; life is hard and death is easy. Finish your own battle, Swallow, and fly out your flight alone," and drawing a knife from her girdle Sihamba laid it upon her knee.

" Do you mean that you will kill yourself if I refuse your prayer? "

" Nothing less, sister, and at once, for I thirst, and would seek some land where there is water, or where we need none. It comes to this, then: if you consent I may live, if you refuse I must die."

" I cannot do it," moaned Suzanne " Let us die together."

Now Sihamba crept to her and whispered in her ear:

" Think of Ralph Kenzie and of what his life must be if you should die. Think of those children who will come, and of that first kiss of love found again which you must miss in death, whatever else it may have to give. Think of the knife's point that you would change for it, or the last sick rush down a mountain height of space. Think of your husband. Hark! I hear him calling you."

Then Suzanne yielded.

" O woman with a noble heart," she murmured, " I listen to your tempting; may God forgive me and God reward you, O woman with the noble heart."

CHAPTER XXXI

THEN they began the work, for much must be done before the daylight came. First Sihamba took a sharp knife, and with it cut off Suzanne's beautiful hair close to the head, over which what was left of it curled naturally. To disguise it further, for though it was dark it was too fine for the hair of a native, she put grease upon it and powdered it with the blue dust that Kaffir women use. This done, the poor girl stripped herself, and with the help of Sihamba smeared all her body, every inch of it down to the soles of her feet, with the ink-like juice mixed with the black earth and grease, which when it was dry made her the colour of a Kaffir. Next Sihamba dressed her in a native woman's moocha made of skin and beads, and gave her an old skin blanket to wear upon her shoulders and hide sandals for her feet, together with anklets of beads and copper wire. Then having examined her all over to see that no sign of her white skin could be seen through the pigments, and burned the long tresses of her hair, Sihamba went to the door of the hut.

"Where are you going?" asked Suzanne.

"To find Zinti," she answered, "for now we must have his help."

"No, no," cried Suzanne, "I am ashamed to be seen thus by any man."

" Wherefore, Swallow, seeing that for some days you are but a Kaffir woman, and this is their dress, of which none think harm? Nay, you must, for remember that if you show doubt or shame, you will betray yourself."

Then with a groan Suzanne yielded, and crouching upon the floor like a native, awaited the return of Sihamba. Presently she came, followed by Zinti, who was in good case, though somewhat thin, for Zinti was clever and provident, and, foreseeing what would come, he had hidden water for himself among the rocks.

" Zinti," said Sihamba, " I would speak with you of secret matters."

" Speak on, lady," he answered—here his eyes fell upon Suzanne crouched on the ground in the full light of the lamp—" but there is a stranger present."

" This is no stranger, Zinti," said Sihamba, " but one whom you know well."

" Indeed, lady, I know her not. Should I forget one so beautiful? And yet—and yet—" and he rubbed his eyes and stared, gasping, " it cannot be."

" Yes, it is, Zinti. There sits the lady Swallow and none other."

Now although there was little mirth left in him, Zinti burst out laughing till the tears ran from his eyes, and Sihamba struck him with her hands, calling him " Fool," and commanding him to be silent.

" Wow!" he said, " this is wonderful. This is magic indeed. She who was white as snow has become black as coal, and yes, she looks best black. Oh! this is magic indeed."

At his words Suzanne sprang up looking as though she were about to weep, and Sihamba stopped his lips with fierce words and blows, though he took small heed of either, but stood staring.

"Zinti," Sihamba said, "you have done me many services, but to-day you must do me the greatest of all. This
morning at the daylight the lady Swallow will pass with
the multitude down the cleft yonder and none will know
her in that disguise. You must go with her, but not too
near her, and cross the plain, meeting her by the saw-edged
rock which stands yonder at the mouth of the gorge in the
Quathlamba mountains. Then you must lead her as fast
as you can travel to that camp of the Boers which is near
the Tugela River, where she will be safe. Do you understand?"

"I understand, lady. But what of yourself?"

"It is my plan to hide on the mountain," Sihamba answered quickly, "in a secret place I know of, seeing that
it is impossible that I should escape because my stature
would betray me. I will join you at the Boer camp later;
or, failing that, you can return in a while—say on the first
night of the new moon—to search for me. But talk no
more, for we have still much to do. Yes, we who have
made a white woman black, must make a black woman
white. Follow me, both of you," and giving Zinti a jar
of pigment and the long goat-skin cloak which Suzanne
wore for an outer garment, she left the hut, carrying in her
hand strips of ox-hide tanned white.

Avoiding the groups of thirst-tormented people who sat
or wandered about in the coolness of the night, they passed
through the gates of the kraal unheeded, and walking
quickly across the wide stretch of tableland reached the
eastern edge of the cliff. Now upon the very verge of this
cliff rose a sharp pinnacle of rock fifty feet or more into
the air, and upon the top of this pinnacle was that stone
shaped like a great chair, in which Suzanne sat day by day,
poised like an eagle over the dizzy gulf of space, for the

slopes of the mountain swelled five hundred feet beneath, watching for the help that never came. Not far from the base of this point Sihamba began to search in the starlight till she found what she wanted, the body of a young woman who had crept here to die of thirst, and whose death and the place of it had been reported to her.

Now she took the jar of white clay, and, aided by Zinti, set about her ghastly task, daubing the stuff thickly upon the cold features and the neck and arms and feet. Soon it was done, for such work needed little care, but then began their true toil since the corpse must be carried up the sharp point of rock, and that by no easy path. Had not Zinti been so strong it could never have been done; still, with the aid of Suzanne and Sihamba herself, at last it was finished.

Up that steep place they toiled, the three of them, dragging the dead body from knob to knob of rock, well knowing that one false step in the gloom would send them to be broken to pieces hundreds of feet beneath. At length they reached the little platform where there was scarcely room for all of them to stand with their burden, and climbing on to the stone which was called the Chair, Zinti drew the dead woman into the seat of it.

Then as Sihamba bade him he wrapped her in Suzanne's long white cape of goat-skin, putting the hood of it upon her head, after which he made the corpse fast in a sitting posture, lashing it round the neck and middle to the back of the stone with the white tanned rimpis in such fashion that it could not fall or even slip.

" So," said Sihamba grimly, " there sits the bride upon whom Swart Piet can feast his eyes while you seek safety across the mountains. Now back to the town, for from this height I can already see light glimmering in the east."

Accordingly they returned to the hut and entered it, leaving Zinti without, none noting them since by now the multitudes were thronging the narrow way. Here Sihamba lit the lamp, and by its light once more examined Suzanne carefully, retouching the dye in this place and in that, till she was sure that no gleam of white showed through it.

"It is good," she said at length; "unless you betray yourself, your skin will not betray you. And now, lady Swallow, the hour has come for us to part, and I rejoice to think that some of the debt I owe you I have repaid. Long ago I told you that very far away I should live to save you as you saved me, and I am sure that I have saved you; there is no doubt of it in my heart. Yes, yes, Swallow, I see you most happy in the love of husband and of children, thinking of all these things as a far-off evil dream, as of a dream that never will return. What more do I desire? What more have I to ask?

"I say that I have repaid to you part of the debt I owe, but all of it I can never repay, for, Swallow, you have given me love which elsewhere has been denied to me. Others have parents and brothers and sisters and husbands to love them; I have none of these. I have only you who are to me father and mother and sister and lover

"How then can I repay you who have taught this cold heart of mine to love, and have deigned to love me in return? Oh! and the love will not die; no, no, it will live on when all else is dead, for although I am but a Kaffir doctoress, at times light shines upon my heart, and in that light I see many new things. Yes, yes, I see that this life of ours is but a road, a weary road across the winter veldt, and this death but the black gate of a garden of flowers——"

"Oh! why do you speak thus?" broke in Suzanne. "Is

this then our last farewell, and does your wisdom tell you
that we part to meet no more? "

" I know not, Swallow," answered Sihamba hastily, " but
if it should be so I care nothing, for I am sure that through
all your days you will not forget me, and that when your
days are done I shall meet you at the foot of the death-bed.
Nay, you must not weep. Now go swiftly, for it is time,
and even in your husband's love be mindful always that a
woman can love also; yes, though she be but a dwarfed
Kaffir doctoress. Swallow—Sister Swallow, fare you well,"
and, throwing herself upon her breast, Sihamba kissed her
again and again. Then, with a strange strength, she thrust
her from the hut, calling to Zinti to take charge of her and
do as she had bidden him, adding that if he failed in this
task she would blast his body and haunt his spirit.

Thus parted Sihamba, the Kaffir witch-doctoress, and
my daughter Suzanne, whom she kept safe for nearly three
years, and saved at last at the cost of her own life. Yes,
thus they parted, and for always in the flesh, since it was
not fated that they should meet again in this world, and
whether it has been permitted to Sihamba—being a Kaffir,
and no Christian—to enter a better one is more than I can
say. In her case, however, I hope that she has found some
hole to creep through, for although she was a black witch-
doctoress, according to her knowledge she was a good
woman and a brave one, as the reader will say also before
he comes to the end of this story.

Outside the hut Zinti took Suzanne by the hand and led
her through the mazes of the town to the open ground that
lay between it and the mouth of the steep cleft which ran
down to the slopes of the mountain.

All this space was crowded with people, for as yet they could not enter the cleft, which nowhere was more than ten feet wide, because it was filled with cattle, some alive and some dead, that, drawn by the smell of the water beneath, had gathered as near to it as the stone walls which blocked the pass would allow.

Suzanne and Zinti mingled with this crowd of fugitives, taking a position almost in the midst of it, for they did not wish to pass out either among the first or the last. There they waited a while, none noting them, for in their great agony of thirst all thought of themselves and not of their neighbours. Indeed, husbands deserted their sick wives and mothers their children, which were too heavy to carry; yes, they deserted them to be trampled by the feet of men and the hoofs of cattle.

Now, the eastern sky grew grey, and though the sun had not yet risen the light was such that a man could see the veins upon the back of his hand and the white moons on his finger-nails. Presently, as though moved by one impulse, thousands of voices uttered a hoarse cry of "It is dawn! Open, open!"

But it would seem that the wall still stood, for the cattle remained packed in so dense a mass that a man could have walked upon their backs, as, indeed, some tried to do.

At last the sun rose, or rather its rays shot upwards across the eastern skies like a fan of fire. Suzanne turned her head and watched till presently the arrows of light struck upon the tall chair rock which was the highest point of all the mountain. Yes, there in the chair sat the white figure and by its side stood what seemed to be a black child. It was Sihamba. Far below other eyes were watching also, the eyes of Swart Piet, for he would not let the people go until he knew that Suzanne and Sihamba stayed behind.

But now he saw them, Suzanne in her accustomed place, and at her side Sihamba.

" Pull down the walls," he shouted to his men, for he was eager to clear the pass of cattle and Kaffirs that he might go up it, and they obeyed him. Before they were more than half down the oxen, pushing and leaping forward madly, cleared what was left of them and, open-mouthed, their lolling tongues hanging from their dry jaws, rushed downward to the water, goring or trampling to death some of those who worked at the wall.

" The schanzes are down," screamed the people, seeing the long line of cattle move, and immediately they began to press forward also.

At Suzanne's side was a young woman so weak with thirst that she could scarcely walk, and on her back a year-old boy, insensible but living, for a red froth bubbled from his lips. A man thrust this woman to one side and she fell; it was that aged councillor who on the yesterday had brought news of the surrender to Sihamba. She tried to struggle to her feet but others trampled upon her.

" Sister, sister! " she cried, clutching Suzanne by the hide blanket which she wore, " I am dead, but oh! save my child."

" Let it be," whispered Zinti, but Suzanne could not deny those piteous eyes, and as she passed she snatched up the boy and the sling in which he was carried by the dying woman, setting the band of it beneath her own breast. So she went forward, bearing him upon her hip, nor did that act of mercy lack its reward, for as shall be seen it was her salvation. Also the child lived, and to this day is a faithful servant in our house, though now his beard is white.

Down the narrow way surged the crowd, scrambling over rocks and dead cattle and crushed women and children, till at the last Suzanne drew near its opening, where stood Swart Piet and some twenty of his followers, watching the multitude pass out.

"Lady," whispered Zinti into her ear, "now I fall behind, for Bull-Head may know me. If I win through I will rejoin you on the plain, or by the saw-edged rock; if I do not, throw away that child, and follow the road of which I have told you, you can scarcely mistake it. Go on, showing no fear, and—stay, let that blanket hang open in front, it is not the custom of these women to wear their garments wrapped so closely."

Suzanne groaned, but she obeyed.

CHAPTER XXXII

THE PASS OF THE QUATHLAMBA

LIKE wild beasts escaping from a pen, that red-eyed, gasping mob rushed and staggered to the edge of the water, and, plunging their heads into it with hoarse grunts and cries, drank and drank and drank. Indeed, several lost their lives there, for some filled themselves so full that their vitals were ruptured, and some were thrust into the river by the cattle or those pressing behind them, to be carried away by the swift stream.

Just at the mouth of the pass Suzanne, laden with the child, was pushed down by those who followed, and doubtless would have been trampled to death, had not one of Swart Piet's men, desiring to clear the way, or, perhaps, moved to pity at her plight, dragged her to her feet again. But when he had done this he did not let her go, but held her, staring at her beauty with greedy eyes.

"Here is a rock-rabbit whom I shall keep for a wife," he cried. "I would rather take her than twenty fat oxen."

Now Suzanne's heart nearly stood still with terror.

"Water, water," she moaned; "let me drink, I pray you."

"Do not fear, I will take you to drink, my pretty," went on the man, still staring at her.

Then, losing command of herself, Suzanne screamed and

struggled, and the sound of her cries reached the ears of Swart Piet, who was standing close at hand.

" What is this? " he asked of the man.

" Nothing, Bull-Head, except that I have taken a woman whom I wish for a wife because she is so fair."

Van Vooren let his eyes rest upon her, but dreamily, for all his thoughts were given to her who sat aloft five hundred feet above his head, and, feeling their glance, Suzanne's blood froze in her veins.

" Yes, she is fair," he answered, " but she is a married woman, and I will have no Umpondwana brats among my people.   Let her go, and take a girl if you will."   For Van Vooren did not wish that the few men who remained with him should cumber themselves just then with women and children, since they were needed to look after the cattle.

" Maid or wife, I choose this one and no other," said the man sulkily.

Then Black Piet, whose sullen temper could not brook to be crossed, broke into a blaze of rage.

" Do you dare to disobey me? " he shouted with an awful Kaffir oath.   " Let her go, dog, or I will kill you."

At this the man, who knew his master, loosed hold of Suzanne, who ran away, though it was not until she reached the water that she noticed a white ring round her arm, where his grip had rubbed the paint off the skin beneath.   Strangely enough Van Vooren saw the ring, and at that distance mistook it for an ivory ornament such as Kaffir women often wear above the elbow.   Still more strangely its white colour made him think again of the white woman who sat aloft yonder, and he turned his face upwards, forgetting all about the black girl with the child.

Thrusting herself through the crowd, Suzanne ran on for a while till she was clear of the worst of it, then terrified though she was, she could resist the temptation of the water no longer, for her mouth and throat felt dry and rough. Climbing down to the edge of the river she drank greedily under the shelter of a rock, and when she had satisfied some of her thirst, she poured water into the mouth of the child, dipping its shrunken little body into the stream, whereon it seemed to increase before her eyes like a dry sponge that is left out in the rain.

While she tended the child thus, and just as it began to find its senses and to wail feebly, she chanced to look up, and to her terror saw that man from whom she had escaped walking along the bank searching for her. Happy was it for Suzanne that the rock under which she was crouched hid her, for the man stood for thirty seconds or more within two paces, so that she was obliged to plunge the body of the boy under water to stifle its crying.

Then, as it happened, the Kaffir caught sight of another woman and infant, more than a hundred yards away, and ran off towards them. Thereon Suzanne, replacing the half-choked child upon her back, climbed the bank, hiding the white mark upon her arm beneath the blanket, and taking such shelter as she could behind stones or cattle, or knots of people who, their thirst appeased, were hastening to escape, she slipped across the shoulder of the slope.

Now she was out of sight of Swart Piet and his men, and for the first time for many a day began to breathe freely. For a while she crept on round the flank of the mountain, then at the best of her speed she struck across the plain straight for the saw-edged rock ten miles away, which marked the entrance to the pass over the Quathlamba range.

From time to time Suzanne looked behind her, but none followed her, nor, search as she would, could she discover

any trace of Zinti, who, she began to fear, must have come
to some harm. One thing she could see, however—the
whitened corpse set on high in the chair of rock, and by
the side of it a black dot that she knew to be Sihamba.
Twice she turned round and gazed at it, but the second
time the dot had become almost imperceptible, although it
still was there. Long and earnestly she looked, sending
her farewell through space to that true friend and deliverer
whose eyes, as she knew well, watched her flight and whose
heart went with her.

Then she travelled on sadly, wondering what was that
plan of escape of which Sihamba had spoken, and why it
was that she stood there by the corpse and did not put it
into practice, wondering also when they should meet again
and where. A third time she turned, and now the dead
woman on the rock was but as a tiny point of white, and
now it had altogether vanished away.

After this Suzanne halted no more, but pressed on steadily towards the saw-edged spur, which she reached about
twelve o'clock, for the grass was so tall, the untrodden
veldt so rough, and the sun so hot that, weak as she felt
with grief and the effects of thirst, and laden with a heavy
child, her progress was very slow. At length, however,
she stood gasping in its shadow, gazing dismayed at the
huge range of mountains before her and the steep rough
cliffs up which she must climb.

"Never shall I cross them without food and weighted
with this child, so the end of it will be that I must die
after all," thought Suzanne as she sank down by the banks
of a little rivulet, resting her swollen feet in its cool stream,
for then, and indeed for weeks after, it seemed to her that
she could never have enough of the taste and smell and feel
of water.

As she sat thus, striving to still the wailing of the hungry boy, suddenly the shadow of a man fell upon her. With a cry she sprang to her feet to find herself face to face with Zinti.

"Oh! I thought that they had taken you," she ex claimed.

" No, lady, I escaped, but I crossed the plain far to your left, for it seemed better that we should not be seen travelling together from the mountain. Now let us eat who have eaten little for so many days, lacking water to wash down the food," and from the large skin wallet which he bore Zinti drew out dried flesh and roasted corn.

Suzanne looked at the food with longing, but before she touched any she took some corn, and having pounded it into a pulp with a stone, she mixed it with water and fed the child, who devoured the stuff greedily and presently fell asleep. Then they ate as much as they wanted, since Zinti carried enough for three such meals, and never did Suzanne take meat with a greater relish. Afterwards, though she yearned to sleep, they pressed on again, for Zinti said it was not safe to stay, since long before this Van Vooren would be seeking her far and wide, and if he chanced to discover the secret of her flight he would travel further in one hour on horseback than they could in four on foot. So they went forward up the pass much refreshed, Zinti carrying the child.

All day long they walked thus, resting at intervals, till by sunset they reached the crest of the pass, and saw the wide plains of Natal stretched out like a map beneath them, and on them, not so very far away and near to the banks of the river that wound at their feet, a white-topped koppie, beneath which, said Zinti, was the Boer camp.

Suzanne sat down and looked, and there, yes, there the

caps of the waggons gleamed in the fading light; and oh! her heart leapt at the sight of them, for in those waggons were white men and women such as she had not seen for years, and with whom at length she would be safe. But even as her breast heaved at the thought of it, an icy, un-natural wind seemed to stir her hair, and of a sudden she felt, or seemed to feel, the presence of Sihamba. For a moment, and one only, it was with her, then it was gone, nor during all her life did it ever come back again.

" Oh! Sihamba is dead! " she cried.

Zinti looked at her in question.

" It may well be so," he said sadly, " but I pray that it is not so, for she is the best of chieftainesses. At least we have our own lives to save, so let us go on," and again they pressed forward through the gathering gloom.

Soon it grew dark, and had her guide been any other man than Zinti Suzanne must have stopped where she was till the moon rose at midnight. But Zinti could find any path that his feet had trod even in the dark; yes, al-though it ran through piled-up rocks on the mountain side, and was cut with the course of streams which must be forded.

In wading through one of these rivulets, Suzanne struck her bare ankle against a stone and lamed herself, so that from this time forward, shivering and wet with water, for her hurt was so sharp and sudden that she had fallen in the stream, she was forced to walk leaning on Zinti's shoulder, and indeed over some rough places he was obliged to carry her. Now again Zinti wished to abandon that heavy child, for strong though he was the weight of the two of them proved almost more than he could bear, but Suzanne would not listen to him.

" Nay," she said, " this child that was sent to me by

Heaven has saved me from shame and death, and shame
and death be my portion if I will leave it while I live.   Go
on alone if you will, Zinti, and I will stay here with the
child."

"Truly white people are strange," answered Zinti, "that
they should wish to burden themselves with the child of
another when their own lives are at stake, but be it as you
will, lady," and he struggled forward as best he could,
carrying the one and supporting the other.

Thus for hour after hour, slowly they crept onward with
only the stars to light and guide them, till at length about
midnight the moon rose and they saw that they were near
the foot of the mountain.   Now they rested awhile, but
not long enough to grow stiff, then hastening down the
slope they reached the plain, and headed for the white-
topped koppie which shone in the moonlight some six miles
away.   On they crept, Suzanne now limping painfully, for
her ankle had begun to swell, and now crawling upon her
hands and knees, for Zinti had no longer the strength to
carry her and the child.   Thus they covered three miles
in perhaps as many hours.   At last, with something like
a sob, Suzanne sank to the earth.

"Zinti, I can walk no more," she said.   "Either I
must rest or die."

He looked at her and saw that she spoke truth, for she
was quite outworn.

"Is it so?" he said, "then we must stay here till the
morning, nor do I think that you will take hurt, for Bull-
Head will scarcely care to cross that pass by night."

Suzanne shook her head and answered:

"He will have begun to climb it at the rising of the
moon.   Hear me, Zinti.   The Boer camp is close and you
still have some strength left; take the child and go to it,

and having gained an entrance in this way or in that tell them my plight and they will ride out and save me."

" That is a good thought," he said; " but, lady, I do not like to leave you alone, since here there is no place for you to hide."

" You could not help me if you stayed, Zinti, therefore go, for the sooner you are gone, the sooner I shall be rescued."

" I hear your command, lady," he answered, and having given her most of the food that was left, he fastened the sleeping child upon his shoulder and walked forward up the rise.

In something less than an hour Zinti came to the camp, which was formed of unlaagered waggons and tents pitched at the foot of a koppie, along one base of which ran the river. About fifty yards in front of the camp stood a single buck waggon, and near to it still glowed the embers of a cooking-fire.

" Now if I try to pass that waggon those who watch by it will shoot at me," thought Zinti, though, indeed, he need have had no fear, for they were but camp-Kaffirs who slept soundly.

Not knowing this, however, he stood at a distance and called aloud, till at last a Hottentot crept out with a gun, and, throwing back the blanket from his head, asked who he was and what he wanted.

" I want to see the Baas of the camp," he answered, " for my mistress, a white woman, lies exhausted upon the veldt not far away and seeks his help."

" If you want to see the Baas," yawned the man, " you must wait till daylight when he wakes up."

" I cannot wait," answered Zinti, and he made as though to pass towards the camp, whereupon the man raised his gun and covered him, saying:

"If you go on I will shoot you, for stray Kaffir dogs are not allowed to prowl about the camp at night."

"What then must I do?" asked Zinti.

"You can go away, or if you will you may sit by the waggon here till it is light, and then when the Boers, my masters, wake up you can tell your story, of which I believe nothing."

So, having no choice, Zinti sat down by the waggon and waited, while the man with the gun watched him, pretending to be asleep all the while.

Now Suzanne was left alone upon the great veldt, and fear took hold of her, for she was broken in body and mind, and the place was very desolate; also she dreaded lest lions should take her, for she could hear them roaring in the distance, or Swart Piet, who was worse than any lion. Still she was so weary that after washing her face and hands in a spring close by, presently she fell asleep. When she awoke the east was tinged with the first grey light of the coming dawn, and it seemed to her as though some cold hand of fear had gripped her heart of a sudden and aroused her from heavy sleep. A sound caused her to look up, and there on the crest of the rise before her, some three hundred yards away, she saw dark forms moving, and caught sight of spears that glimmered in the moonlight.

"Now there is an end," thought Suzanne to herself, "for without doubt yonder stands a Zulu impi; the same that attacked the Umpondwana, for I can see the crane's feathers in their head-dresses," and she crouched upon the ground in an extremity of dread.

CHAPTER XXXIII

Now I must go back to that evening when we learned the great tidings from the lips of the lad Gaasha, whose life Ralph had saved after the attack by the Kaffirs upon the laager. There sat Gaasha on the ground staring, and there, not far away, Ralph was lying in his swoon, while Jan and I looked at each other like people who have suddenly beheld a sign from heaven.

"What evil magic is there in my words," said Gaasha presently, "that they should strike the Baas yonder dead like a spear?"

"He is not dead," I answered, "but for long he has sought that mountain Umpondwana of which you speak. Tell us now, did you hear of any white woman dwelling with the chieftainess Sihamba?"

"No, lady, I heard of none."

This answer of Gaasha's saddened me, for I made sure that if so strange a thing had happened as that a white woman had come to live among his tribe, the man who told him of the return of Sihamba would have told him of this also. Therefore, so I argued, either Suzanne was dead or she was in the power of Piet Van Vooren, or Sihamba had deserted her, though this last I did not believe. As it turned out afterwards. had not Gaasha been the stupidest of Kaffirs, we should have been saved those long days of doubt and trouble, for though he had not heard that Sihamba was accompanied by a white woman, he had heard that she brought with her a white *bird* to the mountain Umpondwana. Of course if he had told us this we should have guessed that the white bird could be none other than Suzanne, whose native name was Swallow.

Well, we set about reviving Ralph, which was done by throwing water on to his face. When he had found his senses again I prayed him not to suffer himself to be carried away with hope, since although Gaasha had heard of Sihamba, he had heard nothing of Suzanne.

To this he answered that now when God had pointed out to him the mountain of his vision and in so strange a manner, he had no fear but that he would find his wife upon it, since God was merciful and did not desire to mock or torment His servants.

I replied that I trusted it might be so, but the ways of the Almighty were beyond our understanding, nor did it become us to pass judgment upon them. Ralph scarcely heeded my words, but, springing to his feet, said:

"Come, let us be going to the mountain Umpondwana."

"First we must consult with the commandant and get aid from him," said Jan, "for it would not be safe that we should wander into these wild places alone, where there are many Kaffirs who doubtless would murder us."

In his eagerness Ralph would not listen to this, for he desired to start at once. But I pointed out to him that we had no horses, all ours being dead of the sickness; moreover, that the night was dark, and we could not trek till the moon rose, so at length he consented. Then we went into the laager, and Jan called the older men together in a quiet place.

"What is it, Heer Botmar?" asked the commandant when they were assembled.

"It is this, cousin," said Jan. "I desire to ask you to go a three days' trek out of your march to a mountain called Umpondwana, whither this servant of mine, Gaasha, can guide you."

"For what reason?" asked the commandant astonished.

"Friend," said Jan, "you have all of you heard the story of how that outcast devil Piet Van Vooren, stole away my only child, Suzanne, the wife of Ralph Kenzie the Englishman here."

"That is an old tale," said the commandant, "and, doubtless, the poor girl is dead long ago; why then do you speak of it now, and what has it to do with your request that we should trek to the mountain Umpondwana?"

"Only this, cousin; we think that my daughter Suzanne is living there among the Kaffirs, and we seek to rescue her. At least this is certain, for only now we have learnt it from the lips of Gaasha that Sihamba, her friend and servant whom we believe was with her, rules over this tribe as chieftainess."

"That may be so," said the commandant, "but did Gaasha tell you that your daughter was there also?"

"No," answered Jan.

"Then how do you know it?"

Now Jan hesitated and turned red as he replied:

"We know it because Ralph Kenzie here saw this very mountain in a vision more than two years ago, and in that vision was told that there he would find the wife who was taken from him on his marriage day."

Now, on hearing this most of the Boers broke out laughing, for, though very religious, we are not a people who place faith in visions. Thereupon I grew angry, and spoke to them more strongly, perhaps, than I should have done, reducing them to silence, for they were all of them a little afraid of my tongue. Also I told them the story of that dream of Ralph's, and of what had just passed with Gaasha, showing them that there was more in it than they imagined. After I had done Ralph spoke also, saying:

"Friends, doubtless this tale sounds foolish in your ears; but I ask what has been my nickname among you? Has it not been 'Man of the Mountain,' because I have always spoken and inquired for a certain mountain which had ridges on it shaped like the fingers of a man's hand, and have you not thought me mad for this reason? Now I have heard of such a mountain and I have heard also that Sihamba, who was with my wife, rules there as chieftainess. Is it strange, therefore, that I, believing now as ever in that vision, should wish to visit this mountain where, as I am sure, I shall find the wife that is lost to me?"

After this the Boers laughed no more but consulted apart till at last the elder, Heer Celliers, spoke.

"Heeren Botmar and Kenzie," he said, "of all this story of a vision we can say little. For aught we know it may be true, but if true then it is the work of magic and we will have nothing to do with it. Should you wish to go to seek this mountain Umpondwana you must go alone, for we cannot alter our plans to trek there with you. But we counsel you not to go, since no good can come of visions and magic."

When I heard this I answered him back, but Jan and Ralph went away, and presently I found them talking together outside the laager.

"Let me go alone," Ralph was saying.

"Nay," Jan answered, "I will accompany you, for two are better than one; also I shall not sleep till I find out the truth and know whether Suzanne lives or is dead."

" Indeed! and what is to become of me? " I asked.

" You, vrouw, can stop with the neighbours here, and we will join you in Natal."

" You will do no such thing, Jan Botmar," I answered, " for where you two go there I can go. What! Am I not sick also with love for my daughter and anxious to learn her fate? "

" As you will, wife," answered Jan; " perhaps it is well that we three should not separate who have been together always," and he went to see about the waggon.

As soon as the moon rose, which was about eleven o'clock, the oxen were inspanned. Before we started, however, several of our friends came praying us not to venture on so perilous a journey; indeed, they threatened even to use force to prevent us, and I think would have done so had not Jan told them outright that we were our own masters and free to go where we wished. So they departed, grieving over our obstinacy, and little guessing that their danger was far greater than our own, since as it chanced just as they had trekked through the Van Reenen's Pass a few days later a Zulu impi, returning from the Weenen massacres, fell upon them unawares and killed more than half of their number before they were beaten off.

So we trekked with the moon, Gaasha guiding us, and did not outspan till dawn. As I have said, we had no horses, but never until I made that journey did it come home to me how slow are oxen, for never before then was I in a hurry, nor, indeed, have I been since that time. It is the Englishmen who are always in a hurry, and that is one of the reasons why we Boers are so superior to them, and when we choose can master them in everything, except shopkeeping, and especially in fighting. Well, at the best the cattle could not drag the waggon over the roadless veldt at a greater rate than two miles an hour, or cover more than twenty miles a day in all. It was pitiful to see Ralph's impatience; again and again he walked on and returned; indeed, had we allowed it, I think that he would have pressed forward on foot, leaving us to follow in the waggon.

At daylight on the third day we inspanned as usual, and trekked through the morning mists until the sun sucked them up. Then Gaasha, who was sitting on the waggon-box beside Ralph, touched his shoulder, and pointed before him. Ralph looked, and far away upon the plain saw what seemed to be a white cloud, above which towered the flat cliffs of a mountain of red rock.

"See, Baas," he said, "yonder is Umpondwana, my home, and now by nightfall I shall know whether my parents are still alive, or, if they are dead, whether they have left any cattle that I can claim by law," and he began to whistle cheerfully.

"And I," said Ralph aloud, "shall know whether my life is to be a heaven or a hell," and all day long, neither eating nor drinking, he sat upon the waggon-box and stared at the mountain, not lifting his eyes from it.

It was about one o'clock in the afternoon when we seemed to be quite close to the green flanks of Umpondwana, that of a sudden we cut a wide spoor trampled by thousands of naked feet. Jan and Gaasha got off the waggon to examine it, but Ralph did not move.

"An impi has passed here," said Jan presently.

"Yes, and a Zulu impi as I think, Baas, but more than one whole day ago," and Gaasha began to hunt about amongst some low bushes which grew near the trail. Presently he held up his hand and shouted, and Jan ran to him.

" Look, Baas," he said, pointing to a bush.

Jan looked, and there beneath the bush lay a man, a Zulu soldier, for his tall grey plume was still fixed upon his head, and near him was his broad assegai. At that moment the man, who was still alive, although he was very near his death from dysentery, seemed to hear, for he sat up and opened his eyes, saying, " *Manzie, umlungho, manzie.*" (Water, white man, water.)

" Bring a pannikin of water, here lies a sick Kaffir," shouted Jan to Ralph, who was still seated on the waggon-box staring at the mountain.

Ralph brought the water, and the soldier drank it greedily.

" Who are you, and how come you here? " asked Jan.

" I am a soldier of Dingaan," answered the man, " but when we were attacking the little people on that mountain I fell sick. Still I came away with the impi, but here my strength failed me, and here I have lain for a round of the sun and a round of the moon. I begged them to kill me, but my brothers would not, for they said that I might recover and join them."

" Where have they gone? " asked Jan.

" They have gone to eat up the Boers in Natal," the Zulu answered in a hollow voice, his empty eyes wandering towards the mountains of the Quathlamba range. " Yes, they have gone to do the King's bidding on the white men, for his word came to us while we besieged yonder stronghold. To-morrow at the dawn they attack the little laager beneath the white koppie by the banks of the Tugela, and I must reach them by then—yes, yes, now I am strong again, and I shall attack with them to-morrow at the dawn.

Farewell, white men, I will not kill you because you gave me the water which has made me strong again," and, rising from the ground, he grasped his spear and started forward at a run.

"Stay," cried Ralph. "I would question you as to what has happened on that mountain;" but the man did not seem to hear him. For thirty paces or so he ran on, then suddenly he halted and saluted with his spear, crying in a loud voice:

"Chief, I report myself, I am present."

Next he stretched his arms wide and fell forward upon his face. When they reached him he was quite dead.

"This is a strange story that we have heard about the Zulus and the folk in Natal," said Jan, rubbing his forehead.

"I think that the man was wandering in his mind," answered Ralph, "still there may be truth in it; but, father," he added, with a gasp of fear, and, catching Jan by the arm, "what has happened on the mountain Umpondwana? The Zulus have been there, and—what has happened on the mountain?"

Jan shook his head, but did not answer, for he knew too well what happens where the Zulu impis pass.

Notwithstanding that Ralph was mad with impatience we halted the waggon for a few minutes to take counsel, and in the end decided to send the voorlooper back to the camp which we had left to warn our friends of what we had learned as to the onslaught on our brethren in Natal, though we had small faith in the story. But either the lad ran away, or some accident befell him, or he failed to find the Boers who had already trekked, at the least our message never reached them, nor did we see him again. Then we went on, Gaasha leading the oxen as quickly as they could walk. All that afternoon we travelled almost in silence, following the spoor of the impi backwards, for our hearts were full of fear. We met no man, but once or twice we saw groups of cattle wandering unherded, and this astonished us, giving us hope, for it is not the custom of a victorious impi to leave the cattle of its enemy behind it, though if the people of the Umpondwana had conquered, it was strange that we should see no herds with the beasts.

At length, within two hours of sunset, we passed round the shoulder of the mountain and beheld its eastern slope.

"It is the very place of my vision," cried Ralph, and certainly there before us were the stone ridges shaped like the thumb and fingers of a man, while between the thumb and first finger gushed the river, upon the banks of which grew flat-topped green-leaved trees.

"Onward, onward!" he cried again, and, taking the long waggon whip, he thrashed the oxen till they bellowed in the yokes. But I, who was seated beneath the tent of the waggon, turned to look behind me, and in the far distance saw that men were driving herds of cattle towards the mountains.

"We are too late," I thought in my heart, "for, without doubt, whether it be the Zulus or others, the place has been taken, since yonder go the victors with the cattle. Now they will fall upon us and kill us. Well, should God will it, so let it be, for if Suzanne is dead indeed I care little if we die also; and to Ralph at least death will be welcome, for I think that then death alone can save him from madness."

Now we had reached the banks of the river, and were trekking up them towards the spot where it issued from the side of the mountain. Everywhere was spoor, but we saw no people, although here and there the vultures were hissing and quarrelling over the bones of a man or a beast.

"There has been war in this place," whispered Jan, "and now the peace of death has fallen upon it," but Ralph only flogged the weary oxen, saying nothing.

At length they could drag the waggon no further, for the path grew too steep for them, whereupon Ralph, seizing the first weapon that came to hand, which, as it chanced, was the broad assegai that Gaasha had taken that day from the side of the dead Zulu, ran forward up the trail followed by Jan and myself. Another two hundred yards and the path took a turn which led to the entrance of the first scherm, the same that the Zulus had captured by forcing the passage of the river. The gateway was open now, and Ralph entered.

At first he could see no one, but presently he heard a voice saying:

"Will you not tell, for death is very near you? Drink, witch, tell and drink."

"Fool," answered another voice, a grating, broken voice, "I say that death is near to both of us, and since she is saved I die gladly, taking my secret with me."

"Then, witch, I will try steel," said the first voice.

Now Ralph looked over the rock from behind which the sound of voices came and saw the body of a little woman tied to a stone by the edge of the water, while over her leant a man, a white man, holding a knife in one hand and in the other a gourd of water, which he now placed close to her lips, and now withdrew from them. He knew that woman, it was Sihamba. Just at this moment the man looked up and their eyes met, and Ralph knew him also.

It was Piet Van Vooren.

CHAPTER XXXIV

THE AVENGER OF BLOOD

FOR a moment the two men stood looking at each other, yes, the shedder of blood and the avenger of blood stood quite still and silent, and looked each other in the eyes, as though a spell had fallen upon them striking them into stone. It was the voice of Sihamba that broke the spell, and it issued from her parched throat with a sound like the sound of a death-rattle.

"Ah! devil and torturer," it said, "did I not tell you that doom was at hand? Welcome, Ralph Kenzie, husband of Swallow."

Then with a roar like that of a wounded beast, Ralph sprang forward, in his hand the uplifted spear. For one instant Swart Piet hesitated, but at the words of Sihamba a sudden terror had taken hold of him and he dared not wait. Like a startled buck he turned and fled up the mountain, but as he passed her he struck downwards with the knife he held, stabbing Sihamba in the body.

Once also he looked round for help, but there was none, for during the long torment of Sihamba all the black villains who served him had slipped away, fearing lest others should secure their share of the stolen cattle. Then he sped on up the pass and never did a man run more swiftly. But after him came one who was swifter than he, the light-footed, long-limbed Englishman with rage in his heart, and an awful fire of vengeance blazing in his eyes.

Up the pass they ran, leaping over stones and dead cattle till at length they reached the tableland at the top.   Here once again Van Vooren paused for an instant, for he bethought him that, perhaps, he might hold the mouth of the cleft against his pursuer.   But his wicked heart was too full of fear to let him stay, so at full speed he set forward across the plain, heading for that chair rock where still sat the whitened corpse, for there he thought he could defend himself.   Ralph followed him somewhat more slowly, for of a sudden he had grown cold and cunning, and, knowing that his foe could not escape him, he desired to save his breath for the last struggle.

For six hundred yards or more they ran thus, and when Van Vooren began to climb the pedestal of rock Ralph was fifty paces behind him.   Presently he also reached the pedestal and paused to look.   Already Swart Piet was standing by the stone chair, but it was not at him that he looked, but rather at the figure which was tied in the chair that he now saw for the first time.   That figure no longer sat upright, draped in its white fur cloak, for it had been disturbed, as I shall tell presently, and the cloak was half torn from it.   Now it hung over the arm of the chair, the ghastly white face looking down towards Ralph and beneath it the bare black breast.

Ralph stared, wondering what this might mean.   Then the answer to the riddle flashed into his mind, and he laughed aloud, for here he saw the handiwork of Sihamba. Yes, that grisly shape told him that his love still lived and that it was to win the secret of her whereabouts that the devil above him had practised torment upon the little doctoress.

Ralph laughed aloud and began to climb the pinnacle. He might have waited till Jan, who was struggling up the pass after them, arrived with his gun, but he would not wait. He had no fear of the man above and he was certain of the issue of the fray, for he knew that God is just. As for that man above, he grinned and gibbered in his disappointed rage and the agony of his dread; yes, he stood there by the painted corpse and gibbered like an ape.

"Your evil doing has not prospered over much, Piet Van Vooren," called Ralph, "and presently when you are dead you will taste the fruits of it. Suzanne shall be mine till the end as she was mine from the beginning, but look upon the Death-wife that your wickedness has won," and he pointed at the body with his spear.

Black Piet made no answer, nor did Ralph speak any more, for he must set himself to finish his task. The Boer took a heavy stone and threw it at him, but it missed him and he could find no more. Then gripping the wrist of the corpse in his left hand to steady himself upon that giddy place, he leant forward and prepared to stab Ralph with the knife as he set foot upon the platform. Ralph saw his plan, and stopping in his climb, he took off his coat and wound it round his left arm as a shield. Then he came on slowly, holding the broad spear in front of him. At the last he made a rush and reached the flat space of rock. Piet stabbed at him, but the strength of the thrust lost itself in the folds of the coat.

Now who can say what happened. Round and round the rock chair they swung, Van Vooren still holding fast to the arm of the dead woman who was lashed in it. Yes, even from where I stood five hundred feet below I could see the flash of spear and knife as they struck and struck again.

At length a blow went home; the Zulu assegai sank deep
into Van Vooren's chest and he hung backwards over the
edge of the abyss, supported only by his grip of the dead
arm—from below it looked as though he were drawing
the corpse to him against its will.   Yes, he hung back and
groaned aloud.   Ralph looked at him and laughed again,
since though he was gentle-hearted, for this man he had
no pity.   He laughed, and crying " That curse of God you
mocked at falls at last," with a sudden stroke he drew the
sharp edge of the spear across the 'lashing that held the
body to the seat.

The rimpi parted, and with a swift and awful rush, like
that of a swooping bird, the dead woman and the living
man plunged headlong into space.   One dreadful yell
echoed down the pitiless precipices, followed presently by
a soft thudding sound, and there, lodged upon a flat rock
hundreds of feet beneath, lay what had been Piet Van
Vooren, though, indeed, none could have told that it
was he.

Thus ended the life of this man, this servant of the devil
upon earth, and even now, after all these years, I can find
but one excuse for him, that the excess of his own wickedness had made him drunk and mad.   Yes, I believe that he
who was always near to it, went quite mad when Ralph
struck him with the whip after the fight by the sheep kraal,
mad with hate of Ralph and love of Suzanne.   Also his
father was wicked before him, and he had Kaffir blood in
his veins.   Ah! for how much must our blood be called
upon to answer, and how good is that man who can conquer
the natural promptings of his blood!

Jan and I were following Ralph when he entered the
river scherm, and reached it just in time to see pursued

and pursuer vanishing up the narrow cleft. I caught sight of Van Vooren's back only, but although I had not seen him for years, I knew it at once.

"We have found the tiger at home," I said, "yonder goes Swart Piet."

"Allemachter! it is so," answered Jan. "Look, there lies the tiger's prey," and pointing to Sihamba he followed them up the mountain side as fast as his weight would allow, for in those days Jan was a very heavy man.

Meanwhile I made my way to the little figure that was stretched upon the rock at the edge of the river. She had fainted, but even before I reached her I saw from her small size and the strange hoop of stiff hair that she wore about her head, that it was none other than Sihamba, Sihamba whom I had last seen upon the eve of that unlucky marriage day.

But oh! she was sadly changed. One of her legs, I forget which, had been broken by a gunshot; the blood trickled from the wound where Van Vooren had stabbed her in the back; her little body was wasted by the want of water, and her face had shrunk to the size of that of a small child, although strangely enough it still was pretty. I knelt down by her, and placing my hand upon her heart felt that it still beat, though very slowly. Then I took water and sprinkled it upon her, and at the touch of it she opened her eyes at once.

"Give me to drink," she moaned, and I did so, pouring the water down her throat, which was ridged and black like a dog's palate. Her eyes opened and she knew me.

"Greeting, mother of Swallow," she said, "you come in a good hour, for now I shall be able to tell you all before I die, and I am glad that I was strong enough to endure the torment of thirst for so many hours."

"Tell me one thing, Sihamba," I said. "Does Suzanne live, and is she safe?"

"Yes, she lives, and I hope that this night she will be safe with your own people, the Boers, for she has crossed the mountains to seek shelter in that laager which is by the white-topped koppie near the banks of the Tugela in Natal."

"The laager by the white-topped koppie——" I gasped. "Oh, my God! that must be the camp which the Zulus attack to-morrow at the dawn."

"What do you say?" Sihamba asked.

In a few words I told her the tale that we had heard from the dying soldier, and she listened eagerly.

"I fear it must be true," she said, when I had finished, "for while he was tormenting me Bull-Head let it fall that Dingaan's regiments had gone hence by order of the King to make war upon the Boers in Natal, but I took little heed, thinking that he lied.

"Well," she went on after resting a while, "they may be beaten off, or—stay, in the glade yonder is the great *schimmel* horse; Bull-Head's people brought him down for him and I know that hours ago he has been well fed and watered. If her husband mounts him at sunset, he can be with the Swallow in the laager well before the dawn, in time to warn them all. Presently, when he returns from killing Bull-Head, I will show him the road, for I shall live till sunset. Give me more water, I pray you."

Now I saw that nothing could be done till Ralph and Jan returned, if they ever should return, so I prayed of Sihamba to tell me what had passed, for I saw that she could not live long, and desired to know the truth before she died. And she told me, with many rests and at no great length indeed, but very clearly, and as I listened I marvelled more and more at this Kaffir woman's love, faithfulness, and courage. At last she came to the tale of how she had disguised Suzanne, and set up the corpse in her place in the chair of rock.

" Step but a few paces there to the right," she said, "and you will see it."

I did as she bade me, and then it was that on looking upwards I saw Ralph and Swart Piet struggling together. They were so high above me that their shapes seemed small, but I could see the light flashing from the stabbing steel and I called out to Sihamba what I saw.

" Have no fear, lady," she answered, " it will only end one way." So indeed it did end as has been told, for presently Van Vooren and the corpse rushed downwards to vanish in the abyss, while Ralph remained standing by the empty chair of stone.

" It is finished," I said, returning to Sihamba.

" I know it, lady," she answered. " Bull-Head's last cry reached my ears, and do you give thanks to the Spirit you worship that he is dead. You wished to know what happened after the Swallow and I parted. Well, I went and stood by the body on the pinnacle of rock, and there, as I expected, came Bull-Head to seek his captive. He commanded us to come down, but I refused, telling him that if he attempted to take the Swallow—for he thought that the body wrapped in the white cloak was she—she would certainly escape him by hurling herself from the cliff. Thus I gained much time, for now from my height I could see her whom I knew to be the lady Swallow travelling across the plain towards the saw-edge rock, although I was puzzled because she seemed to carry a child upon her back; but perhaps it was a bundle.

" At last he grew impatient, and without warning lifted

his gun and fired at me, aiming low, for he feared lest the ball should pierce my mistress. The shot struck my leg where you see, and being unable to stop myself, although I broke my fall by clutching with my hands, I rolled down the rock to the ground beneath, but not over the edge of the precipice as I could have wished to do, for at the last I had intended to escape him by throwing myself from it.

"Leaving me unable to move he began to ascend the pinnacle, calling your daughter Swallow by sweet names as a man calls a shy horse which he fears will escape him. I watched from below, and even in my pain I laughed, for now I knew what must come. Since the Swallow did not answer, Bull-Head, wishing to be cunning, crept behind her in silence, and of a sudden seized the cloak and the arm beneath it, for he feared lest she should choose death and cheat him.

"Then it was that the body rolled over toward him; then it was that he saw the whitened face and the black breast beneath. Ah! lady, you should have heard his oaths and his yell of rage as he scrambled down the rocks towards me.

"'What think you of your bride?' I asked him as he came, for I knew that I must die and did not care how soon.

"'This is your trick, witch,' he gasped, 'and now I will kill you.'

"'Kill on, butcher,' I answered, 'at least I shall die happy, having beaten you at last.'

"'No, not yet,' he said presently, 'for if you grow silent, how shall I learn where you have hidden Suzanne Botmar?'

"'Suzanne Kenzie, wife of the Englishman, butcher,' I answered again.

"'Also,' he went on, grinding his teeth, 'I desire that

you should die slowly.' Then he called some of his men, and they carried me in a kaross to this place. Here by the river he lashed me to the stone, and, knowing that already, from loss of blood and lack of drink, I was in the agonies of thirst, he tormented me by holding water to my lips and snatching it away.

"All day long, lying in the burning sun, have I suffered thus, waiting for death to heal my pain. But in vain did he torture and question, for not one word could he wring from my lips as to where he should seek for the lady Swallow. He thought that she was hidden somewhere on the mountain, and sent men to search for her till they grew tired and ran away to steal the cattle; he never guessed that disguised as a black woman she had passed beneath his very eyes.

"Yet this was so, for I, Sihamba, know it from the talk I overheard between Bull-Head and one of his servants, who had held her awhile wishing to take her for a wife.* Yes, she passed beneath his eyes and escaped him, and I—I have won the game."

Now the effects of the water, which for a little while had given new life to Sihamba, began to pass off, and she grew weak and silent. Presently I saw Ralph returning down the steep cleft, and with him Jan, and went to meet them.

"It is finished," Ralph said, looking at me with quiet eyes.

"I know it," I answered, "but, son, there is still work

* In after days, when there was talk far and wide of the wonderful escape of my daughter Suzanne, disguised as a Kaffir woman, the man who had sought to take her captive told the story of the white mark which his grip left upon her arm. He said, indeed, that both he and Bull-Head saw the mark when she was at a little distance from them, but believing it to be an ivory ring they took no heed.

to do if you would save your wife——," and I told him
what I had learned.

"The *schimmel*," he exclaimed, growing pale to the lips,
"where is the *schimmel?*" and he turned to seek him.

"No, no," I said, "let Jan fetch the horse. Come you
to Sihamba, that she may show you the path before she
dies."

Now Jan went to the glade that I pointed out to find the
schimmel, while I led Ralph to Sihamba. She heard him
coming and opened her eyes.

"Welcome, husband of Swallow," she said, "you have
done well and bravely, yet it was the hand of fate and not
yours that smote yonder on the rock point. Now hearken
——," and she told the road which he must follow across
the Quathlamba, if he would hope to reach the white
koppie camp by dawn.

Before she had done, for the dying Sihamba spoke slowly
and with pain, Jan came leading the *schimmel* saddled and
bridled, for Swart Piet's saddle had been put upon it, the
mare he was riding having been taken by one of his men
whom he had sent to drive in the captured cattle.

The great roan horse, which I rejoiced to see once more,
was somewhat thin, for he had lacked water like the rest,
but throughout the siege he had been well tended by Sihamba and Zinti, and fed with green corn, and since that
morning he had drunk all he would, so that now he was
strong again and fit to run.

"Bring me the *schimmel*," said Sihamba, but there was
no need, for the brute which loved her now as always, had
winded her, and coming to where she lay, put down his
head and fondled her with his black lips. Catching him
by the forelock, she drew herself up, and as once before she
had done when he swam the Red Water, she whispered

into his ear, and as I live the beast seemed to listen and understand.

"Not I, not I," she said aloud when she had finished whispering, "not I but the Englishman, yet, Horse, I think that I shall ride you again, but it will be beyond the darkness. Stay not, stumble not, for you go on your last and greatest gallop. Speed like the swallow to save the Swallow, for so shall you live on when your swift bones are dust. Now, Englishman, away."

Ralph stooped down and kissed the woman, the angel whom God had sent to save him and his, and with her dying lips she blessed him and Suzanne, prophesying to them life and joy. Then he leapt into the saddle, and with a snort and quick shake of its head the *schimmel* plunged forward in the red glow of the sunset.

Sihamba leaned against the rock and watched the light pass. As its last ray fell upon her quivering face, she lifted her arms and cried, " Swallow, I have kept my oath. Swallow, I have served you well and saved you. Sister, forget me not."

With these words upon her lips Sihamba Ngenyanga died; yes, she and the daylight died together, while Jan and I stood over her and wept.

CHAPTER XXXV

THE SCHIMMEL'S LAST RACE

RALPH cleared the mountain slope, but before he had covered a mile of way the darkness began to fall, till presently the night was black. Now he must ride slowly, steering his path by the stars, and searching the dim outline of the mountains with his eyes.

But search as he would Ralph could not see the saw-edged rock. He reached the range indeed, and for hour after hour roamed up and down it, his heart torn with helpless haste and fears, but it was of no use, so at last he dismounted, and holding the *schimmel* by the bridle allowed him to eat a little grass while he waited for the moon to rise. Oh! never was the moon so long in coming, but at length it came, and with it clear, soft light. He looked, and there, not half a mile away, just showing in the shadows, was the saw-edged rock he sought.

"There is little time to lose," Ralph muttered to himself as the stallion swept across the plain towards the rock. "In three hours it will be dawn, and these mountains are sheer and wide."

Now he was in the pass and galloping up its rocky steeps as fast as the horse dare travel and not fall. Up he went through the moonlit silence that was broken only by the distant roaring of lions; up for one hour and for two. Now he was at the crest of the mountains, and beneath him, miles away, lay the dim veldt, and there—yes, there in the far distance—the moonbeams sparkled upon a white-topped koppie and the waters of a river that washed its base. Miles and miles away, and but one hour left to cover them. One short hour, and if it was not enough then death by the Zulu assegai would be the portion of Suzanne and of those among whom she sheltered. For a moment Ralph breathed the horse, then he shook the reins, and with a snort of pride the *schimmel* started upon his last gallop.

Ah! what a ride was that. Had ever man the like of it? Rushing down an untrodden mountain way swifter than others dare travel on a plain, bounding from rock to rock like a buck, dashing through streams, and leaping dim gullies at a stride. On, on went the *schimmel*, with never a slip and never a stumble. On, swifter than a sassaby and surer-footed than a fox; now the worst of the road was passed, and a long, smooth slope, almost free from stones, led them to the grassy plain beneath. The *schimmel* swept down it at a fearful pace and reached the level land in safety, but the strain of that mad gallop told its tale upon him, for he was drenched with sweat, his eye was red with blood, and the breath whistled in his throat.

Ralph raised himself in his stirrups and scanned the sky, which began to brighten with the coming dawn.

"There is time," he muttered, "for the koppie is near, and the Zulus will not attack till they can see the white moons upon their finger nails."

Now he was speeding up a long rise, for here the land lies in waves like a frozen sea. He topped it, and in an instant—almost before he saw them—he had swept through a Zulu impi marching stealthily in a triple line with companies thrown forward to the right and left. They

shouted in astonishment, but before they could harm him
or the horse he was out of reach of their spears and galloping forward with a glad heart, for now he thought the
danger done with.

Down the slope he thundered, and the sound of his
horse's hoofs came to the ears of Suzanne, who, frozen
with terror, crouched in the grass near the spring at the
foot of it. Turning her eyes from the ridge where she
had seen the Zulus, she looked behind her. At first she
could see nothing except a great horse with a man upon its
back, but as she stared, presently she recognised the horse
—it was the *schimmel,* and none other.

And the man. Whose shape was that? No, this one
had a golden beard. Ah! He lifted his head, from which
the hat had fallen, and—did she dream? Nay, by Heaven,
it was her husband, grown older and bearded, but still her
husband. In the piercing agony of that happiness she
sank back half-fainting, nor was it till he was almost upon
her that she could gain her feet. He saw her, and in the
dim light, mistaking her for a Zulu soldier who way-laid
him, lifted the gun in his hand to fire. Already he was
pressing the trigger when—when she found her voice and
cried out:

" Ralph, Ralph, I am Suzanne, your wife."

As the words left her lips it seemed to her as though
some giant had thrown the big horse back upon its
haunches, for he slipped past her, his flanks almost touching the ground, which he ploughed with outstretched
hoofs. Then he stopped dead.

" Have I found you at last, wife? " cried Ralph, in a
voice of joy so strange that it sounded scarcely human.
" Mount swiftly, for the Zulus are behind."

Thus, then, these two met again, not on the Mountain of the Man's Hand indeed, as the vision had foretold, but very near to it.

" Nay," Suzanne answered, as she sprang on to the saddle before him, " they are in front, for I saw them."

Ralph looked. Yes, there they were in front and to the side and behind. All round them the Zulu impi gathered and thickened, crying, " *Bulala umlungu* " (Kill the white man) as they closed in upon them at a run.

" Oh! Ralph, what can we do? " murmured Suzanne.

" Charge them and trust to God," he answered.

" So be it, husband," and, turning herself upon the pommel of the saddle, she threw her arms round his neck and kissed him on the lips, whispering, " At least we have met again, and if we die it shall be together."

" Hold fast," said Ralph, and calling aloud to the horse he set his teeth and charged.

By now the Zulus in front were running down the opposing slope in clusters not much more than a hundred yards away; indeed, the space between them was so narrow that the *schimmel*, galloping up hill under his double load, could scarcely gather speed before they were among them. When they were within ten yards Ralph held out the gun in one hand and fired it, killing a man. Then he cast it away as useless, and placing his right arm about the waist of Suzanne, he bent his body over her to protect her if he might, urging on the horse with feet and voice.

Now they were in them and ploughing through their ever-thickening ranks, throwing their black bodies to this side and to that as a ship throws the water from its bows. Here, there, everywhere spears flashed and stabbed, but as yet they were unhurt, for the very press saved them, although an assegai was quivering in the flank of the *schim-mel*. Ah! a pang as of the touch of red-hot iron and a spear had pierced Ralph's left shoulder, remaining fast in the wound. Still lower he bent his body till his head was almost hidden in the flowing mane of the *schimmel*, but now black clutching hands caught feet and bridle rein, and slowly the great horse lost way and stopped. A tall Zulu stabbed it in the chest, and Ralph gasped, " It is over! "

But it was not over, for, feeling the pain of this new wound, of a sudden the stallion went mad. He shrieked aloud as only a horse can shriek, and laying back his ears till his face was like the face of a wolf, he reared up on his hind legs and struck out with his hoofs, crushing the skulls and bodies of his tormentors. Down he came again, and with another scream rushed open-mouthed at that man who had stabbed him; his long white teeth gripped him across the body where the ribs end, and then the awful sight was seen of a horse holding in his mouth a man who yelled in agony, and plunging forward with great bounds while he shook him to and fro, as a dog will shake a rat.*

Yes, he shook and shook till the flesh gave, and the man fell dying on the veldt. Again the furious beast opened his jaws from which gore dripped and rushed upon another, but this one did not wait for him—none waited. To the Zulus in those days a horse was a terrible wild beast, and this was a beast indeed, that brave as they were they dared not face.

" It is a devil! and wizards ride it," they cried, as they opened a path before its rush.

They were through, and behind them like the voice of

---

* The reader may think this incident scarcely credible, but for an authenticated instance of such behaviour on the part of a horse he may be referred to the " Memoirs of General Marbot."

hounds that hunt swelled the cry of the war-dogs of Dingaan. They were through and living yet, though one
broad *bangwan* was fast in Ralph's shoulder, and another
stood in the *schimmel's* chest.

Not two miles away rose the koppie. "The horse will
die," thought Ralph as he drew Suzanne closer to him,
and gripped the saddle with his knees. Indeed, he was
dying; yet never since he was a colt did the *schimmel*
cover two miles of plain so fast as those that lay between
the impi and the camp. Slowly and surely the spear
worked its way into his vitals, but stretching out his head,
and heedless of his burden, he rushed on with the speed
of a racer.

The Boers in the laager were awake at last, the sound of
the gun and the war-cry of the Zulus had reached them
faintly. Half-clad, men and women together, they stood
upon their waggon-boxes looking towards the west. Behind them the pencils of daylight were creeping across the
sky, and presently in their low rays they saw such a sight
as they would never see again. Fast, fast towards them
thundered a great roan horse, blood dripping from his
chest, and jaws, and flank, and on its back a yellow-bearded
man, in whose shoulder stood a spear, and who held in
front of him a fainting woman.

"Soon he will fall suddenly, and we shall be crushed,"
thought Ralph, and had the horse died while travelling
at that speed it must have been so. But he did not. When
within fifty yards of the laager suddenly he began to lurch
and roll in his stride; then with three bounds he stopped,
and standing still, looked round with piteous blood-shot
eyes, and whinnied faintly as though he heard some voice
that he knew and loved.

Ralph slipped from his back, dragging Suzanne after him, and watched.

For a moment the *schimmel* stood, his head touching the ground, till presently a bloody foam came upon his mouth, and blood poured from his eyes and ears. Now for the last time he arched his neck and shook his mane, then rearing straight up on his hind legs as he had done when he beat down the Zulus, he pawed the air with his fore feet and fell over upon his back to move no more.

Suzanne had fainted, and Ralph carried her to the camp. There they drew out the spear from his shoulder and tended them both, though beyond gasping the words " Prepare, for the Zulus are upon you," it was long before either of them could speak.

Yes, yes, they beat off the impi with the loss of only one man, but Ralph took no part in that fight. Indeed, when we joined them four days later, for after burying Sihamba Jan and I trekked round through the waggon pass, by the mercy of Heaven escaping the Zulus, they still lay prostrate on a cartel, clasping each other's hands and smiling, but speaking little. The Boers, being warned and awake, beat off the Zulus with great loss to Dingaan, for they had the waggons in front, the koppie behind, and the river to one side.

But there were many on that dreadful night whom no *schimmel* galloped to warn. Ah! God, six hundred of them, men and women, maids and children, and little babies at the breast, went down beneath the Zulu assegai in that red dawn. Six hundred of them slaughtered!

Is not the name of the land Weenen—" The Land of Weeping "—to this day?

We avenged them at the battle of the Blood River in-

deed; but could vengeance give us back their lives which it
had pleased the Lord to take thus fearfully?

So, so, that is the end of my story of the forgotten bygone years. As I, old Suzanne Botmar, tell it the shadow
of that white-topped koppie falls upon this house and beneath my feet is the very spot where the brave *schimmel*
died. Ralph and Jan would not leave it—no, not even
when the British hoisted their flag in Natal, making us
English again after all that we had undergone to escape
their usurping rule. We suffered much at that event, Jan
and I, but though he said nothing, for indeed he did not
dare to in my presence, I believe that Ralph did not suffer
at all. Well, he was of English blood and it was natural
that he should like his own flag best, though to this day
I am very angry with my daughter Suzanne, who, for some
reason or other, would never say a hard word of the accursed British Government—or listen to one if she could
help it.

Yet, to be just, that same Government has ruled us well
and fairly, though I never could agree with their manner
of dealing with the natives, and our family has grown
rich under its shadow. Yes, we were rich from the beginning, for Ralph and some Boers fetched back the cattle
of Suzanne and Sihamba which Swart Piet's thieves had
stolen, and they were a very great herd.

For many long and happy years after all these events
that I have told of did Ralph and Suzanne live together,
till at last God took my child Suzanne as she began to
grow old. From that day life had no joys for Ralph, or
indeed for any of us, and he fought with the English
against Cetywayo at Isandlhwana, and fell there bravely,
he and his son together, for his son's wife, an English-
woman of good blood was dead also in childbirth.

Then all the world grew dark for Jan and me, but now in my extreme age once more it lightens like the dawn.

O God, who am I that I should complain? Nay, nay, to Thee, Almighty God, be praise and thanks and glory. Quite soon I must fall asleep, and how rich and plentiful is that store which awaits me beyond my sleep; that store of friends and kindred who have passed me in the race and won the immortal crown of peace, which even now their dear hands prepare for me. Therefore to Thee, Maker of the world, be praise and thanks and glory. Yes, let all things praise Thee as do my aged lips.

Note by the Baroness Glenthirsk, Formerly known as Suzanne Kenzie.

It is something over three years since my great-grandmother, the Vrouw Suzanne Botmar, finished dictating to me this history of her early days and of my grandparents, Ralph Kenzie, the English castaway, and Suzanne Botmar, her daughter. Now, if it be only as an instance of the wonderful workings of fate, or, as I prefer to call it, of Providence, I add this note to her narrative. As I write there stretches before me, not the bushy veldt of Weenen in Natal cut by the silver line of the Tugela, but a vast prospect of heather-clad mountains, about whose feet brawls a salmon river. For this is Scotland, and I sit in the castle of Glenthirsk, while on the terrace beneath my window passes my little son, who, if he lives, will one day be lord of it. But I will tell the story, which is indeed a strange one.

As I think my great-grandmother has said, I was educated at a school in Durban, for, although she was in many ways so prejudiced and narrow, she wished that I should be able to hold my own with other girls in learning as in all things. Also she knew well that this would have been the desire of my dear father, who was killed in the Zulu war with *his* father, the Ralph Kenzie of the story, whom, by the way, I can remember as a handsome grey-headed man. For my father was a thorough Englishman, with nothing of the Boer about him, moreover he married an English lady, the daughter of a Natal colonist, and for these reasons he and his grandmother did not get on very well.

After I had finished my schooling I used to stay with friends in Durban, the parents of one of my schoolfellows, and it was at their house that I met my husband, Mr. Ralph Mackenzie, who then was called Lord Glenthirsk, his father having died about six months previous to our acquaintance.

Ralph, my husband, was then quite young, only three-and-twenty indeed, and a subaltern in a Scotch regiment which was quartered at Durban, whither it had come from India. As the term of this regiment's foreign service was shortly to expire, and as at the time there was a prospect of further troubles in South Africa, my husband did not resign his commission on succeeding to the peerage, as his mother wished him to do, for he said that this was a step which he could consider when the regiment returned home, as it would do shortly.

Well, we met, and since we are now quite old married people I may as well admit at once that we fell in love with each other, though to me it seemed a marvellous thing that this handsome and brilliant young lord, with his great wealth and all the world before him, should come to care for a simple Dutch girl who had little to recommend her except her looks (of which my great-grandmother thought,

or pretended to think, so little) and some small inheritance
of South African farms and cattle.   Indeed, when at last
he proposed to me, begging me to be his wife, as though
I were the most precious thing on the whole earth, I told
him so plainly, having inherited some sense with my strain
of Huguenot and Dutch blood, and though I trembled at
the risk I ran, when everything lay in my own hand, I
refused to become engaged to him until he had obtained
the consent of his mother and relations, or, at the least,
until he had taken a year to think the matter over.

The truth is that, although I was still so young I had
seen and heard enough of the misfortunes of unsuitable
marriages, nor could I bear that it should ever be said of
me that I had taken advantage of some passing fancy to
entangle a man so far above me in wealth and station.
Therefore I would permit him to say nothing of our en-
gagement, nor did I speak a single word of it to my great-
grandmother or my friends.   Still Ralph and I saw a
great deal of each other during the month which I remained in Durban, for it is a gay town, and almost every
day there were parties, and when there were none we rode
out together.

It was during one of these rides on the Berea that I told
him what I knew of the strange history of my grandfather
and grandmother, not all of it indeed, for it was not until
the book was dictated to me that I learned the exact facts,
the matter being one of which our family spoke little.
Ralph listened very attentively, and when I had done asked
if I had the ring and locket of which I spoke.

" Here they are," I answered, for since my father's death
I had always made a practice of wearing both of them.

He examined the ring with its worn device and proud
motto of " Honour first," and as he deciphered it I saw him

start, but when he came to look at the miniatures in the locket he turned quite pale.

"Do you know, Suzanne," he said presently, "I believe that we must be distant cousins; at the least I am sure that I have seen the picture from which one of those miniatures was originally copied, and the crest and motto are those of my family."

Now I became very curious, and plied him with questions, but he would say no more, only he led me on to talk of my grandfather, Ralph Kenzie, the castaway, and from time to time made a note in his pocket-book. Also afterwards I showed him the writing in the testament which was found on the body of the shipwrecked lady, my great-grandmother, and he asked me for an impression of the ring, and to allow the ivory miniatures and the writing to be photographed, which I did.

Within three days of that ride we separated for a while, ·not without heartache on both our parts and some tears on mine, for I feared that when once he had lost sight of me he would put me from his mind, and as I loved him truly that thought was sore. But he, speaking very quietly, said that outside death only one thing should divide us from each other, namely, my own decree.

"Then Ralph, we shall be one for ever," I answered, for at the moment I was too sad for any artifice of maiden coyness.

"You think so now, dear," he said, "but time will show. Supposing that I were not——," and he stopped, nor would he complete the sentence. Indeed those words of his tormented me day and night for weeks, for I finished them in a hundred ways, each more fatal than the last.

Well, I returned to the farm, and immediately afterwards my great-grandmother took the fancy of dictating

23

this history, her reason for doing so being, as I believe, what she has said upon the subject notwithstanding, that she desired me to become acquainted with the actual facts of my descent, and especially with those of the fraud which, in their deep love for their adopted son, my grandfather, she and her husband practised upon the Lord Glenthirsk of that day. This story which (after making every allowance for slips of memory, and for a certain readiness to accept supernatural explanations of events which was characteristic of my great-grandmother, notwithstanding her affected scepticism, I believed to be perfectly true in all essentials), when taken together with my lover's words, gave me much cause for thought. But I said nothing of this either to her or in writing to him, for I felt the matter to be delicate.

By each weekly mail I heard from Ralph, but although his letters were full of love and kindness, he said nothing of coming to see me, and this I could not understand, since I knew that it would not be difficult for him to take a few weeks' leave. Indeed, I was sore upon the point, and hinted as much to him in my letters, but still he made no answer to that part of them, although I told him I thought it only right that he should see me in my Boer home, and there form his judgment of it and me.

Nearly six months had gone by since we parted, when one day I heard that a small body of troops was coming to the neighbouring township to relieve the company stationed there. Further I heard that they were Highlanders, but this I did not believe, for, so far as I knew, Ralph's was the only Highland regiment in the colony, and he said nothing of any such movement in his letters from Durban.

One morning my great-grandmother finished dictating

her history, the ending of which seemed to affect her much,
for when it was done she told me sharply to put the typed
sheets away and let her hear or see no more of them. Then
she rose with difficulty, for the dropsy in her limbs made
her inactive, and walked with the help of a stick to the
stoep, where she sat down, looking across the plain at the
solemn range of the Drakensberg and thinking without
doubt, of that night of fear when my grandfather had
rushed down its steeps upon the great *schimmel* to save
her daughter and his wife from an awful death.

The stead where we lived in Natal was built under the
lea of a projecting spur of the white-topped koppie, and
over that spur runs a footpath leading to the township.
Suddenly the old lady looked up and, not twenty yards
away from her, saw standing on the ridge of it, as though
in doubt which way to turn, a gentleman dressed in the
kilted uniform of an officer of a Highland regiment the
like of which she had never seen before.

"Dear Lord!" I heard her exclaim, "here is a white
man wearing the *moocha* of a Kaffir. Suzanne! Suzanne!
come and send away this half-clad fellow."

Putting down my papers I ran from the room and at a
single glance saw that "the half-clad fellow" was none
other than Ralph himself. In my delight I lost my head,
and forgetting everything except that my betrothed was
there before me, I sprang from the *stoep* and, flying up
the little slope, I fell into his open arms. For a few
seconds there was silence, then from behind me rose a
dreadful shriek followed by cries for help. Freeing myself
from Ralph's embrace, I looked round to see my great-
grandmother hobbling towards us with uplifted stick.
Ralph put his eye-glass in his eye and looked at her.

"Who is this old lady, Suzanne?" he asked.

Before I could answer there came from her lips such a torrent of indignation as I had never heard before.

" What is she saying? " asked Ralph again, who could not understand one word of Dutch. " She seems put out."

" It is my great-grandmother, the Vrouw Botmar," I faltered, " and she does not understand—I have never told her."

" Ah! I see. Well, perhaps it would be as well to explain," he answered, which I accordingly began to do as best I could, feeling more foolish than ever I did before. As I stammered out my excuses I saw her face change, and guessed that she was no longer listening to me.

" Who does the man remind me of? " she said, speaking aloud, but to herself. " Allemachter! his face is the face of that English lord who visited us with the lawyer more than fifty years ago. Yes, his face is the face of Ralph's cousin. Girl," she added, turning on me fiercely, " tell me that man's name."

" His name is Lord Glenthirsk."

" Lord Glenthirsk! The same face and the same name and *you* in his arms. Is God then making a sequel to the story which I finished this day? Come," and she hobbled back to the *stoep*. " Be seated," she said when we had reached it. " Now, speak; no, Suzanne, give me that kaross."

I handed her the rug, wondering what she meant to do with it, and disturbed as I was, nearly burst into hysterics when I saw her solemnly place it upon Ralph's knees saying, " The man has lost his garments and will catch a chill."

" Would you kindly explain," said Ralph blandly, " what the old lady is at now? Really I do not feel cold."

"Your kilt surprises her," I stammered; whereat he began to laugh.

"Silence," she exclaimed in so vigorous a voice that he stopped at once. "Now tell your story; no, I forgot, the man is not educated, do you interpret for him, Suzanne."

"First I have something to say for myself, grandmother," I answered, and in a few words I told that Ralph and I were affianced, though I had said nothing of it, because I wished to give him opportunity to change his mind if he should desire to do so.

"Change his mind!" said the old lady, with a glare of indignation. "I should like to see him dare to change his mind, this Englishman whom you seem to have honoured thus, *opsitting* with him without my leave. A lord indeed? What do I care for lords? The question is whether I should not order the English creature off the place; yes, and I would do it were not his face the face of Ralph's cousin, and his name the name Glenthirsk."

When I had interpreted as much of this speech as I thought necessary, there was a little silence, after which Ralph began to speak very solemnly.

"Listen, Suzanne," he said, "and repeat my words to your great-grandmother. She says that my name is Lord Glenthirsk, but within the last few days I have come to believe that it is nothing of the sort, but only plain Ralph Mackenzie."

"What do you mean?" I asked, astonished.

"I mean, Suzanne, that if your legitimate descent from that Ralph Mackenzie who was cast away about sixty years ago on the coast of the Transkei can be proved—as I believe it can, for I have made inquiries, and find that his marriage to your grandmother to which her mother who still lives can bear witness, was duly registered—then *you*

are the Baroness Glenthirsk of Glenthirsk, and I, the
descendant of a younger son, am only Lieutenant Ralph
Mackenzie of Her Majesty's — Highlanders."

"Oh! Ralph, how can this be?" I gasped. "I thought
that in England men took rank, not the women."

"So they do generally," he answered; "but as it happens
in our family the title descends in the female line, and
with it the entailed estates, so that you would succeed to
your father's rights although he never enjoyed them. Suzanne, I am not speaking lightly; all this while that I have
kept away from you I have been inquiring in Scotland and
the Cape, for I sent home the photographs of those miniatures and a statement of the facts, and upon my word I
believe it to be true that you and no other are the heiress
of our house."

Almost mechanically, for I was lost in amazement, I
translated his words. My great-grandmother thought a
while and said:

"Wonderful are the ways of the Lord who thus in my
old age answers my prayers and rolls from my back the
load of my sin. Suzanne, ask that Scotchman if he still
means to marry you," and seeing me hesitate, as well I
might, she struck her stick upon the floor and added,
"Obey, girl, and ask."

So with great shame I asked, explaining that I was
forced to it.

"Do I still mean to marry you, Suzanne?" he said,
astonished. "Why surely you must understand that the
question is, do you still intend to marry me? When I
begged you to take me some months ago I had much to
offer; to-day if things be as I am sure they are, I am but a
penniless Scottish gentleman, while you are one of the
richest and most noble ladies in Great Britain."

By way of answer I looked at him in a fashion which I trust he understood, but before I could speak Vrouw Botmar broke in, for, as usual, I had translated.

"Tell the man to stop talking about money and rank after his godless English manner. I wish to inquire of his character and religion." And so she did clearly and at length, but I do not think that I need set down her questions or his answers.

At last, when we were both overwhelmed and gasping for breath, I refused flatly to ask anything more, whereon she ceased her examination, saying:

"Well, if he speaks the truth, which is doubtful, he does not seem to be any worse than other men, though that is saying little enough. Is he sound in wind and limb, and what illnesses has he had?"

"You must ask him yourself," I replied, losing patience, whereon she called me a " mealy-mouthed little fool " and laughed. Then of a sudden she said, "Kneel, both of you," and, strange as it may seem, we obeyed her, for we, and especially Ralph, were afraid of the old lady. Yes, there we knelt on the *stoep* before her, while a Kaffir girl stood outside and stared with her mouth open.

"Ralph Kenzie," she said, "whatever else you may be, at least you are an honest man like your grandfather before you, for were it not so you would never have come to tell this child that your fortune is her fortune, and your title her title, though whether this be the case or not, I neither know nor care, since at least you are of the blood of my long-dead adopted son, and that is more to me than any wealth or rank.

"As for you, Suzanne, you are pert and deceitful, for you have kept secret from me that which I had a right to learn; also you have too good an opinion of your own looks, which as I tell you now for the last time, are nothing compared to mine at your age, or even to those of my daughter Suzanne, your grandmother. But this I will say, you have a good heart and some of the spirit of your forbears, therefore "—and she laid one of her heavy hands on the head of each of us—" I, old Suzanne Botmar, bless you both. You shall be married next week, and may you be happy in your marriage, and have children that would be a credit to me and your great-grandfather, could we have lived to see them.

" There, there, Ralph and Suzanne—the first ones, my own lost Ralph and Suzanne—will be glad to hear of this when I come to tell them of it, as I shall do shortly. Yes, they will be glad to hear of it—" and she rose and hobbled back to the *sit-kammer*, turning at the open door to call out:

" Girl, where are your manners? Make that Scotchman some of your coffee."

So we were married, and within the week, for, all my protestations notwithstanding, the Vrouw Botmar would suffer no delay. Moreover, by means of some other interpreter, Ralph, playing traitor, secretly brought my arguments to nothing, and indeed there was a cause for hurry, for just then his regiment was ordered to return to England.

It was a strange sight, that marriage, for my great-grandmother attended it seated on the *voor-kisse* of her best waggon drawn by eighteen white oxen, the descendants of Dingaan's royal cattle that Swart Piet stole to bring destruction upon the Umpondwana. By her side was her husband, old Jan Botmar, whom she caused to be carried to the waggon and tied in it in his chair. He, poor old man,

knew nothing of what was passing, but from some words
he let fall we gathered that he believed that he was once
more starting on the great trek from the Transkei. My
Ralph, he thought, was his adopted child, perhaps because
of some inherited similarity of voice, for he called him
" son," but my own presence puzzled him, for he said
once or twice, " So Suzanne has escaped from that hell-
hound, Swart Piet. Have you killed the dog, Ralph?
Ralph, have you killed the dog? "

Thus we went to the little church where the chaplain
of the regiment was to wed us, the pipers going first, playing
a wild marriage march on their bagpipes. Next came
Ralph and I walking side by side, and after us the waggon
with my great-grandparents, while the rear was brought
up by a guard of honour formed of every available soldier
in the company. Outside the open door of the church the
waggon was halted, and from it the Vrouw Botmar wit-
nessed the ceremony, causing the register to be brought
to her to sign. This she did, resting the book upon the
head of the Kaffir driver, down whose back she managed
to upset the ink.

" Never mind," she said, not the least disturbed, " it
cannot make the poor creature blacker than he is."

" Oh! how can I leave you, grandmother? " I said to her
afterwards.

" Child," she answered, with a stern face, " in my youth,
to keep one I loved near to me, I committed a great sin.
Now by way of penance I part from one I love; yes, being
yet alive I say farewell for ever to the last of my race.
Thus in our age do we pay for the sins of youth. Go,
and God go with you."

So I placed my hand in that of my husband and went.
When we reached this country it was proved that the rank

and estates were mine by law, for the evidence of my descent was too strong to be disputed. I did not wish to take either, but Ralph insisted on it and I was over-ruled. Indeed, had I not done so, it seems that confusion and endless law-suits might have resulted in the future, perhaps after I am dead.

Six months afterwards, in this castle of Glenthirsk, I received a letter, at the foot of which was faintly scrawled the signature of Suzanne Botmar. It was short and ran thus:—

"GRAND-DAUGHTER SUZANNE,

"Last night your great-grandfather died. To-day I buried him, and to-morrow I shall die also, for after being together for so many years I miss his company and mean to seek it again. Till we meet in Heaven, if your pomp and riches will allow you to come there through the eye of whatever needle it has pleased God to choose for you, farewell to you and your husband, whom I love be-cause Ralph Kenzie's blood is in his veins."

As I learnt by other letters on that morrow of which she spoke my great-grandmother, the Vrouw Botmar, did die, for even in this she would not be thwarted, and was buried on the evening of the same day by the side of her husband, Jan Botmar.

THE END

www.ingramcontent.com/pod-product-compliance
Lightning Source LLC
Chambersburg PA
CBHW022205030726
47494CB00019B/444